C000149551

A lifelong history buff, **Georgie L** will one day inherit a title and a ma her dreams of lords, ladies and a stories. When not writing, she ca history or watching any film with a costume and an accent. Please visit www.georgie-lee.com to learn more about Georgie and her books.

Regency Surrender

August 2018

September 2018

October 2018

November 2018

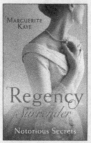

December 2018

January 2019

February 2019

March 2019

April 2019

May 2019

June 2019

July 2019

Regency Surrender: Debts Reclaimed

GEORGIE LEE

MILLS & BOON

First Published in Great Britain 2019
By Mills & Boon, an imprint of HarperCollinsPublishers
1 London Bridge Street, London, SE1 9GF

REGENCY SURRENDER: DEBTS RECLAIMED © 2019 Harlequin Books S.A.

A Debt Paid in Marriage © 2015 Georgie Reinstein
A Too Convenient Marriage © 2016 Georgie Reinstein

ISBN: 978-0-263-26797-6

52-0619

MIX
Paper from
responsible sources
FSC™ C007454
www.fsc.org

This book is produced from independently certified FSC™ paper
to ensure responsible forest management.

For more information visit: www.harpercollins.co.uk/green

Printed and bound in Great Britain
by CPI Group (UK) Ltd. Croydon, CRO 4YY

A DEBT PAID
IN MARRIAGE

A special thanks to RWASD for your inspiration and motivation.

Chapter One

~~~~~~~

London—spring 1817

'**W**hat exactly do you think you are doing?' Mr
Rathbone demanded, his deep-blue eyes fixing on her
through the wisps of steam rising from the copper bathtub. Dark-brown hair lay damp over his forehead. One
drop escaped the thickness of it, sliding down his face,
then tracing the edge of his jaw before dropping into
the tub.

Laura slid her finger away from the trigger, afraid of
accidentally sending a ball through the moneylender's
sturdy, wet and very bare torso. She had no intention
of killing him, only frightening him into giving back
the inventory he'd seized from her uncle Robert. Judging by the hard eyes he fixed on her, he wasn't a man to
scare easily.

'Well?' he demanded and she jumped, her nerves as
taut as the fabric over the back of a chair.

When she'd slipped into the house determined to

face him, she'd expected to find him hunched over his desk counting piles of coins or whatever else it was a moneylender did at night. She hadn't expected to surprise him in his bath with a film of soapy water the only thing standing between her and his modesty. What had seemed like a good plan in the pathetic rooms she shared with her uncle and her mother, when hunger gnawed at her stomach and cold crept in through the broken window, now seemed horrible.

Laura settled her shoulders, shoring up the courage faltering under his steady stare. Beyond this humid room was nothing but ruin and poverty. She had no choice but to continue. 'I demand you return to me the fabric you seized from my uncle.'

The moneylender raised his arms out of the water, disturbing the calm suds, and she caught sight of his flat stomach before the soapy water settled back over it. His hands rested on the curved sides of the tub. They were long but sturdy, like those of the delivery men who used to haul the bolts of cloth off the cart and into her father's draper shop. Mr Rathbone's were smooth and free of calluses, however, and, except for the red of an old cut snaking along one knuckle, the hands of a gentleman.

She took a step back, expecting him to rise from the water and rush at her. He did nothing except study her, as though appraising her market value. 'And who exactly is your uncle?'

Laura swallowed hard. Yes, this was important information to impart if one was to make demands of a naked man. 'Robert Townsend.'

'The gambling draper.' Neither shock nor surprise

broke his piercing stare. 'He came to me six months ago in need of a loan to pay a large debt accrued at Mrs Topp's, among many other establishments. In return for my money, he put up the inventory of the draper business as collateral. When he defaulted, I seized the goods, as was my right pursuant to our contract.'

The floor shifted beneath her. Uncle Robert had lost the business. In the past, he'd stolen merchandise from the storeroom, a bolt of silk or a cord of tassel, and sold it to fund his gambling. They were losses to the business, but not the whole business.

It couldn't be gone, not after everything she'd done to hold on to it after her father's death.

Anger overcame her shock and she gripped Uncle Robert's old pistol tighter, her sweating palms making the wood handle stick to her skin. 'I don't believe you. I know how men of your ilk operate, taking advantage of desperate people with high interest rates until they have no choice but to turn everything they own over to your grasping hands.'

Mr Rathbone's eyes narrowed a touch. What the gun and the element of surprise had failed to do, her smear of his character managed to achieve—a reaction.

'If it's proof you require, I'm most happy to oblige.' He pushed up against the edge of the tub and rose.

'Sir!' Laura gasped and shuffled back until the edge of a table caught her hip. She clutched the pistol tighter, unable to tear her eyes away as fat drops poured down his slender body, catching in the ripples of his stomach before falling into the sloshing water of the tub. The drops were not thick enough to offer any semblance of modesty and she struggled to keep her gaze from wandering from his handsome face to the long length of chest, stomach and everything else beneath. Her heart pounded harder than when she'd crept into the house through the open terrace door, then pressed herself deep into the shadows of an alcove beneath the stairs when a maid had passed by.

He lifted one long leg, then the other over the copper tub and stepped dripping on to the small towel on the floor next to it. Over a nearby chair lay a brown banyan of fine silk—French, she guessed, by the subtle pattern in the weave. She expected him to take it up and pull it on over the long expanse of him, but he didn't. Instead he strode past her, through the wide double doors adjoining the dressing-and-bathing room to his bedroom without so much as a second look, as though she were not standing there threatening his life and he was not stark naked and leaving a trail of wet footprints on the wood floor. He headed to the small desk in the opposite corner of the bedroom, near the windows and across from the tall, four-poster bed hung with expensive embroidered curtains. Behind the desk, he opened one of the drawers. Neither the neat stack of papers on top nor the oil lamp on the corner did anything to prevent her from seeing him as Eve must have seen Adam after they'd tasted the apple. Laura could feel her own judgement coming. What she wouldn't give for a lightning bolt from above, or at the very least a large fig leaf.

'Here is the contract we drew up the day he came to see me.' Mr Rathbone came around the desk, holding out the paper.

Laura forced her eyes to meet his. 'Would you please get dressed?'

'This is my house. You broke into it and threatened me. I may stand as I like. Now here is your proof.' The paper fluttered at the end of one stiff, outstretched arm.

In the flickering candlelight she read the list of her uncle's debts laid out in points in the centre of the page. There were more names than just Mrs Topp's. Most were unfamiliar, but a few she recognised from snatches of conversation she'd caught in the hallways of their ramshackle building. Below the terms were Mr Rathbone's signature and that of a witness, a Mr Justin Connor. Next to them sat Uncle Robert's uneven letters, the wide way he wrote his R and T clear.

It wasn't so much his signing away the shop that shocked her, it was the document he'd put his name to. 'Where did you get this paper?'

'Mr Townsend brought it to me the night he came here seeking a loan.'

'This is mine. I wrote this, it was my plan to save our business.'

'It was an excellent one and, combined with the collateral he possessed to secure the loan, the reason I extended him the sum. He could have succeeded, if he hadn't gambled the money away.' He laid the document on the desk. 'Are you quite satisfied?'

'I am.' *And we're ruined.*

'Good, then you won't need this.' Mr Rathbone grabbed the barrel of the pistol and wrenched it from her hands.

'No,' she cried, as naked as him without the weapon.

'The gun would have done you no good. It was improperly loaded.' He pulled the flint from the hammer and tossed the now-useless weapon on the desk along with the contract. 'Had you fired it, you would have blown your pretty face off.'

She looked to where the weapon lay on the blotter, as useless as her hope and her foolish plans. This morning she had thought her situation couldn't sink any lower. It seemed she had yet to reach the bottom, but all she could think of was her mother. Laura's botched attempt to save them would no doubt land her in gaol. How would her mother survive without her and what would Uncle Robert do to her? 'You should have let me fire it and finish myself.'

He strode past her back to the bathroom. 'You'd have ruined the carpet.'

Anger overcame her sense of loss and she whirled on him. Without concern, he took up the banyan from the chair and slid his strong arms into the sleeves, pulling it shut over his nakedness. Laura's anger flickered, nearly blown out by the sight of his skin caressed by the dark silk, before it flared again. 'I can see all you care about is money.'

He pulled the banyan ties tight across his slim middle. 'I'm a businessman, Miss Townsend. Men interested in financial backing for ventures come to me, as well as those seeking to shore up a struggling business. I offer them finance to be repaid with interest, or, if they default, as your uncle did, I seize their goods and sell them to cover my losses. I have a family and employees whose welfare I must ensure. I am not a charity.'

'No, of course not.' She looked down at the carpet he was so worried about, moving one toe of her worn-out half-boot to trace the swirling curve of a vine. In the brief time she'd spent plotting this ridiculous scheme, she'd failed to work out exactly how she might extricate herself from it without landing in the Old Bailey, or worse. She only hoped the generous nature he spoke of with his family and employees might extend to a very foolish young lady.

'Mr Rathbone, please forgive me for intruding on your privacy and for trying to blacken your good name. I was not in possession of all the facts before I decided to confront you. It seems I was not in possession of my reason either.' She smiled, trying to look the way she imagined a senseless young lady might look, in the hope of saving both her dignity and her freedom. It failed to soften the hard set of Mr Rathbone's mouth.

'Don't play the fool. It's not becoming of a woman of your ingenuity.'

She dropped the smile but not her hope, unwilling to concede defeat. She couldn't, not with her mother shivering at home. 'Then let me offer you a proposal, one that speaks to you as a businessman.'

Mr Rathbone stood silent and she couldn't discern if he planned to listen or to summon a footman to fetch the constable. She didn't give him a chance to answer, hoping her words might at least make him consider her offer and postpone for some time whatever fate he had in mind for her. 'Among the contents of the inventory you seized was a large bolt of cotton woven into a very fine cloth. It's from a special variety, grown in Egypt. It can be rendered, like the Indian kind, into a very fine, almost transparent cloth, but it costs less to produce. I plan to introduce it through Madame Pillet, a modiste to many fashionable and influential ladies. Their orders for the fabric alone could bring in hundreds of pounds. With the profits, I can import more and establish a fine trade. If you return the inventory to me, I'll pay you a portion of the profits until the original debt is settled.'

'I'm afraid I can't entertain your proposal,' he answered without consideration. 'The contents of the draper shop were sold to settle Mr Townsend's debts. I no longer have the bolt of cotton to which you are referring.'

'But you know who has it. You could get it back and we could still reach an arrangement.'

'I cannot.'

'You're leaving us to starve,' she blurted out as even this slim hope dissolved. There was no chance of reviving the business, or doing anything other than sinking into even more degrading poverty.

No sign of sympathy or regret marred the smoothness of his face. 'Your plan has merit, but will not succeed. If the cotton becomes fashionable, those with better connections and more money will race to import it before you can secure more, flooding the market with it and lessening its value.'

'But before then?' she protested meekly.

'I can't afford to gamble my money on the whims of the *ton*. Nor can you.'

'I can't rely on my uncle Robert if that's what you're thinking. He's got everything out of us he wanted, my father's business and what was left of the money,' she scoffed. 'It won't be long before we see the backside of him. Then what will happen to me and my mother?'

'You must have other family?'

She shook her head. 'No.'

'Friends?'

'Uncle Robert saw to it that they were driven away when he borrowed money from them and never repaid it.' She dropped her hands to her sides in imitation of Mr Rathbone, trying to appear as confident and sure as he did. 'I know what I did tonight was foolish and I never meant to hurt you, I only wanted the merchandise back because I couldn't see the business fail. It took my father years to build and my uncle Robert less than a year to destroy.'

If Philip had passed Miss Townsend on the street, he'd have overlooked her. Forced to stare down the end of a barrel at her, he couldn't miss the stunning light of determination in her round hazel eyes. It was undiminished by the faint circles darkening the smooth skin underneath them or the slight hollow beneath the high cheekbones. Loose waves of auburn hair hung on either side of her face and down to the shoulders of her worn-out dress. The sad garment hung loose on her. Regular meals would bring back the fullness of her cheeks and the softness of her waist. Her skin was pale, like Arabella's had been, but where illness had faded his late wife's bloom, only hardship dampened the lustre of the lady before him. 'In business, it's always best to keep facts and emotions separate so one does not cloud the other.'

'I'll remember that when I'm starving,' she spat.

'You won't starve. You're too smart.' There was something of life and fight in Miss Townsend, a trait Arabella had not possessed. Despite his annoyance at being disturbed tonight, he admired it too much to see it snuffed out by gaol fever. He swept the pistol from the desk and held it out to her. 'Thank you for an interesting evening, Miss Townsend.'

Hope flooded her cheeks with a wash of pink. 'You're letting me go?'

'Would you prefer I call the constable and have you hauled before the magistrate?'

'No.'

He moved aside and waved his hand at the door. 'Then go.'

In a flutter of threadbare bombazine, she was gone.

'You there, stop.' Justin's voice sounded through the downstairs hall before the thud of the back door hitting the wall and the squeak of the garden gate let Philip know Miss Townsend was away.

A second later Justin came running in, his pistol drawn. 'Are you all right?'

'Quite.' Philip sat down in his chair, rubbing his still-damp chin with his fingers. Miss Townsend had stirred something inside him—not pity, or even lust, though she was pretty. No, it was curiosity, like the first time he'd seen Arabella sitting across his desk next to her father, Dr Hale. Philip hadn't been able to focus on anything but her while Dr Hale had laid out his plans for a small medical school. The school had failed and Dr Hale had lost both his and Philip's money. It was the only time Philip had allowed emotion to guide a business decision.

'Leave it to you to be so cavalier about an intruder threatening you.' Justin lowered the hammer on the pistol.

'She was never a threat.' Philip curled one finger to rub it along his ring finger still missing the plain wedding band he'd buried with Arabella. No, this was nothing like the day he'd met his wife. There was no emotion to touch his love for Arabella, especially not in the guise of this stranger, no matter how intriguing she might appear.

'You look like the devil.' Justin slid the pistol in the holster under his coat.

'It's been a trying day.' He'd thought the headaches of it were over when he'd sunk down into the hot water. He couldn't have been more wrong.

He stared past Justin to the copper bathtub and the thin tendrils of steam still rising from it. Nothing but problems had plagued him today. A cobbler had called to secure a loan to increase his business. The cobbler's endless words of reassurance and lack of collateral had warned Philip off the venture. The man hadn't reacted kindly to Philip's refusal. He'd only just been ejected from the house when Justin had arrived with news of an import company with an outstanding loan having been declared bankrupt. It'd been a scramble to seize the goods stored in the warehouse before the importer moved them and left Philip with the loss.

With business matters secured, household ones had rushed in to consume the remainder of the day. His

sister, Jane, had tried his patience with yet another demand for an expensive dress too mature for a budding
young woman of thirteen. She'd railed at him with
their grandmother's temper before stomping away after
Philip threatened to cut off her dress allowance. On the
heels of Jane's tantrum came the news that Mrs Marston, his son Thomas's nurse, was moving to Bath to
take care of her grandson, leaving Philip with only a
month to engage a replacement. Jane was too young to
be of assistance and Mrs Palmer, despite running his
house with the efficiency of a factory, was not up to the
task of mothering his sister and son or finding a suitable replacement for Mrs Marston.

What Philip needed was a wife, someone to deal with
these domestic matters.

Justin plucked a small chair from the wall, turned it
around in front of the desk, then straddled it, leaning his
elbows on the polished back. 'So, who was the woman?'

'The niece of Robert Townsend.' Philip smoothed
his hands over his wet hair. 'She wanted her collateral back.'

'Don't they all.' Justin snorted, propping his chin in
his palm. 'I left two extra men to guard the importer's
stock until you can sell it.'

'We'll see to it tomorrow,' Philip said vaguely, his
thoughts consumed with something other than business.

Justin raised one curious eyebrow. 'What did she do
to you?'

Philip straightened a pen on the blotter. 'What do
you mean?'

'Never seen you this cavalier about a full warehouse.

Usually you're all plans until I'm up all night and engaged through most of tomorrow seeing to it, but not tonight. Why?'

Philip studied his old friend and partner. Justin had stood beside him at his wedding and at Arabella's funeral. He balled his hand into a fist. His wife should have had the chance to raise their son and attend to their house. Now, it fell to the people Philip paid to assist him. Not the most ideal of situations and one he would soon correct.

Straightening in the chair, he laced his fingers over his stomach. It wasn't Miss Townsend's disturbance which troubled him now, as much as the opportunity she presented. His father had trained him to assess a client in a matter of seconds. He'd measured up Miss Townsend and, despite the ridiculousness of her attempted threat, found her useful qualities continued to tip the scales in her favour.

It was madness and he knew it. He should recommend her and the mother to Halcyon House, his charitable organisation, and be done with them both, not continue to entertain the plan developing in his mind. He'd chosen Arabella with his heart, ignoring her frailty, believing it wouldn't come between them. He'd been a fool and in the end their love had killed her.

Small footsteps pattered down the long hallway outside his bedroom door before steady, larger ones followed. In a moment, he'd help Mrs Marston get Thomas back to sleep, but first there was business to discuss.

'I have another plan in mind, Justin.' He picked up Robert Townsend's contract. It was sheer luck he'd decided to bring it upstairs with the others, as was his habit, to review before bed or if he was restless in the middle of the night. He handed it to his friend. 'Find out everything you can about his niece.'

'I knew I wouldn't get off so easy tonight.' He rose from the chair and set it back by the wall, then plucked the paper from Philip's hand.

'Speak to anyone who might know her from her lodgings and from the neighbourhood where the draper shop used to be, I'm sure you can discover its location.'

'You know I can.' He folded the contract and slid it into his pocket.

'Get a sense of her reputation, character and situation. Find out any and every detail you can and bring it to me as soon as possible.'

'Is she going to become a client?'

Philip rose, eager to see to his son. 'No. She might become my wife.'

Chapter Two

Laura stared at the worn and splintered door, frozen where she stood, her uncle's dirty tankard in one hand, a cleaning rag in the other.

Someone had knocked. No one ever knocked here. It couldn't be good.

She jumped again as the wood rattled beneath the fist of whoever was on the other side. She set the tankard down and hurried to the door, eager to silence the person for fear they'd wake her mother.

'Who is it?' she hissed through a crack near the centre.

'Mr Rathbone.'

She jolted away from the wood. It'd been two days since she'd fled from his house and there was nothing he could want from her, unless he'd changed his mind about seeing her gaoled. The constable might be outside with him now. She twisted the rag around one hand, then let go. No, the constable would have announced himself. She'd heard him banging on enough doors in the building to know. Mr Rathbone must want something else, but what? The cotton. Maybe he'd finally seen the sense in her offer, found a way to buy back the bolt and was here to discuss an arrangement.

She pulled open the door to find him standing on the other side. Unlike the few others who came here, he didn't clutch a scented handkerchief to his face or look around as though expecting a rat to pounce. He stood exactly as he had two nights ago, businesslike, determined, a dark-blue redingote falling straight from his shoulders to cover his lithe but sturdy body. Her eyes trailed the length of him, from the low hat covering his almost black hair to the tips of his polished boots. Taking in this groomed and dressed moneylender, she tried not to imagine him without his clothes. If she hadn't seen him in such a fashion, she would be more terrified of him now, not mesmerised by the way his high white collar traced the angle of his jaw to where it narrowed to his chin.

'May I come in?' His crisp but polite words snapped her out of her musing.

'Yes, of course.' She waved him in with the rag, closing the door behind him.

In four steps he reached the centre of the room. The faint, citrus scent of his bergamot cologne struck Laura harder than the stench of the street coming in through the window. The richness of the scent reminded her of the perfume shop situated next to her family's old shop and for a moment took her away from the filth permeating her life.

Mr Rathbone glanced down at the table where the

dirty tankard sat, then turned to face her, his scrutiny pulling her back into the mire. 'Miss Townsend.'

'Shh…' Laura gestured to silence him, then caught sight of her dirty fingernails and lowered her hand as fast as she'd raised it. 'I must ask you to speak quietly. My mother is resting. She slept poorly last night and every night before.'

He nodded and removed his hat, holding it against his left side. 'Miss Townsend, I've come to speak to you about a business proposal.'

She twisted the rag tight between her hands. 'You've come to accept my offer? You found a way to retrieve the cotton bolt and return it to me?'

'No. As I told you, it is no longer in my possession.'

'But—'

He raised a silencing hand. 'Mr Townsend knew the consequences when he took my money and he will pay them. He is no longer my concern or yours.'

She perched one fist on her hip. 'Then what is our concern?'

He shifted the hat to his other hand so it rested against his right thigh instead of his left. If she thought the man capable of emotion, she might say he was nervous. 'You managed your father's draper business before Mr Townsend assumed control?'

'Before my uncle stole it from us,' she corrected, more curious than cautious.

'You kept accounts, inventory, credit?'

'I did.' She didn't hide her pride. 'My father thought it better for me to learn the business than attend a lady's school.'

'I know by the speed at which you comprehended the agreement that you can read and understand contracts and your business plan indicates you can write.'

'A fine hand.' She wondered where this line of questioning was leading. Maybe he'd taken pity on her and come to offer work. She smoothed one hand over her hair, wishing he'd given her some notice and a chance to make herself more presentable.

'And you are well, your mother's illness does not extend to you?'

'I am very hearty, thank you. My mother broke her leg a few years ago and, though it healed, she's afflicted with rheumatism. It's nothing food and heat wouldn't ease, but since we have neither, she suffers.'

His eyes dropped down, covering the length of her in a heartbeat before his head rose a touch as though appraising her collateral. She couldn't imagine what he saw since she wore no jewellery and her dress was too old to be of much value to even a secondhand-clothes merchant. 'There is no one, apart from your mother and Mr Townsend, to make a claim on you?'

Worry coiled inside her, fuelled by the memory of him parading before her naked without shame. 'If you've come to make an immodest proposal, you can leave.'

'There's nothing untoward in what I'm about to suggest, Miss Townsend. After a great deal of thought, I have another venture which might interest you.'

From the next room, her mother coughed and Laura tensed, waiting to see if she settled back to sleep or awoke. Hopefully she'd sleep. She needed the rest as much as she needed a decent meal and a proper pelisse to keep out the cold. Eyeing the moneylender, her dread increased. Even if he made her an indecent offer, she couldn't afford to refuse it. With the business lost, there were only more horrors waiting for her and her mother out on the street. 'I'm listening, Mr Rathbone.'

Philip shifted his hat to his other hand. From somewhere outside he heard the cry of an infant. It sounded too much like the way Thomas had wailed in the nurse's arms while Philip had held Arabella in his, clutching her to him as her life had slipped away.

He set the hat down on the table. This transaction had nothing to do with the past, but the more pressing needs of the present. 'A year ago, I lost my wife in childbirth. I'm in need of the services of a woman with your skills.'

Her brow scrunched down over her straight nose. 'You mean as a nurse?'

'No, as a wife.'

'A wife?' Her jaw dropped open before she pulled it closed, her eyes wider than when he'd snatched the pistol from her.

'I assume you're not already married.'

'No, but—'

'And you have no suitors?'

'Unless you consider the drunk who sits in the doorway and pesters me whenever I come and go, no.'

'Good. At present, I employ a capable nurse for my son, but she is leaving at the end of the month. I think it preferable for family to see to the welfare of a child. My sister is thirteen and too young for such things. She is also in need of a guiding hand. She will soon be faced with suitors and I don't have aunts or cousins on whom I may call to assist her.'

'And my mother?'

'I will see to her welfare and care.'

'By placing her in a home with some ill-mannered nurse?'

'She will have a suitable room in my house and a proper maid to attend her. You will learn my business and help me manage it.'

She continued to stare at him as if he'd suggested she be presented to the king. 'I nearly killed you and you wish to trust me with your son and business?'

Her reservations needled him. He'd reviewed the facts last night and they made sense. There was no room for doubt. He pressed on. 'You were never a threat to me.'

A tiny curve appeared at the corner of her mouth and he couldn't tell if she was going to smile or frown. 'How do you know I won't steal from you and run off?'

'Not likely with your mother residing under my roof.'

'There is truth in that.' She uncrossed her arms, the crease beside her lips growing deeper as she silently considered the merits of his offer as any wise client might contemplate the terms of a loan. 'Why me? Why marriage?'

'In my experience, a wife is a better business partner than any other as her interests are my interests. As to why you, you seem a quick wit, except where firearms are concerned.' Her crease deepened into a disapproving frown but he didn't let it deter or distract him.

'Your brazen act the other night demonstrated a degree of courage and strength.'

'Some might call it rash and reckless.'

'It was, but your plans for the fabric demonstrated an innate sensibility and intelligence. Your prior experience in your father's shop is an asset. Your reason for breaking into my house was to protect your mother. That demonstrates a proper degree of concern for those in your care. I have no doubt you can transfer such regard to my sister and son.'

Her brow rose a touch in surprise. 'I have never heard my attributes stated in such a plain way. I'm not sure if I should thank you or chide you for insulting me.'

'I meant it as a compliment.'

She nodded her thanks. 'You may find me a poor partner. I know nothing of moneylending.'

'You will learn so that if anything happens to me, you will know how to successfully carry on until our son reaches an age where he is able to assume control of the business.'

'Our son?'

'He will soon be as much yours as mine, and others will follow. I assume your courses are as they should be.'

She crossed her arms again. 'I beg your pardon.'

'We're making a bargain and, in such deals, we must be frank with one another.'

'They are as they should be.' No blush spread over her pale skin as her eyes dipped down the length of him, pausing near his hips before rising again to meet his gaze. 'Is everything as it should be with you?'

The girl possessed pluck and for the first time in almost a year, he felt the twitch of a smile tug up the corner of his lips before he squashed it. 'It is, as you will discover.'

'I have yet to agree to your romantic proposal.'

'You will.'

'You're so sure?'

'You have no other options.'

She looked at the dirty cloth in her hands, picking off one loose thread around the frayed edge before she faced him again. 'You're right, I have no other options. However, you could present your case in a less business-like tone, with a little civility and charm.'

'You don't strike me as a woman ruled by romantic notions.'

'No, but I'm still a woman and would like to be wooed just a touch.'

For the second time today he wanted to smile but didn't. Instead, he stepped closer, admiring her spirit. She didn't just surrender to him, sign her name on the contract as it were, but demanded his respect, not his money or anything else. Once again, his instinct for business had proven correct. 'Miss Townsend, will you do me the honour of accepting me as your husband?'

Laura stared up at the stranger who stood only an arm's length from her, thankful he hadn't taken her hand or dropped to one knee. She might have demanded a modicum of romance, but with her head still swimming from this unexpected proposal and a lack of food, she wasn't sure she could handle the shock of his touch.

Her parents had raised her to be sensible and she was, but it didn't mean she didn't have dreams. All her life she'd wanted the same happiness she'd seen between her parents, to have a shop and a family with a man she loved and respected. Uncle Robert had destroyed such dreams when he'd ground the shop and their reputations into the dirt. Whatever hope she possessed of reviving them now lay with this gentleman.

Mr Rathbone watched her and she studied him, trying to gauge something of the real person beneath the stiff businessman, but she could see very little. He'd not offered one ounce of warmth since he'd opened his distracting blue eyes in the tub, nor even a brief flicker of sympathy for her plight, yet now he wished to make her his wife and take care of both her and her mother. It defied all reason, except his argument made perfect, rational sense to the practical side of her.

It was the physical realities of marriage which nearly made her sensible side flee. He expected children and there was only one way to get them. The image of him naked in front of her seared her mind and she swallowed hard. After leaving his home, she'd hurried back here and slipped into bed beside her mother, trying and failing to sleep. Mr Rathbone's was the first male body she'd ever seen undressed and the memory of it had insisted on teasing her.

She touched the loose bun at the nape of her neck, the skin beneath suddenly damp with perspiration. Seeing him naked hadn't been an unpleasant experience. If she accepted him, she would see him again in such a state and he would see her, but what would their more intimate moments be like? Her fingers fumbled with the loose strands of hair she gathered up to tuck back in with the others. She'd heard the fallen women cackling together in the hallways. They clearly enjoyed congress with the men they ran after. However, late at night, through the cracked and thin walls of their tumbledown rooms, she often heard the couple next door and the indignities a cruel husband could inflict on his wife. She wasn't sure whether it would be pain or pleasure she'd face with Mr Rathbone, if he would be tender or approach the matter with stiff efficiency. Whatever might pass between them, if she refused his offer, a hundred more degrading things from many strange men most likely awaited her. Their situation was already growing desperate and she knew what happened to desperate women in Seven Dials. There was as much uncertainty with Mr Rathbone as there was without him. At least with him, Laura knew they would be warm and well fed. 'Yes, Mr Rathbone, I accept your proposal.'

'Good. My men are waiting with a cart in the street.' He strode to the window and waved to someone below. 'Ready your things, we leave at once.'

'You were so sure I'd accept.' The man was unbelievable.

He faced her as he had in his room, his confidence as mesmerising as it was irksome. 'I'm always sure when it comes to matters of business.'

Not a second later, the door opened and another young man in a tan coat entered. 'Philip, you kept us waiting so long, you had me worried.'

'Mr Connor, allow me to introduce Miss Townsend,

my intended. Miss Townsend, this is my friend and associate, Mr Justin Connor.'

Mr Connor swept off his hat and made a low bow. He was shorter than Mr Rathbone and broader through the hips and chest. His hair was light brown like his eyes, which revealed his amusement as much as his smile. 'A pleasure, Miss Townsend. It seems you've made quite an impression on my friend.'

Finally, someone with some sense of humour. 'Yes, he was just telling me how much my beauty and charm have enthralled him.'

'Spirited, too. I think it'll be a successful match.' He directed the comment as much to Mr Rathbone as to her.

If Mr Rathbone was needled by his associate's wit, he gave no indication, his countenance the same as when she'd surprised him in his bath. She wondered if he possessed any other expression.

Behind Mr Connor, four burly men in coarse but clean jackets filed into the room. Laura shifted on her feet at the notable tension coursing between them as they took up positions along the wall and near the door. From their thick belts hung clubs like the ones the night watchmen used to carry in Cheapside, where the draper shop was situated. The old watchmen didn't dare wander through these parts after dark. It was a wonder Laura had made it home unmolested after leaving Mr Rathbone's. It seemed whatever luck had led her into his house and out again without landing her in the Old Bailey had followed her home. Hopefully, it would continue to walk with her down the aisle.

'Mr Rathbone, is there some reason for the weapons?' If he was to be her husband, there was no point being shy with him. 'Are my mother and I to be made prisoners?'

Mr Rathbone moved closer, his eyes stern and serious. 'Mr Townsend has proven himself selfish and uncaring. I assume he has held on to you and your mother for this long because he thinks there's still something to gain from you. He won't take kindly to my removing you from his control.'

Laura sank a little, sickened by how accurate a sketch Mr Rathbone drew of her uncle. 'I don't know what he could hope to gain from us. Everything we had, he took.'

'Not everything.' The words were softer than before, just like his eyes. Concern lingered behind his stiff countenance, faint like the subtle weave in a silk pattern, something one could only see if it were held the correct way in the right light. It dissolved some of her fear and made her wonder what other hidden depths existed beneath his stoic exterior.

Mr Connor's watch case clicked closed. 'Philip, we should hurry, he could return.'

The prodding snipped the faint connection between them like scissors against a fine silk thread.

Mr Rathbone's eyes swept the room and, it seemed, deliberately avoided hers. 'Now, Miss Townsend, what should we remove?'

Laura looked over the sad furniture, happy to break his gaze and the odd line of reasoning it created. The setting sun cut through the room and she wished there were curtains to close, anything to hide the mouldering walls announcing the extent of her poverty. Despite how far they'd fallen since her father's death, the indignity of it all still burned. Most of the furniture was her uncle's, from his time with the army in India, where he'd made even less of a success of himself than he had in London. It was all in a sorry state, chipped and scratched. A couple of pieces belonged to her and her mother, the remnants of happier days in the rooms above the draper shop.

'We'll take the portrait of Father.' She motioned to the painting hanging over the sagging mantel. The varnish had turned dark around the edges, but those hazel eyes, so similar to Laura's, still watched over them with the same clarity as they had in life. It was the one aspect of her father the artist had rendered perfectly.

One of Mr Rathbone's men reached up and removed it from its nail, exposing the stained and faded wallpaper beneath it.

'And this?' Mr Rathbone tapped the tip of his walking stick against a locked trunk beside the bedroom door.

'It belongs to my uncle.' She rolled her wrist—the memory of the bruises she'd received when her uncle had caught her trying to pick the lock one night still stung. Whatever was in there, be it valuables or the body of a wife from India, he hadn't wanted her to see it. At this moment, she didn't care. He could have the trunk and whatever comfort he drew from the contents. 'The desk was my grandmother's. My mother will want it.'

Two men took up positions on either side of the desk,

heaving it up and shuffling past the door to her mother's room just as she tugged it open.

'What's going on here?' she demanded, her thin frame barely filling the tilted and sagging jamb. She snapped up her walking stick, laying it across the chest of the closest burly man and stopping both cold. 'Are we being evicted?'

Laura rushed to her mother, gently lowered the walking stick and took her by the arm to steady her. 'No, we're moving. Now, this moment.'

'Moving? Where?' She looked past Laura to the men behind her.

'Mother, allow me to introduce Mr Rathbone.'

Mr Rathbone bowed with respect, not mockery, but it failed to ease the suspicion hardening her mother's pale-brown eyes.

'Yes, I know who he is.' Her mother eyed the moneylender down the length of her straight nose like she used to do with ragamuffins intent on swiping a ribbon from the shop. The fierce look would send them scurrying off in search of easier pickings. Mr Rathbone wasn't so easily cowed. He met her stern glare as he had met almost everything else which had transpired between them, with no emotion.

'He and I are to be married and we are to live with him,' Laura announced. There was no other way to break the startling news.

'Was this the price of Robert's loan?' Her mother banged her walking stick against the floor. 'If so, I won't let you do it. I won't let you sell yourself to pay off one of Robert's debts. Your uncle isn't worth it. I deny my permission for this marriage.'

Laura stiffened. At three and twenty, she was two years past the age when such consent was necessary. However, she could feel her mother's strong will rising, a will which illness, misfortune and widowhood had sapped from her this past year. It gave Laura hope for her future.

'You have every right to object,' Mr Rathbone agreed, his features taking on a more civil countenance. 'As Miss Townsend's mother, I should have consulted you on the matter before making the proposal. I apologise for my breach of manners, but the circumstances of our betrothal are most unusual and allowed no time for a more formal courtship. May we discuss the matter now, in private?'

He moved forward and held out his arm. Beneath the stern set of her mother's expression, Laura caught the subtle arch of a raised eyebrow. He'd won her with his manners, hopefully whatever he intended to say to her would win her favour for the match.

'Yes, for I wish to know how my daughter has so suddenly transfixed you.' Mrs Townsend laid her hand on his arm and allowed him to lead her back into the cramped bedroom and help her to sit on the edge of the broken-down bed.

Laura pulled the door closed on them, not envying Mr Rathbone. It'd been a long time since she'd experienced her mother's chastising scrutiny. It was formidable, but she felt the moneylender equal to the challenge.

In the tiny sitting room, she tossed a weak smile to

the two remaining men flanking the door. They nodded in return before Mr Connor came to stand beside her.

'You're a very fortunate lady, Miss Townsend.' There was a hint of teasing in the compliment.

'Am I?'

'Yes, the widowed Mrs Templeton has been trying to capture Philip's attention for many months now. If I'd known aiming a pistol at him would do the trick, I'd have advised her to try it.' He threw back his head and laughed, filling the room with the merriest sound that had been heard there for ages.

Laura let out a long breath, his humour allowing her to smile. 'You are Mr Rathbone's business partner then?'

'We're friends. Grew up together. My father worked for his father, seeing to the more practical aspects of the business.' He nodded at the men by the door. 'Just as I do. Though not for much longer. I intend to establish myself in a business, once I decide which is the best to pursue.'

'Then I wish you the greatest success.'

'As I do you.' He threw her a wide sideways smile she couldn't fail to meet with one of her own.

'Tell me, is Mr Rathbone always so businesslike?'

'Oh, he's almost jovial today. You should see how stern he is with clients.'

'Apparently, I will.'

The door to her mother's room opened and she and Mr Rathbone stepped through it. His face revealed nothing of their conversation. Her mother, however, beamed, striding in on his arm as though a duchess in Hyde Park.

Laura gaped at them, wondering if there would be any end to the surprises in store for her today. She wasn't sure she could handle too many more.

'You have nothing to worry about, my dear.' Her mother patted her shoulder. 'Now, let's be off. I see they've taken the painting and the desk.' She looked up at Mr Rathbone. 'Would you please ask your men to fetch our trunk from the bedroom? Everything else Robert can have.'

'It would be my pleasure.' Mr Rathbone motioned to the two remaining men. They hurried past Laura into the bedroom, emerging a moment later with the sad trunk holding what remained of Laura's and her mother's possessions.

They were not a foot into the room when another figure staggered into the doorway, the stench of pipe smoke and cheap ale swirling around him.

Uncle Robert.

The air thickened with tension as Mr Rathbone's men slowly set down the trunk and straightened, dropping their hands to the clubs hanging from their belts. Mr Connor stood behind her uncle, his laughter gone as he shifted back his redingote to reveal the smooth handle of the pistol fastened at his waist. Laura's hand tightened on her mother's arm, Mr Rathbone's warning rushing back to her along with a cutting fear.

'What's all this then?' Robert Townsend demanded, struggling through his stupor to pronounce each word. His eyes fixed on the two men carrying the trunk and his sallow face scrunched with confusion before his bleary look fell on Mr Rathbone. At once, his red-rimmed eyes ignited with anger and he advanced on the moneylender. 'What's the meaning of this? I paid my debt to you. I owe you nothing.'

'My business here today doesn't concern you, Mr Townsend.' Philip crossed the room to the older man, preventing him from advancing any further. They were matched in height, but Robert Townsend was wider in the shoulders with a barrel chest made thicker by his large coat. 'Your niece has agreed to marry me. She and Mrs Townsend are removing to my house.'

'My business wasn't enough for you, was it? You had to have everything, you greedy pig.' Her uncle swayed forward on his feet. 'Do you know what Moll Topp pays for a virgin like her? It would have cleared all my debts.'

Her mother's hand tightened in Laura's the way it used to do when she was small and they would cross a busy street. Laura knew her uncle held no love for them, but she hadn't thought he'd sink to such sickening depths to save himself. She trembled as the shadow of another possible fate passed over her.

Only the stretching of Philip's leather glove as his hand tightened at his side revealed his disgust. 'I ask you to remember we are in the presence of ladies.'

'Don't pretend you're my better.' Robert stuck one thick and dirty finger in Mr Rathbone's face. 'I know your kind, feeding off the backs of men like me until you've gained every last shilling from us, then crushing us under your boot heels. Well, I won't be crushed, not by a coward like you.'

Robert pulled back his arm and rammed it forward. Mr Rathbone dipped, dodging the blow, then he came up fast, his fist catching Robert under the chin. The larger man stumbled back across the room, slamming into a small chair, his weight crushing it beneath him. He sat for a moment, stunned sober, and Laura wanted to rush over and add a few kicks of her own in retribution for all he'd done to her parents. There was no time, as Robert hauled himself to his feet, ready to rush at Mr Rathbone.

Mr Rathbone's men stepped up behind him, sticks clasped in their hands. Mr Connor pulled out his pistol and levelled it at the drunk man.

'I wouldn't do that, sir,' he warned.

Laura drew her mother back, ready to flee into the bedroom and bar the door, but no one moved. She barely dared to breathe.

Through the thin walls came the muffled voice of the man next door cursing at his wife.

Robert met Laura's eyes over Mr Rathbone's shoulder, hate twisting his lips into a sneer and drawing tight the red bruise forming beneath the grey stubble on his chin. 'You think you've got the better of me, ya little wench, but ya haven't. Neither have you, Mr Rathbone. Your men won't always be around to protect you. Some day you'll be alone and I'll be there.'

He spat at Mr Rathbone's feet.

Mr Rathbone plucked the hat from the table and settled it over his hair. 'Good day, Mr Townsend.'

He took Mrs Townsend by the arm and escorted both her and Laura around Robert. Laura eyed the old man acidly. Behind them, Mr Rathbone's men filed out, two carrying the trunk while the other two stood guard. Mr Connor was the last to leave, still brandishing the pistol.

Her mother leaned heavily on Mr Rathbone as they picked their way slowly down the stairs. It took all Laura's energy not to sag against the railings as fear pressed down hard on her. As she reached the bottom and stepped out into the chill evening air, she willed herself not to think of her uncle or how horribly true Mr Rathbone's assessment of him had proven. It no longer mattered.

Mr Rathbone settled her mother in the landau and Laura joined her. The hood was open and with the sun dipping, the air had taken on a chill. She drew the blanket over their knees as Mr Rathbone climbed in across from them.

Laura took one last look at the rickety building as the vehicle started to roll away. Robert stood at the filthy window, his obvious hate as searing as if the spring sun were reflecting off the panes. Laura swallowed hard. She might never see this rotting pile of beams again, but she felt certain this wasn't the last she'd see of her uncle.

Chapter Three

If events had proceeded with stunning rapidity in their rented rooms, it was a marvel to see how they moved once they arrived at Mr Rathbone's house. Business pulled him and Mr Connor away, leaving Laura and her mother in the capable hands of his housekeeper, Mrs Palmer. She proved as efficient as her employer, though much more talkative. In a flash she had them fed, their few things arranged in their separate but adjoining rooms, baths drawn and the clean nightclothes Mr Rathbone had procured from a client laid out on the bed.

While Mrs Palmer assisted Laura's mother, her coarse laugh carrying through the walls at various intervals and joined by her mother's higher one, Laura pulled on the cotton chemise. She sighed at the sweep of clean linen against her damp skin, revelling in it too much to be irritated by Mr Rathbone's presumption she would accept his strange suit. When she pulled on the silk banyan lying next to it, she nearly burst into tears. She'd parted with her French one, a Christmas gift from her father, long ago to buy food. She never thought she'd enjoy such a simple luxury again.

If the chemise and banyan felt heavenly, she could only imagine how the clean sheets on the high bed would feel. She touched the turned-back covers, eager to slide between them and give in to the exhaustion heightened by the warm bath, a full stomach and the comfortable night-dress, when the door whispered open behind her.

She turned, expecting to see a maid coming to empty the hip bath. Instead it was a young lady draped in a pale-pink gown, the first small curves of a woman's body just beginning to fill out the lines of it. Her face was round with the slight fullness of youth, but her chin was well defined and her eyes the same deep blue as Mr Rathbone's.

'Good evening, Miss Townsend. I'm Miss Jane Rathbone, Philip's sister.' She dipped a curtsy, pulling out the sides of her simple cotton gown before straightening, arms at her sides just as her brother held himself. 'Philip told me to look in on you and make sure you have everything you need. He also asked me to inform you that you needn't worry about what time you rise tomorrow.'

The girl spoke like her brother, too, but in a childish voice with the hint of a lisp.

'Did he?'

She nodded, her dark curls bobbing around her face and neck. 'You must enjoy it because it will probably be the last time. Philip likes everyone to keep to a schedule.'

'I don't doubt he does.' Nor did she mind. Her parents, with a business to run, had rarely let her dawdle about without purpose. There was always something to do. 'He's very practical.'

'You must be, too, if you agreed to marry him.'

Laura rubbed the soft banyan strings between her thumb and forefinger. 'In this instance, I've proven myself as sensible as your brother.'

'Then it will be a good match.'

I hope so, she thought, though any future now was better than the one her uncle had planned for her.

'In the morning, I'll see to it Mrs Townsend is dressed and has her breakfast. We were speaking earlier and she is eager for me to show her the garden, especially the roses.'

The girl's efficiency was surprising, yet not wholly unexpected. Laura wondered what her mother made of the strange creature. She wasn't quite sure what to make of her herself. 'Thank you, she is very fond of roses.'

'It's time for bed now, Jane.' Mr Rathbone appeared in the doorway behind his sister, his reminder more a firm request than the stern demand of a guardian.

Laura tightened the banyan a touch more about her neck. The chemise beneath stuck to her damp skin, pressing against it with an uncomfortable warmth and making her keenly aware of her undress beneath the silk. It brought to mind how he looked beneath his clothes.

His redingote was gone, revealing a dark jacket woven with a subtle checked pattern paired with tan breeches. Without the bulk of the wool, he seemed leaner, tighter. The well-tailored clothes emphasised his coiled strength, giving a hint of the lithe power he'd revealed when he'd avoided her uncle to land a stunning blow on his chin. Laura hadn't expected Mr Rathbone to be so physical and she struggled to keep herself steady as his masculinity pounced on her.

'Goodnight, Miss Townsend.' Jane hurried out, pausing to rise up on her toes and press a small kiss against her brother's cheek. He bent forward so she could reach him, straightening as she disappeared down the hall.

'Your sister is very charming.' Laura adjusted the banyan, trying to relieve some of the heat beneath it without the garment sliding open and making her appear a slatternly hoyden.

'Don't let her deceive you. She can be very stubborn when she wants to be.'

Laura smiled up at him. 'A family trait, I suspect.'

'Indeed.' He motioned to the room. 'May I?'

No!

'Of course.' Laura stepped back a touch as he entered, wondering at the awkwardness coming over her. The door was open and he maintained a respectful distance. Even his eyes had not wandered away from hers. Laura tried to match his fortitude, forcing her arms to stay at her sides instead of crossing over her chest. Though there was no point in covering herself entirely. In the very near future, he'd see more than her dressing gown.

'I won't keep you from your rest for long. I need to know if you'd prefer the banns to be read or if I should secure a common licence.'

'Do you truly want my opinion on the matter or should I acquiesce to your wishes?' She winced a little at her unsubtle question, but exhaustion, his presence in the room and the uncomfortable weight of the banyan were making her tetchy. She craved sleep and wanted to leave everything else until tomorrow.

If he minded she couldn't tell, his steady countenance not changing, even when he spoke. 'You'll find, Miss Townsend, as my wife, I'll often consult you on many things, this being only the first.'

'Of course. I'm sorry, it's been a long day, a long year in fact.'

'I understand, the past year has been a trying one for me as well.' His hard-set jaw softened and Laura remembered the only other time she had seen this happen, when he'd mentioned his wife. A grief she knew well from losing her father had washed over his face and the same expression crossed it again now. Whatever tragedy had brought him to the position of needing help under such unusual circumstances, it'd marked him as hard as all the trials of the past year had stamped her.

She was about to suggest the ease of the banns, eager to gain the three or four weeks it would take before the wedding to settle in and get to know something of the man she was about to share her life with, when an interrupting cough drew their attention to the door. From further away, Laura heard the wail of a small child.

A thin, middle-aged woman wearing a dark dress stepped into the room. 'Excuse me, Mr Rathbone, I didn't mean to disturb you in the middle of business.'

The woman's gaze jumped back and forth between Laura and Mr Rathbone.

Laura pulled the silk closer to her chin. She could only imagine what the woman must think she'd walked in on.

'Miss Marston, please meet my intended, Miss Townsend,' Mr Rathbone intervened, the stiff mask of business descending over Philip's face and covering the faint hint of emotion Laura had caught. 'Miss Marston is Thomas's nurse.'

'Oh, Miss Townsend, it's a pleasure to meet you.' Mrs Marston's smile was more surprised than relieved. Laura suspected she'd encounter many similar reactions in the days to come. 'Mr Rathbone, Thomas awoke crying and nothing I do will calm him. You always have such a way with him. I thought you might come to the nursery for a moment.'

'Yes, I will.' He started for the door, then paused. 'Miss Townsend, come and meet the gentleman who is part of our arrangement.'

His command given, he didn't wait for her. Mrs Marston wasn't at all surprised by the abruptness and followed her employer out of the room.

Laura walked behind them, the cries of a very young child growing louder as they stepped into the hallway. Mr Rathbone and Mrs Marston made steady strides for the door at the far end, but Laura's progress was slower. When she at last reached the room, the sight inside amazed her. Mr Rathbone stood with the small child in his arms, a little face pressed against his coat, the tears soaking into the wool. One chubby hand clutched his lapel, wrinkling the perfectly pressed crease.

'What's wrong, Thomas? Did you have a bad dream?' Mr Rathbone's steady voice filled the quiet as he shifted back and forth on the toes of his boots. 'You have nothing to worry about. I'm here.'

His deep voice conjured up memories of her father holding her and wiping away her tears after a nightmare. It seemed like such a long time since she'd felt so safe and loved. His words curled around her insides, soothing her as they did the boy until she wanted to lay her head on Mr Rathbone's shoulder and cry away all her frustrations and fears from the past year.

'He has such a way with the boy,' Mrs Marston murmured from beside her.

'Yes, he does.'

Whatever reasons she'd had for wanting to wait a month for the wedding disappeared. Too many things might happen in four weeks. He could change his mind and Laura didn't want to go back to the stinking Seven Dials and the cold, lonely desperation which crept like the damp through those wretched rooms. Even if she never knew the same affection he showed his son, just being in the presence of such love eased the hopelessness and despair she'd suffered for far too long. She didn't want to lose that.

Mr Rathbone buried his face in the child's soft blond curls, lowering his voice, but never stopping his soothing words. The boy sniffed, his eyes growing heavy as his father continued to rock him and stroke his little back. Soon the child's stuffy-nosed breaths gave way to steady, quiet snores. Mr Rathbone kissed his head, then gently laid Thomas back down in his bed. He pulled the blanket up under his chin, then brushed the soft curls with his hand before relinquishing his place next to the bed to Mrs Marston.

'Come,' he whispered to Laura, his entreaty for her to join him as soft as his soothing words to his son. 'We mustn't disturb him.'

In the hallway, with the door closed behind them, he faced her. A circle of wet from his son's tears broke the smooth weave of his coat, but he didn't brush at it or curse the spot. The caring father stood over her, the man of business gone as his eyes swept her face.

Then the look faded and he began to turn and walk away, but she wasn't ready to see him go.

'Mr Rathbone.' She reached out and took his hand.

He whirled, eyes wide, just as stunned as she was by the gesture, but he didn't pull away. A slight connection jumped between them like a cricket hops between two slender blades of grass, bending but not breaking them. One by one his fingertips pressed against the back of her hand and words deserted her as his breath whispered across her forehead. She didn't know if the strange catch in her chest was from the excitement of the move, watching her uncle receive a well-deserved beating or the whirlwind of going from pauper to the expected wife of a well-to-do gentleman in the space of two days.

Swallowing hard, she recovered her wits enough to finally speak. 'I'd prefer the common licence.'

With his son's tears soaking through the wool to wet the linen underneath, Philip could deny Miss Townsend nothing, not even his hand. 'Whatever you wish.'

Something whispered between them, subtle as the faint scent of lavender soap surrounding Laura. This was the first time they'd touched, but it was as comforting as if it were the hundredth. It soothed the panic the unexpected intimacy had sent shooting through him.

'Thank you for all you did for us today.' Her fingers tightened with her gratitude, digging into the bruises colouring his knuckles.

He winced and her grip eased. It was his chance to pull away, but he didn't. He couldn't.

'You hurt your hand.' The sleeve of her banyan slid back as she traced the dark marks on his knuckles, revealing the soft skin and the hint of her chemise beneath.

'It wasn't the first time.' He forced the words through his lips. She stood so close he could see the wet curls at the nape of her neck clinging to her skin. Heat rushed in hard beneath his stomach, making it difficult to stand still, or concentrate on anything beside the green and gold in her eyes. 'Mr Connor and I train with a pugilist. It's imperative my people and I know how to protect ourselves.'

'Will I learn to box?' A playful smile danced along the corners of her full lips.

The sharp twitch of old emotions he'd buried with his wife struck him, as hard as Laura's pulse against his skin.

'No, but you'll learn to properly load and fire a pistol.' He slid his hand out of hers, careful not to jerk away as he struggled to distance himself from her and the memories scratching at his heart. 'Goodnight, Miss Townsend.'

She dropped her hands to cross them in front of her, letting him go. 'Goodnight, Mr Rathbone.'

In the confines of the stairwell, out of her sight, Philip paused. Opening and closing his fist, he tried to shake off the heat of her fingers. There was only one other time in his life when he'd experienced a connection so powerful with a stranger. The first time he'd touched Arabella.

He jerked up straight and descended the stairs. This was nothing like what he'd experienced with Arabella. This was a business deal, a venture plain and simple. He'd researched the lady, spent hours pondering both the good and bad aspects of the union. Yet in the end, it hadn't been the tally sheet which had tilted Philip towards her. It was intuition.

Fear nearly choked the breath from him.

Intuition had failed him before where marriage was concerned. What if it was failing him again?

'If I didn't know you better, I'd say you needed a drink,' Justin chided as Philip stepped down into the hall.

'I need exercise.' Anything to clear the uncertainty pummelling him.

An hour later, Justin swung at Philip, who ducked and came up behind him. The skin over Philip's bruised knuckles smarted as he curled his fingers into a tighter fist.

'Not like you to be so sloppy.' Justin danced around the ring out of Philip's reach. 'What's gnawing at you?'

A bolt of pain raced along Philip's arm as he jabbed

at Justin and missed. They'd been sparring for over half an hour and neither the exertion nor the sweat trickling down the sides of his face had snuffed out the faint spark smouldering in the back of Philip's mind, the spark ignited by Laura's hand. The spark he feared was distracting him from noticing a potential mistake. 'Nothing.'

'You mean nothing as in your soon-to-be wife?' They circled one another, fists raised. The sounds of other men fighting nearby and the pugilists calling out orders to them rang through the high-ceilinged hall. Though not as elegant or well fitted as Gentleman Joe Jackson's establishment, the lessons here were for men like Philip and Justin who needed their skills to defend themselves, not simply dance around their opponents for show. 'You know, if you have needs, I could arrange something less taxing than a wife.'

Justin stepped in to make a hit, but Philip side-stepped out of the way. 'My needs have no bearing on the situation.'

His needs had nearly risen up in the hallway outside Thomas's room to embarrass him and quite possibly her.

'Liar.' Justin circled Philip, whose raw knuckles itched to knock the smug grin off his friend's face. 'She's the most attractive woman yet to appear on your doorstep, demanding her assets.'

Philip swung, his fist brushing Justin's arm as he turned out of the way. 'She wasn't on my step, she was in my bedroom.'

'And she will be again, many times with the way you've arranged it,' Justin taunted, as unguarded with his words as Philip was guarded with his thoughts. 'I still can't believe you're doing this.'

'Why?' Philip jabbed at Justin. 'My son needs a mother, my sister a chaperon and my house a proper steward.'

The tally sheet he'd compiled on Miss Townsend rushed back to him. What was he failing to see? Why was he doubting himself?

'You think it'll be so simple, but mark my words, it won't.' Justin swung at him, but Philip didn't turn fast enough and his shoulder burned from the hit. 'It never is where women are concerned.'

Philip shook out his arm, the pain dull compared to his concern. Justin was right, it wasn't so simple, nothing in life ever was. He'd loved Arabella and she'd loved him. They'd courted and married and she'd fallen pregnant with his child. Simple. The complications had begun with her pains. Then everything had turned into a nightmare.

'We've sparred enough today.' Philip snatched a towel from the hook on the wall and scraped the coarse linen over his face. It wasn't too late to end the venture. He could send Miss Townsend to the safety of Halcyon House or provide her with a few pounds to start another draper business.

He ran the towel over the back of his neck, studying the mix of footprints in the sand on the floor. He couldn't send her away any more than he could leave Thomas to cry in his bed. He'd seen her lodgings, heard Mr Townsend's nasty words. He knew what waited for her beyond the protection of his home and name. He'd made her an offer and she'd accepted the terms of the deal. This would not become the first time he reneged on a contract.

His determination failed to erase his unease. 'What if I'm wrong about Miss Townsend, the way I was with the silversmith I loaned money to all those years ago?'

'Oh, you're wrong. But not in the way you think.' Justin rocked back on his heels and Philip nearly struck him in the gut. 'You think you can keep Miss Townsend in your house, share her bed and still remain the aloof man of business?'

A bachelor with a taste for numerous women wasn't a man to look to for marital advice, no matter how deep their friendship. 'She understands the terms of our arrangement.'

'Perhaps, but you don't.' He smacked Philip on the arm. 'Now come and get cleaned up. You have tomorrow to face. Tonight, I have a very pleasurable venture of my own to see to.'

Justin turned and made for the dressing rooms.

Philip wrapped the towel behind his neck and gripped both ends. Justin was mistaken if he thought there was more to this contract than convenience. Miss Townsend was as practical as Philip, if not a little rash. She understood their arrangement. Or did she?

The idea Justin might be right about Miss Townsend wanting more nagged. He wasn't stone enough not to feel something for her. She was too determined and strong not to admire. In many ways she reminded him of himself, still struggling to find her feet after a reeling loss. As his wife, she deserved his respect and he would give it. He refused to surrender his heart. Doing so was not a part of their bargain.

He strode to the dressing room, flinging the damp towel at the boy attendant near the door.

He'd made the mistake of writing his emotions into a marriage contract once before and had been made to regret it. He wouldn't do it again.

Chapter Four

The steady chirping of birds broke through the haze of Laura's fading dream. First one warbled, then another, until a chorus seemed to sit outside her window. Over the sharp tweets, Laura strained to hear the bell and her father's voice through the floorboards as he greeted customers in the shop below her room. The only thing she heard was the click of the bedroom-door handle and the soft swish of shoes over the carpet. Laura snuggled deeper into the thick pillow, knowing it was her mother coming to chide her for sleeping late. She clutched the clean sheet up around her chin, trying to snatch a few more precious seconds of rest.

'Miss Townsend, are you awake?' Mrs Palmer asked.

Laura sat up, sweet memories of her old room, of her father alive and her mother well vanishing along with the feeling of warmth and love. The loss burned a hole through her chest.

'Yes, I am.'

A fire crackled in the grate. Laura wondered how

she'd managed to sleep through the maid coming in to light it. Perhaps it was the fact she'd slept at all which had allowed her to remain so soundly in her dreams. In Seven Dials, with all the noise from the other tenants and Uncle Robert's drunken mutterings, it'd always been so difficult to sleep. 'I'm sorry I'm still in bed. I should be up.'

'You have nothing to be sorry about.' Mrs Palmer laid a simple blue-cotton dress across the foot of the bed. 'Mr Rathbone had Mrs Fairley, Miss Jane's modiste, send this over. I'm to tell you, you have an appointment with Mrs Fairley at her shop this afternoon. She has a few other dresses from an unpaid order and will alter them to tide you over until a new wardrobe can be made.'

New dresses. Excitement crowded in beneath Laura's lingering sense of loss. The idea of wearing a dress which wasn't practically threadbare proved as irresistible as waking in a clean bed with no sign of rats having traipsed across the floor during the night. Laura picked up the sleeve of the dress and examined the fine stitching. 'I've never had a modiste make my dresses. Mother always did it.'

'You'll like Mrs Fairley. She does good work and is quite nice, too. Came to Mr Rathbone about two years ago seeking a loan to improve her business and has done quite well for herself since. Mr Rathbone prides himself on patronising those he helps who make a go of things instead of wasting the money.'

Laura didn't have to ask what happened to those who wasted Philip's money. She already knew.

She laid the sleeve of the dress down, running her hand over the length of it to press it flat. The dress was sewn from a sturdy but soft cotton, Indian most likely, more utilitarian than silk, but with a few ribbons or the right bonnet it would suit as well for an afternoon at home as it would for attending a small tea. A fond smile tugged at her lips. She could practically hear her father's words in her own thoughts, see the fabric from the bolt draped over his arm as he explained the weave and quality to a prospective lady buyer. Laura's hands stilled and the smile faded. That was all gone now. A visit from the modiste would be the closest she'd ever come to experiencing it again.

'Is something wrong, miss?' Mrs Palmer pressed.

'I'm all right, only a little overwhelmed.' Truth be told, her head was still spinning from everything and it was all she could do to focus. How she would make it through the myriad other, sure to be surprising things which might happen this week, she didn't know. However, if the most troubling thing facing her today was the shock of a new dress, then she really had no troubles at all. After all, she'd dealt with worse problems during the past year, much worse.

Mrs Palmer slid Laura's old black dress from the top of the chair where Laura had draped it last night. If Mrs Palmer was concerned about the tatty dress staining the fine silk upholstery, she didn't reveal it. Her face was all kindness and concern, reminding Laura of the baker's wife who used to give her leftover biscuits from time to time until her husband had found out and put a stop to it.

'I know it all must seem so strange, Mr Rathbone making up his mind so quick about you, but I assure you, Miss Townsend, you couldn't have asked for a better man.'

It seemed Mrs Palmer was as enamoured of Mr Rathbone as Laura's mother. If only she could be so certain about her decision. However, it was a comfort to see the older woman so eager for Laura to like Mr Rathbone as much as she obviously did. It was better than her trying to secretly warn her off him.

Mrs Palmer's ruddy smile returned to her full cheeks. 'Here's me gabbing with the day getting away from us both. There's breakfast waiting for you in the dining room when you're ready. I'll send Mary up to help you dress.'

'I can manage.'

'I don't doubt you can, but Mr Rathbone wants her to assist you. If you need anything, you be sure to let me know.'

Mrs Palmer dipped a curtsy then left as quietly as she'd entered, the nearly frayed edge of Laura's old dress fluttering behind her and almost catching in the closing door. The dress would probably be tossed in the kitchen fire the moment she reached it. Laura was glad to see it go. It was an ugly reminder of how much she and her mother had lost during the past year.

What would the next year bring? She still couldn't say.

Laura flung back the covers and slipped out of bed, determined not to complain or worry, but to face whatever was coming with optimism. At least her uncle had fallen in debt to a young, handsome moneylender and not to one of the many crooked, gap-toothed men she'd seen haunting the rookery in search of payment. It was the only thing of value he'd ever done for her.

A soft knock at the door was followed by the entrance of a young woman with a snub nose and brown hair peeking out from beneath a white cap. 'I'm Mary. I'm here to dress you.'

The girl said little as she helped Laura dress, lacing Laura's worn stays over the crisp white chemise. Holding still so the maid could work gave Laura the chance to take her first real look at the room. It was smaller than Mr Rathbone's, but well appointed with solid, simple pieces of furniture. She wondered if they'd been made by one of the upholsterers who used to frequent the shop. She studied the faint white line running through the flowing silk of the bed curtains, thinking it a familiar pattern, when the image of another room suddenly came to mind.

She wondered how many more mornings she'd wake up here before she found herself in Mr Rathbone's bed.

She breathed hard against the tightening stays, fear and anticipation pressing against her chest. She should have asked for the banns instead of insisting on the common licence. She wasn't ready for such intimacy, not yet, not with everything, especially their future together, so unsure.

Mary tied off the stays then picked up the dress, opening it so Laura could slip inside. She held up her arms and let the blue cotton flow down over her shoulders and body. The soft material made her sigh with delight and eased some of her fears. A man who was so loving and tender with his son wouldn't be cruel to her.

Mary did up the row of buttons at the back, but the dress was too large in the bust. Even Laura's well-formed breasts weren't ample enough to keep the front from billowing and gaping open. While Mary pinned the dress to make it fit better, Laura opened and closed her hand. The shock of Mr Rathbone's touch had remained with her long after she'd blown out her candle and settled into the clean sheets last night. It wasn't his hand in hers which had remained with her the longest, but the conflict she'd noticed coursing beneath his calm exterior. More than once he'd begun to withdraw from her before his palm had settled again, surrendering to her hold. It was as if he both wanted and didn't want to draw close to her. It seemed strange for a man who seemed so determined about everything to be confused about something as simple as touching his intended. Although it wasn't as simple as she wanted to believe.

At Mary's urging, Laura seated herself in the chair before the dressing table and let the young maid arrange her hair. She barely noticed the tugging and combing as she remembered Mr Rathbone's eyes upon hers. There'd been more in the joining of their hands than conveying her desire to wed quickly. There was something she hadn't allowed herself to consider possible when she'd accepted his proposal yesterday—a deeper concern for her than business.

The faint hint of it made her eager to be done with the dressing table and be in front of him again.

With her hair arranged into a simple jumble of curls at the back of her head, Laura made her way downstairs. She felt guilty leaving Mary behind to see to the room. She'd tried to assist her, perfectly capable of making her own bed, but the maid had insisted it was her duty to straighten it and Laura had reluctantly left her to it.

Laura took in the house as she moved slowly down the hallway. Last night, with the myriad arrangements and settling in, there hadn't been time to explore. Her first time here, she'd been too occupied trying not to be seen to admire anything more than the direct route from the back door, down the hall, to the stairs.

The upstairs hall was plain, the length of it punctuated by doors to the various bedrooms and landscapes in gilded frames. The staircase at the far end made one turn before opening into the entrance hall below. It wasn't overly high, but wider than those she'd seen in the few merchants' houses she'd visited with her father when she was a child. Stone covered the floor, leading to a solid door flanked by two glass windows. Through them she could see people passing by in a steady stream along the pavement lining Bride Lane. Some of them entered the churchyard of St Bride's across the street, the rest hurried on to nearby Fleet Street.

Making for the dining room at the back of the house, Laura noted the rich panelling lining the downstairs hall seemed less dark and foreboding in the bright morning light, though it still made her a touch uneasy to be striding so boldly through the house. It was nearly incomprehensible to think she would soon be mistress of it.

She passed the study, the masculine mahogany desk, neatly ordered shelves and solid chairs inside indicating this must be where Mr Rathbone managed his affairs. He wasn't there and she ventured inside. The neatness and fine taste of the appointments matched his attire. Where the back room behind the draper shop had always been cluttered with account books and fabrics, not a speck of dirt or an out-of-place ledger marred the clean lines of this room. Though Laura was by no means slovenly, she wondered how she would be able to keep pace with such a man.

The French doors on the far wall leading to the garden drew her to them. Outside, the sky was clear, with a few wispy clouds floating past the sun. They were only a mile or so from Seven Dials, but it might have been halfway around the world for how different everything appeared here. The air seemed cleaner, the buildings solid stone instead of sagging wood. The whole garden was green, punctuated by the white and red of blooming roses, their brightness a welcome sight after the grime and dirt of Laura's former lodgings.

The moneylender's fortune must be larger than she'd thought for him to possess the luxury of such a garden, one surrounded by a tall, fine wall. Just beyond it, through the iron gate, the one she'd crept through the other night, she noticed a horse staring out from the mews.

In the centre of the garden, Jane escorted Laura's mother around a raised brick bed filled with rose-bushes. Excitement lightened each muffled word as Jane pointed out flower after flower, motioning to them with the pride of a silversmith displaying her finest wares.

As they made a turn, her mother caught sight of Laura. She raised a hand in greeting, her simple gesture joined by Jane's more eager wave. Jane's enthusiasm eased the stiffness in her posture and made her look more like a young girl rather than a female copy of her brother.

Whatever changes Laura's mother had wrought in Jane, the young lady's effect on the older woman was tenfold. Laura's mother wore a dress of dark-blue muslin. It needed to be altered to fit properly, but the clean lines and fine material lent her a measure of dignity which showed itself in the new straightness in her posture. She didn't lean as heavily on her walking stick as before and for the first time in over a year, she appeared rested and happy. Whatever Laura's concerns about herself, they were eased by the smile gracing her mother's thin face.

Laura's stomach growled and she left the window and the room to search out the food Mrs Palmer had promised. The dining room sat across the hall from the study, a shining table with ball-and-claw feet dominating the centre. The panelling didn't extend in here, but gave way to a pale-blue paper on the walls overseen by the portrait of a matronly woman in the dress and cap of a few decades ago.

A footman stood beside a heavy sideboard laden with silver dishes full of eggs, ham and bread. Laura gasped at the plenty of it. During all the weak suppers in Seven

Dials, she never thought she'd ever see or enjoy such abundance again.

Taking the plate offered by the footman, she selected a little food from each silver server, then sat down at the table. She savoured every bite, glad to be alone so she could relish the simple food without the humiliation of revealing the depths of her previous deprivation. After using her toast to wipe up the last bits of her second helping, she rose to get another serving when Chesterton, the butler, stepped into the room.

'Miss Townsend.' Her name sounded so imperious and important in his deep voice. 'Mr Rathbone would like you to join him in the sitting room.'

'Of course.' Laura slid the plate down on to the buffet, suddenly feeling like a thief for indulging so much. The fork scraped and clanked across the porcelain and she winced, wondering when she'd become such a scared mouse. She straightened the knife and fork on the plate, then stood straight, clasping her hands in a businesslike manner in front of her. 'Would you please show me the way?'

'It would be my pleasure.' He almost smiled and Laura caught something of Mrs Palmer's tenderness around his eyes. With everyone silently encouraging her rather than sneering, laughing or pitying her behind her back, it made the idea of easing into her new place as their mistress a great deal easier.

As she followed Chesterton out of the dining room and across the hall, she thought it strange to have so many people thinking well of her presence here and her the only one in doubt.

Jane came bounding down the stairs, carrying a book and Laura's mother's dark shawl, looking more like a thirteen-year-old than she had last night. Spying Laura, she halted and took the last few stairs with the elegance of a woman far beyond her years. 'Good morning, Miss Townsend.'

'Please, call me Laura.' She smiled warmly, trying to put the girl at ease, disliking such seriousness in one so young.

The stiff set of Jane's body eased with Laura's invitation. 'And you may call me Jane.'

'I see you and my mother are getting along well.'

'Very well.' A proud smile spread over her stern lips, bringing back the youthful light which had illuminated her face as she'd come down the stairs. 'We are to visit Mrs Fairley together tomorrow. She was too tired to go today, but you mustn't worry about her. I'll see she gets enough rest.'

'Thank you. It means a great deal to me to have someone keeping her company while I'm occupied.'

'It's my pleasure. I'm going to read to her now. Where are you going?'

'The sitting room.'

'Philip summoned you?'

Laura choked back a laugh. 'In a manner of speaking.'

The girl moved closer as if she possessed something urgent to impart. 'Touch his hand again like you did last night. Miss Lavinia does it in *The Wanderer* and it drives Mr Welton absolutely mad.'

Laura crossed her arms, mimicking the way her

mother used to stare at her whenever she'd offered unasked-for advice or stuck her nose in where it was unwanted. 'Jane, were you spying on us?'

'No, not at all.' Jane possessed too much of her brother's confidence to be cowed by Laura's stern look. 'I peeked out my door and saw you. You two looked just how I imagined Viscount Rapine and Miss Anne must look in *The Lothario.*'

'You're reading *The Lothario*?' Her brother couldn't possibly approve of such a choice.

Apparently he didn't, for Jane clapped her hand over her mouth as if she'd mistakenly revealed a great secret. Her eyes darted to the butler standing a polite distance away, then back to Laura. 'You won't tell Philip, will you? If he finds out I'm reading romantic novels, he might end my subscription to the lending library.'

Laura dropped her stern look and all pretence at reprimanding. 'As long as you reserve your employment of their knowledge to dispensing advice and nothing else, I won't tell your brother and I won't object.'

Jane sighed with relief. 'Good, because Mrs Townsend would be very disappointed. We're going to start reading *Glenarvon* this afternoon and I can't wait.'

'You and my mother are going to read *Glenarvon*?' She never would have been allowed to read such a salacious book. With the exception of the few novels Laura had managed to borrow from friends and sneak into her room, her reading had been comprised of business tracts and the stock pages. While she was grateful for the education, especially now, she wondered when her mother had grown so soft.

'Yes.' Jane moved a touch closer, whispering with Laura in collusion. 'I hear it's quite scandalous.'

'I've heard so, too.' Laura dropped her voice, encouraging the youthful confidence between them. It was a treat to see Jane acting more like a young lady than a stiff governess. 'When you're done with it, I'd like to read it. I might learn a trick or two.'

Jane gaped at Laura. Then a smile broke the line of her lips and she laughed, a good genuine girlish one which brightened the hall. 'I shall be happy to pass it on to you. Now, I must return to Mrs Townsend. I've kept her waiting long enough and she needs her shawl.'

'And I must answer your brother's summons.'

Jane sobered, laying a hand on Laura's arm. 'Don't worry, Philip isn't as stern as he likes everyone to think.'

'I'll keep it in mind.' And she would, for if his sister believed it, it was most likely true.

With a squeeze of her hand, Jane let go and hurried off down the hall, allowing the door at the back of the house leading to the garden to bang shut behind her.

Laura wished she could follow. After a year of looking after her mother, it felt odd to relinquish her duties to someone else, but at least Jane's attention meant her mother wasn't left alone in a strange place while Laura attended to business.

'Here you are, Miss Townsend.' Chesterton stopped at the sitting-room door at the front of the house.

Laura gave him a smile of gratitude and stepped inside.

Mr Rathbone stood near the fireplace, reviewing papers. Through the sheer curtains behind him passed the shadows of people moving on the pavement outside. Laura barely noticed them. The only thing she could concentrate on was the soft light coming through the delicate fabric and spreading over Mr Rathbone's profile. It lightened his dark hair and caressed the strong line of his nose. A fine, camel-coloured jacket draped his shoulders, emphasising the solidness of the long arms arched gracefully in front of him as he reviewed papers. He appeared to her like one of the Greek statues she'd seen in the British Museum. She'd gone there before she'd sold her last decent dress to view the Elgin Marbles and distract herself from her troubles. Like the statues, Mr Rathbone was elegant and refined, yet the memory of his sudden, lethal movements facing her uncle made her shiver. There was an edge of danger beneath his calm facade, one she hoped he reserved only for the worst clients.

'Good morning, Mr Rathbone.' She tugged down the overlarge bodice, which kept rising up as she moved deeper into the room. She wished she looked as fine and well put together as him, instead of unkempt and thin in her second-hand clothes. 'You summoned me?'

He didn't look up from his papers. 'My sister's choice of words, I assume.'

'She has a very interesting sense of humour.'

'She's a hoyden.' He reached up and removed the dagger mounted on two brass hooks to a wood plaque hanging over the mantel. Behind it lay a small safe set into the wall. 'However, Jane is smart and minds herself well enough for someone her age. She shouldn't give you trouble. If she does, speak to me about it at once.'

She wouldn't speak to him. No, she would handle it in her own way and see to it there was more of the spirited young lady on the stairs and less of the dour miss. 'Yes, Mr Rathbone.'

Resting the mounted dagger on the floor, he finally met her eyes. 'Please, call me Philip.'

His gaze was intense, but not stern, inviting her to explore more deeply the slight bond weaving them together like embroidery over fine netting.

'Yes, of course, Philip.' The name was as awkward on her tongue as a button held with her teeth while she was sewing. It would take practice getting used to such intimacy with this stranger. Except he wasn't a stranger, but her husband-to-be.

'And you may call me Laura.' She adjusted the dress again, then dropped her hands, determined to face him with dignity. Her attire was only temporary and, with the modiste's help, she'd soon appear respectable again.

Her confidence wavered. Whatever respectability she regained today, it would be thanks to his coin and effort, not hers. Something in her rankled. She'd struggled so hard to save the business, herself and her mother and in the end she could only do it by falling under this man's protection. She tried to recall her mother's encouraging words, or even Mrs Palmer's simple observation about Philip, but none of them came back to her with enough force to push away the strange regret of not having achieved her own salvation, or the nasty idea she was selling herself.

Philip broke from her gaze to open the safe and slide the papers inside.

'Are you sure you can trust your sister's behaviour to a woman who sneaks into men's houses and threatens them in the night?' It was a flippant question with an edge of seriousness. He was certainly trusting her now by revealing the safe and the key on the small ring in his pocket which opened it. There was nothing to stop her from stealing the key, emptying the safe and sneaking away with her mother while he slept. She would never do such a deceitful thing, but he couldn't know this.

'You aren't a thief.' He swung the safe door closed and locked it.

Apparently, he did know she wasn't capable of robbing him.

She tugged at the dress, wishing she possessed the same unshakeable confidence in herself and her decision to marry as he did in her and his own decisions.

He returned the mounted dagger to the hooks. The silver cufflinks holding the crisp ends of his sleeves together over his strong wrists flashed with the morning sunlight. Only the yellowing bruises along his knuckles kept his appearance from being perfect.

He'd received those bruises for defending her. It was ungrateful of her to stand here lamenting his help because it hadn't come from her own effort, yet she still hated the idea of needing his charity.

His papers secure, this pleasant morning repartee came to an end. 'I asked you to join me because a gentleman is here in need of a loan. It's the perfect opportunity to begin your training.'

'So soon?' The eggs threatened to revolt in her

stomach. Perhaps she shouldn't have enjoyed a second serving.

'The prospective client is a cloth importer and your expertise might be beneficial to the transaction. Before I decide whether or not to invest in his business, I need to know if his proposal has merit.'

'My uncle's plan had merit,' she challenged.

'Because it was yours,' he answered flatly.

'But you didn't know that then.'

'I do now.'

'Yet you still lent to my uncle. Why?' she persisted, her unease making her quarrelsome.

'As I said before, he possessed the collateral to secure the loan. If he'd rebuilt the business, he wouldn't have been the first unlikely client to exceed my expectations.'

She had the distinct impression the remark was directed at her, but it didn't ease the way his past dealing with her uncle Robert continued to chafe. 'Did you know about me and my mother?'

'He failed to reveal your presence when he initially approached me, but in my research—'

'Your research?' Curse it, he was so methodical.

'I research all my clients before extending a loan. I discovered your and Mrs Townsend's presence.'

'And you were still willing to let him ruin us?'

'No.' His expression remained impassive, but the force and sincerity behind the single word was strong enough to wilt her anger.

It didn't stop her from gaping at him in disbelief, not knowing what to think. 'But—'

'I'll explain all to you in good time. Now, we must

see to Mr Williams.' He motioned to the door instead of offering her his arm. 'Shall we?'

'Of course.' It was better to face whatever waited for her in his study than to linger here and pick a fight. Being irritable would get her nowhere and it was a poor way to thank him for all he was doing for her and her mother.

She moved past Philip and he stepped back, as if deliberately maintaining his distance. She was tempted to grasp his hand to see if she could reclaim a little of the connection they'd experienced last night. Instead she strode past him and out of the sitting room, afraid of rattling him with her boldness. With her first taste of this business looming at the other end of the hall, she didn't want him out of sorts. She was anxious enough about facing a man in need of money without disturbing Philip's calm.

Outside the room, he fell in step beside her.

'What should I do?' she asked.

'Listen. If you hear something alarming, speak up at once.'

How strange this all seemed when all her life she'd imagined herself behind a shop counter. It was another item to add to the growing list of things to which she must become accustomed, or perhaps resign herself. 'Do you think him a good candidate for a loan?'

'I don't want to prejudice you.'

His answer was strangely flattering, suggesting he valued her opinion. Hopefully, she wouldn't disappoint him.

Laura followed him into the study. Inside, Mr Connor straightened from where he'd been slouching against the wall next to the French doors. She eyed Mr Connor's dark coat, trying to catch the outline of the pistol she suspected was hidden beneath. How often did he need a weapon here in Philip's home?

The importer who occupied one of the two chairs in front of the desk rose to greet Laura and Philip. He studied her from under bushy black-and-grey brows, his scrutiny unsettling as she took the chair beside Philip's. Something about the rotund man seemed familiar, but Laura couldn't place his face. He appeared to regard her with the same dilemma before giving up and focusing on Philip.

Outside, her mother's muffled voice carried in from where she sat with Jane while the girl read aloud. For the second time that morning, Laura envied Jane, wishing she could pass a leisurely hour engrossed in a story, rather than learning how to lend money.

'Mr Williams, this is Miss Townsend, she will be assisting us today,' Philip announced to the importer as he settled himself behind the desk.

'Don't see why we need a woman here,' Mr Williams said huffily.

'I find her opinions necessary.' Philip rested his hands coolly on the arms of the chair.

'Have it your way.' Mr Williams shrugged and stretched his legs out in front of him as though settling in for an evening beside the fire.

His attitude struck Laura as false. He wanted to look at ease, but the way his foot kept moving back and forth betrayed his nervousness. The small but constant fidgeting reminded her of how Uncle Robert used to face her whenever she'd cornered him about missing inventory.

'Mr Rathbone, I'll come to the point,' Mr Williams began. 'There's a new cotton out of Georgia with a strand so strong it can be woven in half the time and at greater speed than even the cotton coming from Hispaniola. I don't have the money to import it, which is why I've come to you.'

Laura shifted in her chair. She'd heard about men trying to develop such a strand, but she'd never heard of them succeeding. The weak strands of such cotton seemed better suited to making paper than weaving cloth. She looked to Mr William's foot. It moved faster back and forth on the heel. He'd need a cobbler soon if he kept up such fidgeting.

'And your collateral?' Philip asked.

'My shares in a shipping business.' He withdrew a paper from his coat and laid it on the desk.

Philip picked up the certificate, briefly flashing the yellowing bruises on his hand before he settled the document low in front of him to review. Laura studied him as he read, trying to gauge if he saw what she did. Was it only her lack of knowledge about this business and her own discomfort at sitting in a hodgepodge dress in the middle of such an orderly office that was making her uneasy?

At last, Philip folded the paper and laid it in the centre of the clean blotter. She couldn't tell if he approved or disapproved of it. Neither could Mr Williams, judging by the increased pace of his rocking foot.

'And your personal situation? Do you have a wife and children?' Philip asked.

'Haven't much seen the need of tying myself to an interfering woman.' He slid Laura a hard look which she matched with a steady one of her own. 'Though I don't see what difference it makes to a sound investment like this one.'

Laura glanced back and forth between Philip and Mr Williams, wondering if she should say something about the cotton before Philip agreed to the loan. There was nothing sound about his proposal. Philip had asked her to speak out if she had reservations, but what he'd said in the quiet of the hallway and what he wanted from her now with the client staring him down like an overeager bulldog might be a very different thing.

'It makes a great deal of difference to me since it's my money you're seeking to fund your endeavour,' Philip countered. 'If you fail, I'll be the one bearing the brunt of the loss.'

'I won't fail and you'll get back three times the amount I'm asking for.'

Philip paused and Laura shifted in her chair, unsure whether he was preparing to let the man down or accept his offer. 'When would I see the dividends?'

'There's a ship out of Portsmouth ready to sail within the week if I can raise the money. In six months' time it could be back here, the cotton sold and a tidy sum in your pocket.'

Philip paused again and Laura couldn't stay silent any longer.

'You won't see a farthing of what he's promising.'

'This doesn't concern you, woman,' Mr Williams snapped, struggling to twist his large self around in the chair and glare her into silence.

'Miss Townsend, you have reservations about Mr Williams's proposal?' Philip coaxed, unruffled by the importer's outburst.

'Don't matter what she thinks of it,' Mr Williams scoffed. 'You're the man. It's up to you.'

'As the man, I'm eager to hear the lady's opinion.'

Laura swallowed hard, wishing she possessed Philip's composure, but now was no time to lose her wits. 'What he's suggesting won't work. The new cotton from Georgia isn't strong enough to take the pressure of the new water-powered looms. Mr Williams may import the cotton, but he won't be able to weave it as he's indicated and it won't be worth even half of what he's going to pay to buy and ship it.'

'You don't know anything, girlie, except what your dressmaker tells you. Judging by your frock, even she don't know two whiskers about cloth.' The man snorted.

'My father was John Townsend, a draper in Wood Street, Cheapside. I worked with him in his shop my whole life. I know more about cloth, cotton, silk and muslin than you can imagine.'

Philip exchanged a quick look with Mr Connor. Laura wasn't sure if it was admiration or worry.

Mr Williams wasn't as enamoured of her pluck; recognition spread across his face. 'I knew you was familiar. I remember your father. He was a good man, God rest him. What would he think to see you here, meddling with the likes of 'im?'

He jerked his thick thumb at Philip.

'Our business is concluded, Mr Williams,' Philip announced in a low voice as he rose slowly from the chair to stare down at the man. 'I can be of no help to you in this matter. Mr Connor will see you out.'

'You're damned right our business is concluded.' Mr Williams struggled with his large stomach to stand. 'I wouldn't take your money if you offered it to me on a velvet pillow.'

He snatched the shipping share from the desk and shoved it in his pocket before turning a squinted eye to Laura. 'Your father would turn in his grave if he knew his only daughter was now some moneylender's wh—'

'Out, now.' Philip's voice cracked over Mr Williams, stunning the importer silent.

'Come on then.' Mr Connor took Mr Williams by the arm and tugged him towards the door.

Mr Williams jerked free and left of his own accord, a trail of mumbled curses following him.

Philip rounded the desk and closed the door. 'I apologise for what just happened.'

'One would think I'd be used to bullying men after enduring my uncle.' Laura opened her hand, her fingers tight from where she'd gripped the arm of the chair. 'He used to fly into a rage whenever I questioned him about missing money or unpaid bills.'

She studied a deep scratch in the wood floor, following it from where it met the leg of Mr Williams's chair to where it snaked under Philip's desk. The pride she'd experienced when she'd spoken about her father's shop faded like the scratch thinned beneath the desk.

She'd been a fool to think it would be so easy accepting a stranger as her husband. It had been even more simple-minded to imagine they'd touch a few times and it would be as if they were in love and well known to one another. That wasn't how it would be at all. She was going to marry a stranger, live in a strange house and learn a business she wanted nothing to do with. Why? Because she was so desperate, she was willing to sell herself for safety, just as Mr Williams had been about to accuse her of doing before Philip had cut him off.

I'm not selling myself. She closed her eyes and took a deep breath, repeating the truth over and over. It still didn't shift the weight sitting hard on her chest. *I'm trying to make a secure life for me and my mother.*

'Laura?' The sound of her name was soothing, like the sound of Thomas's name on Philip's lips last night. She opened her eyes, expecting to revel in the same softness, but Philip's eyes were firm as he studied her.

'In time, you'll learn to disregard such people.' He took up the stack of papers resting on the corner of the desk and shook them into a neat pile. 'Men like Mr Williams often resort to personal attacks when questioned about their business or finances.'

'I know. People who owed my father and couldn't pay often reacted the same way when pressed.' It wasn't so very different and yet it was. They hadn't looked down on her the way Mr Williams had just done. If they had done, her father would send them off and then remind her afterwards of her worth. What was her worth now? Certainly not what she'd once imagined, back when she'd dreamed of a loving husband standing with her behind the counter of their own shop, greeting clients together the way her parents had used to.

'Many people come here when they're desperate.' Philip laid the papers back on the corner of the desk. 'It affects their better sense.'

Laura wondered if she'd lost hers. Whatever comfort she'd taken in the clean clothes, comfortable bed and good food vanished. She eyed the neat stack of papers, wanting to knock it to the floor, scatter the sheets across the wood and cover the scratch. She'd been desperate enough to come here and turn over the only asset she still possessed to Philip, just as her uncle had been willing to relinquish the business, and Mr Williams the shipping shares. Unlike those men, Laura had been forced by others to part with what little she had left, just as she'd been forced to teach Uncle Robert the business when her father had brought him in, despite her and her mother's protests. Then she'd been forced to watch while he'd taken everything away piece by awful piece. 'I wish you hadn't asked me to join you.'

'I needed your assistance and experience. I knew the shipping shares were worthless. The company refuses to invest in steam engines which I and many others believe are the future, and their fleet is outdated. It was your expertise in cloth I needed.'

She sucked in a deep breath at the blunt statement, struggling to push back the tears pricking the corners of her eyes. She straightened her spine and looked at him. If he could stand so impassively in front of her, she would do so, too, and not dissolve into some blub-

bering girl. 'Surely there are other people you could
have called on.'

'There are, but I need to know if you can see through
what a man says to find the truth of his situation, to
gauge his suitability in case there comes a time when
you must act alone.' He pressed his fingers into the stack
of papers, making them dip in the middle, something of
unease in the simple motion. So he wasn't infallible after
all and he knew it. It was encouraging to know. It made
him at last seem mortal, though no less irritating. 'Your
instincts proved correct, as I suspected they would.'

'And what of my feelings?' She swept the stack of
papers off the desk, sending them fluttering to the floor,
her anger fuelled as much by Mr Williams as all the
frustrations and humiliations of the past year. 'Did you
ever take those into consideration, or how being bullied and brought low by a man like Mr Williams might
hurt me?'

The papers settled over the floor like snow. Philip
watched, emotionless, as a contract balanced on the
edge of the seat cushion before sliding off to cover the
scratch on the wood.

Outside, her mother and Jane passed by the window
as they made their way inside.

Horror rushed in to blot out her anger. What had she
done? This was Philip's house, his business and she was
here at his whim. His generosity could be withdrawn
at any moment and she and her mother would be back
in Seven Dials shivering and starving.

'I'm sorry, I didn't mean to act so childishly.' She
dropped to her knees and snatched up the papers. The

edges flapped with her trembling hands as she tried to force them into a neat pile, but they wouldn't cooperate. The more her hands shook, the more the helplessness widened to consume her. 'It won't happen again, I promise. I don't know what came over me.'

He came around the desk and lowered himself on to one knee across from her. Taking the uneven stack out of her hands, he laid it on the floor beside him. Then he gently caught her chin with his fingers and tilted her face up to his. 'Forgive me. I should have waited to introduce you to the business.'

Concern softened his blue eyes. He was sorry, genuinely so, with no trace of the false, self-serving contrition her uncle used to offer her father. The same faint bond which had slipped between them last night encircled them again. Philip cared for her and wanted her to be happy. The realisation drained the anger from her, but it couldn't erase the hurt, worries, helplessness and humiliations she'd suffered so many times. They pressed down on her and not even Philip's reassuring touch could drive them away.

'I invited you here because you're too strong to be bullied by such a man,' Philip explained.

'I wish I was.' She rocked back on her heels and away from his fingers, then fled the room.

The hall and stairway blurred as her eyes filled with tears. They streaked steadily down her cheeks as she made for her mother's room and pushed open the door without knocking. Thankfully, Jane wasn't with her. Her mother looked up from the chair by the window, her smile vanishing at the sight of Laura's expression.

Without a word, she held out her arms and Laura flung herself into them, burying her face in her chest to cry.

Philip lowered his hand, the warmth of Laura's skin still lingering on his fingertips. It didn't dispel the cold sitting hard in his chest. None of the insults hurled at him by any defaulting client had pierced him as hard as the realisation he'd allowed a client to hurt someone in his care.

He dragged the last few contracts out from under the desk and shoved them down on top of the pile on the floor. He should have followed his instincts and waited to introduce her to someone like Mr Williams. Instead, he'd dismissed his doubts and convinced himself she was fit to face the ugly man. He should have known better. She was strong, but she'd suffered a great deal and, like him, needed time. It was a mistake, one he should have known better than to make.

'I said you didn't understand the terms of the contract and I was right.' Justin slid into the room and settled into his favourite chair by the cold fireplace. 'You can't treat her like a client.'

Philip hauled himself and the contracts off the floor. 'It was never my intention to.'

'Yes, it was.' He reached over to the side table next to him and plucked a crystal glass and decanter of Scotch from it. 'Thankfully, she's no shrinking violet which is good if she's going to marry you.'

'Perhaps I was short-sighted in my assumptions about our arrangement.' And its simplicity. Justin was right, it wasn't going to be as easy as he'd first believed. 'Assuming, after this morning, our agreement still stands.'

'Oh, don't worry, she'll marry you.' Justin poured out a measure of Scotch, then returned the decanter to the table. 'Now you must ask yourself, why do you really want to marry her? And I want the real reason, not your drivel about needing a housekeeper.'

Philip traced the scratch in the floor with his boot. The memory of Laura scrambling about for the papers, as lost and frightened as he'd been the morning Arabella had died, tore at him. That cold morning, he'd come to this room and nearly ripped it all to pieces, gouging the floorboards in a fruitless effort to overturn the desk. If Justin hadn't found him, he might have destroyed the room and himself.

'I lost something when Arabella died; it was as if I buried my humanity with her.' Every day he felt the hardness creeping in where warmth and happiness used to be. It hurt to admit it, even to his closest friend. 'My father always said it was the one thing we must hold on to in this business because it's too easy to lose, as evidenced by so many others in our profession.'

'You've hardly become like them. You never will.'

'I'm not so sure.' After Arabella's death, Philip had shut himself off from his emotions just to move through the day without crumbling. As time passed it was growing more difficult to draw them out again.

'You think Miss Townsend can help you reclaim your humanity?'

Philip didn't respond, but studied the snaking scratch marking the wood. When the workmen had repaired the room, he'd refused to let them sand it away. It was a reminder of his loss of control. Something he'd never let happen again. 'Miss Townsend and Mrs Townsend's influence will do Jane good. I heard her laugh with Miss Townsend earlier.'

'It's about time.' Justin swirled the last sip of his Scotch before downing it. 'She's too serious for a girl her age.'

Philip strode to the table and plucked up a glass. 'I'm to blame.'

'Hardly. Seriousness is a family trait. Your mother was the only one who could enjoy a good joke.'

'She tempered my father.' He removed the crystal stopper from the decanter and rolled it in his palm. 'I worry how my nature might affect Thomas.'

Thomas's happy squeal carried in from outside. Philip set the glass and stopper down and went to the French doors leading to the garden. He opened them and inhaled the pungent scent of roses and earth fighting with the thicker stench of horses and smoke from the streets beyond. 'Arabella should have had time with Thomas. She should have seen him grow.'

'But that's not the way it happened,' Justin gently reminded him.

No, it wasn't. The finality of it was too much like standing at Arabella's grave again, the sun too bright off the green grass surrounding the dim hole in the earth.

Thomas toddled around a square half-pillar supporting an urn. He peeked out from one side of it, and then the other, squealing with laughter as Mrs Marston met him with a playful boo. The sun caught his light hair, making the subtle orange strands shine the way Arabella's used to whenever she'd strolled here.

Philip had used to look up from his accounts to watch her, wanting to join her, but he'd dismissed the urge in favour of the many other things commanding his attention. If he'd known their days together were limited, he would have tossed aside his work and rushed to be with her. If he'd known their love would kill her, he never would have opened his heart to her in Dr Hale's sitting room.

A dull ache settled in behind his eyes, heightened by the bright day. There'd never been a choice between loving or not loving Arabella. He'd loved her from the first moment she'd entered his office looking as unsure as Laura had today. During the first days of their courtship there'd been an unspoken accord between them, as if they understood one another without ever having to speak.

When Laura had reached out to him last night, and when he'd touched her today, something of the understanding and comfort that had so long been missing had passed between them and shaken him to the core.

'Miss Townsend's presence will benefit Thomas,' Philip observed, pulling himself off the unsettling road his thoughts were travelling. His relationship with Laura was nothing like his relationship with Arabella.

'Her presence will benefit you, too.' Justin came to his side and cocked a knowing eyebrow at him. 'Often and quite pleasurably.'

If he wasn't Philip's greatest friend, he would have dismissed him. 'Your experience with women has muddled your impression of relationships.'

'Actually, it's heightened them, which is why I can see matters with Miss Townsend so clearly and you cannot.' He dropped a comforting hand on Philip's shoulder. 'If you let her, Miss Townsend will temper you and more. Just don't resist her when she tries.'

With a hard squeeze, he left.

Philip stepped outside into the shadows of the eaves, watching Thomas without the boy noticing. Thomas hurried around the fountain on unsteady legs, clapping and laughing whenever Mrs Marston surprised him. It touched him to see his son so happy. Philip had forgotten what joy was like.

He looked in the direction of Laura's room, but the portico roof obscured the view. Justin was right, Philip needed Laura to temper him and she possessed the will to do it. He might have misjudged her strength today, but he didn't doubt its existence. When she felt safe, when her life settled into a steady rhythm, she'd find her feet again and he was sure to witness more moments of strength. He looked forward to them.

What he didn't look forward to were the deeper implications of her presence.

In the past year, he'd closed his heart to almost everyone except Thomas and Jane. He wasn't about to open it again and allow anyone to see the hardness which had grown there, or to leave himself vulnerable to having it crushed again. It would be a difficult thing to manage, but he had no choice. There could be no relationship between them without friendship or the most basic of understandings, but he couldn't allow Laura's sweetness to lull him into forgetting the wrenching torment that caring too much for someone could cause. Laura demanded his respect and affection and he would give it, but he would not surrender his heart. He couldn't.

Mother handed Laura her old threadbare handkerchief.

'I'm surprised you still have this old thing, what with Mr Rathbone providing us with all our needs.' Laura rubbed her wet cheeks, widening the hole in the centre of the ragged linen.

'My dear, Mr Rathbone is an excellent organiser, but even he is not capable of remembering everything, much less such a small detail like a new handkerchief.' She smoothed Laura's hair off her face, then caressed her damp cheek.

'At least this isn't his like everything else, like I will be.' Laura leaned back against the wall, worn out from crying. 'It's like being with Uncle Robert again and us helpless to do anything.'

'Mr Rathbone is nothing like Robert,' Mother gently corrected. 'He's willing to share what he has with us and to make you a partner in his life. It speaks to his generosity. And you aren't helpless.'

'Aren't I?' She was a woman with no money, no prospects and almost no family. A proposal from a moneylender was the best she could hope for, even if it made her feel like a purchased bolt of silk. Laura crumpled the damp handkerchief, then threw it to the floor, ashamed again of her foolishness. Better to be a man's wife than to sink to becoming a whore. 'I'm sorry I lost my head.'

'I'm surprised you haven't done it sooner.' She slid

her arm around Laura's waist and drew her up from the bed. 'No one can keep their chin up all the time, not even you.'

Her mother guided her to one of the two stuffed chairs in front of the window, Laura leaning as much for support on her mother as her mother leaned on her. Outside, Thomas's happy laughter carried up from the garden. Through the window, Laura caught sight of his cranberry-coloured skeleton suit darting back and forth between the boxwoods as Mrs Marston chased him.

'Now rest.' Mother pressed her down into the chair. 'I think you need it more than me.'

Laura gladly sank against the well-padded back with a sigh, so weary from everything. 'I don't know if I can do it. I don't know if I can go through with the wedding.'

Yesterday, when standing in the middle of the mouldering room in her worn-out gown, it'd been too easy to accept Philip and the life he offered. Today, it seemed too hard. She wasn't certain she could spend her life without love. It seemed a silly, girlish thing to hold on to when everything else was being laid at her feet, but she couldn't let it go. However, if she rejected Philip, she'd be giving up the comfort and safety of his home, along with her mother's health. 'I'm sorry, I shouldn't be so selfish. Only, I never thought it would all turn out like this. I thought we could save the shop, I believed it until the end. I was wrong.'

'You're not selfish, Laura. You've taken on so much over the past year, things you never should have had to deal with. Now you've taken on this. It's unfair and I wish I could have done more to help you realise some of the dreams you believe are ending with this betrothal. But, Laura, I never would have allowed you to accept Mr Rathbone's proposal if I didn't believe he was a good man.'

'Why? What did he tell you yesterday?' Everyone seemed to believe in him. Why couldn't she?

'He was very honest with me and told me of losing his wife and his hopes for Jane and Thomas. It was like hearing myself speak of you and how it felt to lose your father. Look at him,' she entreated, gently turning Laura's face to the window. From the shadows of the house, Philip emerged into the sun. Light shone in the streaks of red in his dark hair and seemed to widen over the light-coloured coat. He approached Thomas, not with the purpose he'd shown last night, but more slowly, as though weighed down by grief. He knelt and threw open his arms to embrace his giggling son, burying his face in the boy's neck as if he were afraid of losing him. 'He's hurting, Laura, but he isn't without love.'

Jane came out from the house, snapped a rose off one slender branch and tapped her brother on the shoulder. He stood and steadied Thomas on his slender hip as Jane held up the flower to the boy's button nose.

'You can see it in how much he loves his child and Jane. For all the girl's peculiarities, when I speak with her, it's obvious she knows he cares for her.'

Laura remembered the juvenile kiss Philip had received from Jane last night.

'Yes, he loves her, but what am I to him? A contract? A convenient solution to myriad problems?'

'If he truly wanted an easy solution, he would have

hired another nurse and expanded Mrs Palmer's responsibilities. He asked you to marry him because he saw something in you, something he isn't completely aware of himself. It's as if, deep down, he feels you can help him.'

'He doesn't want help. He wants someone to run his house and warm his bed.'

Her mother's shoulders rose with a sigh as they watched Philip set Thomas on the ground. He took one of the boy's hands and Jane took the other and together they led the child to the far wall where a lion-headed fountain spat water into an urn.

'When I lost your older brother, I was heartbroken. I threw myself into the shop, working to near exhaustion to try to dull my grief. No matter how much I tried to bury myself, your father never gave up on me.' She gazed serenely down on the garden, but sorrow laced her words, as palpable as Philip's grief had been when he'd first mentioned his late wife. 'Then one day, the darkness lifted and your father was still there, as loving as ever. Soon you were there, too, and I was happy again.'

Mother slid her hand beneath Laura's and gave it a squeeze. 'Mr Rathbone needs you. I know it's difficult to see right now, but if you're stubborn and refuse to give up on him, you'll capture as deep an affection as he shows to all he loves. I know it.'

Laura studied her mother's long fingers, thinking of Philip's hand in hers last night and the faint connection it'd created between them. She'd experienced it again when he'd apologised this morning, only that time it was him, not her, asking for something deeper. Both moments had been as fragile as fine silk thread. How could she possibly grab hold of something so delicate and make it strong enough to hold them both together?

'I don't even know where to begin.' She waved her hands over her dress, herself. 'I'm hardly going to arouse a grand passion in him.'

'I don't think Mr Rathbone is the sort of man easily ensnared by superficial things like dresses.' Mother's lips drew up in one corner with a mischievous smile. 'Though a finely turned-out figure doesn't hurt where men are concerned.'

'It will be easier to dress myself than it will be to figure out how to catch his fancy.' She knew almost nothing about gaining a gentleman's attention, especially such a stern gentleman.

'Follow your instincts, Laura. They'll guide you well.'

Philip looked up at the window, suddenly meeting Laura's eyes. He didn't turn away or nod, or do anything except study her as he had from the copper tub. She stroked her chin with her thumb and forefinger, almost able to feel Philip's hand on it. If there was one thing she knew to be true of Philip, it was his adherence to the contracts he made. When they stood before the vicar and uttered the vows, he'd be bound by what he said to her, what he stated before all his friends. It would be up to her to see he did more than simply uphold his promise.

'It won't be easy.' He'd fight like a dog to guard the wounded part of himself, but Laura had faced worse battles over the past year and in her own way won them, keeping a roof over her and her mother's heads, even staring down her uncle Robert on more than one occasion.

'Nothing worth having is ever easy.'

Laura nodded in silent agreement. No matter what she might wish for or think she wanted, the truth was, her future lay with Philip. If she hoped to have even a small portion of the life she'd once imagined for herself, a life of love with a true partner in the business and her bed, then she must find a way into Philip's heart.

Chapter Five

Mrs Fairley fastened the last button and Laura turned to face the full-length mirror in the modiste's fitting room, moving slowly so as not to tumble off the small fitting stool. She sucked in a surprised breath at the reflection which greeted her. After a year in tatty black, the light-green muslin dress Mrs Fairley had chosen to alter first was a stunning change. Laura pulled out the skirt, then shifted from side to side to watch the material move. With the swish of the fabric, she caught a little of the excitement of that Christmas morning when her parents had given her a yellow silk dress, her first adult one. For a week afterwards, she'd crept down to the shop mirror at night to admire it.

The excitement of the memory faded and she let the skirt go. The silk dress had been one of the first things she'd sold to pay for the meagre rooms in Seven Dials. More than once while walking through Petticoat Lane with the rest of her dwindling wardrobe, she'd wondered which lady's maid or shop girl wore it now.

'It suits you as if it were made for you.' Mrs Fairley came to stand beside her, a box of pins in one hand. She nodded with approval at Laura's reflection. 'Brings out the green in your eyes.'

Her eyes weren't the only part of her the dress emphasised. The bodice was cut deeper than any she'd ever worn before, exposing the tops of her breasts which rested higher on her chest thanks to the temporary new stays Mrs Fairley had secured for her. It was by no means immodest, but Laura wasn't accustomed to it.

On the *chaise* next to the mirror lay the other dresses Mrs Fairley was to alter. They would keep Laura respectably clothed while Mrs Fairley prepared the rest of the new wardrobe in accordance with Philip's list. The sheer number of garments he'd requested was staggering. It didn't even include the gloves, fans, stockings and various other small items he'd sent instructions to other merchants to secure.

'Do I really need so many dresses?' Laura questioned as Mrs Fairley leaned down to begin pinning the hem.

'If Mr Rathbone says you need them, then I suppose you must.'

Laura tugged up the low bodice again. Even when the draper shop had been a success, her father hadn't spent like this on clothing, not even for his wife. Her father had insisted his family dress well, but simply, and with as few items as they could make do with. He'd believed in selling material, not spending their profits on it. 'I'm not usually so extravagant with my wardrobe.'

'Neither is Mr Rathbone. He never lets Miss Jane indulge in this manner, though she tries.' She slid a sly look up at Laura. 'He must have quite a fancy for you to be so generous.'

'I suppose he must.' Laura fingered the side of the gown, wishing she were a better liar.

'You don't sound so sure.'

'I am, I mean he does. I'm sorry, there's a great deal on my mind right now.'

'I don't doubt it,' Mrs Fairley agreed as she slid a pin in the hem. 'What happened to your things for you to need so many new ones?'

It was an innocent enough question, but Laura's embarrassment flared at the need to answer it. She'd kept her dignity in Seven Dials. Out of it, she didn't want anyone to know the degradations she and her mother had suffered. She was terrified they would judge her, just as Mr Williams had. 'They were lost in an accident.'

'You mean to debt.' Mrs Fairley rose to face her. She was young, maybe only a year or two older than Laura, but with an amiable nature, making her a good friend to anyone in an instant. 'You needn't be embarrassed with me, Miss Townsend. I came close to losing everything once, too. It's nothing to be ashamed of.'

'You won't tell anyone, will you?' She didn't want her shame to reflect on Philip.

'Miss Townsend, a modiste's first task is to help her clients choose flattering dresses to best emphasise their assets.' She tugged Laura's bodice back down into place, revealing more of the tops of Laura's breasts. 'A modiste's second task is to listen to her client's problems and offer advice. I assure you, I'm very skilled in both.'

Laura examined Mrs Fairley, sure that Philip wouldn't hire any woman to dress his sister or his future wife who wasn't both an excellent seamstress and discreet. Given the things Jane had already told Laura and her mother in the short time they'd been here, she could only imagine what the girl must reveal during her private fittings with Mrs Fairley.

What was Laura prepared to reveal? She fingered the small ribbon pinned beneath her bust line while Mrs Fairley waited, as patient as she was buxom. She wore a demure light-blue cotton gown of superior weave with a high chemisette rimmed with delicate French lace. Beneath her generous breasts she'd wrapped a yellow cord, tying the knot just under the small separation almost visible through the sheer netting covering them. It was tasteful yet alluring, the pale blue of the dress matching her soft blue eyes, the yellow of the cord mimicking the rich gold tones of her hair. If there was anyone who might know how to turn a man's head with subtlety, it was this woman.

'What do you know of Mr Rathbone?' Laura began cautiously, still unsure how much she should reveal, if anything. Surely Mrs Fairley would think it odd for Laura to seek advice on capturing the attention of a man she was already betrothed to.

'He's a very fine gentleman.' Mrs Fairly selected a piece of wide netting from a nearby table. It was embroidered with the same flowers as Laura's dress and she draped it over Laura's shoulders to make a fichu. 'A little stiff in the breeches, but his heart is in the right place.'

'How do you know he has a good heart?' She hoped it wasn't for the reason flitting through her mind, but with the slender gold band encircling Mrs Fairley's finger, she suspected the attractive modiste had discovered Philip's better qualities in a less sensual way.

Mrs Fairley stepped back and the glowing smile which had graced her face since she'd first greeted Laura faltered around the corners. 'My husband, John, was a soldier. He was injured at the Battle of Waterloo. He recovered, but it took a great deal of time and I was forced to put aside my business to nurse him. Once he was well, the war with France was over and, with all the soldiers coming home, he couldn't find work. We fell into debt and were on the verge of losing everything. Mr Rathbone loaned me the money I needed to rebuild my business, sent me new clients and, as you can see, has been most generous with his patronage.'

All Laura's objections to the number of items on Philip's list vanished. Mrs Fairley needed the money as much as Laura once had.

Mrs Fairley chose a ribbon from the selection laid out next to the completed gowns and held it up to Laura's face, judging the colour against her skin. 'My husband has found a new life helping me manage my business, keeping accounts and dealing with inventory while I continue to see to clients. Without Mr Rathbone's help, I don't know what would have happened to us.'

Mrs Fairley's voice wavered and Laura recognised her fear of what might have happened whispering through the soft-spoken words. Laura had felt it, too, many times herself in Seven Dials, when each passing day had made their situation worse and lessened Laura's options for changing it.

Mrs Fairley wiped away the tears glistening in the corners of her eyes and fixed a bright smile back on her face. 'What of you? Are you excited for your wedding?'

Now it was Laura's turn to be honest. 'I'm unsure.'

'Unsure?'

Laura was unable to believe what she was about to reveal, but speaking to a married woman closer to her age proved too tempting to resist. 'What do you know of my betrothal to Mr Rathbone?'

Mrs Fairley flipped out the skirt to make it lie better, then examined the line of the hem. 'I know it was sudden and unexpected.'

'It was far more than that.'

While Mrs Fairley knelt down to adjust the pins, Laura told her the story of threatening Philip and the strange proposal. At first Mrs Fairley continued to work but the more Laura revealed, the more the modiste sat back on her heels to listen, her work forgotten.

At last Laura finished, barely able to hear her voice over the noise of her heart beating in her ears. If Mrs Fairley wasn't as discreet as she claimed, if she told every client she possessed about Laura and Philip's betrothal and if he heard of it, she wasn't sure how he would react. She couldn't imagine him being pleased, nor doing anything but hardening him against her and their impending marriage. The task of capturing his heart was daunting enough without her creating more obstacles.

Mrs Fairley clapped her hands together, her eyes

round with amazement. 'If I hadn't heard it from his intended myself, I never would have guessed Mr Rathbone harboured such romantic tendencies.'

Laura nearly fell off the stool. 'It isn't romantic. It's a deal, a bargain.'

'He might have dressed it up in such terms to fool himself and you, but it isn't the real reason for this hasty wedding.'

No. A man who knew his mind so well, who controlled himself with the precision of a tightrope walker like the one she'd once seen in Vauxhall Gardens did not need to invent such excuses to fool himself. Yet hadn't her father created a hundred of them to maintain faith in Laura's uncle? He'd been too honest and giving to realise how wicked his brother really was. Until the end, he'd held on to the idea Robert was still the young boy he'd once protected from street bullies, the one he'd felt guilty leaving when he'd left to apprentice with the draper. 'Perhaps you're right?'

'Oh, I know I am.' Mrs Fairley jumped to her feet, her excitement genuine. Her curls bounced as she snatched the fichu off Laura's neck. 'And I will do all I can to help prove it.'

The cold air sweeping over the tops of Laura's breasts startled her and she moved to tug up the gown again before Mrs Fairley caught her hands.

'You'll catch his attention with it lower, I promise you. And when you approach him, don't scowl with worry. Soften your face.' She pressed her thumb to the crease between Laura's eyebrows, smoothing out the skin. 'He's a confident man and obviously drawn to your confidence.'

'My confidence?'

'Any woman brave enough to threaten him with a pistol is most certainly confident.'

Laura would have called it desperation, but if Mrs Fairley and Philip wanted to believe otherwise, then she'd let them.

Mrs Fairley looked over the selection of dresses, tapping one finger against her chin. 'When will you see him next?'

'Dinner. He's quite busy today.'

Mrs Fairley selected a pale, rose-coloured silk dress and held it up to Laura. 'Then we'll make it a meal he won't soon forget.'

The rich scent of sage and cooked chicken drew Laura to the dining room. Her stomach growled, reminding her how late she was for dinner. She'd sent Mary down earlier to ask Philip and the others to start without her. Given how hungry Laura was, she didn't want to keep others from their meal. However, neither tardiness nor hunger pangs were strong enough to stop her from pausing at the mirror hanging in the hallway to admire again the changes Mrs Fairley had wrought.

She and the young modiste had gone well over their appointed time together. A few stitches through the shoulders of the pale rose-hued dress had tightened the bust, bringing the silk up snug against Laura's breasts. Then Mrs Fairley had arranged Laura's hair, sweeping it up off the back of her neck and using heated tongs to create small curls which danced about her nape.

For such little effort, it'd made quite a difference. Laura appeared elegant, like one of the rich merchant's wives who would occasionally visit her parents' shop whenever her father had acquired a bolt of rare material. Perhaps with a simple necklace and a little more confidence, she would become more like those assured women, and learn to take pride in her position as the wife of a well-to-do moneylender.

Laura turned her face from side to side, pleased with the way the two long curls at the back bounced around her exposed neck. Pausing in her turns, she threw herself a sideways look, trying to mimic the coquettish smile Mrs Fairley had flashed when Laura had asked if Philip would be pleased with the new dress. She'd begged the woman to show her how to flirt, but Mrs Fairley had only laughed and told her she'd know what to do when the time came.

She hoped she was right. Laura's experience with gentlemen was greatly lacking. The stationer's son down the street had once shown an interest in her, but the dalliance hadn't lasted more than a few days. Her father had sent the boy off with a stern warning, reminding him he was in no position to set up house with a wife. She'd railed at her father for driving the boy away until the scandal of the weaver's daughter broke. Afterwards, she'd completely understood her father's concern. A solicitor's apprentice had got the weaver's daughter with child, then abandoned her, leaving her to face the scrutiny of the neighbourhood alone.

No doubt the old neighbourhood would look down on Laura if news of her nuptials to a moneylender became known. Pinching her cheeks to bring some colour into them, she dismissed her concern. Despite the years they'd lived and worked beside the other merchants, not one of their neighbours had helped her and her mother when the business had begun to fail and they'd been forced to hire a smaller, less expensive shop in a sad little neighbourhood many streets away. Instead they'd all stood around whispering while the removers had loaded the cart with what was left of their belongings, blaming Laura and her mother for Robert Townsend's mistakes.

Let them judge her for marrying Philip. Her opinion of them and their behaviour was no better.

Her stomach growled again and Laura reluctantly left the mirror, unable to avoid supper and Philip any longer. For all her thoughts of how to impress her betrothed, she had just as many of eating, especially with the scent of cooked chicken growing stronger with each step she took towards the dining rom.

'The dress is cut too immodestly for a young woman.' Philip's voice carried from the dining room, exasperation thick in his words.

'It's cut exactly like Princess Charlotte's,' Jane protested, sounding much the way Laura had done years ago when she'd wanted an expensive fan and her father had refused to purchase it. 'I altered it myself based on the pattern in the lady's magazine.'

Laura stopped at the dining-room door, unnoticed by the quarrelling siblings or her mother. Philip sat at the head of the table, his frustration with his sister evident in his tight grip on his knife and fork. Laura tried not to laugh at how easily his sister could rattle him when men like Mr Williams didn't seem to trouble him at all. Then again, she knew more than anyone how frustrating family could be. She'd been ready to scream more than once when her father had refused to listen to her arguments against her uncle. He'd always wanted to believe the best of his brother, especially at the end.

'You are not Princess Charlotte, nor are you her age.' Philip cut his food, the knife scraping lightly across the plate. 'You will return the dress to Mrs Fairley to alter at once.'

'I won't.' Jane's foot stamped beneath the table, making the glasses on top rattle. 'I like the dress this way. Tell him, Mrs Townsend, tell him this is the style.'

'It is the style, Jane, but Mr Rathbone is right, it is too revealing for a young lady your age,' Laura's mother responded with measured patience.

'But—' Jane began to protest before Laura's mother laid a tempering hand on hers.

'I think I might have a suggestion which will suit you both. A width of gorgeous French lace along the top edge, like Miss Lamb wears, will encourage more modesty without ruining the line of the dress. It will be quite elegant and modest.'

'May I alter it as she says, Philip?' Jane bit her lip in anticipation, looking back and forth between her brother and the older lady. 'Mrs Townsend is right, it would be modest just as you like and, oh, so in fashion.'

Philip took a deep breath and Laura caught something of relief rather than frustration in the gesture. She wasn't sure if it was the desire to end the debate or his glimpse of the wisdom in the matron's suggestion which led him to nod his head tersely.

'You may keep the dress if you add the lace.' He levelled his knife at her. 'But if you alter one more dress on your own, I won't buy you another until you're sixteen.'

'I promise I won't change any of the others,' Jane stressed, before exchanging a conspiratorial glance with Mrs Townsend.

Philip didn't notice, reaching for his wine glass. Then his hand paused, his attention snapping to Laura.

She tried to steady the rapid rise and fall of her chest, but it was a fruitless struggle. She couldn't stop breathing, not unless she wanted to faint from the same shock she saw in Philip's eyes. They dipped down the length of her. The motion was fast, efficient yet potent, making her feel as if it had been her and not him who had crossed his room the other night naked.

Under the force of his gaze, Laura nearly tugged the ribbon from her hair and escaped upstairs to don a less revealing dress. She didn't flee, but strode into the room, her chin confidently in the air, her mother's words about working to win Philip following her like the swish of her slippers over the wood floor. She'd certainly succeeded in catching his attention tonight.

'My goodness, look at you,' Jane exclaimed.

'Miss Rathbone, that is not an appropriate response.' The older woman nudged the girl with her elbow before raising an approving eyebrow at Laura. 'Laura, you look very lovely this evening.'

'Indeed, you do,' Jane chimed in, fixing her brother with a devilish smile. 'Doesn't she, Philip?'

Philip didn't answer, but rose, his expression as stiff as his posture, except where his eyes widened. Yet it wasn't surprise illuminating their blue. It was something hotter and more potent, like the subtle flash of anger she'd caught just before he'd struck her uncle. This wasn't anger, or anything like what she'd experienced with the stationer's son. The stationer's son had possessed the ridiculous passion of a schoolboy. Philip's reaction was of a man, albeit a man trying not to react.

Heat swept up from the pit of Laura's stomach and burned over the tops of her exposed breasts. She nearly reached out and pulled the napkin from the footman's arm to cover herself before Mrs Fairley's assurance came rushing back.

'Good evening, Miss Townsend,' Philip greeted as she paused beside her chair to let the footman slide it out.

As she took her seat, she threw Philip the sideways look she'd practised in the mirror in the hallway. 'Good evening, Mr Rathbone.'

A muscle in his jaw twitched and his chest paused before he resumed his steady breathing.

Once she was seated, he took his seat again and she withheld a smile of delight, enjoying this new power over him.

Across the table, her mother's and Jane's astonishment was palpable, but Laura didn't dare look at them. It was difficult enough to maintain her composure in front of Philip. She didn't need an interested audience distracting her.

She unfolded her napkin and laid it across her lap, then sat back to allow the footman to present the cooked chicken, small potatoes and asparagus draped in a white sauce. Laura accepted a serving of each dish, trying not to overfill her plate. When at last she had sufficient, she took up her knife and fork and sliced through the potatoes, moving slowly so as not to fall on the food like some ravenous dog. Her concentration was disturbed when Philip spoke.

'Did you enjoy your time with Mrs Fairley?'

'I did. I hope you don't mind it taking longer than expected. I'm not usually one to spend so many hours fussing over my appearance.' Though she'd certainly take more care with her *toilette* from now on.

'Take whatever time you need with Mrs Fairley. I heartily approve of her work.'

'Do you?'

'I do.' He picked up the wine decanter and moved to fill her glass. 'She's exceeded my expectations.'

Laura didn't taste the wine, not wanting it to fuddle her senses any more than this conversation already had. 'No mean feat, I imagine.'

He leaned a touch closer and beneath the clove of the chicken, the faint hint of his bergamot cologne lingered, the scent heady and distracting. 'You've imagined correctly.'

'Then I'll have to discover how else I may exceed your expectations.'

He didn't smile, but she caught the glint of humour in his eyes. 'I anticipate your efforts.'

She focused on her plate, as unnerved as she was emboldened by this flirting. She didn't think it in him to be so charming. Thankfully, Mrs Fairley had promised to alter and deliver two of the other gowns by morning. It would keep Laura from turning back into a vagabond dressed in borrowed clothing and help her maintain something of the heat flickering in Philip's expression.

If the sharp and subtle blend of cloves and parsley sprinkled over the chicken's golden skin wasn't so distracting, she would have tried to be more intriguing. Instead, she set her knife to the bird, eliciting from the tender flesh a thick drop of juice as she pressed down. Spearing the piece with the fork, she raised it to her mouth. Her lips closed over the meat and she slowly drew it from the tongs. She closed her eyes and sighed as the savoury spices melted over her tongue.

After a year of ugly brown gruel, this was heaven.

Swallowing, she opened her eyes, eager for another taste, but Philip's expression made her pause.

He flushed as if his bite had stuck in his throat, except the strangled look suggested he'd been hit somewhere lower. His intense gaze warmed Laura's insides more than the chicken, burning through her like the chilli pepper she'd once tasted from an Indian silk merchant. She'd never thought of herself as a wily charmer of gentlemen, yet without even trying she'd done something, she wasn't sure what, to Philip.

'Is the food to your liking?' Philip coughed, as if struggling through a dry throat. He took up his wine and sipped quickly before setting it at the corner of his plate.

'Yes, very much.' Closing her lips over another bite,

she tried to recall the weaver's daughter and the way she'd flirted with her solicitor trainee. She could recall very little about their relationship except the aftermath. At least whatever came of this odd flirtation, it would do so with a ring on her finger.

'After dinner, I'd like to discuss the advertisement for Thomas's new governess,' he announced, seeming to recover his usual poise.

'I already saw to it this afternoon, before I left for Mrs Fairley's.' She sliced a potato, jumping a little when it rolled out from under her knife. 'Mrs Marston showed me the old advertisement, we discussed Thomas's present needs and I wrote the new one accordingly.'

She speared the potato with her fork to keep it in place as she cut it, watching Philip from the corner of her eyes, waiting for his reaction, unsure what it would be. She'd taken it upon herself to complete the task, eager for something to do and the chance to impress him. For all the advice Mrs Fairley had given her about her physical appearance, she suspected efficiency in handling domestic matters might be the second-best way to gain his admiration.

'You don't mind, do you?' she pressed. 'I thought it best to do it so you had one less item to see to.'

'I don't mind at all.' The stern businessman from this afternoon had vanished, replaced by a more relaxed gentleman, if one could call the straight line of Philip's shoulders relaxed. 'I appreciate your desire to help.'

She hoped it wasn't all he intended to appreciate. Sitting up a little straighter to best highlight the new gown and everything it exposed, she was about to tell him the contents of the advertisement when Jane called out from across the table.

'Miss Townsend, Philip asked Mrs Townsend to serve as my tutor and she's agreed.' The girl was more excited than any thirteen-year-old should be about lessons. 'Isn't it wonderful?'

No, it wasn't. All thoughts of impressing Philip vanished. 'Mother, you aren't well enough for such exertion.'

'I'm not an invalid, Laura,' her mother chided, closing her eyes in delight as she sipped her wine. 'Nor will I be one, not with food this grand and a warm bed.'

She raised her glass to Philip, then turned to Jane. 'I think we should start with Beadman's *Principles of Accounting*, don't you?'

'I think it's a marvellous idea,' Jane concurred and the two fell to discussing the curriculum.

Laura gaped at them. She'd been dismissed, as if she were sitting here in her child's dress, not with her womanly figure filling out every inch of the silk. How could her mother do it? And how could Philip ask her mother to do such a thing without consulting his wife-to-be first? It was arrogant of him to be so presumptuous.

She sliced at her bird, then stuck a larger piece than intended in her mouth. It caught in her throat and she snatched up the wine everyone else seemed so eager to indulge in. The bouquet was as heavenly as the tender chicken, making the bird slide down her throat. If only the continued barrage of surprises would go down as easily.

Setting her wine glass on the table, she caught Philip watching her, his brow wrinkling in question at the

change in her mood. Thankfully, Jane drew his attention away before he could say anything, then the girl
dominated the conversation with her thoughts on wom-
en's education.

Laura focused on her food as the topic changed from
bluestockings to the Prince Regent's latest scandal. Her
mother and Jane exchanged details of it with the same
animation which used to dominate her conversations
with Laura while they'd tidied up the shop in the evenings.

Laura pushed a piece of asparagus through the
sauce, hating to admit she wasn't just worried about
her mother's health. She was jealous of her tutoring
Jane. In a matter of hours it seemed as if Laura had
been tossed aside while a new young lady had been
whisked in to take her place. It wasn't a charitable
thought, but she couldn't help herself. If she lost her
mother's affection and failed to secure Philip's, what
would be left for her?

Laura's discomfort soured her mood, but it didn't
dampen her appetite and she enjoyed hearty helpings
of the next two courses. It was only her fear of looking
like a glutton which prevented her from asking for a
second serving of trifle at the end of the meal.

At last, with her mind still troubled but her stomach
full, Philip rose, as did Jane and Mrs Townsend. Laura
was glad for the end of the meal, eager to be in her room
and to let out her now very tight stays.

'Philip, you must show Miss Townsend Great-Great-
Grandmama's knife,' Jane suggested, mischief in her

eyes. 'You must see it, Miss Townsend, and have Philip tell you the story behind it. It's quite thrilling.'

Laura looked to Philip, expecting him to resist his sister's obvious attempt to see them alone together. She wasn't prepared for him to agree with the idea.

'Would you care to accompany me to the sitting room?'

No. Yes. She wasn't sure. She could almost hear her mother urging her to accept the invitation, but she'd been through so much already today. She wasn't sure she could endure being alone with him dressed so boldly.

'Please, lead the way,' she answered at last, not wanting to leave them all standing in the dining room waiting for her to make up her mind.

He didn't offer his arm as he escorted her out of the dining room. She wasn't surprised or offended. With the exception of last night and this morning, he'd avoided touching her since her arrival. She wondered how he intended to manage their marital relations if he could only be coerced into touching her by an apology. It seemed just another of the many things she'd be forced to overcome if she were to draw them together, yet it might prove the most difficult. She could hardly pounce on him and kiss him the way the stationer's son had done with her in the dark hallway between the shop and the store room. Or could she?

'Why did your great-great-grandmama need a knife?' Laura prompted once they reached the sitting room.

Inside, a warm fire burned in the grate, making the room more intimate and inviting than when she'd met him there that morning.

'She was a moneylender, the one who introduced our family to the business.'

'A woman? I don't believe you,' she teased, but his expression remained solemn.

'She and my great-great-grandfather lived in North Carolina and owned a tobacco plantation.' He removed the slender knife from its place of honour above the mantel and brought it to her. 'After she became a widow, she began lending money to planters and merchants and amassed a sizeable fortune.'

'If your family was so successful, then why did they leave the colonies?'

'My grandparents saw the threat the American Rebellion posed to their business. Well before war was declared, they sold the plantation at a profit and returned to London. The two of them re-established themselves here.'

'And the knife?' Laura's fingertips brushed his palms as she tilted it so the engraving could catch the light. Philip's heat was so distracting, she comprehended not one word of the inscription on the blade.

'Great-Great-Grandmama helped fund Lieutenant-Governor Spotswood's attack against Blackbeard.' They stood so close, she could hear the uneven rhythm of his breathing. 'When Governor Spotswood repaid the loan, he gave her this in thanks. It belonged to the pirate. It was one of many he was wearing when he was killed. It's been in the family ever since.'

'I should have known you were right.' She looked up at him through her lashes and a strange sort of panic flashed through his eyes. Beneath her fingertips, his hands stiffened on the blade. He'd been bold enough to stride in front of her naked when she'd threatened him. Tonight, when he held a weapon and there was no more flesh showing than the curved tops of her breasts, it was as if he wanted to flee. 'You don't lie.'

'I've never had a reason to.'

'Yes, I suppose it is one of the many things I admire you for.'

He arched one eyebrow at her. 'Then I assume you've forgiven me for this morning.'

'I have.'

Something like relief rippled through his eyes. She withdrew her hand from the knife, stunned. She thought nothing besides his sister's strong will could upset him, but it seemed their row this morning had troubled him too.

'I apologise for placing you in a situation you weren't ready for. It won't happen again.'

'Thank you, but what about my mother? Have you placed her in a role she's not ready for?'

'No.' He lowered the dagger, untroubled by her question. 'When I approached her with the suggestion, she readily agreed.'

'I'm sure she felt compelled to.'

'No, not at all.' A moment ago he'd been willing to admit he was wrong. Now he was so arrogantly sure of himself.

'You still should have discussed it with me first.'

'Why?' He returned the dagger to its place above the mantel. 'Mrs Townsend is a woman of mature years and doesn't need anyone's approval to do as she pleases.'

'She's ill. She needs rest.' Laura's voice rose before she brought herself back under control. 'Too much exertion might be bad for her.'

'I must disagree.' He wiped the fingerprints off the blade with the cuff of his sleeve. 'Mrs Townsend, like you, is not used to being idle. With your attention directed elsewhere, she needs an occupation. My sister will gain from the benefit of your mother's maternal care and business knowledge, and your mother from having another young person to guide and teach.'

Laura had no answer for him because he was right. She'd been wrong about him. Once again, he hadn't acted out of arrogance, but concern. If she didn't learn to think better of him, it would undermine everything she was trying to accomplish.

'I'm sorry and I don't mean to sound ungrateful.' She gripped the edge of the mantel. The cold marble corner dug into her palm. 'Only, I've been taking care of her for so long, it's difficult to think I won't have to any longer.'

He laid his hand on the mantel in front of hers. The heat of his skin radiated across the short distance between their fingertips. 'She does still need you. She always will.'

'Just like Jane still needs you.'

He heaved a weary sigh. 'She doesn't believe she does, but, yes.'

If only he needed Laura. Dread made her long to pace. If something happened to her mother, Philip and his family would be all she'd have left. It would be a lonely future if she failed to capture his affection. 'You make it look so effortless, managing your business and your family. If I'd had your talent for it, I might have saved the shop.'

'Then you wouldn't be here.'

She straightened, stunned by the faint hope woven into the words. Maybe it was possible. Maybe she could win his heart. 'Are you glad I'm here?'

After this morning, she wouldn't be surprised if he regretted his proposal.

'I am.' The honesty of his admission stunned her, as did his question. 'Are you?'

She wasn't sure. She'd wanted only the shop for so long. Now she wanted something else, something she wasn't sure she could achieve. If she couldn't win him, at least she was safe here. For that she was grateful. 'Yes.'

He looked down at the marble and traced a dark swirl in the stone. It brought his fingers achingly close to hers. She thought he might take her hand, but then he slid his away.

'It's taken me a long time to become comfortable raising Jane, and then Thomas and managing the business.' Loneliness and heartache tainted his words. Like her, he'd taken care of his loved ones while shouldering the burden of continuing on after a loved one's death. Philip might have been more successful with his business, but grief had left its mark on him just as it had on Laura. 'It wasn't easy. Some days it still isn't. It will help to have someone to assist me. I hope to offer you the same comfort.'

'In many ways, you already have.' She slid her hand over his, eager to chase away the darkness filling his eyes.

Beneath her fingers his muscles stiffened. The easy intimacy of a moment before vanished, the pain straining his expression dampening to something more solid, something she couldn't read.

She expected him to pull away and increase the wall forming between them. To her surprise, he turned his hand over in hers and slid his thumb along the line of her smallest finger. The slow caress ripped through her, as startling as if he'd stroked her nearly bare chest. If the same excitement raced through him she couldn't tell. His eyes remained fixed on hers, serious yet tempting, his true feelings as hidden from her as they were from his clients.

Despite his stoicism, she silently willed him to close the distance between them, to take her in his arms and kiss her until she could think of nothing except his touch, his warmth, his body. The urge frightened her as much as it made her heart race with anticipation, but the moment never happened. She pressed her fingertips against his wrist. His pulse beat a soothing rhythm against her skin. It didn't flutter wildly like hers. It seemed he was reaching out to her, but still holding something of himself back, retreating just when she wanted him to press forward.

The deep bells of St Bride's tolled nine times, marking the hour. Beneath their ringing, Laura caught Thomas's faint cries from upstairs. The sound didn't draw Philip's eyes from hers, but it interrupted the quiet moment and brought it to an end.

Philip slid his hand out from beneath hers, dropping it to his side. 'I must help Mrs Marston settle Thomas.'

'Of course.'

'Would you care to join me?'

'No, I'll stay.' She'd risked enough of herself with him tonight. She didn't have the strength for more.

'Goodnight then.'

'Goodnight.'

He made for the door, stopping just outside it to face her. 'In the future, I'll do my best to consult you on matters pertaining to you and your mother before decisions are made.'

'Thank you.'

His assurance given, he strode away.

Beneath her palm, the marble still radiated with Philip's heat. Nothing had happened between them except the faintest of touches, yet it was as if he'd swept Laura in his arms and kissed the breath from her.

If only he had, then she wouldn't feel so unsettled. For all the passion his fingers had aroused in her, there'd been something rote about his touch, as if he'd known what was expected of him and performed his duties accordingly.

She traced the same marble swirl he had, coming close to the white base of a porcelain shepherdess before retreating. Despite the stiffness in his touch, when he'd spoken of his challenges and his true feelings about her being here, he'd been completely honest. It provided the faint hope that there could be something between them and that he might want it as much as her.

'Did he show you the knife?' Jane strolled into the room, attempting to not look too curious and failing.

Startled, Laura jerked her hand off the mantel, nearly sending the small figurine toppling to the floor. She caught it just in time.

'He did. It was quite fascinating.'

'So was the trick you played with the fork at dinner.' Jane smirked, strolling to join her at the fireplace.

'I didn't play any trick.' To her horror, Laura knew exactly what Jane was referring to.

'Yes, you did. I saw it.' Jane reached up and straightened the statue. 'Philip saw it, too. I've never seen my brother so stunned. You must do it again at breakfast.'

Laura laced her fingers in front of her, trying hard not to laugh at the absurdity of receiving flirting lessons from this sober thirteen-year-old girl. 'Should I die in ecstasy over the eggs just to get your brother's attention?'

Jane failed to see the humour in the remark, regarding it seriously, the way Philip regarded any proposal. The resemblance to her brother was striking. 'No, you're right. One time was good, too many will make it comical. You must continue to employ the subtle approach. Mrs Templeton was quite aggressive and put Philip right off her.'

'Who's Mrs Templeton?' It was the second time she'd heard the woman's name in connection to Philip.

'Mrs Templeton's a widow, all large breasts and red hair. Quite crass, though she doesn't think so. Her husband was another moneylender, an old man. Mrs Templeton set her cap at Philip after Mr Templeton died, but Philip wasn't interested. She wasn't right for him.'

'Am I right for Philip?' Laura felt quite brave with her enquiries tonight.

'You wouldn't be here if you weren't,' Jane stated, as if informing Laura of the day's wool prices.

If only Laura could be so sure. Jane was still a child. There were numerous things she might not know or understand about her brother.

'If Mrs Templeton was married to a moneylender, then she must know the business and still have her husband's clients. Wouldn't it have been prudent on his part to marry her?' Philip was nothing if not prudent.

'Her? Here?' Jane wrinkled her face in disgust. 'It never would have worked. She's too fond of her independence to marry again and she isn't like Philip; she lends to all sorts of questionable people. She's quite nasty when they don't repay. No, he's much better off with you.'

Laura wished she shared Jane's confidence in her suitability for Philip and his uninterest in the widow. He might not have married Mrs Templeton, but what Jane truly knew about Philip's relationship with her was sure to be limited. She couldn't imagine Philip parading his paramour through the house. It was quite possible his proposal to Laura had only come about because Mrs Templeton had rejected his.

The hope she'd experienced earlier dimmed. If his heart lay elsewhere, her chances of securing it were slim. She rubbed her thumb along the tips of her fingers, unwilling to give up so soon after she'd started. There had been something between them tonight, however faint. Whatever his relationship with the widow,

Laura possessed the advantage of being here before him each day. She would use that to her advantage, even if she wasn't precisely sure how.

Philip sat behind his desk, the ledger open, the pen settled in the crease in the centre. He needed to finish the accounts tonight or it would be one more task to do tomorrow. Through the window, the moon grazed the top of the sill, looking down on the garden outside as Laura had looked down on him this morning.

Philip shifted in his chair, the tension low inside him as disconcerting as when Laura had entered the dining room. He'd sent her to Mrs Fairley out of necessity. He hadn't expected the results to be so striking. The pale rose-coloured silk had highlighted the slight blush of her skin and exposed the roundness of her breasts. The effect had hit him hard, as had the sigh of delight when she'd slid the morsel of chicken from the silver tines with her full lips.

Philip tugged at the knot of his cravat, working the tightness off his throat. Justin had told him stories of men with strange tastes, ladies' shoes and stockings driving them to the height of need. Philip had scoffed at the idea, until tonight. If Laura relished every meal in such an uninhibited fashion, he might develop a taste for watching her eat, naked, in the middle of his bed.

He pulled his list of things to do in front of him and wrote a reminder to instruct Mrs Palmer to remove chicken from the menu. He couldn't endure another meal like the one tonight. He might have walked naked in front of Laura when she'd been a stranger, but he was not about to parade his more carnal needs in front of his future mother-in-law or his overly precocious sister.

The item added, he studied the list. Only a few things remained. Almost every one related to Laura. He stuck the pen in its stand, disturbed by how quickly she'd wound her way into his life. Though if any of the tasks on the list wrought the transformation the single visit to Mrs Fairley had achieved, he'd gladly put everything aside to see Laura off to the stay maker.

It was what lay beneath the stays which interested him the most.

His loins tightened again and he stood, trying to pace off the agitating desire. There'd been no one since Arabella. Many times Justin had urged Philip to follow him to his pleasure haunts, but he'd refused. Unlike Justin, Philip didn't allow his carnal cravings to guide his decisions, though he'd come perilously close to letting them influence him tonight. Only the greatest control, and the open door, had kept him from kissing Laura. She'd have allowed him the liberty, he was sure. He'd caught the invitation in the faint parting of her lips and the eagerness in her eyes.

His steps slowed as he reached the centre of the carpet. It wasn't just the unexpected surge of desire which had made him pull back tonight. It was the other, more subtle urge driving him—the craving for her presence as much as her curving body. Her willingness to express her fears and troubles had almost drawn him into revealing his own. It hadn't been false comfort when he'd said he needed someone to share his burdens with. He did. He wanted her here. He wanted her help. How much more he desired was difficult to discern above the cracking of the ice surrounding his heart.

He stopped and removed his watch from his waist-coat pocket and checked the time. It was early still. He and Justin could spar a few rounds at the club and he might shift some of the lingering discomfort distracting him tonight.

He closed the watch case and slid his thumb over the smooth gold, the memory of Laura's skin beneath his as troubling as his behaviour with her tonight. She'd caught the reluctance in his caress as easily as he'd noted the hesitation in her answer to his question about being here. At least her hesitation had been honest and affirmative. It was more than he'd expected after this morning's debacle. Sadly, he hadn't been as unguarded with her.

He dropped the watch back in his pocket and rang for Chesterton, eager to be at his boxing club. He didn't need to bare his soul like some poet to establish a solid relationship with Laura. What he needed was time and knowledge. In the coming days, as he taught her his business and she became further enveloped in his life, they would come to know each other and the awkward-ness they'd experienced today would lessen. He would keep the hardness inside him hidden as well as the sense of failure fuelling it. They would build a relationship on mutual respect and affection, not worries and fears. They would enjoy a solid future together. The past need not trouble them.

Chapter Six

Philip sat in the big chair by the window in the sitting room. Outside, the sunlight was dampened by the darkening clouds beginning to cover the city. They thickened the shadows in the room and made it seem as if sunset had arrived early today. A lively fire danced in the grate and candles burned in the holder beside Laura's chair, flickering in the faint light streaks in her amber hair. Thomas sat snug on her lap, his little head against her full chest as she read the horse story to him for the third time.

Gone was the ragged, desperate woman who'd slipped into his dressing room a short time ago. In front of him sat a poised lady and her confidence increased each day. Whether it was due to the gowns Mrs Fairley sent over every morning or Laura's growing confidence in her place here, he didn't know. He did know the modiste's bill at the end of the month would be substantial and he would gladly pay it.

'You're staring again,' Laura chided with a sideways smile when she reached the end of the book.

'I'm enjoying listening.' Philip laced his fingers beneath his chin. Over the past three days, he'd made a point of spending time with Laura, instructing her on the management of his business or, like tonight, joining her and Thomas in the evenings. 'You have a way with him.'

'He's a sweet boy.' She pressed her lips to Thomas's neck and kissed him, eliciting a peel of baby laughter from the child. Then she threw Philip a teasing look from beneath her long lashes. 'And not nearly as serious as his father.'

Philip lowered one hand to trace the curve of the chair's carved arm, fighting to douse the heat licking through him. 'Good.'

Thomas slapped his little hands against the book, demanding Laura start the horse story again.

'Yes, Master Thomas, I will read it once more.'

Thomas clapped with delight as Laura turned to the first page, ready to begin their fourth reading when Chesterton entered the room.

'Dr Hale,' the butler announced.

Philip's ease vanished as he rose to greet his father-in-law. 'Dr Hale, I didn't expect to see you today.'

'I was on my way to visit a patient. Thought I'd stop in and see my grandson.' Dr Hale reached for Thomas, who held out his chubby arms to his grandfather. 'How is my little man?'

Without hesitation, Laura rose and handed Thomas to the doctor. He bounced the boy on his hip, making Thomas squeal with delight. The two of them shared the same smile, top lips flat whilst the bottom lips spread wide to reveal the gentleman's full set of teeth and Thomas's small scattered ones.

Over Thomas's shoulder, Dr Hale examined Laura with an appreciative eye. 'You must be Thomas's new nurse?'

'No, I'm...' Laura's voice failed as she looked to Philip for assistance.

'Miss Townsend isn't the new nurse. Mrs Marston doesn't leave until the end of the month,' Philip corrected, reluctant to announce the end of his mourning, but he had no choice. 'Miss Townsend, allow me to introduce Dr Hale, Arabella's father. Dr Hale, Miss Townsend is my intended. We're to be married.'

Dr Hale looked back and forth between them so fast, the fine wisps of grey hair at the sides of his head swung out. 'Married?'

Philip's eyes darted to Thomas, then the floor before fixing on Dr Hale. Until this moment, Philip had ignored the guilt lacing this marriage, the guilt which had pricked him when he'd engaged Mr Woodson, his solicitor, to secure the common licence. He didn't want to admit how much this new union felt like a betrayal of the old. 'Yes.'

Dr Hale moved Thomas to his other hip. 'I see.'

'I apologise for not informing you of the situation sooner.' He'd written the note summoning Dr Hale to discuss the matter. It still sat on his desk, unsent, just as the common licence now rested there unopened after Mr Woodson had delivered it this afternoon.

'I'm sorry if the news has come as a shock,' Laura

soothed, dispelling some of the increasing awkwardness threatening to suffocate them all.

Dr Hale stroked Thomas's cheek, then offered her a grandfatherly smile. 'Miss Townsend, I've found there's very little news in this world, good or bad, that doesn't come as a shock to someone. Don't let me make you feel awkward. I wish you and Philip the greatest happiness.'

'Thank you, and please know you may continue to come here at any time. I want Thomas to know his grandfather, and his mother.' She brushed Thomas's hair off his forehead, then squeezed the doctor's arm.

It humbled Philip to see her so welcoming when all he could do was stand there.

Thankfully, Mrs Marston's arrival prevented yet another uncomfortable quiet from settling over them.

'It's time for Thomas to prepare for bed,' the nurse announced.

'Don't want to keep the lad from his sleep.' Dr Hale kissed the boy's chubby cheek, then handed him to the nurse. 'There you go. Sleep well.'

Mrs Marston presented Thomas to Philip. He pressed a kiss to his son's temple, lingering with his eyes closed, seeking comfort, not giving it. Philip was flailing this evening and he hated it.

'I must be going, too. I have a patient expecting me,' Dr Hale announced as Mrs Marston carried Thomas from the room. 'Mrs Linton. Healthy as a horse, but convinced she's dying. I suspect its unhappiness keeping her in bed. Husband ignores her. I do what I can to encourage her to pursue other interests, but instead she focuses on every twinge and cough.'

'Wish her good health from us,' Laura said.

'I will. Congratulations again to you, Miss Townsend.' He turned to Philip, his smile fading. 'Will you see me out?'

'Of course.' Philip might have avoided telling him of the marriage, but he would face like a gentleman whatever harsh words the doctor wished to level at him.

Laura remained behind as Philip accompanied Dr Hale to the entrance hall. The house seemed unusually dark, and when Chesterton opened the front door to let in the fading daylight it didn't dispel the gloom.

'You've chosen well with Miss Townsend,' Dr Hale offered as he accepted his hat from Chesterton and settled it over his hair. 'I can see she'll love the boy as if he were her own. It's the most I could've asked of you in choosing your next partner.'

Philip stiffened, wishing the man would curse at him for all his mistakes and failures the way he cursed himself. 'I do still grieve for Arabella.'

'And part of you always will, just as I grieve for my dear wife.' There wasn't blame in his long face, or hate, or any of the emotions torturing Philip, only a weary mask of resignation, like the one he'd worn the morning of Arabella's funeral. 'But time passes and eventually the pain fades. Let it and give yourself a chance to be happy with Miss Townsend.'

He clapped Philip on the arm, then made for the street, his trim figure silhouetted against the grey wall of St Bride's churchyard as Chesterton swung the door shut.

'Is there something you need, sir?' he asked when Philip didn't walk away.

'No.'

When Chesterton left, Philip didn't move or return to the sitting room. He stared at the carved panels of the door, struggling to push back the guilt threatening to crush him. Dr Hale was right, Philip needed to think of the future, but all he could see was that cold morning cloaked in misery and devastating grief.

'He's a very nice man.' Laura's voice filled the hall from behind him.

'I should have told him sooner. I wanted to, but I couldn't.' He regretted the words the instant they left his mouth. Laura's opinion of him mattered, especially while his own was so low. He'd been a coward and now both she and Dr Hale knew it.

She came to stand beside him and slid her hand into his, twining their fingers together. The gentle grip steadied his desire to stride out of the house and follow the pavement until the hole inside him engulfed all of London.

'My mother told me once that sometimes, after I was born, she would think of my dead brother and feel guilty for being happy with me,' Laura gently offered. 'She loved him very much, she still does, but at times it felt as if letting go of him was wrong.'

Something inside Philip cracked and he tightened his hand in hers. The words rose up inside him, despite every effort to stifle them. She understood and he wanted her to know.

'She wasn't like you, healthy and strong. When she

wanted a child, I refused, but in the end I couldn't deny her and it killed her.'

Laura laid her hand on his cheek and turned his face to hers. 'It's not your fault, Philip. It's no one's fault when people get sick and die.'

'It was my fault. I should have known better. I should have kept her safe and I failed.' He let go of her hand and leaned away from her palm as the hardness rushed back in to surround his heart. He hadn't wanted her to know his gravest mistake. Now she did and he couldn't stand it. 'I have business to see to.'

He made for his office, ashamed of himself and his past.

Laura didn't follow, recognising the grief pulling Philip inside himself. If she tried to draw him out now, he'd only push her away. All she could do was wait until he was ready to reveal more. Then she would listen and help him as best she could, assuming he ever placed as much faith in her as he had in Arabella.

She wandered back into the sitting room and lifted Thomas's discarded book from the chair. Until Dr Hale's arrival, she'd failed to realise how tight a hold the past still had on Philip. It was stronger than any power Laura possessed or could hope to forge in so short an amount of time.

Closing the book, she clutched it to her chest. In a few days, Philip's claim over her had tightened. It wasn't just the food, clothes and his house, it was him and his unwavering presence. She needed him as much as he needed her. Yet tonight he'd strode away from her help and she worried he always would. Then some day, she might take to her bed, focusing on every ailment as she grew old with a man who'd never regard her as more than part of a contract, a deal.

She quit the room, heading upstairs to see to the numerous packages which had arrived today from the glover and the stocking maker. Becoming an invalid like one of Dr Hale's patients wasn't her future. Philip might withdraw from her today, but she wouldn't give up on him, or their life together.

The clock on Philip's bedroom desk chimed nine times. The rain outside had been falling steadily for over an hour, striking the portico below. He barely heard it as he flipped through the papers again, searching the endless paragraphs of agreements and ship's inventory. Everything seemed in order, but experience told Philip something about this deal wasn't right.

'Is everything well with you?'

Philip looked up to see Laura lingering warily in the doorway, her white cotton day dress replaced by one of lemon-yellow silk. It sat snug against her breasts and shoulders, flowing out to cover her hips and sweep the tops of her white slippers.

He set down his papers, cautious of her presence. It'd taken hours of correspondence, accounts and a meeting with Justin to settle him. It might only take a moment with Laura to undo it all. He rose and splayed his fingers on the desk as if to balance himself against any lingering anxiety, but it never came. Instead, something in him softened with her appearance, as if it'd been too long since he'd last seen her and he'd missed her company.

'A potential client has me perplexed.' He waved her into the room.

A small sigh of relief escaped her as she approached his desk. He couldn't blame her for being wary. He'd fled from her in the entrance hall like a frightened debtor from the constable, then sent his excuses for missing dinner. It wasn't Philip's best moment. He'd enjoyed a number of poor moments since Laura's arrival, but she wasn't to blame. The fault was with him. 'The man intends to import a special silk from India. There's no reason why I shouldn't lend him the money.'

'But instinct is warning you off the matter.'

'I need more than instinct. I need proof.'

'Why? It's your money to lend or not. Simply tell him you can't give him what he wants, the way you told me.' She cocked her head at the bathtub visible through the open dressing-room door.

He rewarded her slight teasing with the smallest of grins. She noted it with a subtle rise of her eyebrows. 'It may be that simple, but I prefer to make decisions based on evidence, not suspicion.'

'Perhaps I can help you?'

'If you'd like.' He handed her the papers. 'Read these and see if anything strikes you as odd.'

She sat in one of the upholstered wingbacks flanking the window and set the documents on her lap to review. Beneath the parchment, the yellow silk flowed over her long legs, brushing the slender ankles crossed beneath the chair. Philip tried not to stare as he settled in the chair across from hers. He was glad his actions in the entrance hall this evening hadn't made her shy with him. It spoke to her courage and her concern, something he found endearing and as unsettling as his desire to watch her.

Laura's fingers moved to shift the papers, the whisper of their movement as quiet as her steady breathing. Then she turned to the last page and her brows scrunched a touch.

'You've found something?' he asked.

'I'm not sure.' She shuffled back to the previous page. 'Come and see.'

Philip rose and leaned over the back of her chair, forcing himself to focus on the pages in her hand and not the clean scent of roses and soap heightened by her warm skin.

'Here, in the list of French textile merchants. I recognise only one of the three companies. I've never heard of these two.'

Philip straightened, all but forgetting the alluring little mole he'd noticed just above her collar-bone. He returned to his desk and removed a thick folio from the bottom drawer.

'Did I find something?' Laura twisted in the chair to view him, her hands gripping the rolled and tufted arm.

He looked up from his file and nearly forgot the silk merchant. The eagerness illuminating her face and the way her body turned to tighten the silk of the dress against the points of her breasts struck him hard. It took all his effort to jerk his attention back to the newspaper clippings in the folio in front of him. 'I collect stories about swindles and fake businesses. More than one potential client has tried to present shares in false companies as collateral.'

He held up a newspaper clipping. 'Two years ago, an actress and her husband were caught cheating shops out of goods by offering fake stock in fake companies. The husband served time in the Fleet for the debts the two of them accrued.'

'I remember the story. It seems your investor did, too, and thought it a good idea. What'll you do?'

'Deny his request.' Philip slid the clipping back into the folio. 'Then I'll warn my more reputable colleagues. One of them will start a rumour and within a short time, the man's ploy will be revealed to all.'

'And he'll never know it was you who uncovered his dishonesty.'

'There's a great deal to be said for being discreet.' He strolled to her chair and laid one hand on the back of it, trying to ignore the enticing curve of her creamy neck. 'Thank you for helping me.'

'It was my pleasure.' She looked up at him, the gap between her breasts teasing him as much as her sparkling eyes. If he leaned down, he could sweep her lips with his. Despite fleeing from her earlier, he very much wanted to kiss her now. It was an unsettling urge, made worse by the subtle tilt of her head, the way she seemed to be inviting him to taste her. 'I'm always here to help you when you need it.'

A chill licked up his back at the intimacy curling between them. He strode to the fire, took up the poker and tapped it against the coals as much to elicit a bright flame as to try to regain his usual reserve. 'Good, for there's another matter I'd like your assistance with tomorrow. Mr Connor and I must seize the goods of a bookseller who gambled away my loan and has now defaulted. I'd like you to accompany us so you'll understand the way of it. I don't expect it to be a difficult matter, or a dangerous one.'

Laura's excitement at having helped Philip resolve his troubles with the silk merchant vanished with this request. The manner in which her uncle's other creditors had handled their affairs still burned. The thought of creating such anxiety in another person, even if they deserved it, didn't sit well with her.

'I understand how it might be troubling for you,' he added in the face of her hesitation. 'You don't have to come if you don't wish.'

His recognition of her reluctance touched her. He was trying to be careful of her feelings. As much as she wanted to take up his offer to refuse, she couldn't. Her presence tomorrow wasn't about hurting someone or exacting revenge. It was about his genuine interest in her sharing his life, both the good and the unpleasant, and she couldn't ignore that. She'd accepted him as her betrothed and with it came so many things, all of which she must face.

'I'll come. You're right, it's part of the business and I must learn it.'

'Thank you.' His gratitude was clear. 'I'm sorry for what happened with Dr Hale today, and afterwards.'

He straightened the poker in the stand, staring at it as if it held all the comfort she knew he was searching for.

She came to stand in front of him and laid her hand on his shoulder. Beneath her palm his muscles stiffened. 'You don't need to apologise. It couldn't have been easy for either of you.'

His shoulder dropped a touch, the muscles easing their tightness. 'No, it wasn't, but thank you for trying to help and for your understanding.'

He raised his hand and slid it along the line of her jaw, his solid touch dispelling the uncertainty from the hall along with Laura's ability to breathe. The fire crackled in the grate and somewhere outside a horse whinnied. She didn't move and neither did he. The force of his gaze sent her heart racing until she thought she might have to dart from the room to release the tension.

Then he leaned down, his eyes closing at the same time as hers. His breath swept over the arch of her nose until at last his moist lips met hers.

The taste of him touched places only disturbed once before, when the stationer's son had stolen a kiss from her in the alley behind the draper shop. His lips had been nothing like Philip's. They'd been wet, sloppy, inexperienced. Philip's were controlled, powerful, leading, and Laura was more than willing to follow.

He didn't press his body to hers though her whole being craved it. She didn't dare move too close. She didn't want him to back away, or change his mind, as she knew he could at any moment. His fingers were light on her face, his pulse steady, dizzying, the most wonderful and the most frightening thing she'd ever experienced.

For all her desire to lose herself, she felt him struggling between pushing forward and holding back. It was in the shifting pressure of his mouth against hers, at one moment hard and demanding, the next light and withdrawing until at last it was gone.

She opened her eyes. His face remained so close to hers, she could throw her arms around his neck to pull him close again, but she didn't. His unsteady breath and the way his hand lingered on her face told her they wanted the same thing, but the fight for self-control raged in his eyes. It won, it always did. One day it wouldn't, she'd see to it, but not tonight.

'I'm sorry. You're here under my protection until we're married.' His eyes flicked to something on the desk before focusing on hers again. 'I shouldn't have been so forward.'

She tilted her head and viewed him through her lashes, tempting and forgiving him all at once. 'I think that was quite mild compared to how you acted with me the first time we met.'

'You were much less tempting when you were armed with a pistol.' He withdrew his hand, then made for the desk, the tender lover replaced by the reserved businessman. Laura regretted his absence at once but was also glad for it. The kiss had moved the ground beneath them like an earthquake and they were struggling to find new footing. 'Speaking of meetings, tomorrow evening an associate of mine is holding a dinner party for his wife's birthday.'

The abrupt change in the conversation was startling. 'A dinner?'

'Yes. I'd like to introduce you to some of my associates and friends.' He stepped behind his desk as if deliberately placing the solid wood between the two of them. It reminded Laura of an engraving she'd seen in a magazine once of a man chasing a woman around a table in amorous pursuit. Laura was tempted to try the same with Philip, if only to bring the light of laughter back into his eyes. She wanted to see more of the passionate man she'd experienced during his unexpected kiss, not the one turning to stone in front of her. 'I have no desire to startle anyone else with the sudden announcement of our wedding. Do you mind?'

'I'd be delighted.' *Delighted* wasn't the correct word, but it would do. Hopefully, his friends and associates would be more favourable to the idea of their match than Mr Williams had been. 'What should I say when the wives of your associates enquire as to how we met?'

'Tell them your uncle was one of my clients and introduced us. Our situation is not without precedent. Mrs Moseley was a governess before she married Mr Moseley and Mrs Charton was the daughter of one of Mr Charton's clients.'

'Then we'll be in good company.'

He tapped an envelope beside the blotter. 'Not all of it will be good. Not everyone in attendance manages their loans the way I do.'

'I see.' The discomfort of being associated with such a questionable business filled her again. To think she would have to be on familiar terms with less rep-

utable people and enjoy it almost made her take back
her acceptance of his invitation. However, she could
hardly hold up her head in sanctimonious condemnation. Though her parents had tried to deal only with the
most ethical of merchants, not all of their fellow drapers
and cloth merchants had been so fair minded. Her parents had insisted, however, on dealing with merchants
who did not buy from men who used slaves on their
plantations. More than once she and her parents had
attended some party where a guest or client of the host
was well known for not only supporting slave owners,
but dabbling in the trade themselves.

'I look forward to meeting your friends.' And learning more about him and his life. 'For now, though, I
think it's time for me to go to bed. Goodnight, Philip.'

Before he could respond, or perhaps tempt her to
stay, she hurried back to her room. It was early, but with
her body still vibrating from his firm lips against hers,
it might take hours to fall asleep. The brief intimacy
and what it might mean for their future excited Laura
as much as accompanying him tomorrow troubled her.
He'd surrendered to the passion inside him and kissed
her. It gave her hope that some day he might surrender more.

Chapter Seven

The landau moved quickly through the twisting streets, the morning traffic having eased after the first rush of the day. Laura sat across from Philip and Mr Connor in the semi-darkness, the roof having been kept up despite the fine day. Mr Connor rested with his eyes closed, the dark circles underneath them betraying something of his night-time activities. Philip reviewed a list of goods, shuffling through the papers with all the seriousness of a cabinet member reviewing war plans. It was a harsh reminder of what they were about to do, to ruin a man the way her uncle had been ruined.

No, she reminded herself, it wasn't she and Philip who were ruining the man, but the man himself.

She pulled at the fingers of her new gloves, the fine leather hot against her skin. Philip had apprised her of the situation at breakfast. The man, a bookseller, had gambling debts. He'd sworn to give up the cards if Philip loaned him the money to clear his debt and purchase a very popular selection of novels much in demand. The man had done neither, leaving Philip's house and heading straight for the faro tables to lose all the money and his last chance to save his business. It seemed there were more dishonourable men like Laura's uncle than she'd once realised.

Philip folded the papers and slid them inside his redingote pocket. At the unspoken signal, Mr Connor opened his eyes.

'You're quite serious today, Mr Connor,' Laura teased, trying to lighten the oppressive mood in the coach.

'I'm always serious when we're about to seize collateral. Men in desperate situations can prove unpredictable.' He slid his friend a chiding glance.

'I wouldn't have brought Miss Townsend if I thought it was going to be dangerous,' Philip interjected, his words comforting despite their firm delivery.

In the past few days she'd learned to gauge his moods, to see something of the man behind the sturdy moneylender. He wouldn't hold her in his arms and coo reassuring words, but she could always trust that he meant what he said. Her comfort was short lived as the carriage slowed to turn into a small side street, passing a man standing on the corner preaching universal suffrage. The landau rocked to a halt where the street widened a touch in front of a small bookstore. The store was wedged between a tobacconist shop and a print maker displaying a scathing cartoon of a fat Prince Regent extolling the virtues of the hated Gag Acts. Laura peered through the window at the dark and dirty street. The windows of the shops with eaves were dulled by the grime of London air or streaked with a half-hearted attempt to clean them. The more exposed windows were pocked with brown spots from where last night's raindrops had struck them. The only things each shop had in common were the shabby goods filling their shallow display spaces or overflowing on the rickety carts outside.

Mr Connor hopped out, but stayed near the door, his back to the carriage. Philip stepped down next, waiting by the kerb for Laura to alight. She had to shift to one side as she did to avoid a dead rat. Behind the carriage, the cart driven by Philip's men halted. The burly gentlemen slid down off the sides, disturbing the small puddles dotting the pavement. The sky was clear now and the stench of the street, previously dampened by the rain, was beginning to rise with the heat of the spring sun.

Mr Connor made for the door, Philip following behind him, but Laura paused. A bow-front window with painted green trim marked the shop. The box affixed to the outside of the building spilled over with geraniums glittering with raindrops still clinging to their petals. Behind the flowers, the square panes of leaded glass sparkled with the faint sun reaching down this depressing lane.

'What's wrong?' Philip asked, pausing at the door as she joined him and Mr Connor.

'There's something too genteel about this place for a man in love with the faro tables.' She cupped one of the large geranium flowers drooping towards the door. 'There's a woman's touch here.'

Philip's scrutiny jumped from one point to another, noting the details. He pulled on the top of his glove, stretching the leather tighter over his hand before letting it snap back into place.

'I investigated the man myself. There was no evidence of a woman,' Mr Connor added. 'At least not three months ago.'

'The man's situation has changed.' Laura could sense Philip's fury, yet no one watching them would have caught the subtle shift in him.

They exchanged a look, understanding whispering between them. Despite the change, they must continue, no matter what or who they met inside.

Her heart sank, but with his men waiting by the cart and the neighbours coming out of their shops or pulling back curtains to watch, there was no halting what was about to happen. Even the man preaching suffrage had stopped to watch.

Laura pulled her pelisse closer around her. The gathering shopkeepers' sneers and curious whispers reminded her too much of the morning they'd left the draper shop in Wood Street.

'Come along.' Philip lowered his walking stick, pressing the tip against the ground. 'Let's be done with this.'

Philip opened the shop door, disturbing the bell hanging over it, and Laura and Mr Connor followed behind.

The tinkling noise brought a young woman out from the back room. She didn't have the look of London. The sense of the country was too strong in the cut of her dress and the fullness of her hips. If she wasn't standing behind the counter, Laura might have mistaken her for one of the many milkmaids who walked the streets each morning with jugs of milk hanging off the yokes balanced across their shoulders. Whatever her origins, the freshness of the country had faded from her pale cheeks. The fullness of her body would soon fade, too, Laura predicted, as it had from her when the meals had become sparse.

'May I help you, sir?' The woman's voice was bright and inviting, but there was a strain to it Laura recognised. It was the same tense hope she'd once greeted each customer with when the business had begun to falter and every sale was desperately needed.

The breeze from outside ruffled the pages of an open book on a stand as Philip's men filed in behind them.

The woman's bottom lip began to tremble as Philip approached the counter.

'Madam, my name is Mr Rathbone. I'm here to see Mr Hammond.'

'No, you're not. I know why you're really here.' She twisted her hands in front of her. 'Please do me the courtesy of locking the door so none of the neighbours come barging in to see my shame.'

Philip nodded to Mr Connor, who slid the bolt on the door. 'Where is Mr Hammond? My business is with him.'

'He isn't here. Up and took the King's shilling. Sent me a letter telling me he wasn't coming back. Didn't even say where he was.' Mrs Hammond went white beneath her freckles. The poor woman must have known as little about her husband's failed dealings as Laura had about her uncle's. 'That's what you've come for, isn't it, the money he owes?'

'It is.' Philip's voice softened, but it didn't ease the woman's worry or Laura's discomfort.

'Well, there isn't any to give you.' Mrs Hammond huffed. 'When he wed me, he said he had a good business, a fine shop. It was all lies. He had his fun with me, then left me to deal with his troubles. The coward. I thought I could keep it going, save myself from the streets, but I was sinking before he even left. I don't know anything about running a shop, or keeping accounts. I don't want to end up on the streets.' Mrs Hammond shoved her fist in her mouth to hold back a sob.

Laura rushed to her, recognising herself in the despairing woman and wanting to relieve even a small measure of her pain. 'I'm so sorry.'

The woman dropped her fist to her side, a hard look replacing her tears. 'Are ya?'

'I've been where you are. I know what it's like to lose everything.'

'You haven't lost nothing, not if you're with him.' She waved a finger at Philip, her tone blunt, not cutting. She didn't want Laura's pity any more than Laura had wanted anyone else's. 'I don't have a man like that to save me. Mine's run off, the coward. I hope he gets shot.'

'Mrs Hammond, are there children?' Philip asked.

She shook her head, her dingy blonde hair waving over her forehead. 'No, thank goodness.'

'Do you have family you can go to?'

Again she shook her head, large tears welling in her wide eyes.

'Philip, can't we extend the contract, give Mrs Hammond more time to pay, or loan her more money?' Laura pleaded, hating to see the woman suffer or to think what fate waited for her once she, Philip and his men left with her possessions. 'She's running the shop, she might make good of it yet.'

Philip came to stand in front of her, his body so close she could see the fine needlework around the button-hole of his redingote. Laura tensed, expecting him to pull her from the room like her uncle used to do when-ever she'd question him in front of customers or the more dubious creditors. Philip didn't pull her outside. Instead, he leaned in close to Laura's ear, the heat from his cheek singeing hers. Her heart began to race with more than just the panicked memories brought about by this situation. She stared straight ahead, focusing on the stacks of books just visible behind the counter and the narrow opening between the shop and the storeroom at the back. She was afraid to look at him, not because of what she might see, but because of the primal reaction setting low inside her, a feeling she couldn't explain.

'Making a scene will not make this any easier for Mrs Hammond,' he said in a low voice. It wasn't a warn-ing or a reprimand, but as straight a statement as any he'd ever made. 'I understand your concern, but Mrs Hammond does not possess the skills or experience to make a success of a business which is already flounder-ing. If I fail to seize her goods, one of her many other creditors will do it. They may not treat her as kindly when they do.'

Laura blinked slowly, trying not to let the heat of his firm body so close to hers add to the faint feeling al-ready gripping her. At last she dared to meet his eyes, turning her head just enough to catch his gaze from beneath her lashes. The muscles along his cheekbones tightened, his breath caressing her face in a steady, even cadence to match the rise and fall of his chest. If there weren't all these people watching, she thought he might kiss the fight out of her.

Over Philip's shoulder, Laura caught Mrs Hammond's eye. The woman watched the exchange intensely, hope returning to her tired face. It crushed Laura to think it was about to be extinguished. She was no expert on books, but from here she could see the frayed edges of covers and the dust covering many of the tomes. Philip was correct. Mrs Hammond couldn't revive the business with such sad offerings. 'Yes, you're right. She can't carry on.'

Philip didn't gloat at her acquiescence, but studied her face. That unsettling spark jumped between them again, hidden from the others in the room by his wide back. As she held his stare, part of Laura willed him to step away, to lessen the intensity between them so she could breathe again. As if hearing her plea, he turned and strode to Mrs Hammond.

'Mrs Hammond, if you would please show me where you keep the rest of the inventory, then we may conclude this business and leave you in peace.' The deep tones of his voice were almost soothing.

With a resigned nod, Mrs Hammond led Philip behind the counter and through the small door at the back. Mr Connor went about instructing the men to pack up the books and they began loading them in the cart.

While the men worked, Laura stood in the middle

of the store, watching through the sagging storeroom lintel as Philip quietly spoke to Mrs Hammond. The cadence and tone of Philip's voice was audible, but not the words. Mrs Hammond nodded as she listened, her despair seeming to lift, especially when Philip removed something from the pocket of his redingote and handed it to her. Laura thought it must be a pound or two. It seemed Laura's plea had prompted him to do more than enforce his rights. Mrs Hammond took the item and Philip's hand, showing what Laura thought a touch too much gratitude for such small charity. There was no kindness in extending a few pounds. If the woman didn't have the knowledge to manage accounts, she'd soon spend the money and be no better off tomorrow than she was today.

Laura tugged at her gloves again, wanting to be free of the store and this dirty business, to sit in the dark of the coach and quiet her mind.

She made for the door. 'Mr Connor, I'll be in the carriage.'

'Allow me to escort you.'

'No, I can go alone.'

She slipped outside before he could object, stopping to take a breath.

'Excuse us, Miss Townsend,' one of Philip's men said as he carried a crate of books from the store.

She moved aside, noting the crowd watching, their eyes narrowed with hate and disgust, all of it directed at her. They despised her and Philip just as she'd once despised the creditors, too.

She hurried to the carriage, waving the rising driver

back into his seat. She twisted the brass handle and climbed inside, pulling the door closed with a slam. The horse rocked back and forth, startled by the noise and the driver's voice rumbled as he calmed the animal.

The settling of the carriage didn't calm her, it couldn't, not with the steady clap of footsteps moving back and forth, the clunk of boxes falling into the cart and the loud whispers of all the watchers.

Laura leaned back as far as she could into the darkness of the landau, trying to brace herself against the fear of the strangers in the street and the memories awakened by Mrs Hammond's situation. Today wasn't supposed to be like this. It was Mr Hammond who was meant to suffer for his mistakes, not his wife. Helplessness filled her, just as it had when she'd overheard her uncle Robert downstairs bargaining away the business while her mother had struggled to sleep in the next room. Tears stung her eyes and fell in fat drops of frustration down her cheeks. She hadn't been at the new shop the morning Philip's men had come to claim the inventory, but she'd shaken with anger when Robert had callously told her it was all gone. Despite Laura's engagement to the man who had lent the money, she could no more prevent the end of Mrs Hammond's livelihood any more than she could have saved her own.

She stared out the opposite window, unable to watch Philip's men, eager for this awful morning and her part in it to end. Then, over the shoulder of an old woman whispering fiercely to the thin one beside her, Laura thought she saw a face she recognised. Her heart thumped hard in her chest as she jerked up and pressed her hands to the glass, trying to get a better look, but the man turned and hurried away. His shoulders were wide, his chest thick as a barrel. A shock of salt-and-pepper hair sat below his worn cap as he lumbered down the street.

Uncle Robert.

The day she'd left Seven Dials, he'd promised she'd see him again. The memory of his scowl glaring from the rookery window sent a chill racing through her. With shaking hands, Laura reached down and slid the bolt on the carriage door in front of her, then leaned over to lock the other one.

She returned to the window and caught sight of the man's cap in the distance. She willed him to look back, to confirm or ease her suspicions, but he turned the corner, the profile of his face obscured by the bright light reflecting off the building behind him.

The carriage door on the far side rattled and Laura whirled around to see Philip and Mr Connor outside. She fought to calm herself as she reached over and slid back the bolt.

'Why did you lock the door?' Philip demanded, as he stepped inside and settled himself across from her.

Philip had warned her to tell him if her uncle ever approached her. His intense stare almost demanded it. Out of spite, Laura refused to tell him, though part of her wanted him to know, wanted his protection.

'Mrs Hammond will not have the luxury of a bolt soon,' Laura shot at him, her anger fuelled by the fear threatening to escape from her control.

Mr Connor paused, halfway into the carriage. He

looked back and forth between them, then stepped back out. 'I'll ride with the men.'

Once he was gone and the door closed, the vehicle rocked into motion.

'I'm sorry this morning didn't go as planned,' Philip offered, but she was in no mood for his apology.

'It went exactly as you planned. Mr Hammond failed to pay and you seized his goods. Now Mrs Hammond will starve, or worse.'

'Remember, Laura, Mr Hammond applied to me for help and I gave it. It was his choice to throw the opportunity aside and squander my money.' He settled his walking stick beside him. 'Why did you lock the bolt?'

His return to this subject startled her and she stammered as she answered. 'I was afraid of the crowd. Their hate was obvious.'

'If they understood the amount of good I've done, they wouldn't be so eager for our demise. Neither would you.'

'I have no desire to see us fail,' Laura insisted, wishing he could understand how watching the end of Mrs Hammond's hope had been like reliving the end of hers. 'I only question the good you seem to find in seizing a man's livelihood.'

'I assume your father was forced to collect debts.'

'He was.' Laura shifted in her seat, wishing to be left alone to deal with this tumble of emotions instead of enduring his questions and explanations.

'Then you understand the need to collect mine.'

'No, I don't understand. If my father had seen such a situation, he would have given Mrs Hammond more time, found a way to allow her to make payments, anything but snatch away her things. You see such a situation and it does nothing to alter your course. How can you be so callous?'

The atmosphere in the coach grew as tight as a thread about to break.

'You think me callous?' His question was sharp, slicing away her anger.

She'd pushed him too far.

The carriage rocked to a stop in front of the house. Philip flipped open the latch and stepped down. She expected him to storm inside. Instead he turned, facing her as he had Mr Williams before he'd ordered the man out of his house.

'Join me in the study.' He strode into the house, not waiting for her.

She reached for the open carriage door to steady herself as she stepped down, waving away the footman's offer of assistance. The heels of her half-boots clicked with each step she took up the path. He was going to end their engagement. He was going to throw her and her mother out to join Mrs Hammond on the street. She was going to have to face her mother and tell her they were now going to starve, or worse, because she'd spat on everything Philip was, just because he'd made her face her fears at Mrs Hammond's and that had terrified her.

It was dim inside the hall and the shadows closed in around her as she walked slowly to the study. The prospect of returning to Seven Dials made her stomach roil. It wasn't the cold or hunger she feared so much as the loss of Philip's presence in her life. Over the past few days, he'd been there to support her. He was fast becoming the rock on which everything in her new life was being built. Without his confidence adding to hers, Laura wasn't sure she could face the challenges of poverty again.

She should have thought of these things before she'd let her anger get the better of her. Now it was too late.

Inside the study, Philip stood behind the desk, leaning on his palms pressed flat on either side of a large, open ledger. Even with his eyes fixed hard on hers, she knew she didn't want to lose him, or the closeness she'd fought to build between them. Maybe she was no better than a child, knocking contracts from his desk and hurling insults whenever she was frustrated or scared. Maybe she didn't deserve his trust, respect and affection, but she wanted it, especially now when it was close to being pulled away.

Laura crept into the room, penitent, ready to apologise, grovel, explain, whatever it took to make him forget her ugly words and not cast her out of his life. 'Philip, I—'

'Sit, please.' He pointed to one chair in front of the desk.

She obeyed, more afraid of him now than when he'd disarmed her the night she'd stolen into his house.

'What questions do I ask men who apply to me for money?' he demanded.

'Their collateral,' she squeaked, then cleared her throat, trying to rouse her nerve. 'Their business plan.'

'What else?'

Her memory failed her. She tugged at the lace around

her neck, wanting to rip it out by the seams and clear it away from her hot skin.

'I ask them about their private affairs, whether they have a wife and children and their other household obligations,' he reminded her like a schoolmaster lecturing an unruly pupil. 'Mr Hammond succeeded in keeping the truth of his situation from me. Had I known he'd placed his wife in jeopardy with his poor business practices, I wouldn't have helped him dig the pit deeper. However, having discovered the deception, I'm glad of it.'

'Glad?' It didn't seem possible.

'Because it afforded me the chance to help her.' He turned the open ledger around and pushed it across the desk to her. 'I want you to see this.'

She perched on the edge of the cushion to peer down at the ledger and the long list of women's names. Next to each was fifty pounds and under the amount, a list of withdrawals with notes for the money's purpose. She could make little sense of the entries or who the women were. 'What is it?'

'The accounts for Halcyon House.'

She sat back, stunned. Tales of Halcyon House and the safety it offered women who'd fallen on hard times were rife in Seven Dials. Entrance was by voucher only, but no one knew who provided them. Laura had once tried to discover it but, for all her enquiries, she'd never even obtained the address of the elusive sanctuary. 'Why do you have them?'

'Because I'm the primary patron.'

Laura's heart dropped to the floor and the guilt that

had been steadily rising since her outburst in the carriage increased until she thought it might drown her. Everything she'd believed about him in the landau, all the wrong she'd convinced herself he'd done, ended with this simple admission. She deserved to be tossed into the street.

'I saw you hand Mrs Hammond something. I thought it was money. It was a voucher, wasn't it?'

He didn't answer. He didn't have to.

Laura slumped in her chair wishing she could take back everything she'd said in the carriage.

'My father was one of the primary founders of Halcyon House,' Philip explained. 'Since his passing, I've continued to manage its affairs, extending vouchers when I see fit and helping to raise the necessary funds to feed, house and clothe the women and their children who live there. We employ appropriate teachers in different endeavours, providing the women with the skills necessary to place them in situations to support themselves. When they are ready to leave, we furnish them with the means to establish a shop.'

Laura stared at the figures, unable to look at Philip. 'And their husbands?'

'If they can be helped, we find them a position. If they are dissolute, then we establish a trust for the women, money their husbands cannot squander.' He laid his finger on the ledger. 'This page is one list of those trusts. Two lady patrons, wealthy widows, hold the funds in the women's names for their use so their husbands cannot spend it.'

'I'm sorry, Philip.' She looked at him at last. There

was no anger hardening his stunning blue eyes, only disappointment in her opinion of him. He'd believed in her when no one else would. She'd offered her assistance, listened to his troubles, but deep down, she'd failed to act from her heart. 'You're right. I should have given you the benefit of the doubt. After everything you've done for me and my mother, I should have thought better of you.'

'Yes, you should have.' He rounded the desk. She stiffened, expecting him to escort her from the room, his house, his life. Instead he strode past her, his coldness as brutal as any words he could have thrown at her.

At the door, he paused and regarded her with the same detached reserve she'd come to recognise. 'I would have extended a voucher to you, if I hadn't asked you to marry me.'

He walked away, leaving Laura with the ledger and to reflect on the truth.

She rose on shaking legs and staggered from the room, too agitated to sit still, but not sure what to do or where to go. She wanted to talk to her mother and hear her reassurances, but it would mean admitting her mistake. She climbed the stairs, remorse following her. If Philip cast her aside, she didn't know how she and her mother would survive. Hopefully, Philip would send her to Halcyon House, though she wouldn't blame him if he decided to cast her off with no help at all.

Upstairs, the hallway was empty and she slipped thankfully into her room without being seen. She couldn't face her mother and burden her with worries about their future.

She paced across the thick carpet, her mind flitting from one awful possibility to the next. Making a quick turn, she upset the small stack of envelopes on the corner of her writing table. She dropped to her knees to snatch them up, pausing to look at the names on each one. They were answers to the advertisement for Thomas's nurse.

Laura pulled herself off the floor and settled herself in the chair by the window to read the letters. She might have failed to give Philip her full support, but she wouldn't fail him with her tasks. If she was efficient in this matter and continued to prove her worth, then he might see the value in upholding the engagement. It would give her time to rebuild the trust she'd so thoughtlessly shattered, the trust she hadn't realised was so precious to her until it had gone.

'Shouldn't Mr Woodson have obtained the common licence by now?' Justin's grip tightened on the dummy as Philip pummelled it. 'Your constant need to exercise is impinging on my more pleasurable pursuits.'

'Mr Woodson delivered it yesterday.' Philip punched the dummy hard, but it failed to drive back the anger gripping him.

'Then why haven't you summoned the vicar, set a date and instructed Mrs Palmer to prepare a wedding-breakfast menu? Not having second thoughts, are you?' Justin teased.

Philip jolted upright, dropping his hands to his sides, but not unclenching his aching fists.

Justin's smile wilted. 'You are.'

'Despite the past few days, my intended is determined to see me as nothing more than a grubbing moneylender intent on ruining everyone who wanders across my path.' He slammed his fist into the leather, the blow vibrating up his arm. The control he'd maintained all day, in the bookseller's, then after Laura had thrown her aspersions in his face, nearly failed him. He straightened, closed his eyes and listened to the sounds of the room, concentrating on the slap of fists against flesh, leather and canvas, the shuffle of feet over the dirt floor and the yelling of the trainers until his calm returned.

He opened his eyes and struck the dummy again, his punch controlled and well executed.

Justin clapped his hands on either side of the wobbling figure. 'You can't expect Miss Townsend to possess unshakeable faith in you because you bought her dresses and made her mother happy. It'll take time, which you won't gain by putting off the wedding.'

'Perhaps marriage isn't the best solution to my problems.' Philip shook out the burning in his arms, but couldn't shift the uncertainty which had plagued him since this morning. He's been so certain in his decision when he'd proposed, now he doubted both himself and Laura.

'Breaking the engagement will only cause more problems. Imagine Jane's tantrum when you tell her Mrs and Miss Townsend are leaving.' He pointed a warning finger at Philip. 'That alone should encourage you to set a date.'

Philip turned and strode to the far end of the sparring ring, the potential scene with his sister threatening to bring on a headache. However, it wasn't Jane's disappointment which kept the common licence sealed on his desk instead of discarded in the grate. It was his own. He didn't want to see the light go out of Laura's beautiful face when he told her he'd changed his mind. He didn't want to experience even a small measure of the despair which stung his chest whenever he imagined the scene.

He paced back to where Justin waited with a towel. Taking it, Philip rubbed the coarse cotton between his thumb and forefinger. He was allowing emotions to guide his decision and it unnerved him. Such weakness had allowed him to ignore Arabella's frailty and it had killed her. If he continued on this path with Laura, he might be the one to suffer this time.

'What if marrying her is a mistake?' After her actions in the entrance hall and their kiss the previous evening, he'd thought her concern for him extended further than the mere convenience of his money and name. Today, he wasn't so sure. He despised this confusion. He wanted to see the situation as plainly as he had the day he'd proposed.

'The only mistake you're making is putting off the wedding.' Justin threw one arm around Philip's shoulders, the rogue returning to replace the concerned friend. 'What you need is a wedding night. It'll clear your head.'

The memory of Laura's mouth eager and open beneath his nearly sent him back to pummelling the dummy. Twice yesterday he'd lost control, once after Dr Hale's visit and again in his bedroom. It'd taken the better part of the night and reviewing nearly every contract on his desk to forget the sweet taste of her kiss and how her soft sigh had nearly been his undoing. Not even his embarrassment over his confession in the entrance hall had been enough to drive the unsettling urges her tender cheek beneath his fingertips had raised. How easy it was to forget himself in her presence proved unsettling. 'I don't think the more intimate demands of marriage will make things clearer.'

'I know you don't, but trust me, intimacy is exactly what you need to settle yourself. So take my advice and set the date.' Justin punched Philip's arm lightly. 'Now, come on, we have to get you cleaned up and home before Mr Charton's party tonight.'

'You're coming, then?'

'The lovely widow Gammon will be there. With her, I expect to be very settled by the end of the night.' He whistled as he strolled off to the bathing room.

Philip followed at a slower pace. He was done fighting for the day, fighting Laura, his feelings, himself. He wasn't ready to hurry to the church or to terminate his agreement with Laura, but something had to change before he entered into this most binding of contracts. He needed some assurance his future with Laura would be one of mutual companionship, not derision and disgust. Hopefully, tonight, he would find it.

Chapter Eight

Laura held on to Philip's arm as they walked up to the Chartons' wide front door, careful not to squeeze too tight. Tonight there was none of the warmth she'd experienced in the previous times they'd touched, only an awkwardness she attributed to that morning's row.

Despite an afternoon of attending to household business, worry continued to cling to her like moist linen on a hot day. Not even Mary arriving to help her dress for tonight had eased her concerns. Mrs Fairley had sent over a cream-coloured silk gown with matching elbow-length gloves. A black ribbon edged the bodice, curling down to nip in beneath her breasts before falling in a straight line to her feet. Upon seeing the dress, Jane had insisted on instructing Mary in arranging Laura's hair into a pretty new style displayed in one of her fashion magazines. The tumble of curls gathered near the nape of Laura's neck and spilling over her shoulder to rest on the top of one breast was both demure and suggestive. Mother and Jane had been effusive in their praise of Laura's appearance tonight. Philip had not uttered one word, good or bad about it, nor had he stared at her in the carriage the way he had the night she'd surprised him with her dress at dinner. Instead, his focus had remained on London passing outside the landau window.

Now, as they stepped into the Chartons' columned hall, the fears his indifference raised settled a little. If he was still intent on introducing her to his associates and friends, then it must mean he intended to proceed with the wedding. Perhaps after a few glasses of port and convivial conversation with his associates had put him at his ease, she might gently press the subject of the wedding and put her mind at rest.

'Mr Rathbone, good to see you.' An older gentleman with a round stomach concealed by a fine red waistcoat and dark jacket swept down the curving marble staircase, to grip Philip's hand. 'And you've brought a guest?'

'Allow me to introduce Miss Laura Townsend. We're engaged to be married.'

'I never would have guessed it.' Mr Charton gaped back and forth between them. As reassuring as Philip's announcement might be, she was growing tired of seeing surprise on people's faces when she was introduced. 'But I should have known you'd simply spring her on us. With how close you keep things to the vest, it's a wonder you didn't marry her and then tell us.'

'I wouldn't have wanted to deny the ladies their share of the conversation and excitement.'

Laura tried not to stare at Philip. His near-joke had come out in his usual straightforward tone, but there was no mistaking the humour in it. Mr Charton certainly didn't miss it.

'No, they'd never forgive you.' Mr Charton laughed, then turned to Laura and made a small bow. 'It's a pleasure to meet you, Miss Townsend. You must be quite a lady to catch Rathbone's eye. Well, come up to the drawing room, both of you, Margaret and the others will be all in a flutter when they hear the news.'

Philip inclined his head, the only indication he agreed.

They started for upstairs, Laura struggling to watch her step and admire the fine plasterwork on the ceiling at the same time. She'd thought Philip's house grand until she'd entered this one. Philip's was more modest, his wealth was whispered rather than proclaimed.

Near the top, Mr Charton moved to Philip's other side, mumbling in a voice which wasn't quite low enough for Laura not to hear. 'Mrs Templeton won't be pleased about your engagement.'

'Her opinion doesn't concern me.' It was difficult to tell if Philip's declaration was the truth or merely made for Laura's and propriety's sake.

'No, I don't suppose it does,' Mr Charton conceded honestly.

It did little to calm the anxiety growing inside Laura or the very real fear she would have an enemy among his friends before she uttered so much as a good evening.

Mr Charton led them into the long drawing room just off the top of the stairs.

'Lily, stop playing,' he called out above the chatter

to the young woman seated at the nearby piano forte. Then he looked over his shoulder at Laura. 'My middle daughter, no talent for drawing, but quite the musician.'

Mr Charton raised his hands, making the port in his glass slosh up along the sides. 'Attention, everyone.'

The conversation ceased as the guests turned to face them, their scrutiny and curiosity fixed on Laura, the stranger. Among them she spied Mr Connor lounging near the widow with a buxom woman with deep-brown hair. At least there was one person Laura knew here. She settled her shoulders and stood proudly next to Philip. In time, there would be more, she was sure of it. She had to be sure. The alternative was too frightening to contemplate.

'Mr Rathbone has joined us with some surprising news,' Mr Charton announced. 'He's engaged to be married.'

The gasps of surprise nearly rattled the house to its rafters. Laura's fingers tightened on Philip's arm, digging in hard to the stiff muscle beneath. Neither of them was used to being the centre of so much attention and neither approved of it.

Mr Charton tossed Philip a ribbing smile. 'Now that's out of the way.'

'I would have preferred something more subtle,' Philip chided, both amusement and irritation dotting his words.

Beneath her palm she felt his arm relax, just as her hand tightened as one of the ladies hurried up to them.

'Mr Rathbone, how clever of you to spring such a thing on us,' exclaimed the tall woman in an expensive red silk gown and matching turban. 'Who knew you could be so surprising?'

'I did,' Laura answered, her cheeks burning with her boldness.

'I bet you do.' The woman waved her closed fan at Laura. 'I'm Mrs Charton. You don't know how excited I am to have you here.'

Laura flicked a glance at Philip, wondering if he was excited to be here with her, or if he was regretting it. His demeanour was as unyielding as always and she could discern nothing from it.

'Mr Rathbone, when you wrote to say you were bringing a guest you could have given me at least some hint as to her importance,' Mrs Charton scolded with a laugh.

Before he could answer, they were surrounded by nearly all the other female guests and some of their husbands. The women chattered and chirped, offering excited congratulations. The men were more sober as Philip made the introductions, acquainting Laura with the Moseleys, the Feltons, Mrs Gammon and Mr Jones.

'Enough of this ladies' business, Rathbone, come and give us your opinion on all those uprisings in Manchester. Jones doesn't think the weavers have the right to riot, but I say they do,' Mr Moseley, a lithe man with a long chin, insisted. 'If anyone can get to the meat of the matter, it's you.'

At last Philip turned to Laura, truly acknowledging her for the first time since she'd come downstairs to join him in the carriage. 'If you'll excuse me.'

She gripped his arm, preventing him from leaving.

'What shall I tell the ladies about our engagement?'

she whispered, the women's excited voices keeping her from being overheard. She hadn't dared to broach the subject, or break the silence between them in the landau.

'Whatever you wish. The men aren't likely to ask for details so you needn't worry about me contradicting your version of events.'

This slim reassurance given, he strode off with Mr Moseley, the damage from this morning evident in his swift dismissal of Laura in favour of his friends.

Fear rippled through her, but a comforting hand on her arm steadied her. She turned to find Mrs Charton drawing her deeper into the room.

'I know we must be very intimidating with all our fussing,' Mrs Charton offered. 'But your announcement is the most exciting news we've had at a gathering in some time.'

'It is,' Mrs Moseley chimed in, joining Laura on her other side. Mrs Moseley was near Laura's age with round cheeks and her round stomach indicated she was expecting a baby. 'And for it to come from Mr Rathbone is most unexpected. I don't know what to make of it.'

Neither did Laura, but she resolved to appear happy and excited. It wouldn't do any good to worry and raise pestering and pointed questions among the wives of his associates.

Mrs Charton stopped them before the fireplace. Inside, a cosy fire consumed a thick pile of coal. Despite the warm spring day, the night had taken on a chill. 'Allow me to introduce you to everyone.'

The women formed a tight circle around Laura as Mrs Charton made the introductions. Mrs Felton was closer to Mrs Charton's matronly age, but plump and short where Mrs Charton was slender and tall. Even Mrs Gammon with her wide bosom and round hips had stolen away from Mr Connor to join the conversation.

Only one woman showed no interest in the discussion and Laura guessed she must be Mrs Templeton.

She remained across the room near the escritoire, her willowy form akin to the table's fine legs, her bust as full as the round clock behind her. Her long fingers with long nails sharpened almost to claws tightened on the wine glass she held as she observed Laura.

Laura swallowed hard, wondering at the true depth of Philip's interest in the woman. It was impossible to gauge it when he remained with his back to all the women as he talked with the men.

Whatever disappointment his indifference created, there was little time to entertain it as the women began to question Laura about the proposal. She stammered as she answered, doing the best she could to describe it without revealing the pistol, Seven Dials or her uncle's true financial situation. Then, with a few well-placed answers, she shifted their interest from the proposal to the wedding itself, focusing on the finer points of her dress, the only details of the ceremony she possessed. Nothing else had been settled or, if it had, Philip had not seen fit to inform her. She could well imagine him appearing in her room one morning with the news the vicar of St Bride's was standing at the altar and ready to perform the ceremony. After this morning, she didn't care how it happened as long as it actually happened.

Only that would end the bleak uncertainty hovering around her.

The conversation with the ladies continued until the butler appeared to summon everyone to dinner. Philip and Mr Jones, a well-turned-out bachelor, stood deep in debate. Laura watched as one by one the other ladies' husbands came to lead them down to the dining room, leaving her to stand alone by the fireplace. She feared she might have to go by herself, but at last the gentlemen ended their discussion and Philip came to fetch her.

'How are you fairing?' He held out his arm to her.

She took it with the same hesitation as she had outside the carriage, unsure if his question was driven by manners or genuine concern. She glanced to Mrs Templeton and saw her full lips press thin before she recovered herself and fixed them into a wide, if not cunning, smile.

'I'm doing well. Mrs Charton is very nice, as are all the ladies.' She inclined her head to where Mr Connor and Mrs Gammon sat together on a sofa situated so far at one end of the room it was nearly in the hallway. 'Mr Connor is certainly enjoying himself. He's barely left Mrs Gammon's side since we arrived.'

'Nor is he likely to do so at any time this entire night.' He cocked an eyebrow at her to drive home the meaning of his words.

Laura's eyes widened, but not in surprise at Mr Connor's nocturnal activities. No, she was more surprised at the way Philip spoke to her with the ease and comfort of a long friendship. It gave her hope they could move past what had happened and reclaim some of the intimacy which had developed between them over the past few days.

Mrs Gammon wasn't the only widow looking to snare a bedfellow this evening. Mrs Templeton strode across the room towards them. With each step, her large breasts jiggled above the edge of the blue silk dress, which clung to her round hips. The silk was of inferior weave and not as well cut as Laura's. She guessed Mrs Templeton had paid more attention to the way the colour emphasised the whiteness of her skin and the red curls piled thick against the back of her head than the quality of the material. Her dress reminded Laura of the buxom young women who used to stand across the street from the rookery in their garish second-hand frocks, trying to entice men. Hopefully, Mrs Templeton wasn't as experienced a temptress as those women, or Philip as willing as their clients.

The widow met them near the door to the hallway, all but blocking their way.

'Mr Rathbone, it's a pleasure to see you tonight,' Mrs Templeton purred, standing so close in front of Philip that, if she took a deep breath, her breasts would brush his chest. 'I've missed you at all the dinners of late.'

Laura slid her hand up Philip's arm, making her claim on him clear. If Mrs Templeton noticed, she didn't seem to care, remaining far closer to Philip than propriety dictated.

'I've been greatly occupied.' Philip's even voice and posture offered no clue to his thoughts about the widow's appearance or her proximity.

Mrs Templeton laid one finger on his chest, the large

garnet adorning it sparkling over his dove-coloured waistcoat. 'You're always occupied with the wrong business.'

She slid a wicked glance at Laura before focusing back on Philip.

Laura wanted to pull Philip away from the cat's claws and chide the widow for behaving so inappropriately. Instead she stood firmly beside him, biting her tongue to keep silent. Laura hadn't seen Mrs Templeton in intimate conversation with any of the women, but it didn't mean they wouldn't rally to her defence if Laura insulted her. If Philip still intended to honour their engagement, Laura couldn't afford to make herself an outcast among the wives of his associates and friends.

To her relief, Laura didn't have to pull Philip away. He moved back without any prompting, placing a more appropriate amount of room between himself and the widow's breasts. Whatever dance Mrs Templeton hoped to engage him in, he wasn't rising to the invitation.

'Allow me to introduce my betrothed, Miss Laura Townsend.' He levelled his hand at Laura.

'Miss Townsend. A pleasure.' The slight sneer along the curve of Mrs Templeton's lips told Laura it was anything but pleasurable.

Laura didn't allow her smile to falter and matched Mrs Templeton's shallow curtsy with a deep, polite one. 'It's a pleasure to meet an *old* friend of Philip's.'

'I'm not so old as some are young and inexperienced.' She fixed her eyes on Philip, but he ignored her, turning instead to Laura.

Laura couldn't discern if he was proud or embarrassed by her exchange with the widow. Hopefully he admired her ability to face the subtle sneer of this woman as much as he'd admired her ability to stand up to Mr Williams.

Before any of them could say more, Mr Jones appeared at Mrs Templeton's elbow. A head taller than her, Mr Jones wasn't afraid to inspect the assets the widow so blatantly displayed. 'May I escort you in to dinner?'

'You may.' She took his arm, flashing Philip an enticing smile before following the more accommodating Mr Jones from the room. Mr Connor and Mrs Gammon followed close behind them.

If Philip regretted the widow's departure, it was difficult to tell as he led Laura downstairs to the dining room.

Dinner itself was a far more relaxing affair than the introductions in the drawing room. Laura was seated between the friendly Mrs Charton and Mr Connor, who remained deep in conversation with Mrs Gammon, who sat on his other side. Yet for all the welcome Laura received from the other ladies, she felt Mrs Templeton's attention on her frequently. Philip was unlucky enough to be seated next to the widow, who leaned too close to him as she listened to Philip's conversation with Mr Moseley, offering her opinion on many occasions. Philip kept his gaze on his plate whenever she spoke. Once, he raised his eyes to meet Laura's before shifting them back to the fish. Laura wondered if this reluctant show of attention was for her benefit.

'I'm so happy to see Mr Rathbone entering back into

life again,' Mrs Charton observed, drawing Laura's attention from Mrs Templeton.

'Have you known Philip a long time?'

'Oh, yes, since he was a very young man and his father began doing business with Henry.' She nodded to her husband, who raised his glass to her, the open affection between them touching. 'Mr Rathbone's father used to bring him here when he was teaching him the business.'

'What happened to Philip's parents?' There was so much about his life and past he hadn't told her.

'Fever—seven years ago. Took his father first and then two days later his mother died. It was all so sudden and unexpected.' She shook her head in sorrow. 'After Mr Rathbone's parents passed away, he'd come to Henry for advice. There was one particular occasion when a silversmith he'd loaned quite a sum defaulted. It nearly ruined his entire business.'

'Philip almost lost his business?' It didn't seem possible.

'Oh, yes. It was such a hard time for him after his father died, you understand. And then to lose his mother so soon after. I tried to help where I could with Jane, but I was newly delivered of my twins and could do so much less than I wanted to. Then, after so many years, when all was well, to have another tragedy befall him. The poor soul.' She touched her hand to her chest and threw a motherly look at Philip. 'But to see him tonight, looking so much happier and more like the old Mr Rathbone, it warms the heart.'

'You think him happier?'

'Oh, most definitely and I must say there's no doubt you're the cause. Isn't she, Mrs Gammon?'

The widow leaned forward to peer past Mr Connor. 'Isn't who?'

'Isn't Miss Townsend to thank for the change in Mr Rathbone?'

Mrs Gammon looked from Laura to Philip, then nodded, her pearl earrings brushing her smooth cheeks. 'Oh, yes, I noticed it at once, the moment they entered. I'm so happy for you both.'

She offered a bright smile before returning to Mr Connor.

Laura threw a glance at Philip, struggling to see what the other ladies did. She only noticed how the light from the wide chandelier hanging over the long table softened the set of his nose but deepened the shadow along the edge of his jaw. 'No, I don't think it's me.'

'Oh, indeed it is.' She laid her hand on Laura's, giving it a small, reassuring squeeze.

'What is?' Mrs Moseley called from across the table.

'Almond blancmange,' Mrs Charton answered without hesitation. 'It is one of the best dishes to serve at a wedding breakfast.'

'Oh, yes, you must have almond blancmange.' Mrs Moseley slipped a forkful of fish into her mouth, filling out her already round cheeks. 'It's heavenly.'

Mrs Charton winked at Laura as the conversation turned to the wedding breakfast, leaving Laura to wonder at the woman's comments about Philip. With Mrs Templeton practically pushing her breasts in Philip's face as he passed her the salt, Laura was hesitant to place much hope in Mrs Charton's observation. Maybe seeing his paramour again tonight was the reason for the change in his behaviour. If there was anything between him and Mrs Templeton, perhaps he felt it a welcome relief to be in her presence, rather than facing Laura's doubts about his character.

Throughout the rest of dinner, Laura did her best to enjoy herself despite Mrs Templeton's shameless flirtation across the table. Mrs Charton was the centre of attention at dessert, with a large cake placed in front of her as everyone offered their congratulations. Then Mr Charton presented her with a stunning gold necklace, sweetly fastening it around her neck before leaning in to brush her lips with a kiss. Laura clapped with the others at the presentation, smiling despite the twinge of jealousy at witnessing such love between a man and wife. Before this morning, she thought she and Philip might obtain such happiness. She was no longer so sure.

At last, with the cake eaten and the present given, Mrs Charton rose and led the ladies back to the drawing room. If Laura expected the women to talk of domestic affairs once alone, she was surprised. They settled on the suite of furniture near the fireplace and set to discussing their husbands' business. Laura listened, learning as much about moneylending and dealing with clients as she had from her time with Philip. The conversation only turned to more feminine matters when Mrs Moseley complained to Mrs Charton of trying to manage small children when her husband required so much of her help. Their hostess and Mrs Gammon offered encouraging advice which Laura raptly took in. It was a comfort to know she would be able to draw on these women's experiences to help her manage her and Philip's affairs when the time came. Assuming it came.

Too agitated to sit still, Laura excused herself and made for the refreshment table near the window. If Philip decided not to go through with the wedding, it would only take a few words in private to the Chartons to undo everything done tonight. Then Laura would vanish from all of these people's lives as quickly as she'd come into them. The bitter taste of fear and regret filled her mouth. She wanted to know these people and enjoy the friendship they offered as much as she wanted Philip.

She poured herself a glass of punch, but the tart drink didn't ease the worries determined to needle her. Neither did the subtle rustle of cheap silk joined by a purring voice behind her.

'Tell me, Miss Townsend, when is the happy day?' Mrs Templeton asked, coming around to face Laura.

Laura set down her unfinished punch, viewing the woman with the same detached interest she'd directed at so many of Philip's clients over the past few days. 'The date has not been set yet.'

Mrs Templeton laid her talons over her large chest, her mouth forming a wide O in surprise. 'A sudden engagement, but not sudden enough to secure a date?'

'A date cannot be set until we have the common licence.'

'Strange he hasn't already obtained it.' Mrs Templeton's lips curled into a devious smile. 'Surely if he was so eager to get married, he would hurry things along.'

Assuming an air of carefree indifference, Laura shrugged, not about to let this woman cow her. If she did, it would give Mrs Templeton permission to treat her shabbily every time they found themselves together at such gatherings. 'I'm not concerned. If he had doubts, he would hurry the matter.'

Behind her, Laura heard the deep rumbling of the men's voices as they entered the room to join the ladies.

Mrs Templeton ran her finger over the rim of Laura's half-filled glass sitting on the table, eliciting a low sound from the crystal. 'Nothing is settled until the ring is upon your finger, Miss Townsend, and even then a man may find more tempting entertainment elsewhere.'

She fixed her gaze over Laura's shoulder and the sheer heat in it seemed enough to evaporate the punch from the bowl. No doubt she was eyeing Philip, making her disgusting invitation clear.

Laura didn't turn to see if the invitation was acknowledged. It didn't matter. Whatever happened, Laura wasn't going to allow this woman in the poorly cut silk to knock her down.

'You mustn't know Philip very well if you believe he'll dishonour a vow once it's given, or renege on a contract once it's been made. He has too much integrity to act in the way you've implied, or for me to doubt for even a moment that he will not honour his word. So suggest what you like about the two of you, I refuse to believe it for a moment.'

Mrs Townsend's painted lips twisted together in irritation. Laura had fought her with the truth and she had no answer for it. It *was* the truth. Laura felt it deep in her heart and not even all the fears swirling there since this morning could chase that away. Philip was a man of great integrity, as he'd proven to her time and again. He'd made Laura a promise and he would keep it. Whatever happened between them from this evening on, she would never doubt the man again.

The scent of bergamot swept over Laura and she sensed more than saw Philip beside her. 'Miss Townsend, are you ready to depart? I must rise early tomorrow.'

'Yes, let us go at once.' She held out her hand, ready for him to offer her his arm.

Instead, he slid his hand beneath hers and raised it to his lips. Even through the silk of her gloves the heat of his feather-light kiss seared her skin. He might as well have enveloped her in an embrace and kissed her with the passion of a Gothic hero, his claim on her was so clear.

It nearly knocked the breath out of Laura, especially when his eyes held hers as he rose. With not one glance at Mrs Templeton, he straightened, tucked Laura's hand into the crook of his elbow and led her away.

Philip settled against the squabs, the stiffness in his back he'd experienced on the drive over replaced by a more unsettling stiffness lower down. Laura sat across from him, the dim light from the carriage lantern dancing over her high cheeks and sparkling in the gold earrings Jane had lent her. Ever since Laura had come downstairs to join him in the carriage, the cream dress spilling over her curves, the tender curls of her *coiffure* lying suggestively over one round breast, he'd fought his desire to stare at her. Not even conversation with his friends had set him at ease. He'd spent half the night across the room from her just to avoid the pull of her body over his. There was no avoiding it now.

'Did you enjoy the evening?' he asked, curious about her thoughts on his associates and friends.

'I did. The ladies were very gracious and friendly.' She adjusted one sleeve of her dress. 'Most of them.'

'My apologies for Mrs Templeton. She has a greatly inflated sense of her desirability.'

'Were you ever intimate with her?'

The question startled Philip. He wasn't used to her being so direct. 'No. Mrs Templeton is a handsome woman, but she offers little beyond physical gratification.'

Laura nodded, seeking no further explanation.

Mrs Templeton had tried to snare him early last year, when the darkness of losing Arabella had gripped him the hardest and he'd been at his weakest. It hadn't taken long for him to see through her feigned concern to realise she was more enamoured of his money than him. That he was, even for a moment, tempted by her charms rattled him as much as the mistakes he'd made with Arabella. He'd thought he might be making the same mistakes with Laura until he'd overheard her praising him to Mrs Templeton.

She'd defended him when she hadn't known he was listening. She might have said anything, but instead she'd defended his integrity, his commitment to his word, the one aspect of his character that Mrs Templeton continued to underestimate, judging by her behaviour tonight. It was something Laura might have dismissed after the incident today. She must have believed her words to defend him with such enthusiasm, instead of allowing Mrs Templeton's threat to make her doubt his commitment to her.

Relief filled Philip, strong enough to drive away the doubt the rational part of him had stubbornly clung to. Laura was the right choice. It was time to stop dallying. 'The common licence arrived today.'

The air in the coach thickened and Philip's back straightened along with Laura's. He fingered his watch fob, but the awkwardness he'd expected in the moment didn't come. He'd avoided the subject for days and now it was done the world had not tilted to throw them both off. He was also relieved to find the aching guilt he'd experienced when he'd faced Dr Hale did not return.

'When do you plan to hold the wedding?' More trepidation than enthusiasm laced her question..

Her measured reaction was his fault. He should have told her about the licence sooner, not left her to dangle in a limbo where he held the power to fulfil his promise or to cast her aside. Such a situation would not occur again. 'I thought we might plan it together. It's your wedding as much as mine.'

'Not the most romantic answer, but I suppose it will suffice.' The teasing he'd come to enjoy over the last few days warmed him as much as Mr Charton's port. 'When shall we stand before the vicar?'

'We must wait seven days.'

'Then in seven days we'll wed. It will give Mrs Fairley time to finish my wedding dress.'

He flexed his hand over his knee, as eager to see the dress as what would lie beneath it. 'In seven days it is.'

'You're sure the vicar will be available?'

'Reverend Clare is a former client of mine.'

'Gambling debts?'

'His son needed to purchase a living from a less-scrupulous man of the cloth who consistently ignored his flock.' He rested his ankle on one knee. He caught her surprise at his relaxed attitude in the slight tilt of her head.

'You never cease to surprise me, Philip.'

'It's not my intention.'

'No, I don't suppose it is, but you do it all the same, which I suppose will make for an interesting life with you.'

'I should hate for you to be bored.'

'I don't think it's possible.' She laughed and the sound almost brought a smile to his lips. No, they would not be bored together. She was too intriguing to him, her happiness suddenly too important.

'I'll leave you and your mother to see to the details of the wedding breakfast with cook and Mrs Palmer.'

'If my mother has time. She and Jane are as thick as thieves. I hardly see either of them any more.' Her happiness faded along with these last words.

'It troubles you to see them together so much?'

'A little.' She tugged at the fingertips of her gloves before resting her hands in her lap. 'But you were right, having something to do has made such a difference to my mother.'

'She's affected quite a change in Jane. Not once this week have I been hounded for an inappropriate dress. Also, there is now the tempering influence of Mrs Townsend to counteract the questionable influence of the novels she reads.'

'You know about her books?' Laura rocked forward, looking surprised and, as a deepening blush spread across her chest, a touch guilty.

'There's very little in my house I don't know about.'

'No, I don't suppose there is.' She sat back, pulling one sagging glove tighter over her curving elbow. 'I'm surprised you've allowed her to continue reading them.'

'She's prone to be rebellious. Better she rebel with a salacious book than a more salacious tradesman.'

'A very wise position. Though she'll forget her books once I tell her the wedding date is set. Jane had already told me I must have beef and tonight Mrs Moseley insisted on almond blancmange. I haven't the faintest notion what almond blancmange is.'

'Then be sure to have cook prepare it so you'll know.'

'I would like Mrs Moseley, Mrs Charton and their husbands to be invited, and of course Mrs Gammon. I wouldn't want Mr Connor to feel lonely at such an event.'

'It might inform him how best to proceeded with Mrs Gammon.'

'I think he has ideas of his own.' A tempting smile spread across her lips, bringing a few intriguing images to Philip's mind before he forced them aside.

'What other thoughts do you have for our wedding day?'

Philip listened, enjoying the sweet cadence of Laura's voice. Her hands waved through the air when she was excited or folded quietly in her lap when she became thoughtful. He enjoyed the happiness this control over this aspect of her life gave her, though her confidence took time to cultivate. At first, she searched his face after each proposed wedding detail to see if he approved. When he raised no objections, her subtle apprehension faded. It took many suggestions before she no longer looked to him, but gave full vent to her ideas, her hands moving in time to the rapid cadence of her speech.

As her confidence increased, he realised how unfair he'd been to make so many decisions without consulting her. He remembered the helplessness of not having a say in life. When he'd turned sixteen his father had decided it was time for him to learn the family business in depth. After years of watching his parents, he thought he'd known so much. In truth, he'd known next to nothing. For the first year, when his father had insisted he only listen and learn, it'd frustrated him. Remembering the pride he'd felt at being given his first client still made his chest swell.

Laura wasn't a youth. She was a mature woman with as much experience with hardship, business and struggling as him. It'd been unfair of him to deny her the control she craved, needed and deserved.

Suddenly, without warning, she lowered her hands, facing him with as much seriousness as Jane whenever she was about to ask for something. 'Mrs Charton said you almost lost your business once. What happened?'

Philip dropped his foot off his leg, allowing both feet to rest flat on the floor. He wasn't prepared for this. He felt his reserve returning, a dismissive answer to the question forming before he bit it back. Laura wanted honesty, the kind he should have shown her by sharing the details of Halcyon House sooner. He shouldn't have kept it hidden until revealing it was a necessity rather than a joy. Admitting his past mistakes would not be pleasurable, but she'd asked and he must answer. 'As you know from experience, it's difficult to continue a business when the person you relied on to guide you is gone.'

She twined her fingers together in her lap. 'Yes, it is.'

Philip shifted against the squabs, resting his elbow on the narrow ledge below the window. 'The year after my parents died, I loaned a large sum of money to a silversmith. He'd received a commission from a marquis for an expensive dinner service, but said his young daughter's illness over the last year had left him without the necessary funds to purchase the silver he needed to craft the order...'

'Or so he'd told you,' Laura finished when he paused.

Philip nodded. 'At the time he approached me, Jane was ill, so I sympathised with him. I was also distracted by numerous other difficult clients and didn't properly vet the man's claims. The loan was made and squandered at the faro tables. Had I not taken Mr Charton's advice, and the loan from his solicitor, I may not have proceeded quickly enough to seize the silversmith's shop or the merchandise he'd kept hidden there. The silversmith enjoyed gambling with other people's money instead of his own. The amount I seized was almost enough to pay back what he'd borrowed. If he hadn't hidden his merchandise from more prosperous days, the loss of his loan would have ruined me.'

'I wish you'd told me sooner.'

'Mistakes aren't always easy to admit.'

'No, they're not. I made one this morning.' She stared out of the window at the passing buildings. 'When I saw Mrs Hammond, it was as if I were seeing myself again, losing everything because of something someone else had done. I thought I was over it, I thought it behind me, but it's not.'

The raw pain in her words touched him and he slipped across the carriage to sit beside her. The heat of her body next to his penetrated the wool of his jacket and the linen of his shirt. Without thinking, he wrapped his arm around her shoulders and drew her into the hollow of his arm. She nestled against him, her rose water perfume wrapping around him like a twining vine. He closed his eyes, revelling in the comfort of her body next to his, the weight of her cheek on his chest, the sweet sound of her steady breathing.

'You aren't the only one to blame. I shouldn't have expected you to follow me blindly into a situation I should have known would trouble you. I was as insensitive to you as—'

'I was to you today.' She curled her finger around the lapel of his jacket, the movement tender and trusting. 'I'm ashamed it troubled me so deeply.'

'It will for some time.' Philip rested his chin on her head, curling his arm tighter around her. She didn't fight it, but settled in closer, her breath sneaking in to caress his chest through a small opening at the top of his shirt. 'I can't deny this isn't always a straightforward business. At times it won't be easy for you. If you're ever uncomfortable again, please tell me at once. I will always have your best interests at heart.'

'I want to be able to extend vouchers,' she whispered.

'You will be. I trust your judgement.'

'And I trust yours.'

He wrapped his fingers around hers and squeezed them tight. All would be well between them.

Chapter Nine

As the late morning sun stretched out over the carpet, the savoury scent of beef filled the bedroom. Laura inhaled with a sigh, making Mrs Fairley laugh as she fastened the buttons on the back of Laura's wedding dress.

'I knew I was right to make this dress and all the others a little larger through here.' Mrs Fairley tapped the ribbon beneath Laura's bust. 'I suspected the good food would fill you out in no time.'

'I hope it doesn't fill me out too much. I'd hate to split a seam.' Although a split seam was quickly becoming the least of her worries. It was nearly eleven o'clock and, across the street in St Bride's Church, Philip, the Chartons, the Feltons, the Moseleys and Mrs Gammon eagerly waited for Laura to become Philip's wife.

'I think other things might fill you out faster.' Mrs Fairley hummed as she fastened the last button. 'Mr Rathbone is sure to have quite a surprise in store for you tonight.'

Laura gaped over her shoulder at the modiste, who

shot her a knowing smile in return. Laura wasn't used to discussing such matters so openly. Nor was she completely prepared for the very real future the modiste hinted at. She knew the details; her mother had explained them to her years ago. There'd also been too many conversations between the women of ill repute in the rookery to keep Laura ignorant of what passed between two people in the dark. It was the intimacy it would require with Philip which made her stomach flutter.

'I hope he doesn't surprise me too much.' She shifted the slim gold necklace, an engagement present from Philip, over her chest. Even the delicate metal felt too heavy on her heated skin. As nervous as she was about what was to come tonight, she also craved him.

'Oh, I think he might. You must surprise him as well.' Mrs Fairley withdrew a thin, flat box from her case. 'I have something which will help you do just that.'

Unless it was a book of suggestions on how to please a husband, she couldn't imagine what the modiste might give her to accomplish such a goal.

Mrs Fairley removed the lid and held it out to Laura. 'I brought you these.'

Laura lifted the fine clocked stockings from the tissue paper. As the silk unfolded, the beautifully embroidered roses twining up the back were revealed one after another. They clung to a fine silk so sheer it took on the tone of her hand beneath it. Rubbing her thumb over the wispy weave, she inhaled as much in surprise at the delicate gift as at the thrill of holding such finely wrought fabric.

'It's gorgeous.' A bright red ribbon ran through the embroidery at the top, the satin as smooth as the silk. 'I hate to think of something so beautiful being hidden.'

'They won't be hidden from everyone.' Mrs Fairley winked.

Laura felt her cheeks turn the same colour as the ribbon. She wanted Philip to see these.

'Now, let's get them on you.' Mrs Fairley led Laura to a chair and helped her raise the long hem of her skirt. Laura slid her feet into the stockings, slowly pulling them up over her calves before tying the ribbon just above her knee. The material rubbed her skin like the finest goose down, making it tighten with a shiver. As she stood, the silk of the dress whooshed out around her legs, fluttering the ends of the ribbons underneath against Laura's calves.

'You make sure he is the only one who sees these tonight,' Mrs Fairley instructed, as she picked up the satin slippers and placed them on the floor in front of Laura. 'Don't allow your maid to undress you, let him.'

Laura struggled to breathe, nervous yet excited about what was to come. In the week since the dinner at the Chartons' house, there'd been a new bond between her and Philip. They'd worked together on planning the wedding and other business matters as if they'd been together for years. Even their dinner with Dr Hale last night had been a relaxed affair, the sadness and awkwardness from their last meeting gone. Mr Connor had remarked on the change, thanking Laura for ending Philip's frequent need to exercise.

She slipped her feet in her soft slippers, the silk

stocking pressing down against her toes and up against the arch of her foot. A wicked little smile graced her lips as she wiggled her toes. At least she possessed one advantage over Philip tonight. She already knew what he looked like naked.

She adjusted the necklace again, twining it around one finger before allowing it drop down against her chest. The confidence she'd witnessed in every ripple of his muscles as he'd moved across the room naked in front of her gave her a sense of how it might be with him. It would take great restraint to retain a hold on her senses long enough to display her stockings, especially if he pounced on her with any of the pent-up energy she'd tasted in his kiss the other night. Then, he'd held back for propriety's sake. Tonight, there would be no reason for him to do so.

The doorknob turned and Laura's mother slipped into the room. At the sight of her daughter tears sprung to her eyes.

'Oh, my dear.' Her mother hurried to her, crushing Laura in a deep embrace. 'I used to dream of this day when you were a little girl. When we were in Seven Dials, I thought it would never come, yet here it is.'

Laura hugged her mother close. 'Though not as either of us could have imagined.'

Her mother gently pushed her back, holding her at arm's length and admiring her before fluffing out the flattened lace lining the bodice. 'It's exactly as I imagined. You're young, beautiful and marrying a man of integrity who cares for you.'

She knew he cared as much for her as Laura did for

him. The strength of her feelings for him surprised her. It didn't seem possible to come to care so much for someone in so short an amount of time.

'Look at me carrying on when it is time to go.' Her mother dabbed her eyes with the handkerchief Mrs Fairley handed her. 'Reverend Clare is waiting and the guests are ready.'

Laura's palms went moist and she was glad Mrs Fairley had decided against gloves for this solemn occasion. She said it would be too much trouble with the ring, but Laura sensed it was to keep her nervousness from soaking the fine satin.

'Are you ready, Laura?' her mother pressed.

'Yes.' Excitement swept over her as Mrs Fairley knelt to fluff out the skirt of the dress.

Taking her mother's arm, the two of them made their way downstairs, Mrs Fairley following behind them. Laura walked proudly through the house, not skulking along the shadows of the walls as she'd done the night she'd broken in. What a strange change in circumstances it all seemed, a welcome reprieve after the nightmare of life with Uncle Robert.

Downstairs, they were greeted by the chatter and laughter of the servants gathered in two lines flanking the front door. Quiet settled over the house as they all turned to watch her with bright eyes and wide smiles. Mr Connor strode from where he waited by the front door, appearing in a fine mood. Laura suspected his joviality had more to do with Mrs Gammon's attendance than Laura's wedding ensemble.

'You're beautiful, Miss Townsend, as a bride should

be.' He bowed before her then straightened. 'It's an honour to escort you and to stand beside Philip. Shall we proceed to the church?'

'We shall.' She took his arm, walking with him out of the front door. Two footmen flanked the walk, asking the people rushing by to pause and make way for Laura. Two more halted a cart in the street and Laura and Justin hurried across, Mrs Fairley and Mrs Townsend following closely behind. They moved quickly across the pavement and up the few stone steps to the churchyard.

Laura stepped on to the path leading to the church door, impatient to be inside and beside Philip, but Justin held back, forcing Laura to slow down in order to stay by his side.

'All in good time.' He chuckled at her eagerness. 'I don't want to hurry your happy day.'

'One would think you'd be eager to hand me off and see to Mrs Gammon,' she teased, his good nature only increasing her anticipation. 'When can we expect your nuptials?'

'This will be my second time before the altar and neither time will I have been the groom. However, for now, that will suffice.'

They moved on, passing beneath the tall trees spreading out over the walk and the churchyard. The breeze rustled through the green leaves and the towering branches obscured Christopher Wren's magnificent bell tower. Then at last it came into full view as they made the turn to enter the church. Just as they reached the door, Justin halted.

'Mrs Fairley, would you be so kind as to inform the bridegroom we are here?'

'It would be an honour.' Mrs Fairley hurried around them, her blonde curls bouncing as she slipped into the church.

'And, Mrs Townsend, if you would care to proceed inside,' Justin encouraged, with a wide smile.

Laura's mother turned to face her. She tried to say something to Laura, but the tears threatening to spill from the older woman's eyes left her silent. She placed a swift but tender kiss on Laura's cheek, then followed the modiste into the church.

Laura watched her go, her own eyes blurring, glad of Justin's voice helping to steady her.

'Are you ready, Miss Townsend?'

She took a deep breath which managed to settle the flutter in her stomach, but not the excitement coursing through her. After all the apprehension and excitement of the past two weeks it was at last time to tie her life to Philip's. There was no hesitation this morning. She wanted him for her husband and to share his life. 'Yes, I'm ready.'

Laura followed Justin's steady lead into the church, the excited whisper of the guests calming her nerves as she came down the aisle.

Laura saw almost nothing of the people, the highly polished wood choir stalls, or the white-and-gilded arched ceiling. Not even Jane silently clapping her approval at the dress from where she stood beside Laura's mother was enough to draw Laura's attention away from Philip.

He stood before the altar next to the silver-haired vicar, a dark-grey jacket covering the sharp cut of his shoulders. His hands were down at his sides as always, but the faintest hint of a smile raised the edges of his lips and made his blue eyes dance. As Mr Connor escorted her down the aisle, Laura's smile widened with Philip's approval and the unspoken eagerness hovering between them. Euphoria flooded Laura. In mere moments she would be beside Philip, speaking the vows that would bind them together for the rest of their lives.

Mr Connor escorted her to Philip's side, then stepped away to let the ceremony begin.

The words of the service filled the air as the scent of her rosewater perfume mingled with Philip's bergamot cologne. With his sturdy form next to hers, it was all Laura could to do to focus on Reverend Clare and not shift in her slippers. When they were instructed to face one another, she turned and the ribbons of her stockings grazed the back of her knees beneath the dress. Determined to say her vows with a seriousness to match Philip's, she held his eyes, carefully repeating every word, taking each promise and all their meaning to heart. When he spoke his vows, there was no mistaking his earnestness. He'd been her saviour less than two weeks ago, now he would be her partner.

'The rings, please,' Reverend Clare instructed.

Mr Connor laid the gold bands on the open prayer book. The diamonds in Laura's ring winked in the candlelight from the mantel. She tossed Philip a questioning glance. In the slight incline of his head, she could almost hear him telling her the ring had come from a client, another merchant he'd helped who she would no doubt see when time and need called for it. Reverend Clare blessed the rings, then instructed Philip to take her hand.

Philip slid his palm under hers and raised it between them. Her fingers stretched out over the warm skin of his wrist before she lowered her hand on his. Beneath her fingertips, the quick beat of his pulse mimicked hers. He stood so close that his breath whispered across her forehead. Reverend Clare's august words were lost in the heady strength of Philip's touch as he slid the ring over her finger. She could feel almost nothing of the smooth metal encircling it, only the softness of his skin grazing hers. Nothing in Philip's touch changed and yet, at the same time, everything felt different.

When instructed, Laura took up Philip's ring and held it just beyond his strong fingers. She repeated Reverend Clare's words, ready to abide by everything she was promising today, including the vow made in her own heart to honour the man facing her, the man she loved.

Shock at her emotions forced her to pinch the ring tight so as not to risk fumbling it. Yes, she loved him. It'd crept up on her during their quiet conversations in the sitting room, his study, the garden. It didn't scare her as it might have done a week, or even a few days, ago. There was something between them now. It was slender yet strong, growing sturdier as the days passed, like gentle threads of silk bound together in a twist strong enough to edge even an admiral's uniform.

'With this ring, I thee wed.' She slid the band over

Philip's finger. It caught a bit on his knuckle before she eased it down to fit snugly around his finger, to claim him as he'd claimed her.

Reverend Claire finished the ceremony with his last instruction. 'You may now kiss the bride.'

The kiss in Philip's room the other night seared through Laura's memory as she tilted her face up to meet her new husband's. He bowed forward and she closed her eyes in anticipation, her body tingling as they drew together. When their lips merged, heat leapt between them like sparks flashing between pieces of wool on a hot, dry day. The kiss was tender, light, but in the press of flesh to flesh, she felt him struggling between pushing forward and holding back. Behind her the muffled applause of the guests faded away. There was only Philip, his lips warm against hers, his hand firm and fast in hers, a beautiful, wonderful assurance of their future together.

All too soon, she opened her eyes to watch Philip pull away and she was left wanting more of him and his lips against hers. Without his kiss to muddle her, the sweeping architecture of the church and the presence of the vicar and the guests rushed back. Her cheeks burned with the embarrassment of having enjoyed the kiss so much as she turned with Philip to accept the congratulations of their friends and family.

'Oh, it was so romantic,' Jane gushed as she hurried forward to throw her arms around Laura, hugging her with girlish delight before stepping back to allow Dr Hale to approach.

'Congratulations, Philip.' Dr Hale vigorously shook Philip's hand.

Philip returned the gesture, at ease with the gentleman. 'Thank you.'

'And the very best to you, Mrs Rathbone.' He bowed to Laura. The sound of her new name was startling, but she loved it, just as she'd come to love so many other aspects of Philip's life over the past few days. 'One day I hope to see a little brother or sister joining Thomas in the nursery,' he said, stepping away to speak with Mrs Townsend, as a faint flush of embarrassment rose to Laura's cheeks.

'Shall we return home for the wedding breakfast?' Laura asked Philip.

Philip raised her hand to his mouth, pressing his lips to her skin. He gazed up at her, the promise of the night to come heavy in his gaze. 'Yes, please.'

Laura shifted on her feet and felt the stocking ribbons ruffle again. She didn't know how she would make it through the next few hours with such anticipation pooling deep inside her.

After the register was signed, Laura and Philip led a chatting and laughing parade of guests out of the church and back across the street to their house. The lively wedding breakfast extended well into the late afternoon, the conversation flowing as steadily as the port.

The cook had prepared a scrumptious meal and Mrs Moseley raved no end about the almond blancmange while Mrs Charton and Laura's mother discussed the challenges of raising a daughter. Mrs Charton had seen her eldest daughter married last year and talked at great length about her new grandbaby. As they spoke, the older women tossed Laura more than one suggestive look.

If Philip was anxious about the wedding night, it didn't show in his spirited discussions with Mr Charton and Mr Felton. Even if he never quite smiled, in the midst of such warm-hearted and festive people, he was cheerful and his dry humour flourished to Laura's and everyone's delight.

At last, when the best of the French wine was gone and the candles needed to be lit, Mrs Charton rose, sending a secret signal to the other ladies. Mrs Felton, Laura's mother and Jane stood as well, the women forcing the men to their feet.

'We do not wish to intrude on the rest of your celebration tonight,' Mrs Charton explained, barely containing a mischievous smile. 'Mr and Mrs Rathbone, we wish you all the best.'

'Hear, hear,' Mr Charton chimed in, raising his wine glass before finishing the last of the deep-red liquid and staggering after his wife into the entrance hall.

All too soon the guests were gone. Mr Connor and Mrs Gammon melted away along with Laura's mother, Jane and the servants, leaving Laura and Philip alone at last.

In Philip's room, they stood across from one another. The fire crackled in the grate and a candle sputtered. Mary worked near the dressing table, laying out a chemise and robe.

'Shall I leave you to prepare for bed?' Philip trilled

his fingers against his thigh, one foot turned as if he intended to go.

Laura's bravery nearly fled. It would be easier to meet him beneath the sheets with the room dark than to face him in the soft glow of the candles. She curled her toes in her shoes and the silk stockings slid along her skin. She wouldn't deny herself, or him, the pleasure of seeing the fine needlework.

She reached out and stilled his fingers. 'No, your assistance is all I require tonight.'

Without being asked, Mary removed herself from the room, closing the door behind her.

Philip drew Laura to him, step by slow step until they were nearly touching. As he looked down at her, a strand of dark hair fell over his forehead. She reached up to brush it aside, then stopped, still hesitant to be so intimate with him. His hand squeezed hers, as if nudging her on, and she stroked the faint lines of his forehead. With the backs of her fingers she traced the angle of his cheek, dropping to the smooth jaw below. He remained steady beneath her touch, not alarmed or uncomfortable at her caress. Heat began to build in his eyes and he ran his thumb tenderly across her palm. At last she slid her hand along the skin above his collar, bringing it to rest in the short hair at his nape.

Accepting her subtle invitation, he leaned forward and Laura closed her eyes, waiting, expecting. She wasn't prepared for the intensity of this kiss.

He didn't hold back this time, but covered her lips hard with his. His arms encircled her waist, pressing her stomach to his need rising beneath the fine material of his breeches. The ribbons from one of the garters brushed the back of her leg as her form curved to fit into the arch of his. The strength of his embrace kept her from falling on to the carpet he'd been so worried about ruining the night they'd first met.

Twining her arms around his neck, she held on tight, not frightened but excited by the passion building between them. His tongue traced the line of her lips, nudging them open. She took in the firmness as it teased and tasted her, urging her to do the same. She surrendered to the thrilling caress, heeding nothing but his body against hers, his breath on her cheeks, his fingers sliding over her shoulders. His desire reverberated through her and she didn't hold back, eager to ride the crest of it into the unknown.

It wasn't until the first prick of cool air on her back awakened her from this delicious fugue that she noticed he'd undone the buttons of her dress. Whatever fears she'd had of coming together with him dropped like the silk pooling around her feet. Breaking away from his kiss, she stepped out of the circle of the garment, noting how his eyes widened at the sight of her near undress.

'Your stay-maker does excellent work,' he choked, sliding his hand along the curve of her waist to rest on her hip. His shock emboldened her and she clutched the edges of his lapels in her hand.

'Your tailor is very talented, too.' She touched her tongue to her top teeth, feeling quite bold as she peeled the fine wool away from his chest.

He didn't help, but watched her, his chest rising and falling fast as she set to work on the buttons of his waistcoat. She slipped each one through the holes until the garment hung open over his trim waist. Her palms grazed his hard muscles as she pressed both the jacket and waistcoat off his shoulders and down over his arms.

He made the task easier by lowering his hands and allowing them to rest on either side of him as he always did, but tonight his stance was different. His fingers loosened from their fists to let the jacket and waistcoat slide free. They didn't curl back under when the clothing fell away, but reached for her urgently, as if she'd been away too long, drawing her to him so he could kiss her. Yet even in his grasp she felt Philip's steady self-control while her urges ran wild beneath the taste of his tongue against hers.

His lips never broke from hers as he pulled each tie of the new stays through the eyelets, loosening the fine garment. With the last few strings still fastened, he turned her around.

'Don't I get to see you?' She glanced over one shoulder, trying to tease him though she could barely speak through her nervousness. His warm cheek came up against hers, his body achingly close though just far enough away for his fingers to continue their work.

'You've already seen me naked. Now it's my turn.' His playfulness surprised her and increased the warmth spreading inside her.

Her stays opened and her heavy breasts bounced lightly as he moved the restraints away and let them fall forward on to the floor. The chemise billowed out around her naked skin, teasing the tight tips of her breasts. There was nothing separating her from him except the thin layer of cotton and a delicious heat radiated between them. His hands didn't retreat entirely as he moved up close behind her. He swept the curve of her hips through the cotton before his fingers tangled in the material and he began to draw it over her head. Her arms stiffened, the unfamiliar making her resist a moment before she raised her arms to let the chemise come free of her body. Philip was her husband now, there was no reason to hide herself from him.

Husband. The word curled around her heart. Now she was his, she would give her entire self to him tonight.

Cold swept over her, tickling her hot skin like his breath whispering across the back of her bare shoulders. She turned to press her body against his, something deep and primal she didn't understand urging her on, but he stepped back. The same passion burning low inside of her flared in his eyes as his gaze dropped lower and lower to the garters, red ribbons bold against her legs.

The sheer fabric and fragile silk were the only things still covering her and the vulnerability in her nakedness nearly struck down her bravery. He could pounce on her, satiate his lust and be done, leaving her confused and wanting. Instead, the control which dominated Philip's life kept him planted to the floor. It increased her courage and she turned on the balls of her feet, rising on her toes to give him a better view of the embroidery and her round derrière.

'Do you like them?' Her voice wavered as she lowered herself to rest the heels of the clocked stockings against the plush carpet. The ribbons fluttered a touch as she moved, sweeping her skin with the same feathery heat she'd witnessed in his gaze.

'I must remember to pay Mrs Fairley more the next time her bill is due.' His voice sounded strained, making Laura bold, her confidence in this new power growing ever stronger as she met Philip's burning gaze.

She turned again, faster this time so the ribbons danced against her knees before settling back to grace her calves. 'Add a little extra to thank her from me.'

It wasn't the ribbons Philip watched now, but her breasts as he moved forward, cupping the weight of each in his palms. 'I shall jump to comply.'

The heat of his touch stole her playfulness and a heady need rose up inside her as his palms kneaded the full flesh. She reached out and undid his cravat, revealing the firm Adam apple's punctuating the fine length of his neck. Loosening the laces of his shirt, Laura spied the sweep of dark hair on his chest. She ran her fingers through the coarseness of it, feeling his heart beat a quick pace beneath her touch. Then she grasped the sides of his shirt and tried to raise it over his head. He was too tall for her to manage and he slipped his thumbs beneath the linen, helping her to free him from it.

She'd been too stunned to truly appreciate his body the night they'd met. Now she could fully admire it. The hours at the boxing club had tightened the muscles of his stomach and chest and they rippled as he raised his arms to crush her softness against his solid body.

The thickness in his breeches pressed against her bare stomach as his lips claimed hers again, his kiss more hungry than before, but with the marked restraint she'd come to know so well. The maiden in her was glad for his contained reaction. The curious woman who'd already seen his body slick with water wanted his careful control to crack and for him to ravish her passionately as she'd read about in novels. She had no real knowledge of the act, but the yearning deep inside her offered a heady hint to the pleasure waiting for her under Philip's guidance. If his touch elsewhere proved to be anything like the delicate circles his thumbs made across the tender tips of her breasts, she didn't know how she would survive the night.

'Raise your leg,' he growled in her ear.

She did as she was told and his hand slid over the curve of her breast and down the length of her thigh to the satin ribbon. In one fluid move he pulled it free of the bow. With his wide hand, he pushed it over her calf, drawing it from her foot before dropping it to the floor. Without prompting, she raised the other foot, clutching his shoulders as he guided the second stocking over her pointed toes, his movements controlled and agonisingly slow.

As she lowered her leg, his fingers graced the length of her inner thigh. Her body tightened as he neared her need, anticipation making it all but impossible to stand as his feathery touch graced the top of her womanhood before sliding down to settle inside her.

She gasped at the fire ignited by his touch, which welled up inside her until she could barely breathe from the sensations racing through her.

'Philip,' she gasped, leaning hard against the hand at

her back holding her steady and keeping her from falling into the tide of pleasure rushing in to consume her.

Then he withdrew his fingers and she settled against his chest, panting, her need heightened but not quenched.

She lowered her hands to his waist, tracing the skin above his breeches as she trailed her fingers to his front. The pressure of his hips against hers eased as he shifted slightly to give her access to the wool. She fumbled with the buttons, trying to undo them, but with him so close, his masculine scent as sharp as his breath that raced across her nakedness, she could barely grasp the round ivory. He brought his hands over hers, assisting her and sliding the buttons through the holes. Then he let go, inviting her to do the rest.

She didn't quite possess his grace when it came to lowering his breeches, but they soon lay around his feet and he stepped out from the fabric. As she rose to face him, she paused, taking in the sight of his hardness.

Nervousness filled her, but there was little time to entertain it as he stepped forward to press against her once more. She nearly jumped back at the slight twitch of him against her stomach, before settling herself into the circle of his arms, his hands firm and steady against her back.

He led her to the bed and pressed her down on to it, his weight against her bare skin even more heavenly than the clean sheets and chemise had felt on her first night here. In the past week, a happiness she'd thought had died with the shop had consumed her and Philip was the cause of it. The thought moved her just as deeply as his unexpected kiss against the tender tip of her breast. His fingers began to play over her skin as they trailed down her stomach and over the curve of her thigh. Then at last, when she thought she might expire from the steady teasing of his tongue and fingers, he settled himself between her legs. He didn't press forward, but paused, and she felt him hot against her skin as he silently waited for her invitation. She opened to him, drawing in a sharp breath as he slid slowly into her depths. He moaned as she accepted his body into hers, bringing them closer together than she'd ever believed possible.

He moved slowly at first, each stroke filling her, until she thought she might shatter from the intense pleasure. She moved her hips to match his thrusts, wanting more, to give to him as much as he'd given her in their brief time together. Wrapping her arms around him, she held on to the hard muscles of his back, pressing her chest against his. With his heart so close, there seemed nothing to stop it from becoming hers.

Philip groaned, his restraint faltering under her silent demands as he plunged into her. Pinned in the circle of her arms, he felt free, the guilt of leaving the past behind lost in her softness. He surrendered to his passion and hers, grasping her around the waist to hold her steady as she tightened around him, her pleasure evident in her soft whimpers. As his desire began to crest, he mustered his control to wait, to hold back until at last her body exploded around him in spasms. Then he surrendered to his release, crying out as it pulsed to meet hers.

Philip clutched Laura to him as the ripples of pleasure uniting them began to fade. Rising up on his elbows, he brushed the hair from her forehead and pressed his own against it. Breath after breath laced with the sweet tang of her perfume caressed his face.

At last he dropped down beside her and slid his arm under her to draw her close. He caressed the length of her arm, following the arch of it to where her hand rested on his stomach. Their wedding bands clinked together and his hand stiffened at the noise before he settled it firmly over hers. He resisted flexing his fingers or raising them to examine the band. The weight of the gold against his skin was familiar and yet unfamiliar, comforting and awkward.

He pulled Laura closer to drop a kiss on her forehead, pushing away all other thoughts.

'What's wrong?' Laura asked, her ability to sense his unease disturbing.

'Nothing.' Guilt stabbed at Philip for holding back. Each day it was growing more difficult to withhold his whole heart from Laura. He cared deeply for her, but there still existed a part of him he couldn't relinquish, not even to her sweet charm. He ignored the shame just as he'd banished the melancholy thoughts threatening to taint this moment. She was happy and it was all that mattered.

'Liar,' she challenged, stroking his chest.

'I was thinking about today and how beautiful you looked,' he said, not wanting the past to intrude and deny either of them their happy wedding night. 'Justin was escorting you so slowly up the aisle, I didn't think you'd ever reach me.'

'Perhaps he was afraid Mrs Gammon would step in to spring the parson's mousetrap.' She giggled against him and he felt the joy of her humour welling up inside of him, pushing away the dark memories and nagging shame.

'I'm glad he took his time. It gave me the chance to admire you.'

She raised her head to him, her lips drawn into a seductive smile matched by her inviting eyes. 'Careful, Philip, I might become used to such flattery.'

'Good, for I intend to flatter you often.' He smothered her smile with his lips. In the whispered breath of their kiss, a calm settled over him. There was no logical reason for this feeling, nothing about it he could explain or rationalise beyond Laura's presence. He lost himself in it and the pleasure of her embrace.

Chapter Ten

Laura sat at the desk in Phillip's bedroom, combing through the columns of numbers on the ledger in front of her. She'd spent the past quarter of an hour trying to tease out why the expenses for beef did not match those of the bills stacked in the pile next to her. Picking up the butcher's last bill, she was careful not to disturb the neat stack of contracts next to the blotter. The writing table in her room was elegant, but too narrow, and while Philip was downstairs with Mr Connor, she'd decided to come in here to work. Though she doubted he would mind her little intrusion, this was his space and she didn't want to completely upend it.

Below, in the garden, Thomas's happy giggles were punctuated by one of his high-pitched squeals as Mrs Marston, Jane and Laura's mother played with him. Laura longed to be outside with them enjoying the fine day, but the ledger needed to be balanced, not because Philip demanded it, but because she did. He was a fine manager, but in the past year he'd been pulled in so many directions, one or two things had gone errant, like cook overspending at the butcher. Laura was determined to address these small issues, no matter how much she wanted to crawl into the large bed, pull the covers up to her chin and fall asleep.

She stifled a yawn, struggling to continue on, but the figures blurred before her, the totals making no more sense than before.

'This is impossible.' She tossed down the pencil and fell back against the chair in a huff, then laughed at herself. Two weeks ago she'd have given her teeth for such a simple problem. Now all she could do was complain.

The breeze fluttered through the open window, making the fine curtains billow out. The small crystals dangling from the candlesticks over the fireplace shivered with the wind, creating little rainbows in their depths. They spilled over the tendrils of the vines woven into the carpet. She slipped out of her shoes and rubbed the bottoms of her feet over the thick pile. Then, folding her hands over her lap, she closed her eyes. It wasn't the figures which vexed her as much as the lack of sleep. Since the wedding, more pleasurable pursuits than rest had occupied her and Philip's nights. She curled her toes at the memory of last night and the delicious things he'd done to her. In the dark together, they were open and vulnerable with one another. It was only afterwards when the intimacy seemed to fade.

She relaxed her feet, trying not to worry. The hint of the reserve she'd detected during their wedding night had come over Philip again last night, intruding on the quiet conversation between them. One night, she hoped, that reserve would be gone for good.

The breeze filled the curtains again. The ruffling fabric soothed her along with the sounds of the birds and her mother and Jane's steady conversation outside. There was only one more thing she needed to ease the concern dancing along the back of her mind.

'Have you become a woman of leisure?' Philip's teasing question drew her from her silent reverie. His lips lilted in a near-smile and Laura's toes pressed deeper into the carpet, anticipation making her lick her lips before she recovered herself and straightened.

'If only I could be, but the accounts won't allow it.' She waved her hand over the open book. 'It seems I've dropped a figure and can't find it.'

'Let me see.' He closed the door and came to stand beside her and examine the ledger.

All thoughts of the accounts flittered out of her mind. There was only him, strong and masculine, his scent permeating the smell of warm earth drifting in from the garden outside.

He bent over the book, hands flat on the desk as he studied her work. While he was occupied, she leaned back a touch to admire his solid buttocks hugged by his buckskin breeches. Her fingers trilled on the arm of the chair, the activity keeping her from stroking the firm roundness, but she wanted to, badly.

'Having trouble concentrating?' He looked back at her, his eyes inviting. He pressed one finger to the ledger, but she longed to employ it in another, more sensual activity. 'You didn't carry the four on line twelve.'

She slid her fingers over the open neck of her gown, drawing his eyes to her breasts, as daring this afternoon as she'd been the night she'd first slipped into his room. Only today she was his wife, not a client. 'Does it matter?'

'Not at all.' In one easy move he turned and drew her from the chair into his arms, his body hard against hers. She leaned languidly into him, twining her hands around his neck and arching back as he bent forward.

'And here I'd come to ask you to join me on a walk through the park.' His voice rumbled between them. 'I have something to discuss with you.'

She traced the line of his jaw with one finger as his hand found its way to her behind, gripping it tight and pulling her closer against him. 'What?'

'I can't remember.' He leaned forward to claim her mouth, but Laura didn't surrender, not yet, wanting to tease him a little longer.

'But I have things to do.' Her fingers twined in the knot of his cravat, drawing the ends out from beneath the waistcoat.

'They can wait.' He leaned forward again. A growl of frustration escaped him as she denied him yet another kiss.

'It must be a special day if you're asking me to put aside work.' She enjoyed this teasing and the unexpected reaction it elicited from him.

'One cannot work all the time.' There was mischief in the remark as his frustration turned to determination.

Rising up on her stocking-clad toes, she finally surrendered her lips to his.

* * *

Whatever matter Philip had sought her out to discuss vanished. There was urgency in her wanting, a demanding need to match the one welling inside him. This would be no leisurely afternoon lovemaking, but a fast coming together. He surrendered to the moment, channelling his restlessness into the hunger drawing them together.

He tugged up the sides of her dress and slid his hands beneath the fine cotton chemise. Tracing the line of her silky thigh, he found her centre. She tilted her head back, as he slid one finger inside her. She was ready for him and he almost lost what little control remained. Holding back, he ran his tongue over the sweet skin of her neck while his finger worked her pleasure until she was near panting, her hands tight on his shoulders. He drew her earlobe between his teeth, his fingers steady and firm in their work, withdrawing just before she reached her release.

Opening her fevered eyes to meet his, she caressed his chest, then undid the buttons on his breeches. She slipped her hands beneath the buckskin to stroke his hips, her touch as teasing as the kisses she pressed against the skin above his cravat. The feather-light brush of her fingertips over his hardness sent a tremor racing through him. He splayed his fingers on his thighs, allowing the woman who'd been little more than a stranger to him two weeks ago to explore his body, relishing her growing confidence and her gentle touch. When at last she took him in her hand, he groaned, clenching his teeth as she slowly began to stroke. Remaining still, he gave himself over to her until the quickening pace of her palm proved his undoing. He shoved the ledger aside and the contracts fluttered to the floor with it as he lifted her up to rest on the edge of the desk. She pulled up the hem of her gown, as eager as he was for their joining.

Her fingers wound through his hair and she stifled her cry of pleasure in the curve of his neck as he entered her. The window was open, the breeze teasing them both as he plunged into her, all other thoughts lost in the storm of his desire. His thrusts were hard and greedy but she matched each one with a subtle shift of her hips, drawing him in deeper. The swelling pleasure pushed them higher until with one last thrust his body shuddered into hers and they fell together in a slow descent of light and darkness. Only her curves against his kept them from toppling over the top of the desk in exhaustion.

Moments passed, until the room, the breeze, the sound of people outside came back to Philip. He slid his hand up the curve of her back. Twirling one dark curl around his finger, he treasured the soft sweep of her hair over his skin. On the floor around them lay the scattered contracts and the upended ledger. He ignored the urge to break from Laura to clean up the mess.

'I should tease you over figures more often,' Laura murmured into his neck, her hand making lazy circles over his exposed body. 'Though I fear I may not be able to join you on a walk today, or even perhaps tomorrow.'

She laughed, the bright sound as lovely as the whimpers which had met her release. He let go of her curl and it bounced back against her neck.

'It was not my intention to exhaust you.' He kissed her damp forehead, pushing the strands of hair which clung to her radiant skin, ready to dress and proceed with the day.

'Oh, please do.' She wrapped her legs around his waist and all thoughts of business were gone.

It was a full two hours before they finally left the room and arrived in Hyde Park. Laura held Philip's arm as they made their way leisurely over the paths crossing the wide swathes of grass. A few fashionable folk were out riding or enjoying the fine day in their open-topped landaus. The rest of the park occupants were retired soldiers and their grandsons or young governesses running after children.

Laura tugged her hat down a touch to shield her eyes from the low sun. She strode beside Philip in a new walking dress of deep puce, the glow from their love-making still fresh on her skin. After their adventure on the desk, they'd closed the window and drawn the curtains to take advantage of the comfort of the bed. Deep inside, Laura's body quivered at the memory and she was tempted to drag Philip back to the landau and away from whatever he'd brought her here to discuss. She smiled wickedly at her wantonness and the shock Philip was sure to greet such a suggestion with. However, after their afternoon intimacy, he might just surprise her and agree to a romp in the carriage.

'I have a proposal for you,' Philip announced, jarring her out of her pleasant daydream.

Her hand froze at her neck and she wondered if he'd entertained the same scandalous thought as her.

'Yes?' she braved, knowing she couldn't resist him if he ask her to do such a thing.

He brought them to a halt, turning her to face him. It clearly wasn't lovemaking he wanted to discuss, but something more serious.

He didn't speak right away, but studied her, increasing her curiosity. At last he moved them back into a walk. A week ago she wouldn't have understood his hesitation and would have fretted over it. Today she recognised his careful ordering of his thoughts and waited patiently until he was ready to say them.

'You've told me a great deal about your parents' business and how they built it. It reminds me of my father. After his death, had I lost my business, it would have been like losing him again.'

'Yes, at times, after everything was gone, it felt as if I'd somehow failed him and my mother.' She adjusted her hands on his arm, touched by how well he'd come to understand her.

'I want to offer you the chance to revive your father's business.'

This time it was Laura who brought them to a halt, surprised out of her steady step. It was what she'd wanted the most when she'd first stolen through his house, the one thing she'd been forced to give up the moment she'd accepted his proposal. Now the chance was before her again.

'I spoke to the gentleman who bought the contents of the shop after I seized them from your uncle,' Philip continued, squinting against the low sun behind Laura. 'He doesn't possess everything, but he's willing to sell back a generous portion of what is left. I can instruct Mr Woodson to find a suitable location for the shop and you and Mrs Townsend can manage it.'

'What about being your partner, understanding your business? How can I do that if I'm running my own?'

'I want you to be happy.' He guided her into the shade of a tall tree, its branches spreading out over the grass and the gravel path. 'After the incident with Mrs Hammond, I'm concerned you may not be.'

She laid her hand over his. 'You'd really do such a thing for me?'

'Yes.' He didn't waver in his declaration and she knew this wasn't a hollow offer. He was determined and ready to act if she accepted it, but she couldn't.

'Thank you, Philip. You don't know how much it means to me to hear such an offer, but I don't need the draper shop any more.'

'But it's your father's legacy. It's as important to you as my father's business is to me.'

'It was at one time, when I had nothing else to hold on to during all the cold nights in Seven Dials. Since then, you've given me so much more to cherish and to strive for. Going back to the draper business would be like sliding into the past when all I want is to move forward, with you.'

He raised her hand to his lips, the kiss tender and

heartfelt. He'd offered her a gift and in refusing it, she'd given him something even more meaningful in return. It seemed strange to leave the past so firmly behind, but she wouldn't go back. Philip was her future now and though parts of him still remained hidden from her, with each passing day they drew closer together.

In the distance, a church bell chimed. Philip plucked his watch from his waistcoat and clicked open the gold case, the businessman Laura knew so well overtaking the caring husband once again. For all his sudden change, there was a new softness around his eyes and at the corners of his mouth.

'I'm afraid we must return home.' Philip clicked the watch closed and dropped it back in his pocket.

'I knew you wouldn't linger too long,' she chided with a laugh, running her hand over his back. 'Though at home, might I tempt you to dally for a time with me, upstairs?'

He met her daring question with a tempting look. 'I can always make time in my schedule for you.'

He dropped a searing kiss across her lips, heedless of them standing in the open where anyone who happened by might see them.

When at last they broke from their embrace and returned to the gravel path, they could not walk back to the carriage quickly enough. There was a great deal they could accomplish inside with the curtains drawn, even more when they arrived home.

Hand in hand, they neared the tall gates of the park entrance. Across the street, the landau waited by the kerb. A wide-shouldered gentleman in a rough coat peered inside it through the open window. Laura jerked to a halt at the sight of him, trying to catch a glimpse of his face, but a large town coach lumbered between her and the landau. Her desire shrivelled into cold fear as she realised the strange man ogling the carriage reminded her of her uncle Robert.

'What's wrong?' Philip slid his arm around her waist and drew her close.

'I thought I saw my uncle near the carriage.'

He peered across the street as the town coach wobbled away on its springs, but the man who'd ignited her fear was gone.

'Mr Rathbone, I must speak with you.'

Laura jumped at the deep male voice calling out to Philip from across the grass. They turned to see Mr Jones hurrying towards them, dressed in a finely tailored coat of expensive light-blue wool.

'Mr Jones, of course. Walk with us if you will,' Philip urged, but Mr Jones hesitated.

'What I wish to convey would best be spoken out of your wife's hearing.' He tipped his hat to her. 'My apologies, Mrs Rathbone.'

'She may hear anything you wish to discuss,' Philip insisted.

Mr Jones's troubled eyes darted back and forth between her and Philip. 'I don't wish to alarm your wife unnecessarily.'

Philip stood stiffly as ever, making it clear he intended for her to stay.

'Philip, I can wait inside the carriage,' Laura offered, recognising Mr Jones's unease. He would speak quickly and more freely if she was away and Philip could relay the matter to her once they were done.

'All right.' They left the park and crossed the street in silence. Philip helped her into the landau. 'I'll only be a moment.'

He closed the door and she settled herself against the squabs, her nerves tightened by Mr Jones's strange warning. Whatever he'd drawn Philip to the back of the carriage to discuss, she couldn't hear it over the steady clop of horses and the creaking wheels of the numerous carriages beginning to arrive with the *haut monde* for the fashionable hour.

She shifted to the back squab to try to catch something of the conversation when the sound of crunching paper drew her attention to the floor. Against the dark treads lay what looked like a ragged bit of old broadsheet tracked in on her half-boot. She plucked it up, ready to fling it aside when the dark, sprawling letters on the unprinted side made her freeze.

You owe me.

The carriage door opened and Philip stepped inside, his face set hard. 'The man you saw was Mr Townsend.'

'I know. I found this on the floor.' She handed him the note.

He offered it only a glance, his lips drawn tight across his teeth.

'It isn't the first time he's approached us,' she confessed cautiously. 'The morning at Mrs Hammond's, I thought I saw him in the crowd. It was the reason I'd locked the carriage door.'

He settled his hands on his knees, his displeasure obvious. 'Why didn't you tell me before?'

'Because I wasn't sure. I didn't get a proper look at him. With everything happening in the bookshop and how upset I was, I thought it was only my mind playing a trick on me.'

'If you'd told me, then I could have done something to prevent the present situation.'

'The present situation?' Her stomach clenched with worry.

'Last night, your uncle approached Mr Jones about trading a gold necklace for money. During the transaction, he asked Mr Jones if he wanted to see me ruined and hinted at helping him achieve it. His suspicions raised, Mr Jones pretended to entertain the idea and tried to garner more details, but his questions made Mr Townsend suspicious and he left.'

Laura felt her misstep as sharply today as she had in his study that day he'd shown her the Halycon House ledger. It was an awful reminder of the lack of faith she'd displayed in Philip. 'What'll we do?'

'Mr Jones believes the necklace is stolen. I'll contact a thief taker I know who'll see to it Townsend is arrested and we'll be rid of him.'

For once, Philip's confidence didn't put her at ease.

'I don't think the necklace was stolen, I think it was something he had hidden away, in the trunk he brought back with him from India. I tried to pick the lock once, convinced he was keeping valuables from us, but I couldn't open it.' Her wrist tingled at the memory of her uncle's rough grasp as he'd pulled her from the floor when he'd found her kneeling in front of the chest, hairpin in hand.

'Now you know what he was hiding.'

'I wonder what else he kept squirreled away while my mother and I sold what we had to pay the rent and buy food. The selfish pig.' She plucked the note from Philip's hand and crushed it between her palms. 'I never let him bully me before. I won't let him bully me now.'

She flung the wretched paper out of the window.

'Laura, not all moneylenders are as honest, or on as good terms with us, as Mr Jones,' Philip warned, dampening her resolve.

'What are you saying?'

'I don't know how serious Mr Townsend is, or how determined, but he may find someone to assist him with whatever he has in mind.'

'He can't be serious, or sober enough, to do anything. He couldn't even keep himself fed without my help.'

'I agree, but we must still be cautious.'

'And do what? Hide in your house in fear?'

Philip flexed his fingers over his knees. 'There is a press-gang boss I've dealt with before, a Mr Walker.'

'You'd have him sent to sea?' Her uncle had hated the discipline of the army and returning him to service would be like Philip sending her back to Seven Dials with all the deprivations and uncertainty it entailed. She shifted against the squabs, unsure if she could wish such an awful fate on anyone, even her uncle.

'Only if Mr Townsend continues to pursue whatever plot he's concocted. I'll have Mr Walker locate him tonight and threaten him with being pressed. It should be enough to scare him away from implementing whatever foolish plan he has in mind.'

'And if it isn't?' Robert Townsend wasn't known for being rational, especially when drunk.

'Then he has no one to blame but himself if he wakes up aboard a ship.' Philip tightened his hands into fists, his determination and unease subtle, but none the less evident. 'Most likely, the encounter with Mr Walker will encourage Townsend to leave London and it will settle the matter.'

She hoped Philip was right.

'My uncle isn't the first person to threaten you, is he?' She knew about Philip's weapons and his boxing, but in all the time she'd been with him, she'd never felt in danger, until now, and that was due to her, not some indignant client.

'No.' He moved across the squabs to sit beside her, wrapping his arm around her waist and pulling her close. 'Not everyone who has threatened me is as lovely or talented as you.'

Laura smiled, his confidence raising hers. She might have doubted him at Mrs Hammond's, but she didn't doubt him now, nor his determination to protect her and keep her safe.

His brief spark of humour faded as he stared down at her. Philip slid his hand beneath hers, his grip tight with his concern. 'Until the matter is resolved, promise me you'll only leave the house escorted by me, Mr Connor or one of my men, and you are not to see clients by yourself.'

'I promise.' She didn't know if her uncle would resort to violence. Judging by his fury the day Philip had removed her and her mother from Seven Dials, she knew it was within him to lash out. Only it wasn't just herself she was worried about. It was Philip. 'What about you?'

'I'll be careful. I promise.'

She rested her head on the soft wool covering his chest and closed her eyes, breathing him in as if they were alone together in his bed and all the troubles of the day were put away in the darkness. Whatever juvenile ideas about revenge her uncle possessed, she knew Philip would deal with them.

The landau rolled up to their front door and Philip stepped out first, stopping to look up and down the street before beckoning her out. She took his hand, holding her head high as they strode up the front path, pulling Philip back when he wanted to hurry forward.

He paused and threw her a questioning glance.

'I won't let him intimidate me,' she answered defiantly and Philip's lips drew proudly to one side.

'Nor should you.'

Together they strolled into the house. Once inside, Philip handed his stick and hat to the butler and asked him to summon Mr Connor.

While Philip and Mr Connor sequestered themselves in Philip's study, Laura went about the activities of her day. She tried to focus on each task, but she was so distracted Mrs Palmer, and even Laura's mother, asked more than once if something was wrong. Mrs Palmer didn't pry out of deference to Laura's new position as head of the household. Laura's mother wasn't so shy.

'Come, dear, what is it? You look worried,' her mother pressed. They sat together with Thomas in the shade of the house, watching Jane direct the gardener as he tended the roses.

'I'm tired, that's all,' Laura lied. She didn't want to frighten her with the truth.

'As a newly married woman, I don't doubt you are,' she observed knowingly. 'But your distraction is more than marital bliss.'

Thomas struggled to slide off Laura's lap, but she wouldn't let go of him. With its high walls, the garden seemed safe enough, but her nerves were on edge. She felt as if her uncle might appear at the iron gate at any moment, the pistol she'd left behind gripped in one hand and this time packed correctly. She didn't want this beautiful life torn apart or to see Jane, Mother or Thomas suffer yet another tragedy. Guilt hit her hard. If only she'd trusted Philip sooner, this threat might not be hanging over them.

'It's only the household accounts.' She glanced at the study windows and the back of the drawn curtains. She wished Philip had left them open. She needed to see him, wanted to see him. His presence would calm the flutter of worry making her stomach turn over. 'They're in worse shape than I first thought.'

'I see. You're married now, so it isn't my place to pry, but if you wish to speak to me, I will listen.'

Her mother rose, taking Thomas and carrying him across the grass to join Jane.

Another wave of guilt hit Laura. Her mother had a right to know if they were in danger and she'd never kept anything from her before. However, as it might all come to nothing, there seemed no reason to disturb her peace. If only she could settle herself.

Chapter Eleven

The day passed in a blur for Laura. There seemed no time to be alone with Philip until at last, long after supper, when Thomas, her mother and Jane were asleep. Laura lay in his bed, every noise in the garden and from the street shaking her from her light sleep. She didn't want her uncle to have such power over her, but she knew how frail one's position in life was, how everything which seemed so solid and reassuring for years could come crashing down around her. She didn't want to go back to such a precarious and terrifying life.

Rolling over, she pounded her fist into the warm pillow before flipping it over in search of the cooler side. Uncle Robert had ruined so much already. How much more did he plan to lay to waste now that he was done wrecking his own life?

At last the door opened and Philip slipped into the room. The tension in Laura eased as he made for the bed, shedding his coat and cravat as he walked. He draped the garments over the coverlet at the foot of the bed before unfastening his cufflinks and dropping them into the crystal bowl on the dressing table. He sat gently on the edge of the sheets, thinking her asleep, as he pulled off his boots and set them carefully on the floor.

'Where have you been?' she whispered. She'd sent word she would sleep in his room tonight, wanting to be close to him and the comfort he provided.

He looked over his shoulder at her, the faint orange glow from the coals in the grate flickering in his hair. 'You're awake, then?'

She sat up, wrapped her arms around his waist and laid her head on his back, his shirt soft against her cheek. 'I couldn't sleep until you were here.'

He twisted around in her embrace, stroking her back through the chemise. 'Justin and I have just returned from Mr Walker's. He's going to visit your uncle tonight. By morning, if he's smart, Townsend will be far from London and out of our lives.'

'I'm sure he will.' She shifted up on to her knees, her arms draped loosely around him, her hair falling forward to brush her cheek. 'I'm sorry again I didn't trust you.'

'I understand why you didn't.' He pushed a lock of hair behind her ear, his hand lingering against her jaw. 'Besides, it's in the past now. There's no reason to dwell on it.'

If only she could forgive herself so easily. 'But I put us in danger by being foolish.'

'We all make mistakes.' He pulled out of her embrace, propping one arm against the mattress to lean hard against it. Guilt and anger shadowed his face, just as it had in the entrance hall the night he'd told her about his late wife's death. 'I don't want to fail you like I failed Arabella.'

'And you won't.' Taking his face in her hands, Laura forced his eyes to meet hers, refusing to let him retreat into his pain. 'You've done so many things right, Philip: maintaining your business, managing Halycon House, taking care of Thomas, Jane and me. Look to those and let the rest go, for your happiness and all of ours.'

She held her breath, waiting for him to trust her as she trusted him. If here, in the middle of the night in his bed, he couldn't be completely open with her, he might never be.

Then, at last, the pain faded from his expression. He slid his hand along her cheek and nestled it against the back of her neck. 'Perhaps some day, with your help, I will be able to.'

He drew her to him, covering her lips with his. Relief flooded through her and all thoughts of danger faded with the sweep of his tongue across hers. Tonight, he was hers and his past wouldn't pull him away.

Philip covered her body with his, protecting as much as seducing her. Anger had burned inside him from the moment Mr Jones had told him of Townsend, to the moment he'd entered the stinking air of Mr Walker's grimy lodgings. It wasn't danger to himself which fuelled his rage. He'd faced worse and survived. It was Townsend's threat against Laura and the happiness they'd found together which made Philip seethe.

His thumb grazed the hard point of one breast

through Laura's chemise and her fingers dug into the muscle of his back. Cupping the full mound in his palm, he slid his other arm around her and pressed her hard against him, lowering them both into the soft sheets. The fears awakened by Townsend's threat shadowed Philip even as he caressed the tantalising roundness of Laura's hip and slid the soft cotton from her body. The worry demanded that he pull away and guard his heart. Intoxicated by his need for her, he couldn't.

He pressed himself into her, eager for the calming comfort of her soft curves. As they moved together as one, their intimacy and her fierce possession of him swept through Philip. He twined his fingers with hers, raising their hands above her head, both resisting and craving this closeness. She was here now beneath him, but nothing was certain, nothing guaranteed. He kissed her hard, the exquisite taste and heat of her driving back his worries. The word *love* lingered on the tip of Philip's tongue as he inhaled her delicate rose scent, but his breath came too hard, his body was too demanding to allow him to free the word. So instead he showed her, grasping her around the waist as her body tightened. She met his frenzied thrusts, drawing him deeper and deeper into her until they both cried out with their release.

It was a long time before Philip withdrew and settled in beside her. He said nothing as he held her, listening to her short breaths grow longer until it was evident she was asleep. Sleep eluded him and he stared at the folds of the canopy above the bed, refusing to disturb her though he wanted to rise, pace, exercise, do anything to shift the agitation burning a hole in his gut.

It wasn't until Laura had shown him the threatening note from Robert Townsend that Philip had realised the depths of his feelings for her. In the past week she'd become more than his wife, but a part of him, a part he could not survive without. With her, he'd been free to put aside the control he'd exerted over himself for so long and enjoy the passion of her body and being. It had lifted him above his past troubles and all the sorrows which had turned him to stone. The feeling hadn't come at once, but crept over him bit by bit. He'd failed to see it because it had simply become part of his life, like breathing or eating, and just as necessary.

'I love you,' he whispered, disturbing the fine wisps of brown hair arching over Laura's face.

'Hmm,' she murmured against his chest, snuggling closer to him before settling back to sleep.

He closed his eyes, struggling to join her in rest. He'd been this happy with a woman once before and she'd been ripped from him. He didn't want to face such torment again. A noise in the garden jerked him from his light sleep and panic loomed before he beat it back. Philip listened, but heard nothing except the faint whinny of a horse in the mews.

He stroked Laura's back, drawing from her peace to regain his own. He couldn't allow his worries to taint his time with her, or make him scurry back to the hardness inside him. He didn't want to live for ever in that cold, lonely place, but here with Laura and her love. He settled down closer to her and closed his eyes. Laura believed in him and his ability to keep her safe. He would prove himself worthy of her faith.

Loud thuds echoed through the room. Laura raised her head groggily from Philip's chest, thinking someone must be racing up the stairs and wondered who could be about at this hour. Then the bedroom door rattled on its hinges and Mr Connor's voice called through the wood.

'Philip, wake up. There's trouble at the warehouse.'

Philip flipped back the covers, snatched his banyan from the foot of the bed and flung it on before he cracked open the door.

Laura clutched the sheets to her, straining to hear. She couldn't make out the words of their muffled conversation. At last, Philip closed the door, then marched to the grate, lighting a reed and setting it to the candles on the mantel. Orange light filled the room, settling over the smooth skin of Philip's chest as he slipped off the banyan and made for the clothes laid at the foot of the bed.

'What's wrong?' She tugged the sheets up higher over herself, to ward off the chill of fear licking at her.

'There's a fire at the warehouse where I store collateral.' He pulled his shirt on over his head, then reached for the breeches. 'I must see what can be salvaged and ensure the two guards I pay to watch it aren't hurt.'

She snatched up her dressing gown from the chair beside the bed, wrapped it around her and pulled the ties tight across her waist. 'You shouldn't go. Send your men.'

'They'll come with me.' He tugged up his breeches.

Laura hurried to his side, trying not to panic. 'What if it's my uncle who set the fire? What if he's trying to get you there so he can hurt you?'

Philip sat in the chair and pulled on his boots. 'Most likely it was some sailor who was trying to keep warm. It's happened before, to Mr Charton and Mr Felton.'

'And if it isn't a sailor?'

He rose and cupped her face with his large hands. 'Even if your uncle did it, he was probably drunk at the time. He could barely strike me when he was sober. If he's inebriated, it should make it easier for Mr Walker to find him.'

He pressed a sweet kiss to her lips. She laid her hands at his waist, wanting to clutch him to her and not let go. Instead, she believed in his confidence and used it to bolster her own.

'I'll have my men with me. I'll be fine.' He stroked her cheek, revealing only a hint of worry in the gesture. 'I'll leave two men with you. While I'm gone, don't open the door to anyone except me, Mr Connor or my men, do you understand?'

'I do.'

'Then I must go.' He pulled on his redingote and hurried to the door.

Laura followed him out into the hallway. They weren't the only ones awakened by Mr Connor.

Jane rubbed her eyes as she staggered out of her room. 'Philip, what's wrong?'

Across the hallway, Laura's mother watched from her bedroom, her long braid falling out from under her nightcap and over one shoulder.

Philip took Jane by the shoulders and guided her back to her room, giving her a little push inside. 'Only some trouble at the warehouse. I won't be gone long. Go back to bed. All will be well.'

His fatherly tone settled Jane and she returned to bed with far less resistance than Laura had expected.

Laura's mother remained. She wrung the end of the braid with her hands, throwing Laura a silent question with her eyes.

Philip closed the door to Jane's room, then made for the stairs. Laura followed, pausing to whisper to her mother, 'I'll tell you more once he leaves.'

'I'll wait up to hear it.' Her mother faded back inside her room as Laura and Philip hurried downstairs.

At the foot of the stairs Mr Connor met Philip. 'The fire company has been summoned. I've sent Mr Phelps with most of the men and the cart to try to remove what they can and make sure the guards are all right.'

'There isn't much there except the bookseller's stock and the remaining wine from the vintner.'

'The crates will make it easier to remove them, unless the fire has already reached them.'

'Let's hope it hasn't.' Philip looked to the two men flanking the door. 'Mr Reed, Mr Marsh, stay here and keep an eye on things. I'm not expecting trouble, but be alert.'

'Yes, Mr Rathbone,' the two men answered in unison.

With a last, terse look at Laura, Philip strode out to the waiting landau.

'Take care of him, Mr Connor,' Laura instructed.

'Don't worry. I'll see to it he's back in your bed by morning.' With a saucy bow, Justin swung around on one boot and followed Philip out the door.

Mr Reed swung the door closed and slipped the lock, then both men took up positions on either side.

Laura made her way back upstairs, eager to put some of her mother's concerns to rest, though she didn't know how she'd accomplish such a feat with her own mind a tangle of fretting. She knew she wouldn't sleep until Philip was safely back home.

Philip stood at the kerb, the heat of the fire warming his face as a roar of flames raced up the east side of his building. Around him were stacked crates of books and barrels of wine his men had managed to save before the flames had overpowered them. His men now stood about, hands on their clubs, keeping an eye on the crowd. They'd been warned about Townsend and were on alert for any additional trouble. Philip might have worked to convince Laura it wasn't her uncle who'd set the fire, but he had his doubts. So far, there'd been no sign of the drunk. Philip imagined Laura waiting anxiously at home for him to return, the image of her fretting for his safety feeding his anger.

Nearby, two burly firemen pulled and pushed on the pumps while the rest directed the water from the river into the flames. Dark smoke alternated with white as one plume was extinguished only for another to sprout up nearby. The stench from the foul river water mixed with the acrid smoke filled the air. Philip's grip tightened on the walking stick he held as he watched the flames lick at the roof. He almost wished Townsend would stagger from the shadows and confront him. The buffoon deserved a beating for the fears he'd raised in Laura.

Mr Cramner, the stocky fire captain, approached Philip, his face greasy with sweat and soot. 'The flames are putting up quite a fight, but I don't think they'll win, not with the moist air tonight. You're lucky you got the books and wine out. If those had caught, it might be worse.'

'Good work, Mr Cramner.'

'Fight isn't over yet, Mr Rathbone.' He pointed at one of the men manning the pumps and stomped off towards him. 'Adams, put your back into it. I want the whole damned Thames sucked through there before the other brigade gets here and starts interfering. We don't want the whole block catching.'

Justin came to stand beside him, serious for once as the light from the fire wavered over his face. 'Neither of the guards saw or heard anyone before the fire broke out. Hard to believe Townsend could sober up enough to stagger here and do something like this.'

'Even if he did, by now I'm sure Mr Walker must have found him. I paid him plenty and he's never failed to find a man before.'

'Mr Rathbone,' a gruff voice called out over the roar of the flames. 'Mr Rathbone.'

Philip and Justin turned to watch Mr Walker push his way through the crowd and hurry over to them.

'Did you find Mr Townsend?' Philip demanded, eager to know if his plan had worked.

The press-gang boss shook his head. 'He doesn't live in the rooms in Seven Dials any more. I searched all the other places a man like him is likely to turn up, but he was nowhere to be found, not even at Mrs Topp's. Then I heard about this.'

He waved his hand at the flames.

Justin looked to Philip. 'Where do you think he went?'

The faint noise Philip had heard earlier from the garden came rushing back to him along with a sickening realisation. 'Townsend didn't do this to get me here and strike at me. He did this to pull me away from Laura. I have to get back home.'

Philip ran for the carriage, Justin close on his heels.

'My house, at once,' Philip called to the driver as he and Justin jumped inside.

The carriage took off in fits and starts, men hurrying to shuffle out of the way as the horses danced with agitation at the flames. A cracking noise filled the air, and through the window Philip watched as a portion of the warehouse roof collapsed.

At last the carriage broke free of the confusion and tore down the dark streets, passing the whores and drunks littering the shadows.

'I should have known. I should have guessed what Townsend was up to.' Phillip banged his fist against the carriage side.

'Mr Marsh and Mr Reed are there,' Justin tried to reassure him. 'They'll see to it he doesn't get in.'

'If he got past the warehouse guards, he can get past them.' The same wrenching fear he'd experienced the morning Arabella had told him she was pregnant choked him again now. He tried to force it away, to keep it from distracting him from whatever needed to be done, but he couldn't shake free of it.

He balled his fist over his knees. If Townsend dared to touch Laura or anyone else in his house, he'd kill the man himself.

Laura sat by the window in her mother's room, the lantern hanging over the doors to the mews just visible beyond the garden wall.

'Watching won't bring him back any faster,' her mother reminded her, though she, too, kept glancing out at the darkness beyond the garden gate.

'I know, but I can't sleep until he's home safe.'

'You can't sit up all night worrying either.'

'I won't. I'll do the accounts. Do you mind if I bring them in here?'

'Not at all. I'm not likely to sleep any more than you are. I'll read Jane's new book.' She slid the slender tome off the table beside her chair and flipped it open. 'I like to know what happens before she does so I'm not too shocked by the content.'

'I'll return in a moment.' Laura made for her room, eager for the work to take her mind off Philip and what might be happening at the warehouse. Even if the fire wasn't her uncle's fault, there were other dangers to threaten Philip: a spreading inferno to trap him and his men perhaps, or a carriage overturned by a spooked horse.

Laura paused outside her room and took a deep

breath, banishing the images of doom threatening to overwhelm her. Everything would be fine and in the morning this would be just another business matter to deal with. Philip was well protected by his men and experience. There was little her drunk, bumbling uncle could do to hurt him.

Laura pushed open the door, the chill inside cutting through her thin banyan. She hugged the dressing gown tighter to her chest as she went to the window and shoved the sash down to meet the sill. Then she took up the poker next to the fireplace, kneeled down and jabbed at the coals, sparking them back into life.

The flames danced in the grate as she rose, ready to return the poker to the stand when something in the mirror over the fireplace made her heart stop.

Uncle Robert's cold, red-rimmed eyes met hers from across the room. 'Hello, me darling niece.'

She whirled around, her fingers tightening on the iron. 'What are you doing here?'

He pushed away from the dark wall beside the thick bed curtains where he'd been waiting for her. In the light of the fire, she caught the dull nose of a pistol in his hand by his side. 'I couldn't miss the chance to congratulate me own flesh and blood on her advantageous marriage.'

He swept into a mocking bow, staggering a little, in danger of tipping forward on to the carpet before he righted himself.

'Laura, why is it so cold in here?' Her mother entered the room, then jumped to a halt, the book falling with a thud to the floor at her feet. 'Robert.'

He levelled the gun at Laura. 'Come in and don't say a word or I'll shoot your precious daughter and find a less pleasant way to silence you.'

The older woman hurried to stand behind Laura and the poker which offered them both slim protection.

'Whatever you think you're doing, you won't get away with it.' Laura seethed. 'Philip's men are downstairs. They'll kill you for this.'

'But they ain't up here, and they ain't likely to get to me before I send a bullet through you and the poker through your ma's head.'

'What do you want?' Laura demanded, determined to remain calm and steady as she knew Philip would. Then, when the moment presented itself, she would be able to give them a fighting chance to escape.

'I want what I'm owed for keeping the two of ya for the last year.'

'We owe you nothing,' Laura countered, refusing to show an ounce of the fear tightening her hold on the poker. 'You stole enough from the shop.'

'Don't think you're going to cast me out so easily, girl.' Spittle escaped with the words, a large drop sliding down through the thick grey stubble on his chin. 'You think you're so high and mighty, living here with your filthy moneylender, a man who makes his living off the backs of men like me. Tell me, how many weeks did ya both spend planning to ruin me?'

'You ruined yourself.'

'Don't think I didn't guess what the three of you were up to with this proposal coming so fast after he stole everything from me.' Her uncle took a step forward, his red-rimmed eyes blazing, and Laura and her mother backed up. Laura nudged her mother to the side, away from where they would be trapped against the fireplace and towards the open bedroom door. Hopefully, one of them could slip through it and alert Philip's men. 'Do you know what I've had to suffer since you two rode away laughing at me in your hoity carriage? I've been sleeping in gutters, bitten by rats and fleas, while you're here lounging in your silk sheets.'

'You could have sold your necklace to help yourself, but instead you used it to try to ruin us, wasting it like you wasted the chance my father gave you to make something of yourself.'

'Your father gave me a chance?' He snorted. 'He and our parents never gave me a chance. They shipped me off to hell before I was even a man while my brother was taught a trade, given a business, a wife and family. They were so eager to be rid of me they never stopped to think what I might have wanted.'

'Killing us won't change the past, it'll only make things worse for you,' Laura countered, careful to keep her words low and steady so trembles of fear didn't warble them. 'You think Philip will just let you go if you hurt us? You think life in gaol or swinging from the end of a rope will be any better?'

'My life will be better and you're going to make sure of it.' He jabbed his thumb against his dirty shirt. 'I want my share of the money from the sale of the inventory and whatever else the rat paid to take your virtue.' He moved a step closer and Laura and her mother took another cautious step back. 'You thought you could cut me out of whatever deal you made with the money-lender—well, you're wrong. You'll pay me and you'll do it now.'

'We don't keep money in the house.'

'Liar. He gave me a lot when I visited before so there must be something here.' He waved the gun in a large circle at the room. 'So fetch it.'

'I can't.'

He stepped forward again and Laura and her mother backed achingly close to the door. 'Don't think I won't send a ball through you.'

'The safe isn't here. It's downstairs, in the sitting room.' She said nothing about not having the key. All she wanted was to escape and alert Philip's men.

He waved her towards the door with the pistol. 'Then get to it and don't tell anyone what you're about or I'll kill your ma, do you understand?'

She adjusted her grip on the poker. 'You would stoop so low, wouldn't you? You're disgusting.'

'Look at both of you, cornered and still looking down your noses at me.' Her uncle's lip curled, revealing one dark tooth before his mouth twisted into a sneer. 'Now get me my money.'

Laura nodded. Her heart pounded in her ears as she turned slowly, gripping the poker tight. He was so focused on his hate and bent on revenge, he hadn't thought to tell her to get rid of it. Or he just didn't see Laura as a threat, dismissing her as he always had. Tonight, it would be to his detriment.

Laura took one step forward, shifted her weight to her legs, then swung the poker in an arc to slam against her uncle's arm. The pistol clattered to the floor as he clasped his wrist and howled, his heavy eyes flaring with hate and anger.

'You bitch!'

'Mother, run!'

Her mother fled, screaming out for Philip's men.

Laura bolted for the door. Her uncle grabbed her by the arm and tugged her back, flinging her at the other side of the room. Her feet left the floor before she stumbled and slammed hard against the wall. An explosion of light and pain ripped through her head and she sank to the floor, catching her head on the edge of the table and sending another sharp pain tearing along the tops of her eyes. Weakness washed over her and she reached up to feel warm blood slipping down her forehead. It streaked against the side of the chair as she rested her head against it, exhaustion settling over her like a heavy blanket. She fought against the sensation and the room spun as she rose to her knees to face the man storming towards her.

'You never respected me like you should've.' He swept the gun from the floor, his form growing larger and more menacing as he came to tower over her. 'You thought yourself too smart and too good for your own uncle. Well, I'll show you who's smart.'

Laura sagged against the soft side of the chair, aware of the dark end of the pistol barrel dancing before her. The thud of footsteps and deep voices sounded from somewhere down the hall. She'd be dead by the time her mother and Philip's men made it up the stairs. Regret and pain pounded hard through her head and her stomach clenched, threatening to revolt.

The pistol swam in front of her, the barrel dark, menacing, ready to swallow up her whole life the way the throbbing along her temples and the light dancing around the corners of her vision had swallowed the room. Somewhere down the hall Thomas let out a wail. No, she thought, she would live for Philip, for Thomas, and the life they would build together. She grabbed the arm of the chair, trying to haul herself to her feet, refusing to give up and be shot like a dog in her own house.

Her uncle stepped closer, eyes burning with hate and satisfaction for what he was about to do. 'Now you're going to pay, you little bitch, for everything your father did to me, for everything he denied me.'

The trigger clicked and the hammer hit the pan. A deafening roar filled the room, followed by the sharp stench of smoke and burning wood, metal and flesh. The mangled pistol dropped to the floor in front of Laura, the cracked barrel and singed handle smoking. Behind it, her uncle tipped back, his bulk dropping to the floor with a thud.

A commotion of voices clattered through the swaying room, increasing the throbbing in Laura's head. Her mother's high-pitched voice stood out among those of Philip's men, but she couldn't see her. All she saw was the worn-out bottoms of her uncle's shoes before everything went black.

Philip was out of the carriage before it stopped, racing across the front walk and through the open door. The emptiness of the hallway confirmed his worst fear.

He started for the stairs when Jane swung around

the banister at the top, her braid flying to one side. 'Philip! Philip!'

She rushed down the steps as he flew up, the two of them meeting on the landing. 'He came. He tried to kill her.'

Philip's hand tightened on the banister as he faced his sister, trying to guess what had happened from her expression.

'He didn't,' Jane whispered. 'But she's hurt, badly. I summoned Dr Hale. He's with her in your room.'

Philip raced past his sister, barely aware of her soft footsteps falling in quick succession behind him.

He flung open the door to the bedroom, coming up short when he reached the poorly lit scene before him. In the centre of the carpet lay Robert Townsend, his face a mess of black powder and blood. The mangled pistol lay at his feet. Philip's stomach clenched, but not from the gore. It wasn't the first time he'd seen a man in such a state.

It was the scene greeting him in the four-poster bed that rattled him. Laura sat up against the pillows, Mrs Townsend rubbing her back as she retched into an old porcelain basin. A white bandage with a dark spot of blood covered her forehead. Dr Hale stood on her other side of the bed, his grey hair wild at his temples, his face grim.

It wasn't the blood or the vomit which nearly sent the contents of Philip's dinner up to join the mess on the floor. It was the terrifying familiarity of it all.

Philip rushed forward, but Dr Hale rounded the bed to stop him.

'Move aside,' Philip commanded.

Dr Hale clenched his arm, refusing to let him pass, his grip just as firm as it had been that fateful morning a year ago. 'Come with me into the hallway and keep your voice down. The noise will only disturb her and increase her suffering.'

'You can tell me here,' Philip insisted.

'The cut on her forehead is more bloody than serious, but she's suffered concussion. She's confused. The best we can do is to keep her awake tonight, not let her sleep. I saw too many men during my two years in the army fall asleep after hitting their heads only to watch them slip into a coma and pass before the night was out.'

Laura retched again, crying despite Mrs Townsend's soothing words. Philip looked to her, eager to be by her side. Dr Hale's hand tightened on his arm, keeping him where he stood.

'Will she be all right?'

'Her eyes are responding well to light and she's behaving as I would expect after such an injury. By morning she should be better, assuming there isn't some deeper wound which prevails. Sadly, all we can do is wait.' Philip tore his gaze away from Laura to meet Dr Hale's eyes. In the grey depths was the same sickening seriousness he'd used to deliver the news which had changed all their lives. 'She must not be allowed to sleep tonight.'

'I'll make sure of it.' Philip wasn't going to relive that dreadful morning.

'Brace yourself, Philip, she's confused. She may behave strangely.'

Philip nodded, drawing in a steadying breath before Dr Hale let go of his arm. He strode to the bed, barely aware of Dr Hale taking up his former position on the far side.

Mrs Townsend rose as Philip approached, removing the bowl Laura had been hunched over. The older woman's worried eyes met his, the concern in them so deep it was nearly Philip's undoing. He saw no blame in her gaze, but none the less he felt deeply responsible. He should have guessed, he should have sensed what Townsend was up to and prevented it. He should have kept Laura safe, but he'd failed her as he'd failed Arabella.

Philip settled on the bed beside her. 'Laura, I'm here.'

'I'm so tired.' Her eyes began to close and Philip slid his hand in hers. It was cold, deathly so. The terror of it struck him deep in his soul.

'You can't sleep. Dr Hale says so.'

'Who?' Her half-mast eyes cast about the dark room in confusion, alighting on Dr Hale.

He cast a smile at the patient, but she didn't offer one in return.

'I don't know him.' She looked to Philip to ease her confusion. 'Should he be here?'

'Yes, he should.'

Out of the corner of his eye he caught sight of his men moving in with a blanket. Philip shifted on to the bed, sitting in front of Laura to block the view of his men cleaning up the mess that was Robert Townsend's body. He'd send Justin for the constable and have him see to the legal matters. Helping Laura heal was all Philip cared about tonight.

'What's this on my head?' Laura tugged at the bandage.

Philip gently pulled her hand away from it. 'You've hurt yourself.'

'How?'

He looked to Dr Hale, who shook his head, warning him off the truth. 'You slipped and fell.'

The explanation left her more confused than before. Soon her eyes began to slide closed again.

Philip patted her hand. 'Stay awake.' *Stay alive.*

'Philip?' Jane's shaky voice carried through the semi-darkness. He twisted around to see his sister standing at the doorway, just as she'd done that morning a year ago, sniffing back her falling tears. The sound of her young, frightened voice rattled him, her fears too much like his own.

'I'll see to her.' Mrs Townsend laid one hand on Philip's shoulder and offered a light squeeze before going to Jane. 'Come, come, my dear, everything will be all right.'

Her reassurance seemed as much for Philip's benefit as Jane's.

Jane's scared sobs were muffled by Mrs Townsend's embrace as she escorted her into the hall.

'Why is it so dark in here?' Laura looked around the room in confusion, her voice weak and tired.

'We can light some candles if you wish.'

'No.' Dr Hale's objection stopped Philip from rising to see to the matter. 'The darkness is better. It helps the mind to rest.'

'Then what should I do?'

'Talk to her. Keep her awake.'

Philip settled in across from Laura, telling her first of the fire, his success in retrieving the merchandise and how his guards were safe. She didn't seem to comprehend, asking him who set the fire and where it had been. Casting about for something, anything to say, he studied her small hands in his. The clock chimed sweetly and the crystals on the candlesticks clinked together in the soft breeze from the slightly opened window. Philip wasn't a man to chatter, to fill the air with words, but once he began speaking to Laura tonight, he couldn't stop.

He spoke to her constantly as the hours wore on, surprised to find there were so many things inside him to say. He described his father and mother and his many happy memories of them both alive and in love. He spoke of the awkwardness of hearing, at sixteen, that his mother, after so many barren years, was with child again. He described the worry he'd experienced the night she'd been delivered of Jane. It was the same worry nipping at him now. His father had sent him to the boxing club with Justin to keep him away. Justin had made many jokes about the horror of his parents being intimate at their age while Philip had pummelled a dummy so hard, his hands had hurt for days afterwards. Then Chesterton had arrived with the news his mother and new baby sister were safe. In the midst of his relief, he'd realised how pernicious fear could be.

Laura listened, sometimes asking questions in her

struggle to follow the thread of Philip's stories. He told her of warm Christmases in the sitting room with his parents and cuddling a very young Jane, who'd cried because she couldn't reach the red berries on the mistletoe hanging in the doorway. He asked Laura about her Christmas memories, hope filling him as she began one story about receiving a yellow dress she'd wanted so badly. Then her voice drifted off, along with all memory of the happy day.

'What was I talking about?' she asked and Philip's hope faded as another minute of this long night fell away.

Philip ran his hands over his face, exhaustion pulling at him, but he fought it, determined to keep his vigil, to keep talking, to keep Laura awake.

The clock chimed four times. Mrs Townsend slipped quietly back into the room, taking the chair next to the bed.

'How's Jane?' Philip asked.

'Sleeping. She's very shaken. We all are.' She leaned forward. 'How are you, Laura?'

'My head hurts.' Laura tugged at the bandage again before Mrs Townsend took her hands and laid them in her lap.

Judging by the questions Laura peppered her mother with about why she was in bed and why her head was bandaged, Philip guessed she would have little memory of the evening. He was glad. Glancing at the dark, stained wood floor, he wished he could remove tonight from his memory as easily as his men had removed the ruined carpet.

'You should get some sleep, Mr Rathbone,' Mrs Townsend urged.

He raised Laura's hand to his lips, pressing a kiss to the soft skin. 'I won't leave her.'

He'd lost one wife. He couldn't lose another, or face Mrs Townsend the way he'd faced Dr Hale that ugly morning.

'Then I'll sit with you and read.'

Mrs Townsend read aloud from one of Jane's novels. It was a simple story, but Laura kept losing the thread of it. It shook Philip each time Laura stopped her mother to ask a question. Mrs Townsend answered them with patience, often rereading a sentence two or three times until at last Laura seemed to grasp it.

Philip couldn't help Laura with the plot. He couldn't focus on anything but Laura's eyes and keeping them open and fixed on him. She blinked hard against the exhaustion making her shoulders sag and darkening the skin beneath her lashes. From time to time she would offer him a weak smile, propping up his spirits, only to make them fall again when she looked at him with puzzlement, unsure for a moment who he was or why people were gathered around her in the room.

Dr Hale's soft snores from the stuffed chair by the window punctuated the noise of a nightingale perched in one of the bushes outside.

Then slowly the darkness began to turn to grey, and the nightingale's call was replaced by the trills of songbirds. Dr Hale awoke and leaned over to look into Laura's eyes, holding up a candle to examine first one and then the other. Laura watched the flame move across her line of vision, the confusion which had so disturbed Philip a few hours ago replaced by a more concentrated scrutiny of Dr Hale.

The doctor blew out the candle and set the brass holder on the bedside table. 'I think we can let her sleep now.'

'Thank heavens,' Laura breathed, as if at last aware of the long hours which had passed.

Philip was relieved to hear something of the usual Laura in the remark, but it didn't ease the worry stiffening his back.

With Philip and Mrs Townsend's help, Laura settled down into the bed. She was asleep before Mrs Townsend could even draw the coverlet up to her chin.

Down the hall, Thomas's loud wail broke the morning quiet.

'I'll help Mrs Marston see to the lad,' Dr Hale offered. With his grey hair in some disarray, his cravat wrinkled and his waistcoat undone, he staggered out of the door, a sigh escaping him as he turned the corner. Philip recognised the release of tension in the subtle sound, and envied it.

His worry only increased with the daylight filling the room.

Mrs Townsend kissed her daughter on the cheek, then moved around the bed to the window. She tugged the curtains shut. The rings rattling against the rod made Philip flinch.

'Rest, Mr Rathbone. You won't help her by wearing yourself thin.'

'I'll sleep in a little while.'

Mrs Townsend studied him from across the bed. 'Thank you for all you've done for her.'

'I couldn't have done anything else. I love her.' The admission hurt because he hadn't yet told Laura. Somehow, for Philip, the intimacy they shared together in the darkness at times seemed just as terrifying as the sickroom.

'I know.'

'She doesn't.'

Mrs Townsend came around the bed, grasping one post. 'She does know, Mr Rathbone. She has for some time.'

She patted his shoulder, then left. The sweep of her feet over the floor reminded him of the quiet leaving which had taken place after Arabella had passed away. Mrs Palmer had shut the curtains as everyone who'd worked so fervently to try to save Arabella had drifted out of the room.

Only Laura wasn't dead. She was alive.

She shifted beneath the covers, mumbled something, then settled back to sleep.

Philip came around the bed, unable to take his eyes off her for fear that if he looked away she might drift away. He sagged down in the chair still warm from where Dr Hale had rested most of last night. It was the same chair he'd occupied a year ago when he'd watched Arabella and willed her chest to rise once more. Down the hall he heard his father-in-law's deep voice soothing Thomas, just as he'd tried to soothe him after Arabella had died.

Philip grasped the sides of his head, his fingers digging into his temples. It was all too much like before.

Something inside him shifted, solidifying around his heart like hot metal when it cooled, creating a shield between him and the emotions threatening to undo him. He'd been determined from the start to maintain his distance with Laura, to enjoy friendship and companionship, but not this soul-wrenching closeness which had cost him so dearly before. He'd allowed himself to stray from his original intent, like one of his clients who, holding the money in his hands, wanders back to the gaming table instead of his shop, squandering his second chance and all hope of salvation. Last night had been a warning, like the first lost shipment cautioning an investor from buying more shares.

Philip wouldn't walk away from Laura. He wouldn't abandon her or the promises he'd made. Neither would he continue to surrender his heart. He'd given it away as casually as some of the less-reputable moneylenders gave away sovereigns. It was a mistake, a dangerous one. There were more tragedies which could befall a person than the loss of their assets. He knew. He'd suffered through that loss once before. He would not do so again. He'd pull back his heart, guard the investment of his emotions as stringently as he did his business. Loss would not shatter his world ever again.

Chapter Twelve

Laura opened her eyes and the room spun. She squeezed them shut, but it didn't block out the strange wavering light around her vision or the pain radiating from the back of her head. Her stomach flopped. If it hadn't been empty, she would have lost the contents of it.

Against the dark canvas of her eyelids, she caught flashes of images: her uncle, a looming circle of black. None of it came into detail, but wavered like a busy pattern of silk viewed from across a room. Nothing made sense to her now, not the pain, the strange light or whatever must have happened to leave her so hurting and confused.

Beneath the confusion, the image of Philip sitting on the bed beside her, the candlelight stroking the sharpness of his jaw and straight nose came to her. As the wavering light crowding her vision began to fade, the sense of Philip's presence and love enveloped her.

Love.

She could almost hear him speak the word, but

couldn't untangle the memory of it from all the confusion smothering her like a heavy down coverlet.

The floorboard squeaked. Someone was here.

'Philip?' She didn't open her eyes. She didn't want to disturb the faint respite from the pain.

'No, my dear.' Her mother's voice came as both a comfort and a disappointment.

Laura opened her eyes. The room was dark, her mother's form shadowy as she came to sit beside Laura, the bed sinking under her weight. 'Where is he?'

'Resting. It was a long, difficult night.'

'Is he all right?'

'He is. And how are you? You've slept away most of the day.'

'Not well.' It hurt to talk, to think, to lie here.

Her mother draped a damp cloth over her forehead. Laura felt a little sting above one eyebrow, but the coolness eased some of the tension along her temples. 'You took quite a nasty bump last night.'

'What happened? I keep seeing snatches of things, Uncle Robert, a dark circle, but nothing makes sense.' She opened her eyes and took a deep breath to steady her rebelling stomach. In the air lingered the faint aroma of smoke and gunpowder beneath the tart scent of lemon scouring soap. Whatever images she'd seen, they weren't part of a dream, but something real.

'Uncle Robert broke in here last night and threatened us.'

Laura's eyes flew open and she turned. A fresh wave of pain crashed through her and she gripped her head. 'What happened?'

Her mother reached up to adjust the disturbed cloth. 'I'll tell you all about it when you're better.'

Laura reached under the cloth and her fingers brushed the cut on her forehead. 'Is Thomas fine? Is Jane and everyone safe?'

Her mother removed her hand from the cut and laid it at her side. 'Everyone is fine, but if it will put your mind at ease, Robert is in no position to trouble us again. The poorly packed pistol killed him.'

'Then he's dead?' She was ashamed of the relief sliding through her.

'Yes.'

Laura closed her eyes, trying to recall what had happened, but nothing came to her except the image of a dark hole and smoke. 'I don't remember anything.'

'It's better that way,' her mother reassured her, offering no more details about the events of the previous night. Laura didn't press her. She was too drawn out and hurting to take in any more than the facts she already knew.

'Is she awake?'

Laura's heart skipped a little at the sound of Philip's voice. She forced her eyes open and reached out, inviting him to hold her, to press his sturdy cheek against hers and wrap his long arms around her. The craving made her heart ache, but it didn't sting as much as the reluctance which whispered through Philip's eyes.

He moved forward slowly, as if compelled by duty, not by desire.

Her fingers curled over her palm and she nearly pulled her hand back, stunned and wounded by his reticence. Her mother had said he was fine, but something else had happened, something she could faintly detect, but couldn't work loose. It was all too tangled in her mind, like a tightly knotted thread.

Philip stopped by the bed, taking a chair beside her, staring at her hand as if reluctant to take it. When he finally did, Laura felt like she was holding a dead fish. 'How do you feel?'

'As if I've been struck by a carriage.' She rubbed her aching neck, then ran her fingers through her hair to feel the tender bruise beneath.

'Dr Hale assures me you'll make a complete recovery.' His words were as they should be, low, comforting, but even through her haze of pain she felt something missing. It was as if he spoke because it was expected, not because he wanted to.

She willed back the light obscuring her vision to fix on his face. He didn't look at her, but focused on her hand in his.

'Philip, what's wrong?'

At last he met her eyes. Warmth curled through her at the tenderness in his face. He softened his hand in hers until she thought he would take her in his arms and kiss away the fear seeping through her.

Then it was like a metal gate banged shut between them. He sat up straighter, something of the man she'd first met in this room, the stranger, coming over him.

'Nothing's wrong.'

Laura exchanged a look with her mother, who turned away to fuss with a basin of water. It wasn't the wound or exhaustion making Laura see things which weren't there. Her mother had caught his reserve, too.

She let go of his fingers, hating the stiff coldness of his grip. She laid her hand on his chest, startled at the way his heart raced beneath her palm. 'I'm sorry you had to suffer, too.'

'Your mother and Dr Hale were with me. It was a long night, but you're better now.' His face remained rigid as he leaned away from her touch. She lowered her hand back to the bed. It reminded her of the first time she'd touched him, outside Thomas's room. He'd struggled so hard to keep his distance then and again over the next few days. He was doing it again.

'Will you sleep here with me tonight and keep me company?' If she could hold him in the darkness, she might drive away whatever was hardening him against her.

He shook his head, resisting her. 'Dr Hale says you need rest. I would only disturb you. I'll sleep in your room.'

'What if I need you?'

Agony flashed across his face, as though he were fighting with himself to refuse her. The stoic man in him won the battle. 'There's a bell here on the table. Ring it and you'll have what you need.'

'I need you.' Weakness coloured her words, but Laura wasn't ashamed. She wanted him to know what he meant to her.

'You need rest.' He rose and laid his hands on her shoulders, pressing her gently down against the pillows.

She yielded, not possessing the strength to fight him.

* * *

Outside the bedroom, Philip sagged against the wall in the hallway, the pain so intense he struggled to breathe. She'd reached out to him and he'd pulled away and she'd seen it. Guilt gripped him hard as he felt the anguish of turning away from her when she needed his comfort the most.

'Are you all right, Philip?' Jane's voice cut through his agony.

He straightened, facing his sister as she approached him. She appeared less like a woman today and more like a child. Fear still danced around the edges of her round face and he knew it would be some time before the events of last night faded from her consciousness, just as it had taken months for her to recover from the shock of losing Arabella. 'I'm fine.'

'You don't look fine. You look as though you were the one who was thumped on the head.'

He rubbed his hand against his coat, Laura's warmth clinging to his skin, reminding him of everything he'd done wrong. 'Why don't you sit with her for a while? I'm sure she'd enjoy the company.'

'Why aren't you sitting with her?'

Curse her directness. 'A man from London Insurance will be here soon. I must speak with him.'

'Let Mr Connor or Mr Woodson deal with him.'

'It's my warehouse; I'm the one who must meet with him.'

He tried to slide around her and make for the stairs, but Jane blocked his way.

'She needs you.'

He studied his sister standing so defiantly in front of him. She was as determined as their mother had been whenever their father stubbornly refused to yield. 'And I'm here.'

'No, you're not. You haven't been here all morning. It's just like after Arabella died, like this whole year had been until Laura arrived.'

'What do you mean?' There was no need to ask. He already knew.

'You're distant, like no one and nothing can touch you, not me or Laura or anyone.'

Philip tapped his thigh. He'd pushed everyone out of his heart except Thomas and Jane. Or so he'd thought. A fresh wave of remorse struck him. 'It's been a difficult night.'

It was a poor excuse for what he'd done to Jane this past year and what he was doing to Laura now. He was hurting those who loved him the most, but he couldn't stop it or the increasing hardness encasing him.

'Everything will be fine, Philip, you'll see.' Jane threw her arms around his waist and hugged him tight, comforting him the same way he used to comfort her. 'Laura is going to get better and then she'll teach me to recognise fine silk, like she promised she would.'

He wrapped his arms around Jane and laid his cheek on her soft hair, revelling in her innocence. It shamed him to think she could take in the horrors of last night, of this past year, better than he.

He removed her arms from around his waist. Her eager eyes met his, waiting for him to agree with her that all would be well. He wanted to share her belief, but he couldn't. She was young. She'd been even younger when they'd lost their parents. She possessed no real understanding of the depths of suffering that loss could inflict on a person.

'Yes, everything will be fine.' But not the way she and Laura wanted it to be. 'Now, go in and help Mrs Townsend. I must see to the insurance man.'

He descended the stairs, cursing the pain crushing his chest. He didn't want this agony. He wanted everything settled as it had been before Laura had arrived, before Townsend had burst in and shattered their tranquillity, before he'd been foolish enough to fall in love.

Dropping off the last step, he strode to his office, squaring his shoulders as he struggled to regain something of the man he'd been two weeks ago, the one he both hated and needed.

Laura could neither wake nor fully sleep as the images haunting her semi-consciousness pulled at her like thick mud. Last night, Dr Hale had given her laudanum to dull her headache. The tonic tainted her dreams, turning them dark. Her uncle returned to harass her, threatening her and Jane and Thomas again and again until she cried out. As she struggled to free herself from the tortuous nightmare, she thought she saw Philip's face above hers and felt his hand on her forehead. His tender voice had soothed her back into a dreamless sleep which ended with the birds chirping outside the drawn curtains and her alone in bed.

Through a crack in the curtains, a thick shaft of sunlight fell over the desk. She peered through to the dressing room beyond, thankful the strange, flickering light from yesterday no longer obscured her vision. Everything in the room was as it should be, the desk neat, the coverlet wrinkled over her, the chair beside the bed empty and the bottle of laudanum corked on the table beside it. There was no evidence Philip had been here last night except her hazy dreams and the lingering memory of his voice.

A knock at the door made her roll to one side. The room swam a little, but to her relief the aching along the back of her neck and above her eyes was nearly gone. 'Come in.'

The door cracked open and Jane peered around it.

'Oh, you look much better this morning. The circles around your eyes are not nearly as dark.' She threw open the door and strode in, followed by Laura's mother and Mary carrying a breakfast tray.

Laura's mother marched to the curtains and pulled them open. 'What you need is some fresh air and sunlight.'

Laura blinked against the bright light filling the room, but it didn't increase her pain.

'How do you feel?' her mother asked as she raised the sash.

The cool air flowing in from outside drove away some of the exhaustion pulling at Laura. 'My head doesn't hurt as much, but I still feel so tired and sometimes dizzy.'

'Dr Hale says you probably will feel like that for a while,' Jane explained. 'He suggested broth and bread for today. Tomorrow you may have eggs.'

'Then I look forward to tomorrow.'

With her mother and Jane's help, Laura sat up. Mary rested the tray across her lap, then set to tidying the room.

While Laura removed the silver lid from the bowl, Jane plunked down on the bed in front of her, making the coverlet puff up around her knees. 'The coroner and the constable were here yesterday.'

'Were they?' Laura stirred the thick broth with the spoon, the rich, meaty scent of it heavenly. She tried a small amount, pausing to see if it would stay down. When it did, she eagerly ate the rest, thankful once again for the comfort of good food. If only Philip were here, it would help settle the lingering disquiet of her nightmares.

'Philip wouldn't tell me anything about it, but Mr Connor told me the constable wasn't surprised to see the end of your uncle.' In the quick clip of Jane's words, Laura sensed her unease over what had happened and her desire to be brave and cheerful for Laura's sake. It was the same way Laura used to speak to her mother when her father was ill. 'According to him, in the past two weeks Mr Townsend got into trouble with at least two other moneylenders and someone named Mrs Topp. Who's she?'

'The owner of a bawdy house,' Laura mumbled through the last bite of the soft bread.

Jane's eyes opened wide. 'Oh, how exciting.'

'Laura, Jane isn't old enough to hear such things,' Laura's mother chided, removing the tray and handing it to Mary to take away. 'What happened at Mrs Topp's?'

'Mr Townsend was tossed into the gutter for fighting with one of her best clients,' Jane eagerly relayed. 'I think it's exactly what he deserved. I told Philip so, but he only said Mr Connor shouldn't have told me about it.'

'Where's Philip?' Laura asked, trying not to sound concerned. A man wasn't expected to attend the sick room, but his absence this morning was glaring and troubling.

Jane shifted hesitantly on the bed, looking unsure about speaking for the first time since entering the room. 'At his boxing club.'

Laura picked at the sheet. 'I see.'

'He thinks he's being brave by staying away,' Jane rushed, as though revealing a bigger secret than the things Mr Connor had told her. 'And that if he is, then no one will know how scared he was for you, but of course we all know. We were all scared.'

Laura was also scared, not for herself, but for her relationship with Philip.

Before she could think on the matter further, Dr Hale appeared at the door, interrupting their conversation.

'Good morning, ladies.' He looked more rested than he had last night, his usual good cheer evident in his wide smile. 'How are you doing today, Mrs Rathbone?'

'She's much better. Ate nearly everything cook sent up for her,' Jane answered for Laura, jumping to her feet to stand at attention by the bed.

Dr Hale approached, setting his leather bag on the floor before leaning in to examine Laura's eyes. 'And the pain?'

'Mostly gone.' Laura followed his finger as he moved it in front of her eyes.

He examined her forehead. 'The cut is healing nicely. I'd say in a few days you'll be back to your old self with this whole ordeal behind you.'

She wasn't as confident as the doctor. She might be the same as before, but things with Philip wouldn't be. She sensed it in his absence. She leaned back against the pillows with a sigh. It was all too much to think about right now, yet it was nearly the only thing occupying her thoughts.

'You're tired so I'll leave you.' He picked up his bag. 'Jane, I was so eager to check on Mrs Rathbone, I didn't have my breakfast. Would you be kind enough to escort me to the dining room?'

'It would be my pleasure, then I can tell you what Mr Connor told me the constable said.'

Laura's mother shook her head as Jane and Dr Hale left the room, arm in arm. 'She enjoys gossip far too much.'

'So do you,' Laura teased, the levity lightening a little of the weight in her heart. 'Philip hasn't been in to see me since yesterday.'

'Yes, he has.' Her mother lifted a shawl from the back of a chair and began to fold it. 'He was in here with you last night while you were sleeping. I heard you call out and came in to sit with you, but he was already here. He didn't notice me. I don't think he wanted anyone to see him, so I didn't disturb him. He stayed for a very long time.'

Tears welled in Laura's eyes at the image of him

holding his silent vigil. He was still caring for her as he had since the moment she'd come under his protection, but hiding it. 'Why wouldn't he want anyone to see him? Why is he avoiding me?'

'He's had quite a shock, my dear.' Her mother perched on the bed next to Laura, crumpling the shawl against her stomach. 'We all have.'

'Tell me what happened.'

'Dr Hale doesn't think it a good idea for you to know just yet.'

'I don't care, I have to hear it.' It was the only thing which might explain Philip's sudden distance.

In short sentences, her mother relayed her uncle's threat, Laura's bravery with the poker and finally his death caused by the poorly packed pistol. Laura looked to the now bare floor near the fireplace, noticing the dark circle staining the wood, the lingering scent of vinegar and lemon soap explained. None of it moved her like her mother's description of the long night afterwards and how Philip had sat beside her, determined to keep her awake and alive.

The throbbing behind her forehead increased and Laura closed her eyes. She struggled to remember the events her mother described. Only the vague awareness which had come to her late into the night, the peace and comfort of Philip sitting next to her and old memories of Christmas in their rooms above the shop revealed themselves.

She couldn't believe the same man who'd sat with her making her feel so warm and safe could be so distant now. What had happened between the darkest part of night and just before dawn to change him so much?

'Is she worse?' Philip's voice pierced the cloud of confusion swirling around her.

Laura opened her eyes and lifted her head from the pillows, wincing at the stab of pain at the back of her neck.

'No, she's much better,' her mother replied.

The bright statement didn't ease the firm set of his mouth. He didn't move into the room, but lingered by the door, hands stiff at his sides, just like yesterday.

'Laura was only worrying over you. She hasn't seen you this morning,' her mother remarked. It wasn't a chastisement but a reminder, a pointed one.

If Philip experienced any awkwardness he didn't reveal it, waiting near the door as her mother rose to give Laura a hug.

Her mother leaned in and whispered in her ear, 'See, he's here now. There's nothing to worry about.'

She made for the door, pausing in front of Philip. 'Go and sit by your wife.'

She drew the door closed behind her as she left.

Philip didn't move, but studied Laura as he had the night she'd first faced him in this room when he'd been wearing nothing but soapy water. She smiled a little at the memory.

'It's good to see you smile,' he offered, cautiously approaching.

'I wish the same might be said for you.'

'When you're completely recovered, I will smile.' The words were tender but his tone was a little cold, like some posy of flowers obliged to be delivered. He sat down on the edge of the bed, near her waist, close but somehow distant.

'My mother told me what happened.'

He turned his hand over, bringing his thumb in to touch his wedding band. Nothing else about him changed. 'She shouldn't have.'

'I insisted.' She watched him stroke the ring, her worry sharp, pain thudding along her temples. 'When Uncle Robert was at his worst in Seven Dials, I used to wish for him to meet with some accident. I didn't think one would befall him here.'

'He never should have been allowed to creep in.' Philip's fingers curled until his nails dug into the lines of his palms and his knuckles turned white.

'There was no way either of us could have known what he was planning.'

'I should have known. I should have guessed it.'

'It's not your fault, Philip.' She laid her hand on his cheek, wanting to comfort him as he'd comforted her during her nightmares. 'Everything is well now.'

'No, everything is not well.' He jumped to his feet and paced back and forth beside the bed. 'I should have done more to prevent last night. I should have made sure Mr Walker found Townsend before I left, I should have insisted Townsend be pressed instead of being lenient and waiting for him to strike. If I had, you wouldn't have been hurt. I failed you, just as I failed Arabella.'

'You didn't fail me.'

'I did. Can't you see it?' he blurted out, the shame in his eyes more powerful than it had been the evening he'd stormed away from her in the entrance hall. He jerked back his shoulders, the fight to regain control evident in the tightness along his jaw. He paced to the mantel, then turned and strode back to the foot of the bed, stern reserve descending over him. 'Now isn't the time to discuss it. I'll leave you to rest.'

He made for the door.

'I love you,' Laura cried, desperate to make him stay and not knowing any other way to pierce the wall encasing him.

He halted, but didn't turn around. The sun brought out the deep hint of blue in the darkness of his coat and another darkness threatened to consume them both. 'You shouldn't. You don't know who I am, how incapable I am of—'

'Love? You're wrong, Philip. I know you love me as much as I love you. I heard you say it when you sat with me and kept me awake through the night. I thought it was a dream, but it wasn't.'

She twisted the sheet, waiting for him to answer, to acknowledge at last what she'd suspected since their wedding night. Instead he stood in silence, his hands tightening into fists at his sides. She willed him to face her, to reveal the scarred and battered Philip he was fighting so hard to hide, but he didn't.

'It was a mistake to make our relationship more than an business arrangement, a bargain.' He reached for the doorknob, his words as chilling as the morning breeze that flew in through the window. 'I can't be the husband you want. I'm sorry if I led you to believe otherwise.'

Then he was gone.

Laura stared at the empty hallway and the painting of a dog hanging on the opposite wall. Tears made the room waver and she squeezed her eyes shut against them. Everything she'd fought for, everything she'd done to win Philip's heart came crashing down around her. She lay back against the pillows, her head hurting, her body too weak to do more than sink into the soft down. She cursed her uncle again. He'd severed Philip from her and Philip was all too willing to allow it.

She rolled on her side and opened her eyes. The bottle with Dr Hale's laudanum mixture sat on the table beside the bed. She was exhausted, but she didn't want to sleep, to face again the cloying dreams which had left her so ragged this morning. However, if sleep was the only way to bring Philip back to her, then the elixir was just tempting enough to taste.

She clasped the bottle, tilting it back and forth to make the liquid dance inside. For the first time she understood why some of Dr Hale's patients took to bed and the easy peace of the drug. Sleep was more comforting than the cutting loneliness of watching a once-loving husband turn away.

She ran her thumb up to the cork, ready to remove it and enjoy the sweetness inside. Her nail dug into the soft bark, peeling back a thin layer before she stopped.

She didn't want to be like Dr Hale's patients, trapped in a lifetime of loneliness, abandoned by the one man who'd vowed to love her the most. She set the bottle back on the table and pushed herself up on one elbow. This was not how it would be between her and Philip.

She flung aside the covers and swung her feet to

the floor. The room spun as she sat up. She gripped the thick wood of the bedpost until everything stopped swaying. Then she pushed herself up, wobbling as she took her first step, catching the back of the chair to steady herself.

With her fingernails digging into the chintz, she wasn't sure how she would make it downstairs, or muster the strength needed to face Philip, but she knew she must. Another day could not go by like this, not another hour could pass with him retreating from her.

Her mother appeared in the doorway, stopping so quickly, the water in the pitcher she carried sloshed over the top and dribbled on to the floor. 'What are you doing out of bed?'

'I must see Philip.'

'You can't.' She deposited the jar on a low bookshelf and rushed to Laura's side. 'You'll make yourself worse.'

Her mother tugged her back towards the bed, but Laura fought to stay standing. 'No, I have to. You told me once you tried to push Father away because of your grief. Philip is doing the same to me now. He's retreating inside himself and I can't let him do it. I have to fight for his love, like you told me to do. I can't let him pull away.'

Philip sat across the desk from Mr Charton. Word of the fire and Townsend's demise had circulated among his friends and the affable man had paid a visit to make sure everything was all right. Assured by Philip that it was, he lingered now, sharing one of his many humorous stories. Philip was eager to draw the visit to a close, but he didn't want to insult his friend.

'And that's when I said he should try it and he did.' Mr Charton slapped his knee and let out a loud guffaw.

Philip laced and unlaced his fingers together in front of him, unable to share Mr Charton's humour. If he let even one harmless emotion through, then everything else he held back would come rushing out with it. Before Laura, it'd been so easy to shove everything, his pain, his fear, into the deepest corners of his mind. Then Laura had unleashed it. Now it took all his effort to keep the tentacled beast in its box.

'Don't you agree, Mr Rathbone?' Mr Charton prompted eagerly as he waited for an answer to something he'd said.

'I'm sorry, Mr Charton. I failed to follow you.'

'I'm not surprised, not with you worrying about Mrs Rathbone. I always worry about Mrs Charton when she's ill, never so much as when she was delivered of our children. Soon, you'll have the same reason to worry and then another strapping boy in the nursery.'

Philip forced himself not to bolt from the study, hurry to the boxing club and pound the first dummy he saw into a pulp of feathers and leather. After last night, he knew he wouldn't be able to sit with Laura in her confinement, pacing the room until she and the child were either safe and well, or dead.

He snatched up the pen lying across the top of his desk and clutched it hard, working to ignore the beast inside him rattling against its cage. He'd been careless with Laura since the wedding, risking getting her with child instead of holding himself back. He set the pen down, lining it up with the ledger as Mr Charton prattled on about his children. When Laura was well, Philip wouldn't return to her room. To be alone with her in the dark was to risk both her safety and himself with their intimacy. He couldn't do it again.

A slight commotion in the hallway made him look up and the wind was knocked from him.

'I say, are you ill?' Mr Charton looked alarmed, before following the line of Philip's stare to turn in his chair and face the door.

Laura stood there, exhaustion clear in the darkness beneath her eyes. Mrs Townsend was beside her, helping her to stand.

At the sight of Laura, Philip's chest clenched, not with fear, but excitement. The life flaring in her eyes took hold of him, bringing him to his feet. He wanted to jump over the mahogany desk to reach her, hold her, kiss her, but he didn't move. The angry gash on her forehead was a reminder of everything she'd been through, everything he couldn't face.

He pressed his fingertips into the polished desktop, as if they might take root there and keep him anchored against the storm of emotions roiling inside him.

Laura ignored the other men who rose to greet her, focused as hard on Philip as he was on her.

'Everyone leave, now,' she commanded.

Justin pushed off his perch by the window and made for the door. 'Shall we, Mr Charton?'

'We shall.' Mr Charton moved fast on Justin's heels,

following him around Laura. 'I've been married long enough to know when there's trouble brewing.'

Laura let go of Mrs Townsend and moved into the room, stepping cautiously. With surprising strength, she swung the door closed, then winced at the loud thud it made. Her heavy breathing betrayed her determination as she gripped the back of the chair before his desk, struggling as much as Philip to steady herself.

'You shouldn't be up. You should be resting.' Philip hurried around to her side and took her by the arm. The beast inside him roared at the touch and her nearness. The intensity of the moment was everything he didn't allow himself to be: irrational, unexpected, uncontrollable.

She resisted the gentle pressure he placed on her arm, her body trembling under his hand, not from weakness but conviction. 'No, Philip. You won't push me away so easily.'

'I'm not pushing you away.' He balled his free hand tight at his side. He'd tried for so long to hide the ugliness inside him. Now she was seeing it and the awful man it made him.

'I know exactly what you're doing, even if you won't admit it. I won't let you crawl back into your stoic castle or live with me as a partner, but not as a true wife or companion.'

Philip scraped in a ragged breath, struggling for the strength which had carried him through the last two nights, determined not to crumble under the force of her determination. 'If you don't rest, you won't get better and then you might—'

'Die?' She stuck her chin defiantly in the air. 'Is that what you're afraid of, Philip?'

He didn't answer. He couldn't speak through the rigid exertion of beating down the helplessness and pain welling up inside him. It was a battle he was slowly losing.

She slipped her hand behind his neck, leaning heavily on him as she drew his forehead down to touch hers. The fortitude blazing in her eyes singed him and he dropped his gaze to the floor. Beneath her feet, the scratch on the floor snaked under the desk, white against the deep brown of the surrounding boards, a glaring reminder of his failings. He screwed his eyes shut, understanding for the first time why men swung or cursed at him when he came to collect their debts. He forced them to face their mistakes and the consequences just like Laura was forcing him to face his.

'Life is about risk, Philip, you can't hide away from it.' Weakness sat hard in the pull of her fingers against his neck and the faint struggle between breathing and speaking. Her bravery shamed him. She was stronger than he. 'It was a risk to accept you when you proposed to me, to give you my future, my happiness, my body. I had to trust you would be a man worthy of them all and you have been. You've been kind and good, even when I doubted you. You stood by your word, even when I thought so low of you. I wouldn't have blamed you for giving me over to Halcyon House. Instead you took me as your wife, showed me your heart and your soul.'

He jerked up straight. She didn't understand. The Philip she wanted was dead, crushed by dread. He was ugly and hard and damaged, incapable of loving her, his sister, maybe even his son. 'The man you want never existed.'

'No, he's right in here in front of me. He always has been.' Warm hands slid along the sides of his face, drawing him in, comforting, tender. Her belief in him was more powerful than his doubts, the whisper of her touch stronger than anything he'd ever done to maintain the cairn of stones crushing his heart. Like water, she slipped between the cracks, penetrating him until the stones began to tumble and light filled the darkness. 'I love you, Philip, and I know you love me, too.'

'I do.' He opened his eyes and took her by the waist, pulling her into the arch of his body, his strength supporting her in her weakness. 'I have since the night you first barged in here.'

He brought his lips down hard to cover hers. They dropped to their knees together, clinging to one another, life, love, happiness in every mingled breath. He couldn't push her away or live without the deep connection of their embrace. She believed in him, loved him, even when he hated himself. He couldn't deny her his belief and love in return, nor did he want to.

Laura broke from him, leaning into his chest and clutching his jacket. He hugged her tight, supporting her. For the first time, her exhaustion didn't frighten him. Eventually her weakness would fade like the nasty stain on the floor of their bedroom and the horrid events of the other night.

'I guess I wasn't as strong as I thought,' she stated without submission to her listlessness but in jest of it, defying it. She wasn't afraid of her injuries, wouldn't surrender her life or their future together. Neither would he.

'No, you're so much stronger.' Philip laid his forehead against hers, gently so as not to cause her pain, his body aching to be close to hers. In time, when she was recovered, they would be as one once again, and from it would come children and a future that he'd almost surrendered to his fear. 'But now, you must rest.'

He bundled her into his arms and lifted her up. The firmness of her against him was a reminder of her life, her strength and her love. He'd been so wrong to think he could close himself off to the woman he'd known from the first was meant to be his.

He carried her out of the room, past Mr Charton and Justin.

Mr Charton nudged Justin with his elbow. 'It's a beautiful thing.'

'Yes, it is,' Philip murmured to Laura, kissing the soft hair framing her face. She didn't look away as he carried her upstairs, her love for him as sure as her arms around his neck, her slender form in his hands.

At the top of the stairs, Jane and Mrs Townsend stood outside the nursery. Jane gaped at the sight of them. Mrs Townsend's hands flew to her heart, her besotted expression almost as sweet as Jane's.

'Isn't it romantic?' Jane sighed, her childish excitement feeding Philip's.

'Hush now, Jane,' Mrs Townsend chided with a laugh, taking her by the shoulders and drawing her back into the nursery.

'But it is, isn't it?' Jane insisted.

'Yes, it is.'

Thomas's happy coos joined their conversation as Mrs Townsend closed the door behind them.

Philip carried Laura into his room, the place which encompassed their first meeting and the first trial they'd been forced to overcome. He knew there would be more difficult times ahead as well as good, life never flowed so simply, but they would face them all together, without fear of the future.

'Will you stay with me this afternoon?' Laura asked, as he laid her gently on the bed, kneeling beside it to keep her arms around his neck, unwilling to let go.

'I will stay with you. Always.'

Epilogue

'May I have your attention, everyone.' The ring of a knife against crystal faded into the clear, late summer air. Mr Charton stood with a full glass of punch near the fountain, his nose a little red from one too many glasses.

Everyone mingling through the Rathbone garden stopped their conversation and turned to him. Philip watched him raise his glass, wondering what he was about. Overhead, paper lanterns glowed brightly, the candles inside flickering like the stars in the evening breeze.

'I want to offer my congratulations to Jane on her fourteenth birthday. She's becoming quite the charming young lady.' Mr Charton pointed at his lanky son, who stood beside Jane. The young man was clearly besotted with her. 'You mind your manners with her, Milton, or you'll have Mr Rathbone to answer to. He's quite the boxer. Why, I remember once when we were near Portsmouth, preparing to inspect some collateral. My, what collateral it was. I've never seen statues in such positions. They were—'

'I think we should save your story for another time, darling,' Mrs Charton interrupted, tugging her husband's arm just hard enough to make her point.

'But I—' he began to protest before a stern look from his wife finally sobered him. 'Yes, of course, another time. To Jane.'

Everyone raised their glasses and chimed in unison. 'To Jane.'

Philip nodded at his sister, who glowed under both the guests' attention and that of the young Mr Charton. Dressed in a pale-blue gown with an appropriately high neckline, she appeared the confident young lady she was quickly becoming under Mrs Townsend's tutelage. Young Mr Charton whispered something to her. Her eyes sparkled as she listened, then a hearty laugh escaped her. In the past few months she'd shed much of her seriousness. As had Philip.

'Jane looks very lovely tonight, my compliments to you and Mrs Fairley,' he said to Laura.

She stood beside him, dressed in a silk gown in a shade of green as rich as the leaves of the rose bushes. 'Oh, I had nothing to do with it. She chose the pattern all on her own.'

'She selected a modest dress without a fight?'

'She did.'

'You and your mother have worked a miracle.' Though the miracle was more in the change in Jane's temperament than her attire. He couldn't remember when she'd last stood in front of his desk, hands balled at her side, punctuating each demand with the stomp of her left foot. He vaguely remembered enduring such a tantrum during Laura's first night in his house, before Laura's love had brought him back to everyone who surrounded him.

Mr and Mrs Charton passed Philip and Laura as the wife drew her husband from more libations. Mr Charton paused, almost swaying into Philip. 'Portsmouth was one strange evening, wasn't it, Rathbone?'

'Indeed it was,' Philip agreed, before arching a knowing eyebrow at Laura. 'Though we've had stranger, haven't we, my dear?'

'Indeed we have.'

'Though nothing can top the printer's shop. You remember him, the one who use to sell all those portraits of women—'

'Another time, Henry,' Mrs Charton insisted, twining her arm in his and leading him off to where the Moseleys stood.

Laura crossed her arms beneath her breasts, drawing the silk tight over their roundness and stirring Philip's interest. 'Why haven't I heard the story of the statues or the prints before?'

He caressed her elbow just above the glove, making her shiver. 'Because they're quite stunning.'

'Then I look forward to hearing them tonight.' She squeezed his arm, making it clear the story was not all she expected from him that evening.

Philip returned the silent hint with a wink, wondering if they'd be missed if they disappeared upstairs for a while. With Jane ensconced by the fountain with the two Felton girls and young Charton, she wouldn't likely search out her brother or sister-in-law. Mrs Townsend could serve as chaperon, though she was too much involved in a discussion with Dr Hale to take much notice of her young charge.

Laura rose up on her toes, resting her hands on Philip's shoulder to whisper in his ear. 'Come with me, I have something to tell you.'

He turned, finding her lips temptingly close to his. 'Does it have anything to do with clocked stockings?'

With a devilish smile she lowered herself from his shoulder. 'It might.'

'Then lead the way.'

She took his hand and pulled him into the shadows of the portico, seeking out the darkest corner near the study where the rose bushes were highest. Orange light from inside the house spilled over the stone still warm from the late afternoon sun.

'Are we to abandon our guests?' Heat settled low in his body, the idea of creeping away enticing.

'Not just yet.' She wrapped her arms around his waist, leaning her body into his until it was all he could do not to press her against the wall and shock anyone who might happen by.

'Then what surprise do you have for me?' He touched his cheek to hers, her gardenia perfume intoxicating.

'Quite a large one,' she whispered, her breath teasing his hair. 'I'm with child.'

His fingers tightened on her waist, crinkling the silk. He leaned back, studying her eager eyes. 'You're certain?'

'Dr Hale confirmed it this afternoon.' She arched back, a wide smile making her glow as bright as the lanterns. 'In a few months' time, we will be keeping Thomas's new nurse quite busy with another charge.'

Philip stroked her forehead and the faint red line that streaked over her eyebrow. It was the only thing which remained of the terrible night last spring. Philip tightened his arms around her, bringing her in closer to him. The darkness of the past was far behind him. All there existed now was a future with Laura and their child. He wanted both more than anything he'd ever wanted before.

'Are you happy?' she pressed at his silence, nervously biting her lower lip.

He met her eyes, the hazel depths which had first caught his notice, capturing him again. Elation rose from deep inside him, welling up until the sternness of his cheeks eased and a smile wider than any he'd ever experience spread across his lips and through his entire being. 'It's the most wonderful news I could receive.'

Her mouth fell open at the sight of his grin before her pretty lips turned up into a radiant smile to match his. 'Philip, I've never seen you like this!'

'And you will again, and again and again!' He picked her up and whirled her around, his deep laugh filling the evening air. It was joined by Laura's as the two of them twirled together, heedless of their guests and anything but each other and their joy.

* * * * *

A TOO CONVENIENT
MARRIAGE

To my husband who believes in me and my dreams.

Chapter One

London—May 1818

'Marry you?' Helena Gammon sat back from Justin Connor, her ungloved hand stilling on his chest beneath his shirt. A horse snorted from somewhere outside his chaise where it sat parked in a long row of conveyances in front of Vauxhall Gardens.

'I'm quite serious. We get on well together, especially at night,' Justin murmured against the buxom little widow's neck. 'Soon, I'll have the resources to establish myself in the wine trade. I'll need a wife who can manage as well in my business as in my bed.'

She shifted out of his embrace and laid her hands in her lap as though they were at tea. 'There are other matters to consider.'

Her lack of enthusiasm wasn't how he'd imagined this proposal unfolding.

'Such as?' Justin leaned back against the squabs, sure he wasn't going to like what he was about to hear.

'You aren't likely to make a go of it.' She shrugged as though his failure was predetermined. 'Not after what happened with the last one.'

'The storm sank the ship.' *And my business.* He pulled his gaping shirt closed. He thought everyone understood that little fact. Apparently he was wrong. 'There was nothing I or anyone could have done to prevent it.'

Despite months of careful planning, researching, investing, hiring the most capable captain and the sturdiest ship, his first foray into business had dropped to the bottom of the English Channel, taking with it a considerable amount of his money. He hated ships.

'Even if you did manage to make a go of it, I'm tired of being some unpaid servant to my husband's ventures. I worked myself to the bone with Mr Gammon. Now I want to be free of such concerns.' She tugged her bodice up higher over her ample breasts. 'Mr Preston asked me to marry him this morning and I accepted.'

'You did what?' He hadn't realised the old furrier was sniffing around the widow, much less falling on his knees in front of her in infatuation.

'He's rich and has people to take care of his business for him.'

'He's well over sixty and not likely to keep you amused in the evenings.'

'That's why I'm here.' She laid her hand over the open flap of his breeches. 'I thought we could continue.'

He caught her fingers. 'After a year, you should

know I won't dally with another man's wife, or help a woman break her marriage vows.'

She pulled back her hand. 'When did you become so serious about anything except Mr Rathbone's business?'

'I tend to be serious when there's the possibility of violence,' Justin growled, seeing Helena's true colours for the first time and despising them. He'd thought their convenient arrangement was based on some measure of respect and affability. He'd been mistaken.

'Well, if that's how you're going to be.' She flicked her skirt down over her calves and ankles. 'Mr Preston is waiting for me inside.'

'You'll regret marrying him.' Justin pushed open the chaise door. 'He might be making a lot of promises now, but once you're his wife, they'll all disappear.'

'You know nothing of the situation.' Mrs Gammon hopped down from the chaise and stormed off across the walk and into the gardens.

Justin slammed the chaise door shut and slumped against the squabs. It galled him to think she'd waited until he'd proposed to reveal her true impression of him, though he supposed it was better now than after the parson's mousetrap was sprung. Justin roughly stuffed his shirt back in his breeches and did up the fall, not bothering to button his coat or redo his cravat. Outside, the excited chatter of ladies and gentlemen passing too close to the chaise as they filed into the gardens filled the air.

Then the door swung open. He jerked upright, thinking Helena had come back, but it wasn't her.

A stunning woman with eyes the colour of the emeralds he'd once handled as collateral fixed her gaze on him, not with the coy calculation of a vixen, but determination. She opened her full lips as if to say something, then changed her mind, pressing them tight together. Gold earrings swung from the small lobes as she raised her foot to step inside the chaise, then paused, as she took in his partial undress and began to back away. Male voices outside the carriage caught her attention and, in a sweep of chestnut curls, she looked to the sound of the noise, then climbed inside and pulled the door shut behind her.

'Drive away, at once,' she commanded, pressing herself against the squabs and out of view of the window.

'No.' Justin pushed open the door, inviting her to leave. Whatever nuisance this was, he wasn't in the mood for it, no matter how pretty it might be.

'Please, you must.' She leaned out of the chaise to pull the door closed, bringing her face much too close to his. A few freckles dotted her nose and her eyelashes were thick and dark above her vivid eyes. She licked her lips nervously, making the red buds glisten in the low light. Her jasmine perfume encircled him like the cool night slipping in through the open door. She was tempting, but she was trouble, he could feel it.

'I've had enough female companionship for one night and don't intend to pay for more.'

She closed the door and sat up across from him with unwarranted indignity. 'I don't want your money, or anything else.'

She waved a bare hand at him, making the gold bracelet adorning her wrist slide down.

'Then what do you want?' He dropped his elbow on the sill of the window and touched his fingers to his chin, more intrigued than annoyed. She wasn't dressed in the flamboyant colours of the night birds, but in a silhouette of shimmering green material which hugged her high breasts, the tops of which rose in lush half-circles above the bodice.

'To be away from here, as fast as possible.' She could barely sit still, but still he didn't give the order to the driver.

'Why?'

'It's none of your business.' The irritation mingling with anxiety in her eyes made them sparkle even brighter.

He levelled one finger at her. 'You're in my carriage, so I think it is my business. Besides, you don't strike me as the kind of woman whose family approves of her jumping in a strange man's vehicle.'

She glanced out of the window, a new panic dimming the slight sweep of pink across her fine nose. 'You don't know the half of it.'

'Enlighten me. I have nothing else to do this evening.'

There was no time for her to tell him as the door swung open again. Two men stared inside, too finely turned out to be whore minders. The older man sighed and clapped his hands over his eyes. The younger man heaved like a bull as he studied first the woman, then Justin and his undone cravat and coat.

'How dare you.' The bull reached in and grabbed Justin by the lapels, hauling him out of the chaise.

Justin's boots hit the step before he regained his footing. He brought his arms up between the bull's and knocked them aside, then pulled back his fist and rammed it into the younger man's face.

The bull dropped to his rear in the dirt, sending up a puff of dust. Stunned but not beaten, he hauled himself to his feet, staggering as he glowered at Justin. 'You'll pay for that.'

'Why don't you stay down?' Justin moved one foot back for balance, then raised his fists. 'It'll hurt less.'

The man rushed at Justin, who slammed his fist into the bull's stomach, making him double over. Then Justin brought his elbows down on the man's back to knock him face first into the dirt. He groaned and rolled over, clutching his middle.

Justin straightened one cufflink. 'I warned you to stay down.'

'No, Father,' the woman yelled from behind him. 'It's not what you think.'

Justin whirled around to see the older man rushing at him with his walking stick raised. The woman jumped between them, spreading out her arms to stop them, her steadying hand meeting Justin's chest. He looked down at the lithe fingers spread out over his loose shirt, her thumb just slipping into the open V to kiss his sweaty skin. It was the lightest of touches, but it could have knocked him across the garden.

She turned her piercing eyes on him and they opened wide with a shock to match his. Tense breaths raised and lowered his chest beneath her palm as he waited for her to pull away, the danger from the other men fading beneath the subtle press of her skin against his. Helena's touch had never rattled him to his boot heels like this woman's, which was igniting him like a reed set to the coals.

'Then what exactly is it?' the older man demanded, lowering his stick, but not easing the hard glare he fixed on the woman.

At last she pulled back her hand and it was almost a relief as the tension between them ebbed, although not completely.

From the ground, the bull coughed and hauled himself to his feet. He staggered over to stand beside the older man. A nasty bruise marred his cheekbone and he failed to fully straighten as he continued to cradle his stomach.

'Is this the man you've been compromising yourself with?' the bull wheezed.

'I've never seen this woman before in my life,' Justin spat out, levelling his gaze at both men and daring either of them to pounce again. Whatever connection he'd experienced with the strange woman was gone.

'This isn't him. I forced my way into his carriage to hide from you.' The woman threw an apologetic look at Justin over her shoulder before turning to face her family. 'I wasn't here for a tryst. I was waiting for Lord Howsham. We were to be married, but he never arrived.'

Her defiance began to wilt beneath the truth and her father's condemning stare. Despite his stinging knuckles, Justin felt a twinge of pity for her. He knew a little something about disappointed hopes.

'Then who is he?' The bull pointed at Justin.

'Who the hell are you?' Justin shot back. This whole situation was growing tiresome.

The older gentleman stepped forward, asserting his authority the way Justin had seen his own father do so many times. 'I'm Horace Aberton, Duke of Rockland, and this is my son, Edgar, Marquess of Sutton, and my daughter, Miss Susanna Lambert.'

Justin raised an eyebrow at the hesitation which met Lord Rockland's admission of the woman's relationship to him. Justin supposed if he gave a fig for what the upper classes got up to when they weren't trying to thump him outside Vauxhall Gardens, he'd understand the hesitation, but he didn't and therefore didn't care.

'If you expect me to be impressed, I'm not.' Justin had helped collect enough debts from men like Lord Rockland to not be cowed by their grand titles and lack of manners.

'How dare you?' Lord Sutton stomped forward, ready for another beating.

'Stop.' Lord Rockland's booming voice pulled him back, muzzling but not completely checking the bull's anger. 'I think we've had enough fighting for one night. I believe an apology is in order, Mr—?'

'Connor.' Justin jerked straight the lapels of his coat.

'I'm sorry for offending you this evening and for holding you responsible for an inappropriate situation in which you were not involved.' Lord Rockland laid a large hand on his chest, his diamond ring flashing in the lantern light. 'Surely you understand how easy it was to make such a mistake.'

'No, not particularly.'

'Then perhaps you can understand the need for discretion.'

'It's not my discretion you need to worry about.' He flung a look at Miss Lambert, who boldly faced him. He had to give the woman her due; she was no cowering miss.

'True, but I'd like us to come to some understanding about your tact in this matter. If you'd be so kind as to pay a call on me tomorrow at noon, I believe I can make it worth your while.'

Justin wanted nothing more to do with this trio, but he did need money to finally put his last venture behind him and start again. He recognised opportunity when it came crashing through his chaise door. 'I believe you can.'

'Good. Until tomorrow.' Lord Rockland bowed to Justin before ushering his wayward progeny away.

'He doesn't deserve—' Lord Sutton sputtered.

'After the beating he gave you, I recommend you shut your mouth.' Lord Rockland's admonishment silenced any further protest.

Only Miss Lambert dared to turn and watch Justin as she strode away with her father and brother. It was a plaintive glance, but Justin wasn't in the mood for extending more pity or forgiveness. With his plans for the evening in tatters, he stepped back into his chaise and made for home. With any luck, tomorrow would be better. He'd receive a tidy sum of an apology from the duke, the kind he needed to repay Philip for the money he'd invested and lost in Justin's last venture, and secure the necessary merchandise to establish himself in the wine trade. Nature had defeated him last time. It wouldn't happen again. He'd succeed, no matter what Helena or anyone else thought.

'What did you think you were doing?' Lord Rockland roared at Susanna from across the coach as it spirited them away from Vauxhall Gardens.

'Acting like a slut,' her half-brother sneered. 'What else do you expect from a bastard?'

'Shut your mouth, Edgar.' Lord Rockland trilled his fingers on his knees. 'Well, Susanna? Why were you throwing yourself and my promise of your dowry away?'

To have a home, life and family of my own instead of constantly being reminded of how grateful I should be to you for nothing, she thought, but she didn't dare utter it. She was too ashamed of her foolishness to make the situation worse with the truth. 'I told you, I went to meet Lord Howsham. We were to leave for Gretna Green.'

'With the rumours of debt circling him, I'm not surprised he ran after you, or I should say your dowry. Did he compromise you?' Lord Rockland pressed, though she didn't know why. Her father wasn't about to force the earl's hand, not for his bastard daughter.

'No, I'm not as stupid as you believe,' she lied. The truth would see her banished back to the country with all hope of escape lost. Thankfully, the darkness of the carriage kept the shame from lighting up her face. She'd been a naive fool to believe Lord Howsham's false compliments, but she'd been so lonely and he so attentive and insistent. Lord Howsham hadn't cared for her. He'd only been after her dowry. She pressed her fingertips to her temples, chastising herself more than her father ever could.

'If I'd known bringing you to London to try and make a good match would result in you throwing yourself at the first man who flattered you, I'd have left you at Rockland Place.'

She wished he had, but remained silent. It was best not to provoke him. Instead, all she could do was play the dutiful daughter, bite back her anger at his and his family's treatment of her in what they considered the name of generosity and humble herself once again. 'I'm sorry, you're right, I didn't think.'

'Indeed you didn't. Whatever he might have promised you, Lady Rockland told me this morning he's marrying the Earl of Colchester's daughter in a fortnight.'

'Seems he'd rather have a nobleman's wife and her considerable inheritance than a bastard and her meagre dowry,' Edgar mocked.

Susanna balled her hands in her lap, wanting to pound on her thighs, the carriage, her father's chest and her half-brother's swollen face. Lord Howsham hadn't just abandoned her for a woman with a more robust lineage and fortune, but he'd told her the deepest of lies a man could tell a woman. She'd fallen for them like some kind of country simpleton, allowing Lord Howsham to press himself on her in the hope he might love her. In the end, it'd gained her nothing but more scorn.

'You'd better hope Mr Connor and Lord Howsham are both willing to keep their mouths shut about this. If not, what little I've been able to achieve on your behalf will be gone,' her father threatened.

Susanna almost wished it was gone. For all the effort he thought he was extending on her behalf, she'd seen very little love or true concern about her and her future. All he and his wife, Augusta, seemed to care about was getting rid of the taint hanging about their house in the form of her.

'I can't believe you're going to entertain a common man like him.' Edgar rubbed at the dark bruise forming on his cheek. 'If I were you, I'd have him thrown in jail for what he did to me.'

'If I were you, I wouldn't want such an embarrassing beating made public for all of London to read about in the papers,' their father answered. 'As it is, I believe Mr Connor can be of some use to us.'

'What could he possibly do for us?'

'He might be the solution to the new problem Susanna has presented us with.'

Susanna's stomach tightened as it had the morning after her mother's funeral when Lord Rockland had stepped through the door of their simple wine shop and looked down his aquiline nose at her. She'd known by the way he'd studied her, as he did now, her life was about to change. The little love she'd enjoyed with her mother, who'd done all she could to protect her daughter from the taint of being a bastard among their friends, relatives and neighbours, had ended. Instead of leaving her with all the people she'd ever known, although they weren't any more loving than the Rocklands, Lord Rockland had taken her into his household to have her moulded into heaven knew what. She'd never been like Edwina, her half-sister and his legitimate daughter, coddled and dressed and paraded through court and the ballrooms. Instead she'd been a barely tolerated companion and chaperon who was now being thrust into society in the hope her family might foist her off on someone else. Lord Rockland should have left her in the wine shop.

'Whatever you have in mind, I want no part of it,' Susanna said and was scolded with a cold glare.

'You'll go along with my wishes or you'll find yourself cast out of my house, with the promise of the dowry rescinded and you left, like any little whoring bastard, to fend for yourself. Do I make myself clear?'

'You do,' she answered with feigned meekness. Tonight was a setback, but it wasn't the end of her plans. Her father wouldn't decide her future as he had when she was thirteen, nor would he get his way. She'd make a life for herself somewhere, somehow, get her thousand pounds of dowry and be free of the Rocklands for ever.

Chapter Two

Justin stepped into the Rocklands' ornate Grosvenor Square entrance hall, unfazed by the painted cherubs and knights peering down at him from the gilded ceiling. This wasn't the first time he'd been in a grand man's home. In the many years he'd helped his friend and employer, Philip Rathbone, collect debts, there'd been a few titled men who'd defaulted. They'd face Philip and Justin to either return the money or hand over whatever cherished family silver or priceless paintings they'd set up as collateral.

'Good day, Mr Connor, and thank you for coming,' Lord Rockland greeted Justin as the butler showed him into the wide study situated near the centre of the house. The books lining the many shelves held little interest for Justin. The experience he'd gathered from his years as Philip's assistant was more practical and valuable to a man interested in trade than a book full of theories or pretty poetry.

There was no sign of Miss Lambert as the duke led

him to a pair of wingback chairs in front of the fire. Between the chairs stood a table laden with a selection of liquors. Now here was something Justin could appreciate.

'What will you have?' Lord Rockland asked.

'Something expensive.'

The surprised arch of Lord Rockland's eyebrow didn't trouble Justin as the older man picked up the decanter with the silver brandy tag hanging on a delicate chain around its neck and poured out a healthy measure. He handed the thick glass to Justin, who took a taste, impressed. This was fine drink, not the rotgut he usually endured when he was sent to extract information from common men regarding the suitability of Philip's potential clients.

Lord Rockland poured himself a glass, then motioned for Justin to take a seat across from him. Once both men were settled, the duke wasted no time getting to the matter. 'A man like you with such a fine chaise must do well in business.'

'I do well enough,' Justin answered with a shrug. The chaise was Philip's. Justin had been forced to sell his to repay a few investors after the ship had gone down. The loss of his fine vehicle and the matching grey horses had hurt almost as much as the loss of his business.

'And what exactly is it you do?' Lord Rockland enquired.

'I'm in business with a man who loans clients money. I investigate the quality of their collateral and assist my employer in obtaining payment if their debt goes unpaid.'

'It certainly explains your skill with your fists.'

He pinned the duke with a sharp look. 'I don't extract payments in such a way. I use it to defend myself against uncalled-for attacks.'

'My apologies again for last night.' Lord Rockland swirled the brandy in his glass, then took a sip. 'Our emotions were running high after my daughter's ill-advised adventure. I'm afraid neither my son nor I was thinking straight.'

'I see.' Justin didn't, but he could play along. 'I don't intend to continue in my present occupation. I mean to establish myself as a wine merchant, once I have sufficient funds.'

It wasn't a subtle hint, but he wanted the man to come to the point. He didn't have time to lounge in Grosvenor Square, drinking a duke's brandy all day.

'I see.' The older man tapped the side of his glass. 'Then allow me to propose an offer, one, as a man of business, you're sure to appreciate.'

Justin took a deep drink, savouring the rich liquor, then set the glass aside. 'I'm listening.'

'As you might know from gossip, Miss Lambert is not my legitimate daughter.'

Justin hadn't known, nor did he care. Half the people he dealt with were born without the vicar's blessing. It didn't matter to him.

'Before her mother died, I promised to give Susanna a thousand-pound dowry if she married a gentleman I approved of,' Lord Rockland explained.

'How very generous of you.' And worrying. He was starting to wonder what exactly Lord Rockland intended to offer him.

'I'm a man who takes responsibility for my mistakes.' He enjoyed another sip before continuing. 'Susanna, as you might have noticed, is a headstrong woman who often acts before she thinks. It's made finding her a respectable husband difficult, even with the promise of her dowry. She nearly threw away the money last night with her impulsive behaviour and now I must hurry to rectify the situation before all is lost.'

'For you, or for her?' Justin asked, suspecting it wasn't the young lady Lord Rockland was worried about as much as the taint her escapade might leave on his family.

'For both of us, and you. I'm prepared to give you Miss Lambert's thousand-pound dowry if you agree to marry her.'

Justin stopped the glass halfway to his lips and stared at the man from across the aromatic brandy. 'You want me to marry your daughter?'

'Assuming you're not already married.'

'I'm not.' Justin frowned, the memory of Helena's rejection stinging as much as his knuckles after the beating he'd given Lord Sutton last night. Justin took a long drink, barely tasting it as it burned past his tongue. It was her loss, not his.

'Good. As a man of business, I'm sure you won't dismiss such a tempting offer so lightly and will keep the details of last night private. I possess grave concerns about Lord Howsham's ability to remain silent on the matter.' Lord Rockland sighed as though they were discussing a troublesome horse which wouldn't trot properly and not a young woman and her future. 'It's only a matter of time before Susanna's reputation is called into question and all chances of her making a more advantageous match are gone.'

Justin opened his fingers over the glass, then closed them, one by one, trying to ignore Lord Rockland's unintended insult. Justin was no nobleman's son, only the common son of a man who'd served Philip's father the same way Justin served Philip. Despite the way Justin's father and Helena derided him for wanting to be more, he wasn't about to make something of himself off the back of some young lady. 'She doesn't need a husband. She needs a better chaperon.'

Lord Rockland's chiselled cheek twitched. 'I don't think you clearly understand what I'm offering you.'

'I understand exactly. Money and a connection to the Rockland family. I know what these things are worth. I also understand the price your daughter would pay for me to obtain them. I won't ask it of any woman.'

Lord Rockland gaped at Justin as though it'd never occurred to him Justin might refuse what he considered a magnanimous gesture. 'I assure you, she's quite amenable to the idea.'

'You don't know me, she doesn't know me and neither of you know what kind of man I am.' Although Justin was coming to understand clearly what kind of family this was.

'From what I've seen, you're a man of honour and integrity who'll treat my daughter as well as any man is expected to treat his wife.'

Lord Rockland's love and concern for his child was enough to make Justin sick. 'No.'

'Perhaps if you were to speak to her, you might see how much you have in common?' Lord Rockland rose and strode to the door leading to an adjoining room and pulled it open. 'Susanna, please join us.'

'I'm afraid you're mistaken.' Justin stood. He had better things to do than sit here and humour this ridiculous idea.

Then, in a swish of silk skirts the young woman appeared and whatever it was he needed to do today was forgotten.

If Miss Lambert's eyes had captivated him in the dim light of the lanterns hanging from the trees above Vauxhall Gardens, in the sunlight, they blazed with a green which nearly knocked him out of his boots. She strode closer, sparing not a glance for her father, but focusing entirely on Justin. The rich chestnut hair framing her face bounced a touch with each step, making the soft ringlets graze the long line of her neck and high cheeks. He envied the curls, especially the one resting over the swell of her breast. The creaminess of her skin was just visible beneath the fine netting of her fichu while the rest of her supple roundness was covered by a brown-silk gown in a tone to match her hair. It heightened the colour of her skin with a warmth he longed to bury his face in and inhale.

Despite the allure of her full curves, it was her eyes

which continued to command him. They were intelligent, quick, hiding her thoughts, but telling him they existed, and not one was concerned with the frippery of dresses or gossip. She was playing the demure, dutiful daughter for her father's sake, but Justin caught the steely resolve beneath the polished manners. It was the will of a woman with a plan she was as eager to implement as Justin was to establish his wine business. She'd been foolish last night, but Justin sensed it was a momentary weakness, like his proposal to Helena or the five pounds he'd spent on a bottle of wine last week, or what he was very near to agreeing to do.

He settled his shoulders, determined to resist the fleeting temptation of an attractive woman, confident she couldn't change his mind about this match, even if the part of him low down wanted her to win him over.

'I'll leave you two to discuss the matter,' Lord Rockland offered.

The duke's words broke the spell cast by Miss Lambert's eyes.

'And then cry foul once the two of us are left alone. No, thank you,' Justin protested.

It wasn't the first time a father had tried to get him alone with his daughter in an attempt to snare her a husband.

'I won't cry foul. She's been compromised enough already,' Lord Rockland flung off as he slid the doors closed behind him.

'Quite a charming father you have there,' Justin remarked.

Miss Lambert dropped her hands from where she'd

been demurely holding them in front of her and rolled her pretty eyes. 'He's the envy of the *ton*.'

She walked over to the small selection of drinks and picked up the brandy. She splashed a tiny drop into a glass, then tossed back the contents, shivering as it went down.

If this was meant to shock Justin it did, but there was something in the confidence of her movement, the surety with which she was executing what he felt was a clear plan, he had to admire.

'Shall I pour you some more?' she asked.

'No.' He needed a clear head for this encounter. 'I gather you're in favour of your father's suggestion.'

She set the glass down with a clunk. 'How very intuitive of you.'

'It's part of my job to guess what people will do before even they know. It helps me to avoid trouble.'

Her full lips turned down at the corners. 'I'm not the trouble my father has made me out to be if that's what's worrying you.'

'I'm not worried about anything, since I have no intention of marrying you.'

'But you will.' She crossed her arms under her breasts and the slight rise of the full mounds was distracting.

'I assure you, I won't.' Justin forced himself to focus, surprised by the ease with which Miss Lambert affected him.

'I don't think you fully comprehend the benefits of the agreement.' She rolled one graceful hand in the air between them, her nails short and neatly buffed.

'Oh, Miss Lambert, trust me, I understand very well the benefits.' He caressed her lithe body with his eyes, following the faint trace of a small waist and rounded hips beneath the flowing dress. He took the last fortifying sip of brandy to ease the heat rising inside him. He needed to reason with his brain, not his member.

She squared herself at him, sure in herself and her goal. Her confidence was currently her most appealing and annoying trait. 'I heard most of the conversation between you and my father. I know you think I don't want this marriage, but I do.'

'You don't even know me. For all you know I could be a drunk who likes to beat women.'

'You aren't such a man. You have too much integrity. If you didn't, you'd have accepted my father's offer without bothering to talk to me, set a date for the wedding and rushed through to the bedding as fast as possible.'

Justin tipped his empty glass to her. She was flattering him, a somewhat effective tactic. 'Perhaps, but even with you standing here demanding we wed I won't take you.'

'What if I could be of use to you?'

He winked at her. 'I don't need to be married for that.'

She frowned then, the small pursing of her lips as tempting as the subtle rise and fall of her chest.

'I mean in business. I can make my father increase his offer, especially since he's so eager to be rid of me.' A pain Justin recognised rippled through her eyes. She wasn't alone in enduring the condemnations of a demanding and stubborn father. Justin knew a little something about it, too. 'A word of support from him will have clients lining up at your door.'

'I'm aware of this, Miss Lambert, but it's not so much the clients I'm worried about as it is my wife.' He set his glass down. 'I don't want to look around one day and find you back in Lord Howsham's bed or in some other man's.'

For the first time since she'd entered the room her eyes dropped from his and a flush of red washed over her creamy skin. Her shame didn't last as she raised her head to meet his gaze again with a will as seductive as the faint scent of jasmine gracing her skin. 'I don't blame you for being suspicious of me and my motives, so I'll be as honest with you as you've been with me. I didn't run after Lord Howsham out of lust. I did it because I believed he'd offer me the things Lord Rockland never has, the freedom of my own home and a place as something more than a bastard. You're worried I'll chase after every lord who comes my way. The truth is I want nothing more to do with any of them, not even my father. If you agree to the marriage, I will maintain contact with my father in an effort to help you. I could be quite an asset to your wine business.'

'What do you know of trade, Miss Lambert?' She didn't look like one to sit behind a counter all day or wander through a cellar in search of a bottle.

'My mother's family owned a wine shop in Oxfordshire. I assure you, I didn't spend my girlhood learning to draw on plates, but to manage customers, inventory and accounts at my mother's side. She was an excellent negotiator. It's how she managed to extract Lord Rockland's promise to support me, even after she passed.' She swallowed hard. Justin pitied her and wanted to reach out and take her in his arms to soothe her. His grief for his own mother was as raw as hers, but he didn't move. 'I can garner for you the same type of deal.'

'Can you now?' She was certainly more experienced in the wine business than he'd imagined. He wondered what other surprising traits and talents she possessed.

She strolled over to him, allure and innocence wrapped up in the slow swing of her hips. 'Judging from your willingness to start your own business, you're a man not averse to taking risks. A betting man as some might say.'

'I've been known to wager from time to time.' Justin remained still, as intrigued by her offer as he was tempted by her full lips and what they would feel like beneath his.

'Then let me offer you one now. I'll prove to you today I can be an asset to both you and your potential venture. If you're suitably impressed, you'll agree to my father's offer.'

'And if I'm not?' He was ashamed to admit it, but she was already halfway to impressing him up the church aisle. However, he wasn't ready to tie himself to this strange woman, not yet.

'Then you're free to go. I'll leave the decision up to you.'

* * *

Susanna waited for the tall gentleman with the brown hair to answer, ignoring how her chest caught every time his amber eyes caressed the length of her body. Lord Howsham's hurried, fumbling touch hadn't made her insides melt as they were doing now with Mr Connor standing mere feet away. He smelled of leather, sawdust and musk, a more masculine scent than the lemongrass preferred by the society fops. It wrapped around her, drawing her to him until she almost forgot it was she who was here to win him over. She was close, her victory revealing itself in the hold of his eyes on hers and the twitch of his jaw above his cravat as he struggled between detached uninterest and desire. For all his rejection of the proposal, he wanted her as much as Lord Howsham had, only this man possessed the self-control to deny himself. She wished Lord Howsham had done the same and not pressed her into an intimacy she hadn't truly wanted. However, if he'd shown some restraint, she wouldn't be in this position, with her freedom only a conversation away. 'What do you say, Mr Connor? Are you willing to accept my challenge?'

He settled his muscled thighs covered by buckskin breeches against the edge of a small table and crossed his arms over his wide chest, his ease of manner both annoying and rousing. He reminded her of a tiger she'd once seen at the Tower lounging in the sun, relaxed but laced with an edge of danger one could almost touch. 'How do you know I won't simply say I will and then walk away?'

'Because you're the kind of man who keeps his word once it's given.'

He tilted his head in silent agreement. 'Are you the kind of lady who keeps hers?'

'I am.' She raised her chin, determined, in spite of the actions which had landed her in this muddle, to demonstrate her integrity. She might have made a drastic misstep with Lord Howsham, but she wasn't a woman to cuckold a man or break her vow once it was given. 'I promise you, when I change your mind, you won't regret it.'

He tossed a cocky smile at her which made her toes curl in her half-boots. 'No, I don't believe I will.'

She held out her hand to him. 'Then we have a deal?'

He eyed her fingers with the same amusement he'd demonstrated during their entire discussion. Embarrassment eroded her confidence as her hand hung in the air waiting for him to take it. For all his glib light-heartedness, she sensed the serious streak lying just beneath the humour. He was considering her offer and whether or not she was worth the risk. He wouldn't be the only one taking a chance with this challenge. She would be, too, but it was worth it if it meant ending her time with the Rocklands and escaping the taint of being a mistake and an unwanted intrusion.

At last he slid his hand in hers, his hold hot and hard. Her heart began to race and she took a deep breath to steady herself, willing her body not to tremble. If he experienced any measure of the heat sliding through her at the joining of their skin, he didn't reveal it, his eyes crinkling at the corners with an enticing smile. How the woman who'd leapt from his carriage last night could have walked away from such an alluring man Susanna didn't know, but she was thankful she had.

'We do.' He smiled with a wickedness to nearly make her faint. 'Now do your best.'

Reluctantly, she let go of his hand and strode to the double doors, struggling to make each step sure and to not peek back at him. It felt too much like something Edwina would do in the presence of the Earl of Rapping, gazing longingly at him from across the theatre, making a fool of herself as she all but drooled over a man who barely acknowledged her existence. The same couldn't be said for Mr Connor. Without turning she knew he watched her and it gave an even greater purpose to her goal. If she succeeded, there'd be no need for all this girlish mooning about. She'd have the rest of her life to stare at his sharp cheeks and strong nose. It wasn't an unpleasant thought.

She gripped the brass handles hard, as much to steady herself against Mr Connor's influence as to prepare to face her father, and opened the doors. Everything depended on the success of what she was about to do. 'Father, please return, we have a few more things to discuss.'

'You've both seen the sense in the proposal, then?' Lord Rockland asked as he returned, appearing quite pleased with himself.

'Not until you agree to raise the dowry to two thousand pounds.'

This startled her father out of his usual imperiousness. 'One thousand pounds is a very generous offer.'

Clearly he hadn't intended to engage in a negotiation, but to hand her over to Mr Connor with little trouble and no further thought. She wouldn't allow him to get off so easily. He was the man who'd helped make her a bastard, now he'd make her a legitimate woman, but not without some pain.

'One thousand, five hundred, and you'll purchase the wine for Lady Rockland's masque from Mr Connor and see to it we're both invited so Mr Connor may make the connections necessary to ensure the growth of his trade.'

'Lady Rockland will never allow such a thing,' her father scoffed and she wasn't sure which he dreaded most, his wife's wrath or the thought of connecting himself so publicly with his potential merchant son-in-law.

'If you agree to this, in writing, I'll marry Mr Connor and create no stir which might result in a scandal where Lord Howsham is concerned.'

Tense silence settled over the room as her father mulled through the points of her demands. She slid a glance at Mr Connor. If her negotiations couldn't open his eyes to the benefit of having her as a wife and a partner in his business, nothing could. His admiration for what she'd done showed itself in the impressed half-smile he offered her. Freedom was within her grasp.

'All right, I'll do what you've asked.' Lord Rockland looked to Mr Connor. 'Are these terms amenable to you?'

She waited, hands tight at her sides for him to answer. It wasn't so much the thought of freedom which captured her now but the sun from the window illuminating his hair and falling over the tan wool of the jacket covering the width of his shoulders. She shivered a little at the sight of him, tall, solid, a rock of a man next to her father, yet with a humour to soften his edges. She'd witnessed his strength last night when he'd flattened Edgar, but he wasn't all unthinking, uncompassionate brawn. When her pain had welled up during their discussion, sympathy had whispered through his eyes. For reasons she couldn't explain, she knew he understood her loneliness, not in the mocking way Lord Howsham had pretended to understand, but in the way of a man who had shared something of the same kind of experience. If they married, she would come to know both the serious man and the one smiling at her father now, the one she desperately hoped would accept the offer.

'They are,' Mr Connor said at last. 'I will marry Miss Lambert.'

Susanna unclenched her hands, relief sweeping through her followed by a new anxiety that tightened her neck. Her course was set, for good or for bad. Mr Connor was right, she knew nothing about him, but he was now her intended and no matter what, she must make the best of things, although being with him would surely be better than staying here.

Mr Connor turned to her, gracious in his surrender. He reached for her hand, bending his tall frame as he slid his fingers beneath hers and brought them to his lips. He pressed the firmness of them against her skin, raising a chill which raced up her arm to crash inside her against the fire his gentle touch ignited. She'd never experienced such a reaction to a man and she rocked a touch before the squeeze of his fingers steadied her.

'I'll call for you later this afternoon for a carriage ride,' he offered, his breath whispering over the back of her hand.

'Please do.' She could barely utter the words through the dryness in her mouth. It wasn't like her to want a man so powerfully, not after the awkward way Lord Howsham had introduced her to the physical side of love, but Mr Connor was no Lord Howsham. There was tenderness beneath his teasing, something she'd never experienced with the earl. This man wouldn't be rough with her. It would be smooth and easy like sliding into the warm water of a bath.

'Until this afternoon.' At last he released her and with reluctance she lowered her hand, wanting him to take her from this house now, tonight, so she could delight in the fire filling his eyes and the comfort of his good nature.

Mr Connor left with more confidence than he'd entered with, when she'd watched him through the crack in the door, listening eagerly for what he might say.

'Well, there's one matter resolved,' her father sighed with relief once they were alone. Then he turned to her, his expression clouding with the disapproval he'd meted out to her last night. 'Now you've accepted Mr Connor, there'll be no calling off the wedding, no matter what happens, or I'll cast you out of this house without a penny. Do you understand?'

'I do.' She stared at Mr Connor's empty glass and the faint outline of his lips along the rim. In her desperation to escape the Rockland house, she'd misjudged Lord Howsham. She hoped she hadn't misjudged Mr Connor. If he proved even a tenth of the man she gauged him to be, he'd make a good husband. She'd do her best to deserve him and put all of the unfortunate incidents of the previous day, and her life, behind them.

Chapter Three

'Was your meeting with Lord Rockland a success?' Philip asked as Justin strode into his friend's study.

'You have no idea.' He explained to Philip the events of the interview. When he was done, he leaned back against the French door, feeling the sun warming his back through the glass. 'I suppose you think I'm crazy.'

'I'm the last person to judge a man for taking a wife so quickly, or for the most ephemeral of reasons,' Philip admitted from where he sat ramrod straight in the chair behind his desk. Philip had proposed to Mrs Rathbone after she'd held him at gunpoint demanding the return of some collateral. It'd been a strange start to a very successful marriage, one Justin hoped to emulate.

'Mr Connor, your father would like to see you in the morning room,' Chesterton, the Rathbones' butler, announced with more apology than efficiency. This wasn't the first time Justin's father had come here in search of him.

Justin looked at the liquor on the side table before eschewing the drink. Smelling alcohol on his breath would only give his father another reason to criticise him. 'I'll be back.'

He strode down the panelled hallway of the Rathbones' house which was situated in Bride Lane just off Fleet Street. Across the street, the bells of St Bride's church began to toll the noon hour. In a matter of days, he'd have his common licence and a date fixed at the church. It amazed him how the green-eyed hellcat had managed to snare him in a matter of minutes, though he'd rather be back with her than preparing to face the man pacing across the Rathbones' fine sitting-room rug.

Mr Green, the young man Justin paid to reside with his father and keep him out of trouble, sat on a bench near the front door. He jumped up at the sight of Justin. 'I'm sorry, Mr Connor, I tried to talk him out of it, but he insisted on coming here to see you.'

'It's all right, Mr Green. You do your best.' Justin waved the young man back on to the bench. It was hard for anyone to deal with his father, much less dissuade him from any course, including ruin.

''Bout time you came to me,' his father grumbled as Justin approached. 'Thought I was going to have to wait here all day.'

'And a good afternoon to you, too, Father.' He should have taken the drink.

'I waited all morning for you to come and tell Mrs Green to stop shoving those damned tonics on me, but you never showed.'

His father's housekeeper was a saint for putting up with him, as was her son.

'I'm sorry I failed to arrive for our appointment. I was meeting with a young lady and her father to finalise the details of our engagement.' There was no other way to make the announcement except the direct one. His father wasn't one for polite conversation, though once he'd been charming and suave, able to talk a stranger into buying him a drink as well as putting down the pistol when he and the elder Mr Rathbone had arrived to collect a debt.

'Finally making that little widow your wife, heh?'

'No. She's accepted a proposal from another man. I'm marrying Miss Susanna Lambert, the Duke of Rockland's illegitimate daughter.'

Shock lengthened the deep lines of his father's face before he drew them tight into his usual scowl. He marched up to Justin. He was a good head shorter than his son, but it didn't stop him from waving one thick finger in Justin's face.

'So a widow of your own class ain't enough for you—you want to raise yourself up. Think you're too important for your station and the life I've given you. Well, you aren't. Reach too high and you'll fall fast enough.'

'Your faith in me is astounding.' Justin laced his fingers behind his back. The insulting man was his father and he'd honour him, but no commandment could make him like him. The most he could do was tolerate him, much as he'd seen Miss Lambert tolerate her father. He'd admired and revered him once, but his father's acerbic tongue had killed those feelings ages ago.

'What have you ever done to give me faith in you except drink, lay about with easy widows and squander your money on ridiculous shipping schemes? How much of my blunt did you lose in that harebrained venture of yours?'

'Not one ha'penny. Now, as much as I'm enjoying this conversation, I must ask you to get to the point. Mr Rathbone and I have business to attend to this afternoon.'

'Well, la-de-da.' His father made a mock curtsy, his hands trembling as he held them out. It was lack of alcohol which made them shake, a situation he'd soon remedy. 'Knew sending you to school was a waste. I've come for money, since you think me too great a fool to manage it myself.'

Justin withdrew a few coins from his pocket and handed them to his father. He didn't bother to point out he was acting in his father's best interests. The older man wouldn't understand any more than he understood Justin's desire to emulate Philip and be more than another man's assistant.

'Taught ya' everything ya' know and this is how ya' repay me, handing out a pittance as if I was a child.' His father scowled as he plucked up the coins and shuffled into the hall. 'Come along, you,' he barked at Mr Green. 'No-good son of mine thinks he's better than his old father.'

A trail of mumbling curses followed him out the

door until Chesterton closed it and brought the noise to an end.

Justin turned his hand over, studying the dark bruises on his knuckles. He wasn't sure he should subject Miss Lambert to his father, but judging by the brief treatment he'd seen meted out to her by Lord Rockland, she more than anyone might sympathise with the necessity of managing a difficult relative.

'Is your father gone already?' Mrs Rathbone stepped into the sitting room, concern for Justin in her caring eyes. Her infant son slept on her shoulder, one small hand curled tight by his tiny mouth.

'Not even pleasant company with me could keep him from his other errands today,' Justin said glibly, hating to be pitied. This wasn't the first spat Mrs Rathbone had witnessed between father and son. They were a regular occurrence.

'You must recall the better times and ignore his taunts,' she urged, rubbing the sweet baby's back.

'I do.' He sighed out the lie, barely able to remember his father from before his mother's death. Afterwards, his father had turned to drink, growing more callous and quarrelsome with each passing year. It'd come to a head last summer when Justin had taken over the management of his father's finances after the older man had woken up in a ditch in Haymarket with no memory of the night before and a nasty bruise under one eye. His father had been so enamoured of his son's desire to help him, he'd turned on Justin like a wounded dog.

'I know he still loves you.' Mrs Rathbone laid an

encouraging hand on his arm. 'But he has his demons to struggle with.'

'Don't we all?' Justin flashed Mrs Rathbone a wide smile, stamping down on the anger and pain chewing at him.

'On a happier note, I understand congratulations are in order.' Mrs Rathbone beamed as her son snored lightly.

'Indeed they are. I'm about to join you and Mr Rathbone in wedded bliss.' Although the idea he might not enjoy a union as happy as theirs taunted him. Hopefully, the force to be reckoned with he'd witnessed this morning wouldn't turn into a haranguing fishwife once they were married. He could only tolerate one person calling him a failure at a time.

Mrs Rathbone tapped a finger to her chin. 'I understand it was a most peculiar proposal.'

Justin matched her sideways smile with one of his own. 'It wouldn't be the first in this house now, would it?'

'Certainly not.' Mrs Rathbone laughed, the cheerful sound driving away the curses still ringing in his ears and making the baby let out a small cry before he settled back to sleep. 'I only hope Jane doesn't surprise us like that some day.'

'If our examples are anything to judge by, I wouldn't be surprised if she did.' Jane, Philip's fourteen-year-old sister whom he had raised since their mother's death, was too precocious and sure of herself for her own good, just like her brother.

Philip stepped into the room, dressed in his redingote and carrying his walking stick. 'Shall we be off?'

'We shall.' A vintner had fled back to France to avoid repaying a loan. They were going to seize his stock, the wine which Justin would purchase from Philip and use to establish the business his father and Helena had so callously dismissed.

'Be careful,' Mrs Rathbone cautioned, squeezing Philip's arm.

'I always am.' Philip laid a kiss on his son's little forehead. Then he pressed his lips to his wife's, in no obligatory peck, but a deep meaningful kiss. Philip, the most rational man Justin knew, had raced headlong into his union and all had been well. Hopefully, Justin would enjoy the same luck in his hastily negotiated engagement.

Chesterton handed Justin his gloves and he tugged them on. He flexed his fingers beneath the supple leather and pushed away the memory of Miss Lambert's hand in his. She'd transfixed him as much with her ability to bargain as with her presence and the faint catch of her breath when they'd touched. As much as he enjoyed the charms of women, they usually didn't have such power to sway him. If they had, he'd have failed to seize half the collateral from Philip's clients. Yet with a few glances from beneath her dark eyelashes, and a walk to mesmerise him, she'd wrangled him into one of the most binding contracts he'd ever entered into. He looked forward to discovering more of her hidden charms.

He tapped the pistol in the leather holster beneath

his coat, the agitation biting at him fuelled by more than the task facing him and Philip. He didn't usually relish the physical aspects of his position as Philip's assistant, but today he wouldn't mind if a man took a swing at him and he could swing back. It would take a row, or an hour at his pugilist club, to work off the frustration from his encounter with his father, and the more pleasant tension roused by Miss Lambert.

He followed Philip to the waiting carriage, ready to be done with business and enjoy his drive with Miss Lambert. He wished to discuss with her tonight the vintner's inventory and his plans for it. She'd wrestled a duke for his support of Justin's venture while his own father and previous paramour had dismissed it. If nothing else, it was a positive omen for what their future life together might entail. She'd share his success and he would succeed, despite what anyone else believed.

'I think French silk would be beautiful for the dress,' Mrs Fairley, the young modiste, suggested as she draped a sample of the fine cream-coloured fabric over Susanna's shoulder.

'English silk will do,' Lady Rockland barked from her place on the sofa where she watched the fitting. Lady Rockland had grudgingly summoned the modiste at Lord Rockland's command to discuss Susanna's wedding dress and a suitable costume for the masked ball. If only he'd ordered her to be pleasant. 'The future wife of a merchant won't need such an expensive gown.'

'Yes, Your Grace.' Mrs Fairley folded the sample

and laid it with the others in her case. Lady Rockland hired Mrs Fairley to dress Susanna while she and Edwina patronised a much more fashionable and expensive French modiste.

Susanna exchanged an awkward glance with the comely Mrs Fairley, who blushed on her behalf. It wasn't the first time the kind young woman had witnessed this sort of conversation, but it would be the last. Even if Susanna's desire for freedom had made her misjudge Mr Connor, surely the life of a merchant's wife must be better than a duke's unwanted bastard daughter.

'I don't see why you're buying her a new dress for her marriage when one of her old ones will do for a wine merchant.' Edwina, Susanna's half-sister, selected another sweet from the box on her lap and popped it into her round mouth.

'He won't even be a merchant until he's received your father's money,' Lady Rockland was kind enough to point out, looking down her nose at a man she hadn't even met who probably had more honour in his right hand than she possessed in her entire stick-thin body.

'Then why are they coming to the masque?' Edwina whined, her exasperation as annoying as the way she chewed her sweet. 'We've invited no other common people.'

'It doesn't matter if they come. Everyone will be wearing masks—no one will recognise them anyway,' Lady Rockland explained, as though Susanna were not standing in her suddenly too-tight stays and chemise right in front of them.

'I hear Cynthia Colchester is going to have the finest French silk gown and a ceremony in St George's in Hanover Square.' Edwina licked the tips of her fingers with a smacking noise before smiling smugly at Susanna.

'She's having it because her family can afford it, unlike her husband-to-be. Lord Howsham is up to his neck in gambling debts and on the verge of losing his estate.' Susanna bit down on her irritation at her half-sister. It was she and not Lord Howsham who'd gained the most from him breaking his promise. He'd wanted her money; now he had someone else's.

'He still has his title, as does his wife, which is more than some people possess.' Edwina smirked, her pudgy face squishing up with her arrogance.

'Edwina, leave us,' Lady Rockland commanded.

'Whatever for?' Edwina rubbed a bit of marchpane from her cheek.

'Don't question me,' the duchess snapped.

Edwina, who was only one year younger than Susanna's twenty, stomped from the room like a toddler.

Lady Rockland didn't dismiss Mrs Fairley, who knelt on the floor packing up her box. The woman was too far beneath Lady Rockland's notice for her to believe whatever she was about to say needed to be kept from her.

Susanna prepared herself, imagining this exchange would be no more pleasant than any of their previous encounters. Her expectations weren't disappointed.

'Given your behaviour with Lord Howsham, I assume I needn't tell you what will pass between you and your husband on your wedding night,' Lady Rockland blurted out with all the concern of a fish.

Mrs Fairley paused in her packing before returning to her work.

'My mother was kind enough to explain it to me when I was thirteen, before she died,' Susanna answered, the idea of this woman acting in any kind of motherly way as revolting as her haughty attitude.

'Yet another of the many mistakes she made in regards to you, mistakes others are now forced to endure.' Lady Rockland screwed up her face as if smelling something foul. 'When you and Mr Connor are wed, and after the masque, don't think you'll be allowed back into this house. I've endured the shadow of Lord Rockland's marital weakness and been forced to parade it in front of all of society for the past seven years. I won't do it any longer.'

'You needn't worry. I won't pollute myself with the taint of society by coming back here as a married woman.'

The duchess's lips drew back across her teeth. 'Oh, you'll come crawling back eventually. Men of Mr Connor's class never forget where they can obtain money, but you've both got all you're going to get out of Lord Rockland. I'll see to it you don't get a shilling more.'

Her imperious dictate given, Lady Rockland gathered up the hem of her skirt and swept from the room.

Susanna let out a low, frustrated sigh. If she could pack up her things and make for Scotland tonight. she would, but Mr Connor had been guaranteed her father's help and she'd make sure the duke kept his word.

Then she'd do everything she could to help Mr Connor succeed and prove Lady Rockland's nasty prediction wrong. She only needed to bear this a little while longer, then she'd be free of the woman for good.

'Congratulations on your engagement,' Mrs Fairley offered as she rose. 'Did Lady Rockland say you were to marry a Mr Connor?'

'I am.'

'Is he the associate of Mr Rathbone, the money-lender?'

'I believe so.' They hadn't discussed many details of their lives and, in fact, she knew very little about him except for his ambition in the wine trade and his willingness to accept a deal on which both of their futures hinged.

'I'm familiar with the man and his employer and they're both very honourable gentlemen.' She picked up her case, holding it in front of her. 'You'll be very happy with him.'

'Thank you. I'd like to retain your services, if I can, when I leave here.'

'I should like that.' With a polite curtsy which made her light-gold curls bob, Mrs Fairley took her leave.

Susanna slipped on her banyan and began to pace. It boded well that Mrs Fairley thought highly of Mr Connor. During the fittings in which Lady Rockland had been absent, Susanna had shared many confidences with the young woman who understood as well as Susanna what it was like to be looked down on by a duchess. The modiste was the closest person to a friend Susanna possessed. Lady Rockland had seen to it there were no other people on whom Susanna could hang the title.

Despite the fact she'd lived with the Rocklands since her mother's death, they'd only grudgingly treated her as a member of the family within their home. Outside of it, she was virtually ignored. At the few teas or country parties she'd been allowed to attend, the duchess had always given her strict instructions to keep her mouth shut and make herself as invisible as possible. It wasn't the most ideal way to forge friendships with other young ladies, though most daughters of the other country families didn't deign to talk to her. They were too afraid the taint of bastard would rub off on them to attempt so much as a discussion of the weather with Susanna.

She went to the wardrobe and began to rifle through her dresses, looking for one to wear for tonight's ride, as eager to see Mr Connor as she was to escape this house for an hour or two. She'd thought of little besides him since he'd taken his leave this morning, and had eaten even less at nuncheon than she'd been able to choke down over the last two weeks. It wasn't just his commanding presence or the deep roll of his voice, which was both powerful and playful, but what the agreement they'd entered into meant. She'd be his wife, his property as much as a helpmate in his business.

Her body would be his, though she doubted he'd fall on her as Lord Howsham had done in the forest at Rockland Place. There'd been something distasteful in Lord Howsham's pressing need for intimacy and the speed with which he'd slaked his lust and left her confused and wanting. Mr Connor wouldn't rush through the bedding; she'd felt it in the smooth slide of his hand beneath hers, the gentle pause when his lips had met the back of her hand and the drawing humour in his eyes which had invited her, instead of forcing her, to think of what was to come.

She clutched the dress to her chest, shivering at the idea of his broad chest and flat stomach against her skin, wondering what it would be like to linger with him in the dark, the sheets tangled around them as their bodies melded together. Though there was more to a marriage than the bedchamber to consider. The hours between rising and sleep were long ones in which a man could ignore his wife, much as Lord Rockland did to his, giving rise to a bitterness of spirit Susanna had felt the brunt of many times.

She sagged down onto the edge of her bed, releasing her tight grip on the muslin. With any luck, the isolation she'd known at Lady Rockland's hands and the indifference of her father were about to end, assuming Susanna hadn't made a grave mistake. Even if she'd chosen poorly and Mr Connor turned into a monster, she'd have to stand beside him at the altar or find herself penniless on the London streets.

Rising, she rang the bell for her lady's maid, ready to dress and face her intended. This wasn't a poor choice, but the best she could make. She'd have a home of her own and a respectable husband and at last a station in society where people couldn't look down on her or whisper behind her back. She'd already proven to Mr Connor she could be useful to him and had gained something of his admiration. If he never grew to love her, or even cherish her, she'd at least earn his respect. It was the most a bastard like her could hope for in a marriage. If something more came of their union, it would be a gift of providence, although providence had never been so generous to her before.

Chapter Four

'I believe you have no more business here with the family, sir.' The balding butler looked down his crooked nose at Justin as though he'd been discovered sleeping on the Duke of Rockland's front step. Apparently, between this morning and this afternoon, the family had failed to inform the man of Justin's change in status or his appointment to ride with Miss Lambert.

'Miss Lambert is expecting me.' He tried to step around the lanky man who shuffled to stay in front of him. This wasn't the first time a servant had tried to rebuff him at the front door. Usually it meant their master was slipping out the back with the best of his goods, where Justin's men were sure to be waiting for him.

'Let him in, Netley. Mr Connor and Miss Lambert are engaged.' Lady Rockland's voice slid out from behind her dedicated servant, the announcement made with as much enthusiasm as if Justin had arrived to clean the chimneys.

Netley offered no congratulations, but grudgingly stepped aside to allow Justin entrance.

Justin dismissed the overly pompous fop whose pedigree was probably no better than his and approached the duchess. She stood on the landing in the middle of the grand marble staircase like a crow on a gable, her dark dress as thin as the risers were high. 'Your Grace.'

He swept off his hat and bent into a deep, well-executed bow. When he straightened, she arched one eyebrow at him, betraying her surprise at his manners. More than likely she'd expected to find a lout with the grease of his cart and the smell of fish clinging to his coat. Ah, the better sort were such a charming lot. 'I've come to take Miss Lambert for a drive.'

The woman's gaze shifted from Justin to the large windows on either side of the door. Outside sat Philip's curricle with the hood down, the chestnut horse pulling it held by a well-tipped boy. There was nothing about the vehicle to bring down the tone of the house or the occupants. Again Lady Rockland's eyebrow twitched and Justin wondered if she'd swoon from the shock of having her lowered expectations so utterly confounded. An examination of the tall woman with the rigid back, square chin set in a long face and hair arranged in tight rows of curls against the front of her head told him she wasn't a swooner, but a silent striker. Like a snake, this lady would take a quick bite, then slither off to let her wounded victim suffer a slow death. A most charming woman.

'Good afternoon, Mr Connor.' A more melodious

voice carried over the crow's stony silence as Miss Lambert came down the stairs. The pale blue muslin swung about her thighs as she moved and the pastel colour heightened the subtle hue kissing her cheeks. Pert breasts gave shape to the fitted bodice of a matching blue spencer which was cut away at the chest before dipping in to fasten just under those tantalisingly full mounds. Elegance marked her movements, but something of Lady Rockland's lineage was missing, betraying a childhood spent among more humble people, her airs and graces learned too late to make them completely natural. Still they captivated Justin, weaving a spell around him which took away his speech and all awareness of Lady Rockland eyeing him as though he were a rat about to be smacked with a broom.

'Miss Lambert.' Justin bowed again, but more shallowly this time, unwilling to cease watching her.

She paused and reached for the banister as if to brace herself before she pulled back her hand and resumed her steady descent. With each drop to the next step, the curls along the arch of her neck just peeking out from beneath her bonnet shivered and he flexed his fingers, envious of the way the locks brushed her smooth skin.

Lady Rockland was not so enamoured of her ward's regal entrance and scowled at her as Miss Lambert passed by on the way down. Miss Lambert met the woman's contemptuous sneer with a challenging glance of her own. To Justin's astonishment, it was the duchess who flinched first.

Justin nodded his silent congratulations to Miss Lambert. She lifted her chin a touch, taking on an air of confidence, but the shift of her green eyes betrayed the vulnerability he'd caught in his conversation with her earlier. In a flash, compassion rose up to overwhelm his desire. He'd been like her once, trying to appear brave while struggling to stand firm against those who wanted to tear him down, especially his father.

'Shall we?' Justin proffered his elbow when she reached him.

'Please.' Miss Lambert laid a gloved hand on his arm, the expectation in her wide eyes helping him to dismiss his sour memories. He'd learned long ago to laugh and not care what others thought.

'Try not to embarrass the family while you're out,' Lady Rockland warned as she snatched up the edge of her skirt, flung it behind her and flitted off to whatever business consumed her day.

'I'm sorry,' Susanna mumbled, the excitement fading from her bright eyes as they left the house. The door nearly slammed shut behind them, Netley clearly as eager as his employer to see the back of them.

'Don't be. It's not your fault her curls are too tight.'

Miss Lambert hid a subdued laugh behind one gloved hand and Justin was heartened by the return of her cheer. Whatever her treatment at the Rocklands' hands, it hadn't destroyed her spirit, or her sense of humour. It would be an interesting challenge to draw it out fully, as intriguing as the promise of her alluring curves beneath the straight dress.

* * *

The sunshine piercing the trees along the front path spread over Susanna, melting away the chill of the Rockland house. Despite having more fireplaces than servants, the stone mausoleum was never warm and neither was the company it kept. In the fresh air, Susanna felt as if she could breathe at long last, though Mr Connor's arm beneath her hand and his tall figure beside her made each breath shallow and unsteady.

'Lady Rockland is quite the charming lady,' Mr Connor remarked as he helped Susanna into the vehicle.

She gripped his hand tightly, more to steady herself from the surprise rocking of her body in his presence than at the twitching springs of the chaise. 'She was practically polite today, though once we're wed, I don't think we'll have many dealings with her.'

If it wasn't for the promise she'd extracted from her father to help Mr Connor, she doubted she'd ever see her father again after the wedding. It wouldn't surprise her. Her grandfather and uncle had breathed a sigh of relief when Lord Rockland had arrived to take her away the day after her mother's funeral. They'd washed their hands of her, just as Lady Rockland would. Susanna didn't give a fig about the duchess, but her grandfather and uncle's utter rejection, after she'd been raised in their presence, had nearly shattered her already mourning heart.

'I assume, then, we won't have to entertain august guests at Christmas?' Mr Connor climbed in beside her, raising her mood despite the old pain biting at her.

It felt good to laugh with someone who wasn't afraid to poke fun at her dour relations. It was a refreshing change to the parade of sycophants who usually wandered into the house.

'I don't think we'll tarnish our dining room with their company.'

'Good, because I hadn't intended on purchasing a new dinner service this year.'

He winked at her, then snapped the reins over the horse's back, urging the fine animal into motion. While he focused on the traffic filling the street, she studied him. A fawn-coloured coat and matching hat set off those teasing brown eyes which had nearly made her stumble on the marble staircase. However, it was the approving nod he'd tossed at her when she'd silently challenged Lady Rockland's sneer which had filled her with more delight than the sight of his light grey breeches stretching over his strapping thighs. This near-stranger had supported her more in one moment than anyone had in the seven years she'd lived with the Rocklands. She drew her spencer a little tighter over her chest, chilled to realise how narrowly she'd missed being tethered to Lord Howsham, who held as little regard for her as anyone else in her life. The promise of freedom from the Rocklands must have been overwhelming to make Susanna ignore all of Lord Howsham's faults. Hopefully, it wasn't blinding her to Mr Connor's.

'Speaking of dining, my friends, the Rathbones, have offered to host the wedding breakfast. We're to join them for supper tomorrow night. They're eager to meet you.'

'I'd be delighted to meet them.' And nervous. As much as society looked down on her, those of the class she'd been born to were usually more vocal in their disapproval of her. For Justin's sake, she hoped his friends would at least be grudgingly cordial and save their most cutting remarks for after she left. It didn't matter what they said about her behind her back. She was used to the whispering and it had lost most of its sting long ago.

'They aren't the only ones I intend to introduce you to before the wedding.' He shifted his feet against the boards and for the first time in their brief acquaintance, she suspected he might be nervous. It didn't seem possible, and yet if she were permitted to wager on it, she felt sure she would win. 'I'd like to introduce you to my father.'

She wondered what it was about his father that disturbed his ease, though she could well imagine. There was little chance of mentioning anyone in her family without it setting her teeth on edge. 'I'd be honoured to meet him. I'm curious about the man who's given you your jovial attitude.'

'It wasn't him. That came from my mother. She died when I was fifteen and my father's good nature died with her.' The small lines between his eyes deepened with a pensiveness she hadn't thought possible as he explained how he'd gained control of his father's affairs and how ungrateful his father had been afterwards.

Then the story ended and with it Justin's seriousness, which was replaced by a devil-may-care attitude which piqued her curiosity. To all, it appeared as if he didn't possess a single concern, but no amount of flippancy could completely conceal how deeply his father troubled him, or the hole his mother's death had left in his life. She knew about such grief; she still lived with it, too. 'You'll see what an amiable fellow my father is when you meet him. Prepare to be charmed. He's more Lady Rockland than Father Christmas and I won't be shocked if he makes you cry off.'

Her hands curled tight over the edge of the seat as he merged the curricle into the crush on Park Lane. 'I won't cry off and you needn't worry about me meeting your father. I'm used to dealing with difficult relations, Mr Connor.'

'I'm glad to hear it because I need you.' He slowed the horse as they made a wide turn on to Kensington Gore. 'And please, call me Justin. Mr Connor reminds me too much of my father.'

'And you may call me Susanna.'

He slid her a charming smile. 'A pretty name for a pretty woman.'

His compliment shocked her, adding to her alarm as he turned the curricle into Rotten Row. 'No, we can't go in there.'

'Why not? You're a duke's daughter. I thought the toffs loved to see the high born's progeny paraded about.'

If it weren't for the boning in her too-tight stays, she'd have slumped with her displeasure. 'Not the illegitimate ones, at least not without his Grace present to keep the daughters' tongues firmly in their heads.'

His curricle joined the stream of carriages entering the park and driving down the wide, dirt path. Mr Connor sat up straighter in the seat, motioning at her to do the same, seemingly oblivious to everything but the direction of his horse and the ribbons in his wide gloved hands.

Susanna tugged her small hat a little further down over her forehead, wishing the brim curled like a poke bonnet instead of up to reveal her face. At least then she might tilt her head and hide behind the straw.

'If you continue to pull on your bonnet, you'll tear it,' Mr Connor chided her good-naturedly.

She let go of the brim. 'We shouldn't be here. People are staring.'

She had no desire to be made a spectacle of, especially not with Edgar riding by and scowling at them as though they were beggars who'd happened in on his supper and didn't belong here. She didn't. She didn't belong anywhere.

'I'm not surprised since I'm alongside the most beautiful woman in the park.'

Her heart fluttered at the compliment. It wasn't flung off or studied as Lord Howsham's flattery had been when he'd worked to seduce a naive young woman starving for attention.

Then four young married women passed by in a landau, gaping wide-eyed at her before dipping their heads together to whisper.

'Ignore them. They mean nothing to us,' Justin instructed.

'Then why are we here?'

'I want you to enlighten me about these people. I know many wealthy merchants. It's my acquaintance with the better sort which is lacking.'

'I'm not sure what I can tell you. I don't really know them any better than you do.' Invitations weren't regularly extended to bastards, no matter how influential their father.

'I'll wager when you're sitting silently in your fearsome stepmother's midst, she talks past you to her husband, or her friends as if you weren't there. During those conversations, some interesting things must slip out.'

'Careful, you lost our last wager,' she warned with a smile.

'I don't see it as a loss, but a very interesting gain.' He turned the horse to avoid an oncoming phaeton with its hood open and its springs strained by the very rotund Lord Pallston.

'I thought these people meant nothing to us,' she challenged.

'Their sensibilities don't, but their business does. If I can claim one or two great men as clients, it might ensure our success.' It surprised her how easily *our*, instead of *mine*, rolled off his tongue. 'Now tell me, who's the round gentleman driving the phaeton as ruddy as his nose? He looks like a man whose thirst could make a wine merchant rich.'

'I thought you already possessed means.'

'I used to possess a great deal more before my last venture sank.' The humour in his eyes hardened, telling her all she needed to know about his last attempt at business. It was admirable of him to keep trying, despite what must have been a considerable setback, and it was more than those around them were capable of doing. It was another trait she and Justin shared—the ability to pick themselves up and continue on. The alternative was too upsetting to consider.

'He won't make you rich. He's Lord Pallston and he doesn't pay his debts. Few of these great men do. They pride themselves on owing almost every merchant in London.'

Justin rubbed his chin thoughtfully. 'I know something of collecting debt. I haven't let a man run out on Mr Rathbone yet.'

'It's not worth the effort or the uncertainty. My grandfather was foolish enough to deal with men like Lord Pallston. All they did was drink the wine while we watched our dinners grow thinner and the bills go unpaid.' She hated to disappoint Justin's ambition, but if the business was to be hers, too, she knew better than to build their hopes for success on the fickleness or insolvency of the peerage. A need for money often played a part in all these people's decisions, including Lord Howsham's, whose debt was about to consume his family estate. She hoped it did. He deserved to be ruined.

Susanna warning him off pursuing the nobility as clients wasn't what Justin wanted to hear. If the voice saying it wasn't so sweet he might have disregarded it, but he understood her reasoning. Philip employed the same logic, rarely lending to great men. When he did, it was only after they'd laid out the silver for Philip to hold until their debt was paid. Justin wasn't likely to convince any lord to leave a soup tureen as collateral for wine, not when there were a hundred other merchants willing to risk bankruptcy to supply a peer with his Madeira. He'd planned on using Lord Rockland's influence to bolster his name and perhaps even match Berry Bros. in their success. Now it was clear this part of his business plan might not work as he'd expected.

With one avenue to expand his trade quickly narrowing, the idea he might not succeed in this venture as his father and Helena believed drifted over him like the faint notes of Susanna's jasmine perfume, only rather less pleasant. He flicked the reins and guided the horse past a lumbering town coach. No, he would succeed and damn his father and Helena. Justin's desire to capture the business of the *haut ton* through Susanna might come to nothing, but it didn't mean he didn't have more plans or other possible clients. There wasn't a pub owner or merchant near Fleet Street he hadn't had some dealings with and most of them were pleasant. He'd make a go of this if he had to call on every man who owed him a favour from here to Cheapside.

'Does your grandfather still have his shop?' Justin asked with some hope for his own venture. It might be good to have contacts outside London.

'I don't know, though if he and my uncle were on

the verge of sinking, I'm sure they'd deign to write to me begging for money, and to remind me how much I owe them for all of their years of *kindness*. They'll get nothing if they ever show up on my doorstep.'

'They sound as warm as mounting blocks.' Justin laughed.

'Just like the Rocklands.' She sighed.

'I'm curious—why did Lord Rockland take you in instead of placing you with another family?' He pulled on one rein to make the horse turn at the end of the row. 'I have a difficult time believing Lady Rockland was amenable to the idea.'

'I've never really asked.' She shrugged. 'Out of gallantry, perhaps, or a desire to prove he's so far above everyone else he can claim paternity to any child he's sired no matter how much it irritates his wife or shocks his peers.'

'I imagine Grosvenor Square was alight with other grand ladies warning their husbands not to follow Lord Rockland's lead.'

'And children of questionable parentage all over London breathed a sigh of relief at not being thrust into this world, always hovering on the fringes, a lady and yet not a lady, a duke's daughter and his bastard all at the same time.'

'You aren't to refer to yourself in such a way. Do you understand?' He refused to hear her speak so meanly of herself.

'But it's what I am and how everyone here and in Oxfordshire has always seen me.' Her green eyes clouded with a loneliness he understood. He knew what it was like to be derided by those who should care for you the most. 'It's how Lord Howsham viewed me.'

'Hang Lord Howsham and all these idiots. It's not how I see you or how I want you to view yourself. You're my affianced and very soon to be my wife, a respectable woman who no one has the right to look down on.'

She tugged at the bonnet ribbons beneath her pert chin. 'About Lord Howsham. I think I should explain.'

'No, I don't want to know. Neither of our past amours interest me.' He gathered her time with the earl hadn't been good and, despite never having met the man, Justin wanted to pound his face for the insults he'd heaped upon Susanna. How he could have abandoned such a woman, especially after the promises he'd made, he didn't know. It didn't bode well for his honour, or that of any other man of his class.

Justin settled his shoulders and his hackles, allowing the more pleasant sensation rising beneath to come over him. He wished he had a man to drive them so he could sit with Susanna and bask in her intelligent eyes and the way she admired him with respect and interest no other woman had ever shown.

If they weren't sitting in view of all of Hyde Park, he'd lean across the bench, take her parted lips with his and shock everyone passing in their carriages. He was tempted to bring the curricle to a halt near the line of trees, place his hands around her trim waist to help her down, and then feel the curve of her breasts against his chest as he led her behind a tree while he freed her hair from the bonnet. It was a giddy, boyish desire, one she'd sparked the moment she'd appeared at the top of the stairs. He hadn't experienced a craving like this since his youth and it filled him with an anticipation he'd never known with a woman before, one he wasn't about to act on.

Soon she'd be his wife and they'd be free to take their pleasure at their ease. He'd make her sigh with passion instead of sadness. She wasn't a jaded widow or spurned paramour, but a lonely woman in need of affection. He'd see to it she had what she needed both in body and spirit. He looked forward to drawing out the bold woman who'd faced him yesterday, instead of the unsure, hesitant one sitting beside him today.

Susanna stared out at the passing carriages, thankful Justin didn't intend to press her or judge her for her mistake with Lord Howsham. Justin's lack of interest in the matter wiped the slate clean. If only she could brush away the nasty chalk marks of her illegitimacy and the way it tainted her in the eyes of everyone riding past. Justin might urge her to think more of herself, but after a lifetime of being reminded of a sin of which she was not guilty, she couldn't simply put it aside. The taint was too much a part of her, like her hair colour or eyes, although perhaps in time, with his help she could forget it.

She slipped Justin a curious look, admiring how straight he sat on the seat, the edge of a smile drawing up the corners of his mouth until it seemed he might whistle in delight. Despite his joy, he wasn't some silly lout with more fluff than brains, or a thug for his employer who thought of nothing more than his own pleasure. There was a depth to him she'd caught earlier in the mention of his father, and again just now, a sense of honour and loyalty to those in his charge, including her.

'When do you think we'll wed?' She was eager for the date to be set and the vows to be spoken, suddenly afraid something would rise up to take this opportunity and the happiness it offered away from her.

'Eager for the wedding night, are we?' His subtle, teasing words curled around her and sparked an excitement deep inside her she hadn't experienced since the time she'd stood alone in the woods with Lord Howsham. With the earl there'd been an edge of uncertainty and danger. With Justin, it was like craving the cool rush of water over burning skin on a hot day. It made her bold and she tilted her head, eyeing him through her lashes.

'Among other things.'

'Such as?' He glanced at her from beneath the shadow of his hat and she licked her lips. She *was* eager for the wedding night, though she didn't want to appear like some hussy and admit it, not in the middle of Rotten Row.

'Having my own house,' she announced wistfully. 'It'll be nice to belong somewhere instead of being made to feel as if I'm some unwanted guest by the Rocklands, and even by my mother's family.'

The admission itself shamed her as much as the ease with which she'd made it. It wasn't like her to air her grief because there was never anyone there to listen, or to care, but something about Justin made it difficult for her to be reserved.

'You'll never be unwanted at my house, though it isn't as grand as your father's.'

'It could be a hovel for all I care.'

'It's not quite so humble.' He laughed, his good mood lifting hers. 'But it needs a woman's touch.'

'I don't wish to intrude on your space.' Outside of the colour Lady Rockland and Edwina's rooms were painted, her father had rarely allowed Lady Rockland any say in the decor or even the management of the four houses he owned. It was another of the many things which stuck in the woman's craw and increased her bitterness.

'Intrude all you want, except in my study.' He slowed the horse as they made a turn, his mastery of the ribbons as appealing as his confidence in the seat and his openness with her. 'A man has to have his space, just as you'll have a room of your own to do with what you please. I want you to be happy with me and for us to work together in both our home and the business.'

'Thank you.' She settled her hands in her lap, fingering the fine embroidery on the back of her glove. Of all the things she must soon become accustomed to, his concern for her, not just his physical desire, would be the most difficult. She would offer him the same regard, although it wouldn't come as easily to her as it did to him. She'd spent so many years hardening herself against attacks, it was difficult to imagine letting down her guard enough to trust another person with her life and possibly her heart, but she must. He offered her a future free of guilt and derision, a future she never could have imagined before today. She would do everything she could to be worthy of it and embrace the life he promised her.

Darkness began to settle over the city as Justin strolled with Philip through the warehouse set on the banks of the Thames. They examined the casks and bottles they'd seized from the vintner earlier in the day. There hadn't been time before Justin's appointment with Susanna for them to take stock of what was about to become Justin's first inventory. Mr Tenor walked behind them, listening and observing as always. Before Justin's ship had faltered, he'd been training Mr Tenor to take his place as Philip's assistant, much to the elder Mr Connor's grief. Justin's father had served the elder Mr Rathbone faithfully, prospering under the family as Justin had done, but Justin wanted more for himself and some day his own son. However, judging by the quality of the casks, it would be a while before Mr Tenor received his promotion.

'The vintages aren't as good as I'd hoped.' Justin frowned as he held up the lantern to read a label. When the vintner had run off to escape his debt, he must have taken the best of his stock with him.

'There are a few fine ones here.' Philip examined the bottles packed in straw in a crate. 'They should turn a nice profit.'

'Not as nice as I'd like. I can sell the rest to public houses and a few merchants of less discerning taste.'

It wouldn't bring in the money he needed. Those funds would come from Lord Rockland's order for the masque and whatever other great men's wishes Justin could fulfil. Despite Susanna's wariness about cultivating some of the peerage's patronage, he hadn't given up entirely on the idea.

'When I have the shop, I'll have you transfer these to it,' he instructed Mr Tenor.

'Yes, sir,' the brawny man answered, scratching at the holster and pistol under his thick arm.

Justin looked over the casks. To his amazement, he was more excited for his upcoming nuptials than this first foray into his new venture. The afternoon with Susanna had been far more pleasant than he'd expected, her humour and plain speaking as charming as it was captivating. He wished he hadn't needed to cut their drive short, but there was as much business to see to as pleasure. Very soon there'd be a wonderful meeting of both.

'When will you have the building?' Philip asked as they stepped out into the misty night and Mr Tenor locked up the warehouse.

'In a few days.' With it would go the last of the money the sea hadn't claimed. If he couldn't make a go of the business, he could sell the building, hopefully at a profit. If his losses were too large, he'd be forced to continue in Philip's employ. It had taken a great deal for Justin to swallow his pride and apply to his friend when failure had beset him the last time. It wasn't an option he wished to entertain now, no matter how much he admired Philip.

'Do you need any assistance?' Philip asked tactfully as they strolled to the waiting carriage. Mr Tenor fell back to the cart where the other men who worked for Philip transferring goods stood smoking pipes and chatting.

Justin rested his hands on his hips and pushed back the edges of his coat, revealing the butt of the pistol in its holster beneath the wool. Though Philip would never allow him to fall into debtors' prison, or worse, Justin wanted to be his own man and emulate his friend's success through his own efforts. 'You helped me enough the last time and lost a pretty penny in the bargain. I won't put your money at risk again.'

Nor would he risk Susanna's dowry until it was absolutely necessary. He wouldn't use it to fund his business, but keep the money safe. It would be a hedge against his losses, protection against total ruin in case nature decided to flatten his business with a grape blight or a sudden fire. Remaining on land was no guarantee one wouldn't be sunk.

'Bastard, you ruined me.' A man's voice rang out from the deep shadows between the buildings.

They whirled to see a man rushing at them, pistol raised. His face was black with grime and his long hair reached down to touch the dirty red soldier's coat with its black shoulder boards.

Justin stepped in between his unarmed friend and the man, brandishing his weapon. 'Move an inch closer and I'll take the top of your head off.'

The man jerked to a halt, fear widening his eyes. Justin recognised him as a bookseller who'd used Philip's loan for drink instead of paying off his debt and whose business had failed last year. He'd since accepted the king's shilling to feed himself and apparently to buy more gin. Justin could smell it over the stench of the river.

'I'll kill you both for what you did to me.' The man kept the pistol aimed at them, refusing to back down, too drunk to be afraid.

'Drop your weapon and walk away and we'll all forget this ever happened,' Justin suggested, not wanting trouble with either this man or the constable.

'Not until you've paid for ruining me.'

Justin squeezed the trigger of his gun. In an explosion of smoke and noise the ball fired, skimming the man's shoulder and tearing off one black shoulder board, but leaving him unscathed.

The man's face went white in the moonlight as he pressed his free hand to the hole in his uniform, amazed to find himself unharmed.

'You missed,' he jeered with a high, nervous laugh.

'I hit exactly what I aimed for and it wasn't your head,' Justin corrected as he exchanged his empty pistol for Mr Tenor's loaded one and levelled it at the man. 'Now, I'm aiming at your forehead. Put your weapon down, or I'll put a ball through it.'

The man blanched and the end of his pistol began to shake. Justin tightened his grip on his weapon, afraid the man's fear would trigger his gun. He'd drop the man with a shot before risking it if he didn't surrender soon.

At last, reason seemed to overcome the bookseller's

muddled senses and he threw the pistol down and bolted into the darkness.

'Should we go after him, sir?' Mr Tenor asked.

'No, he won't be back.' Experience told him when a man had been scared off his taste for revenge. He lowered his weapon and strolled over to snatch up the pistol from the puddle it'd fallen into. Shaking off the water, he handed it to Mr Tenor. 'Unload it, then give it to one of the men.'

'Yes, sir.'

Without a word, Justin and Philip made for the carriage. Once they were inside, the driver set the vehicle in motion.

'Thank you again,' Philip said across the semi-darkness, his voice as even as ever though a certain strain lingered in his tone.

It was always a challenge to shake off the anxiety after an incident, but it'd never clung to either of them quite like this before. Usually Justin would make a joke or comment to break the tension, but nothing came to him tonight. It wasn't just his future wrapped up in this kind of encounter now, but Susanna's, too. Once they were married, he couldn't be so casual about being on the wrong end of a pistol.

'How do you handle it, now you have a wife?' Justin asked.

'I've surrounded myself with exceptional people. You'll do the same in your business.'

Justin pressed his fist to his chin and stared out of the window as the warehouses along the Thames gave way to the dark shops and houses. One of those bow-front windows glittering with wares would soon be his and it couldn't come too soon. The risks of working for Philip had never troubled him before, not even when he'd been a child. His mother had always been stoic in her support of his father, never fretting whenever he was called away to assist the elder Mr Rathbone. Her bravery had fed Justin's and he'd carried it with him when doing his duty. Now he was about to be wed, it seemed an altogether different matter.

He fingered the smooth handle of the pistol beneath his coat. He shouldn't fret about his position like an old lady, not when the risk of childbirth was greater to a woman's life than an unhinged client. He knew more women, including his mother and Philip's first wife, who'd perished in their travails than he did men who'd been brought down by a man's misplaced anger at the moneylender. Still, the threat he'd encountered tonight, for the first time ever, gave him more encouragement to do well than his desire to prove he could manage a business of his own. In a few days, Susanna's livelihood would rely on his success and he didn't wish to leave his wife and whatever children they had alone. She'd agreed to stand beside him for better or for worse. He'd make sure it was better.

Chapter Five

'How exciting to be dining with Mr Connor and his friends,' Mary, Susanna and Edwina's shared lady's maid, gushed while helping Susanna into her emerald-green silk evening dress. Lady Rockland refused to hire a lady's maid for only Susanna and in a small way she was glad. She'd soon be able to don her clothing without another woman fluttering around her, returning to the days when she was quite capable of dressing herself.

'Yes, very exciting,' Susanna lied, too cautious around Mary to express her concerns as she sometimes did with Mrs Fairley. The young woman with the button nose was more relaxed and open in Susanna's presence than she ever was with Edwina. However, Susanna was never quite sure how much of what she said remained with cheerful young Mary and how much was repeated to the woman's demanding employer.

'The bodice is a little tight, miss,' the maid said as she tugged it flat against Susanna's breasts in order to do up the buttons along the back. 'You must be enjoying too much of the good London food.'

'Nonsense, I've hardly eaten these past few weeks.' There'd been too much for Susanna to worry about with her secret relationship with Lord Howsham, and then Mr Connor. The anxiety had curdled her stomach every morning until she could barely stand the smell of eggs and ham. 'You must not have tied the stays tight enough. Try them again.'

'Yes, miss.' The maid began undoing the buttons and Susanna took a deep breath as the dress dropped away from her body and she stepped out of it. The comfort was short-lived as the maid began to tighten the stays and the cotton and boning pressing against Susanna's breasts made them sting. She rubbed her chest, surprised at the tenderness. It must mean her courses were coming on for her breasts were always sensitive when they arrived, though they'd never been quite so sore.

'There we are, now let's try the dress again.' Mary helped Susanna step into the dress, then raised it over her hips to settle it against her bust.

Susanna turned so the young woman could do up the buttons and it was then she noticed Lady Rockland watching from the doorway. How long had she been standing there, hand on the doorknob, dark brows knitted tight together as she watched the maid struggle to do up the dress.

'How does it feel now, miss?' the maid asked, oblivious to the observing duchess.

'Much better.' Though it didn't fit as well as it had when she'd last worn it in the country a few weeks ago.

'It must have been the stays, then,' Mary concurred.

'Yes, I'm sure you're right,' Susanna said more to Lady Rockland than to the maid, afraid the ill fit of the gown might reflect poorly on Mrs Fairley's skills. While Susanna doubted the imperious woman would send so much as her lady's maid to the blonde modiste after Susanna left, she hated to think of the young woman with the kind eyes missing out on any work. As the daughter of those in trade, she knew how important each order was, especially those such as the Rocklands', which tended to be large.

'Mary, go and see to Edwina,' Lady Rockland commanded and the girl scurried away.

Lady Rockland strode into the room. Her dress hung like mourning crepe on her shoulders and increased the sternness of the dark ringlets arranged over the top of her head. 'You were feeling ill at breakfast this morning, and most of last week.'

'As any woman so close to marriage might be expected to feel,' Susanna asserted. Lady Rockland was probably worried Susanna would take ill and never leave the Rockland house. Even if she were on her death bed, Susanna would find a way to make it down the aisle and away from these people for good.

Lady Rockland came to stand incredibly close to her, far closer than she'd ever stood before, but Susanna didn't move back. She met the duchess's dark eyes as she always did, but this time Lady Rockland wasn't cowed. 'I hope you didn't do anything to jeopardise the wedding, for if you throw off this suitor, you'll be tossed in the gutter where you belong.'

Susanna said nothing about Lord Rockland having already made such a threat. She didn't want Lady Rockland to learn she and her husband were, for the first time ever, in agreement about Susanna's future. The woman was tiresome in her hate. 'I assure you the wedding will take place as soon as possible and you may have the pleasure of watching me wed.'

'I don't think it necessary for either Lord Rockland or myself to attend such an event.'

Susanna remained firm in front of the woman, despite her sagging spirits, and was relieved when Lady Rockland at last flounced away. For all the gold in England Susanna wouldn't have her stepmother at the wedding, but the girlish part of her which still craved her father's affection wilted. He wouldn't be there to give her away. He'd already done so the morning Mr Connor had accepted the offer and made his proposal.

Augusta marched down the hall to her husband's room. She barged in without knocking, coming upon the duke in his breeches and waistcoat as he held out one hand to the valet who fastened his cufflinks.

She fixed hard eyes on the skinny valet. 'Get out.'

Without a word, Rawlings made a hasty retreat.

'What is it now, Augusta?' Horace drawled, as he finished fastening his cufflink.

'That brat of yours is with child.' Augusta stormed up to her husband, explaining about the tight dress, Susanna's lack of appetite and her suspicions. 'I should have known she'd do something like this, the little whore.'

'What does it matter if she's expecting?' He took up his coat and slid his long arms through the sleeves. 'She'll be married in a few days and the child will be Mr Connor's to deal with. No one will be the wiser.'

'What about her lady's maid? She might suspect something and then how long will it be until the cheap woman tells every maid in Grosvenor Square? It'll taint Edwina. People already wonder why she wasn't married last Season. You never should have brought Susanna to us in the first place.'

'If you'd spent more time worrying about Edwina and less time concerning yourself with Susanna, you might have succeeded in marrying her off.' Horace tugged his cuffs out from beneath the jacket sleeves.

'I've done my best.' Failure struck Augusta, bruising her pride more than any motherly sense of duty. She wasn't blind to her overweight daughter's lack of grace and elegance, but she hated to be reminded of it every time Susanna entered a room and fixed her with those hateful green eyes, Horace's eyes. The morning Augusta's mother had informed her of her own arranged marriage, she'd known Horace's heart wasn't part of the contract, but she'd expected his respect. He'd denied her even that courtesy and there was nothing she could do about it.

'Then do better.' Horace rolled his chin over his collar, straightening the cravat, his signet ring glinting in the candlelight. 'I want Edwina well settled by the end of this Season or you'll have more to worry about than any rumours surrounding Susanna. Do I make myself clear?'

'Yes.' Augusta bit back a more forceful retort. If Horace failed to take her concerns about Susanna seriously, there was nothing she could do, overtly at least. After many years, she'd learned to accomplish a great deal in more subtle and effective ways.

'Good, then send Rawlings back in. I'm expected at my club.'

'We wouldn't want you to be late for your club.' She snorted, knowing very well Horace wasn't going to White's but to Drury Lane to fawn over his actress mistress. At least in this affair he was maintaining some discretion, but if he got this mistress with child, Augusta would insist on a separation before she allowed the filthy little mongrel into her house. She'd borne enough embarrassment among her friends and society because of Susanna. She wasn't about to endure more.

There seemed little difference between Fleet Street and Oxfordshire except for the number of establishments crammed together, their bow-front windows displaying all the items available inside. Were Susanna allowed to, she would have gladly walked through this neighbourhood to the Rathbones' house. She felt more at home among these shops than in any of the ballrooms or salons she'd been forced to accompany Edwina to in the more fashionable district of Mayfair. Instead, she remained in the Rockland town coach, the one without the duke's arms, noting as another person on the street outside paused in the stocking of their cart to admire the maroon coach lumbering by. From inside, Susanna met their eyes, catching a sense of their curiosity as they wondered which grand lady had dared to venture into this section of London.

She was nobody and she settled back against the squabs, giddy to know she'd soon be allowed to travel these streets like a common woman once again. It would be a relief to return to the world in which she'd been raised. Whether these people would accept her remained to be seen. In Oxfordshire, the butchers and grocers had looked down their noses at her for being born without benefit of a marriage ceremony, reserving their greatest disdain for her mother, who had held her head up proudly at her daughter's accomplishments instead of shrinking away with her shame. She wondered if Justin's friends would treat her the same way. He might not wish her to refer to herself as a bastard, but it wouldn't stop anyone else from flinging the word at her.

Worry over what awaited her at the Rathbones' made her stomach tighten, but she took a deep breath, forcing herself to relax. Given the generous way Justin treated her, it was difficult to imagine his friends behaving so meanly, or him tolerating any snide comments, especially after his insistence no one would look down on her. It still baffled her how a near-stranger could regard her with more care and concern than either of her natural families ever had. It wasn't the money making him attentive. She'd seen too many titled but poor men offer only the faintest attention to their wealthy intendeds to think money could make a man love a woman. With Justin, his concern was a genuine part of his character, one which urged her to reveal more to him in their brief time together than she'd told to any of the Rocklands in the years she'd lived with them. She trusted him not to hurt her and he really wanted to know about her.

His interest, and her willingness to confide in him, didn't scare her as much as the plan to become Lady Howsham had. It'd kept her awake the entire night before Vauxhall Gardens. When she'd lain awake thinking of Justin last night, it certainly wasn't worry which had warmed her body, or made her dream of his hands upon her skin. She wanted to see him tonight, to be beside him and indulge in the deep tones of his voice and the power of him beside her.

It was the memory of him smiling at her which strengthened her courage as the carriage turned on to Bride Lane. The old stone church sat on one side, towering over the line of houses and shops on the other and throwing them deep into shadow as it blocked the light from the setting sun. The carriage rocked to a halt in front of a plain but stately home in the centre of the terrace. A moment later, the door opened and Susanna took the footman's hand and stepped down from the coach. It was a peaceful place, with the noise from nearby Fleet Street fading in the rustle of the large trees in the churchyard.

'Shall I escort you to the door, miss?' the footman asked, eyeing their surroundings as if unable to believe it was so genteel and no footpads were lurking nearby to attack her.

'No, I'll be quite fine on my own.'

She moved up the path to the house, eager to leave behind the trappings of her father's status and embrace again the simplicity of the merchant's life, assuming the Rathbones were welcoming. She still had no idea what to expect.

What she didn't expect was for the front door to open and a young woman with auburn hair a few years older than herself to appear in the frame. Not once did her lively hazel eyes flicker to the carriage to gape at it as her grandfather had done the morning it'd pulled to a stop in front of his shop. To this woman it seemed not to exist; only Susanna mattered.

'You must be Miss Lambert. We've been expecting you. I'm Mrs Rathbone. Welcome and congratulations.'

She pulled Susanna into a sweet hug. Susanna stiffened before at last relaxing enough to awkwardly return the greeting. She barely received any acknowledgement at home. She wasn't accustomed to so much affection from a stranger.

'Mr Connor has told us all about you.' Mrs Rathbone held her at arm's length. 'You don't know how surprised we were by your and Mr Connor's engagement.'

Susanna eyed her warily, wondering just how much the woman knew about everything, including Lord Howsham. 'Yes, it was most unexpected.'

'As was mine to Mr Rathbone.' She linked her arm

through Susanna's as though they'd been fast friends for years and guided her into the house. While the butler helped Susanna out of her pelisse, she took in the simple yet elegant entrance hall. The Rathbones' wealth was evident in the high polish of the panelling on the walls and the quality of the furniture, although it lacked the ostentatious gilding and overwrought ornamentation the duke and those of his station favoured.

From a door along the side of the hall Justin emerged, accompanied by a tall, slender gentleman with a boy of about two perched on one hip.

Susanna saw only Justin and her feet nearly carried her to him before she restrained herself. The desire to be near him startled her. During her unfortunate yet brief time with Lord Howsham, it had been the freedom he'd offered which had filled her with yearning, never truly him. It was different with Justin. His sweep of her figure with his eyes, the glance both fiery and impressed, and the broad smile which softened the square set of his jaw and lit up his expression called to her more than any promise of a future. His wide chest practically demanded she wrap her arms around his waist and lay her head on his tan coat, the hue of which nearly matched his copper-coloured eyes. She craved the weight of his arms around her and the steady sound of his heart beating beneath her ear. She hadn't expected to feel such a powerful reaction to a man she barely knew, but in all the uncertainty of her life he was in a very short amount of time becoming something very secure.

'Good evening, Miss Lambert, and welcome to our home. I'm Mr Rathbone.' The tall gentleman came forward, his face more severe than Justin's, but with a friendliness which eased his sternness. 'And this is my son, Thomas.'

The boy resembled his father, with dark hair and a watchful expression which took in everyone while he sucked on two fingers.

'Good evening,' Susanna answered with a curtsy, but her attention flicked back to Justin as he approached.

'I see you made it in one piece,' he joked, coming to stand before her as Mr and Mrs Rathbone kissed the boy goodnight and gave him to the nurse to lead upstairs.

'I did, though I'm sure my father's driver was worried we'd be robbed by ruffians once we turned off Fleet Street. He hasn't ventured much further than Hyde Park.'

'Of course he has, he's been with his lordship to Drury Lane,' Justin countered.

'Why would he be in Drury Lane?' A young lady with Mr Rathbone's eyes and something of his stance asked, coming to join them in the entrance hall. Susanna was eager to know the reason, too, though she could well guess.

'There's a certain actress there the duke—' Justin began before a matron who reminded Susanna a little of her mother stepped up behind the young lady and shot Justin a silencing, yet mirthful glare.

'You shouldn't speak of such things in front of Miss

Rathbone, or Miss Lambert,' she chided, wrapping her arm around her young charge's shoulders.

Mr Rathbone introduced the young lady as Miss Jane Rathbone, his younger sister. The matron was Mrs Townsend, Mrs Rathbone's mother and Miss Jane's companion.

'I'll be sure to send out some food and drink to the driver for his troubles. Since he may be bringing you into this part of town for the wedding, we want to be in his good graces,' Mr Rathbone announced as he wrapped his arm about Mrs Rathbone's waist. Their unashamed intimacy was touching.

Lord Rockland didn't offer his wife affection in public and, judging by the woman's sour nature, not in private either. Growing up, Susanna had never had a father to show tenderness to her mother. She'd once caught her grandfather hugging her grandmother in the garden behind the house. He'd even smiled at the small bent little woman who had been his wife. The brief moment was the single time Susanna remembered seeing her grandfather happy. What little love and good nature he'd possessed had been buried with her grandmother.

Susanna's throat constricted at the memory of her grandmother's lavender-scented cotton dress. She'd been the only person in the house who'd cherished Susanna as much as her mother had. She used to wrap her gnarled arms around Susanna to comfort her after the village children had taunted her. They were the only warm memories Susanna possessed besides those of her mother holding her, or reading to her at night before she fell asleep. All too soon her grandmother had passed away and a few years later her mother had followed, death stealing from Susanna what little love she'd ever experienced.

Swallowing past the lump in her throat, she looked to Justin. As if sensing her pain, he took her hand.

'Are you well?' he asked with concern.

'Perfectly.' She smiled, hoping with all her being he'd prove to be as caring as his tight clasp of her hand promised.

'Dinner is served,' the butler announced.

It was then Susanna realised everyone was watching them. She tried to let go of Justin but he held her tight. She wondered what everyone thought of her being so bold, but there was no hint of judgement in their eyes. It was as suprising as her hope for Justin's affection.

'Shall we?' Justin shifted her hand to his arm, his solidness beneath her palm settling her remaining worries.

'Please.' These were good people, worthy of being his friends and she would come to know and appreciate them as much as he did.

He led her down the hall behind the Rathbones, as comfortable here as if it were his own home. She possessed little idea of what his abode looked like. Surely it was nothing like this one with its richly panelled walls leading down the hall past an orderly study. Inside, French doors opened out on to a garden where pink, red and white roses bounced on their bushes in the breeze. The company turned left away from the cheerful beauty and into the dining room across the way.

'You'll be sure to tell me about the duke and Drury Lane later, won't you, Mrs Townsend?' Miss Rathbone pleaded in much too loud a whisper from behind them.

'Of course, but not in front of your brother or our guest,' Mrs Townsend answered and the two of them indulged in a conspiratorial giggle before quieting to take their places at the mahogany table.

The dining room proved as refined yet understated as the rest of the house. Blue paper covered the walls, the colour bright with the light of the candles in their elegant silver holders in the centre of the table. On the polished surface sat a set of china, stemware and silver fine enough to make even Lady Rockland take notice.

To Susanna's pleasure, she found herself seated between Mrs Rathbone and Justin, with Mr Rathbone at the head of the table and Mrs Townsend and Miss Jane across from her.

The conversation didn't wane as dinner began and Susanna marvelled at the convivial atmosphere. Here, the knives and forks didn't clank against the plates to echo off the plasterwork, and the sound of chewing didn't replace the conversations as it did in the Rocklands' town house.

'Miss Lambert, Mr Connor was telling us your family is in the wine trade?' Mrs Rathbone asked with genuine interest. There was no hint of condemnation or criticism in her question.

'In Oxfordshire. My grandfather provides most of the dons and too many of the students at the university with their fare.' It was how Lord Rockland had met her mother, but she didn't say it, not wanting to remind them of her illegitimate status and risk losing their good favour. Though she doubted these friendly people, who probably already knew most of her background and still welcomed her at their table, would be so mean. They didn't strike her as petty like the Rocklands, who tore down even those they considered their greatest friends when they troubled themselves to speak during meals.

'How do you find the wine?' Justin asked as some topic of Miss Rathbone's choosing drew the attention of the others away from Justin and Susanna.

Susanna took up her goblet and tilted it to her lips. The fine vintage slid across her tongue, smooth and easy, unlike the old swill her grandfather used to sell to the students. She peered at Justin from over the top of the crystal, his interest making her take her time, sensing it was more than waiting for her opinion which kept him enthralled.

At last she set the glass down. 'It's excellent.'

'I chose it.' Justin's already formidable chest swelled beneath his fitted coat. The flickering candlelight caressed his face and danced in his eyes, revealing the small dark flecks mixed with the copper of his irises.

She touched the rim of the crystal goblet. 'If this is the measure of your tastes, then you possess a bright future as a merchant.'

'It's my goal to impress in this…' he lowered his voice and leaned in closer to her, his breath against her cheek as intoxicating as the spirits '…and all other matters.'

She didn't blush, but answered him with lowered lids and the tilt of her head, as though teasing and inviting him all at once. 'I have no doubt you'll succeed.'

The look in his darkened eyes nearly melted her already heated insides. 'I appreciate your faith in me.'

She licked her lips, wondering if he would taste as heady as the wine. 'It's well deserved.'

'Good.' He set his wine glass on the table, the red sparkling like one of Lady Rockland's grand rubies. 'I've secured the common licence and spoken to Reverend Clare at St Bride's. He's prepared to perform the service on Monday morning. Lord Rockland and I are meeting the day after tomorrow with his solicitor to ensure everything in regards to your dowry is in order.'

Susanna touched her napkin to the corners of her lips, trying to maintain some control over her excitement. In three days she'd be free of the Rocklands, and her time with Justin would become much more intimate. She crossed her ankles beneath the table, wishing the ceremony was tomorrow. 'It sounds perfect.'

'Indeed, it does.' He slipped his fingers beneath her palm where it rested on her thigh. The subtle stroke grazed the top of her leg, teasing the skin beneath her skirts. She drew in a deep breath, making her breasts swell against the tight stays holding them and drawing his eyes down for the quickest of moments before they rose to hold hers.

'I must make sure Mrs Fairley is done with my dress,' she stammered, though at the moment, she'd walk down the aisle in her chemise if it meant marrying him and—to her shock—reaching the bridal chamber faster.

'I'm sure she'll be done in time,' Mrs Rathbone assured her, overhearing the conversation. 'She's had practice at doing up a wedding dress in a hurry. She did mine and it was excellent.'

Susanna reluctantly let go of Justin, remembering her place as both the Rathbones' guest and an unmarried woman who shouldn't be touching a man. She should have known better, but under Justin's tempting spell, she'd forgotten herself and where she was.

'She does all of our clothes,' Miss Jane added, as though this alone was enough to recommend the young modiste.

'Mrs Rathbone, you said you and your husband had an interesting courtship?' Susanna asked, her curiosity and the amiable atmosphere making her as bold as Jane.

'Oh, very interesting.' Mrs Rathbone exchanged a conspiratorial glance with her husband, bringing a sly smile to the man's lips and easing the strict set of his features.

Susanna listened in amazement as Mrs Rathbone described how, after she'd threatened Mr Rathbone with a pistol, he'd made a proposal a day later. She'd accepted him on his odd terms and had come to live here with her mother. She went on to explain how her mother, having been a draper's wife, now acted as Miss Jane's tutor, teaching the young girl all she'd need to know to some day become a prosperous merchant's wife, or perhaps the wife of a fellow moneylender's son. These things were told to her as if she deserved to know them because she belonged here and was one of their friends. It was a great pleasure for Susanna to not be judged in their midst, and if her bodice wasn't so tight, she'd have sighed with relief. Instead she listened and chatted and ate, admiring Justin and the small arch of bronze hair curving over his smooth forehead.

'Do you like being a duke's daughter?' Miss Jane bluntly asked.

'Miss Jane, such a question isn't appropriate,' Mrs Townsend gently corrected, although she tilted her head at Susanna as though waiting for her to respond, her curiosity as great as her young charge's.

'It's tiresome,' Susanna answered, wondering what the girl thought when she didn't regale her with magical stories of balls and masks.

Miss Rathbone, proving herself as sensible as her brother, merely nodded, then speared a piece of meat with her fork. 'I thought as much.'

Her curiosity satisfied, she didn't press Susanna further on the subject and she was glad. She wanted to be here with them tonight, not pulled into memories of the shivering loneliness waiting for her when she left this jovial family.

All too soon dinner ended and Susanna expected to follow the ladies into the sitting room and leave the men to their port. To her surprise, Mrs Rathbone didn't rise and it was Jane who dictated the course of the evening.

'Mr Connor, you must show Miss Lambert the roses. They're in full bloom now and quite beautiful.'

'Miss Rathbone and my mother are very proud of the garden,' Mrs Rathbone added, seeming to encourage the idea instead of rebuking the young lady for speaking out of turn as Lady Rockland would have done. 'You must see them.'

'And we will.' Justin rose from his place, as ready as Susanna for them to be alone. What the Rathbones thought of their eagerness to depart to the darkness of the garden, Susanna couldn't say. Given Mrs Rathbone's tale about her introduction to Mr Rathbone, Susanna doubted anyone here would criticise her too harshly for slipping away with Justin.

She laid her napkin beside her plate and rose as Justin slid the chair out from beneath her. He offered her his arm and she took it, following him through the dining room and across the hall into the well-ordered office. Given the masculine furniture and the way not one item appeared out of place, she guessed this was Mr Rathbone's domain.

'Your friends are very kind and welcoming,' she complimented. 'Have you known Mr Rathbone long?'

'I grew up with him. He's like a brother to me.'

She released Justin's arm as he stepped forward to open the French doors. The night air poured in, the heady scent of the roses mixing with the mist of the evening to cover the more pungent smells from the surrounding streets. The dark green leaves of the rose bushes shimmered with the orange light spilling out from the house. Susanna moved past Justin to the nearest rose bush. Taking one full flower in her hand, she dipped her nose down to the centre to inhale its sweet fragrance.

'They remind me of my grandmother's garden behind the shop in Oxfordshire.' Her voice caught in her throat. Too many memories danced in the scent.

Justin said nothing, but stood close beside her listening, the faint moonlight playing along the edges of his shoulders.

'Wildflowers used to bloom there, too, in the spring and she tended them as lovingly as she did her roses, until she died.' She let go of the flower and it bobbed back up to join the others, knocking a few petals off the fading bloom above it. 'Afterwards, I tried to maintain the bushes and the pretty little blossoms, but the work of the wine shop and my grandfather's demands took up most of my time. Eventually the plants withered. The last time I saw the garden there was nothing but weeds and dandelions.'

Tears stung the corners of her eyes. It'd been years since she'd spoken to anyone of her grandmother, or even her mother.

'My mother loved roses, too. When she was alive, she used to help Philip's mother in this garden since she didn't have one of her own.' Justin took her hand, offering her a comfort the painful memories and years of loneliness had denied her. She stroked the back of his hand with her fingers. Like her, he'd experienced the sharp edge of loss. Unlike her, it hadn't stolen his humour. 'She would have liked you—you have her spirited nature.'

'My mother would have liked you, too. She enjoyed laughing as much as you do. It was the only merriment I ever enjoyed in my grandfather's dour house.'

'My mother and Mrs Rathbone used to get up to all sorts of things here. They might have married serious men, but they both had a wicked sense of humour.'

She offered him a wry smile, thankful he wasn't allowing her to wallow in her grief. 'It explains a great deal about you.'

'And probably Philip.'

'If Mr Rathbone is such a great friend, why do you wish to leave his employment?' Susanna asked, eager to change the subject. Justin was her future and she didn't want the past to drag at her or sour her happiness.

Justin plucked a petal off the bloom and turned it over to examine the slight darkness on the underside. 'If I was content to remain a humble man like my father, to stick to the station in life I was born to as he thinks I should, I'd gladly spend the rest of my days in Philip's employment. But I want to be something more than a hired man and achieve my own success.'

'Your father doesn't approve of your efforts?'

'He hasn't been my most ardent supporter.' He flung the petal away, darkness clouding his eyes at the mention of his father, just as it had yesterday in the curricle.

It made her realise why he insisted she see herself in a better light than everyone else did He was forced to do it, too. They weren't so very different from one another and he, more than anyone else, might understand what she'd struggled against all her life.

'I'm glad you're defying him and I envy you. I've only ever been the disgraced daughter of a disgraced daughter, someone who belongs neither in a merchant's shop nor a duke's home. They've never seen me, who I am, what I'm capable of. I want to prove to all those people who thought I was nothing better than a little whore, destined to follow her mother into ruin, that I'm so much more.'

'You will.' He brought her hand up to his chest, his fingers entwining with hers. 'We both will.'

With a small tug he drew her closer, then let go of her hands to allow them to lie on the fine wool covering his shoulders. The heat of him wasn't lessened by his clothes or hers and her tender breasts tingled under the pressure of his chest against hers. Lower down, the firmness of him sent a primal shiver racing through her as his large hand touched the small of her back and pressed her closer. She tilted her head and closed her eyes as he brought his face near to hers. The tang of his breath mixing with the heady aroma of the roses made her knees weak and she parted her lips, waiting, wanting and wondering why he hadn't kissed her.

She opened her eyes to see his head tilted to one side, his eyes fixed on the upper storey of the house as though he were listening for something. She followed his gaze, catching a small shadow at one of the windows overlooking the garden.

'The curious Miss Rathbone is watching us.' Releasing her, he caught her hand and pulled her under the small portico off the office.

They slipped into the deep shadow in the corner, where the privacy was made more complete by the large bushes growing in front of this dark, tucked-away spot. Justin turned her, placing himself between her and any curious eyes from the garden or the house. Slight panic welled up inside her. She'd been alone like this with Lord Howsham and the thrill had quickly turned to anxiety and then regret. She shifted on her feet, unsure if she should stay or flee.

'What's wrong?' he asked, his voice a near whisper in the darkness as his hand on her back eased, placing a slight distance between them. 'We can go back inside, if you'd like.'

In the comfort of Justin's embrace, the tenderness with which he held her close banished her fears. He wouldn't treat her so roughly, not tonight or any of the many to follow. 'No, I'm fine.'

She laced her fingers behind his neck and drew him down to her. He caught her lips with his, the moist heat of his mouth against hers making her quiver. Beyond the walls of the garden, a horse whinnied in the mews and the roll of carriage wheels and the call of a driver carried over the house from the street at the front. The sounds faded beneath the beat of her heart in her ears as Justin savoured her mouth. There was more in his kiss than simple lust for their coming wedding night. There was understanding, as deep as the caresses of his tongue, as firm as the press of his fingers against her back. In the brief time she'd been with him he'd shown her a glimpse of her future with him and she was eager to rush to it, though he asked no more of her tonight than kisses. In his restraint, this son of a simple man was proving himself more of a gentleman than Lord Howsham had ever been.

Twining her hands in his hair, she longed to convey to him not only her gratitude but her belief in him and their future together. With him she would enjoy true affection and the companionship of someone more like her than anyone she'd ever known before. The lonely days which had marked her life would end and she'd at last be with someone who cared.

The soft whisper of slippers over the portico stone slid in beneath the rapid beating of her heart. The subtle sound warned her to pull away, but she couldn't. She didn't want to be separated from Justin, to leave this bliss and return to the uncertain world waiting for her, the one where promises were easily broken, affection withheld instead of given and almost anything might come to snatch away her future.

'Mr Connor, are you out here?' Mrs Rathbone's clear voice carried over the night, but there was no missing the note of anxiety in her words.

Was she worried she and Justin were setting a bad example for Miss Rathbone? Had she come here to chastise them for acting like a common street whore and her client? Susanna's heart fluttered with worry. She wanted these people's respect and friendship, not their contempt. If Justin was concerned he didn't show it as he dropped a quick kiss on the tip of her nose, then released her and turned around, his wide body shielding her from Mrs Rathbone's sight.

'Yes, Mrs Rathbone?' he asked with more amusement than embarrassment, making the effortless transition from ardent suitor to deferential employee faster than lightning.

Susanna remained behind him, glad for the shadows, for they hid the blush singeing her cheeks. Here she was wishing for people to think more of her and she was acting like a tart.

'I don't mean to interrupt you,' Mrs Rathbone said with strained amusement, 'but your father is here.'

Justin marched with Susanna to the sitting room, opening and closing his free hand in frustration as he prepared to exchange her soft sighs for the old man's tiresome insults. Mr Green offered him an apologetic nod from where he stood just outside the sitting room. Inside, Justin's father paced back and forth across the carpet, his hands trembling at his sides, his grey hair in disarray, his hat having been discarded on a chair near the fireplace. The felt appeared as rumpled and worn as the old man.

Shaking off the last of the desire which had been doused by his father's arrival, Justin entered the room, his hand tightening over Susanna's when she tried to remove it. Despite what he'd told her of his father yesterday, there was no preparing her for what was sure to be an uncomfortable encounter. Perhaps in the presence of a stranger his father might show some restraint, though he doubted it. The old man would snarl and bite like a badger no matter what Justin did. Susanna had said she was used to dealing with difficult relations— it was time to test her skill, and Justin's.

'Good evening, Father.'

Mr Connor jerked to a halt and turned hard eyes on Justin. 'About time you showed up. Do you enjoy making me crawl and bow before you like some kind of prince?'

Justin exchanged a 'See what I mean?' look with Susanna. 'Father, allow me to introduce you to my fiancée, Miss Susanna Lambert.'

She stiffened beside him and he offered her a slight apologetic shrug. It was best to do this quickly. There was no way to ease her gently into an acquaintance with her future father-in-law.

His father's rheumy eyes jerked up and down Susanna before his lip curled with the usual look of disgust he always wore when it came to anything concerning Justin. It hadn't always been like this. Justin could still remember a time when his father had smiled at him, then thumped him on the back in proud congratulations.

'Mrs Gammon would've been more use to you than this hothouse flower. Though I suppose this one brought you money. Not sure what else she could do except warm yer bed.'

Justin moved to respond, refusing to let his father insult Susanna, but her restraining hand on his chest kept him still, for the moment.

'This hothouse flower has spent a great deal of time behind a counter, keeping accounts and managing inventory. I assure you I won't wilt under work,' Susanna shot back, refusing to shrink from Mr Connor's frank appraisal.

Justin was impressed, but not surprised. Judging from all she'd told him of the Rocklands and her childhood, this wasn't the first time she'd faced a grouchy old man with a few insults on his tongue.

Mr Connor's bushy eyebrows rose in surprise and his lips worked to answer, but no response seemed to come to him. Frustrated in his efforts to insult Susanna, he turned his wrath on his favourite subject, his son.

'I've come for me money,' he snapped, then held out his hands to Susanna as though pleading with her for sympathy. 'Look at me, forced by my son to beg like some kind of common street urchin. Would you allow such a thing, Miss Lambert?'

'If it were in a gentleman's best interest for someone else to handle his affairs, then, yes, I would.' Her polite but firm opinion of the situation impressed Justin, but not his father.

'Well, look at the bastard putting on airs,' the old man mocked and no feminine hand could restrain Justin this time.

He grabbed his father by the arm and pulled him into the hall. 'You'll mind your tongue in my soon-to-be wife's presence.'

'Don't you dare order me about.' His father shook out of his grasp, remarkably strong for someone who took no more exercise than walking to the pub.

'Take your money and be gone.' Justin dug a few

coins from his pocket and held them out, his hand shaking with rage. 'I have no patience for you tonight.'

With rough fingers, his father plucked the money from his palm, ignoring the coin which fell to the floor as he stuffed the rest in his greasy coat pocket.

'You and your charity can go to hell.' He stomped to the door. Chesterton rushed to open it, but Justin's father shoved him aside. 'Get out of my way. I don't need your help.'

The stench of the misty streets wafted in and with it the faint, sweet scent of gin clinging to his father's coat.

'Mr Connor.' Susanna's patient voice carried over the tense silence in the entrance hall.

Justin's father paused, peering back at her from over his shoulder with one squinty eye. 'What?'

'You almost forgot your hat.' She approached him, holding the hat as though it were a fine Wellington and not a battered old cap. Her stride wasn't clipped or insulting, as though she intended to throw the thing at him so he'd be gone. Neither was her expression condemning, but she smiled, charming him as Justin had charmed many a tradesman's neighbour's wife to ferret out a potential client's situation or solvency. 'Here you are.'

Mr Connor cautiously turned, eyeing her and the hat as if she would strike him if he dared to touch it, his insults seeming to flee from him in the face of her manners. Then at last he took the battered thing, more gingerly than he'd plucked the coins out of Justin's hands.

'Thank you,' he offered grudgingly.

'Our wedding is set for Monday. I'd very much like for you to attend,' she announced to Justin's astonishment.

The white whiskers on the end of his father's chin rose and fell with the way he chewed as he considered Susanna's invitation. Then he pointed his hat at Justin. 'He don't want me there.'

There was certainly truth in that, but Justin held his tongue, refusing to display any lack of solidarity with Susanna and give his father more musket balls for his continued attacks. He intended for Monday to be a memorable day for Susanna, but not for the wrong reasons.

'Then consider yourself my guest,' Susanna offered with all the poise of a duchess.

Mr Connor turned the hat over in his hands, pondering her request. In the gesture, Justin caught for the first time in years something of the thoughtful, intelligent man his father had once been before Justin's mother's death and the gin had done their damage. Then the image was gone, like a shadow chased away by lamplight and the grizzled, mean old man was before him again.

'Ain't making no promises. Never been one for the likes of church.' He narrowed his eyes at Justin. 'Unlike some, I don't give myself airs, or try and look down on others.'

He smashed the hat on his head and stomped out, with poor Mr Green following on his heels.

Chesterton rushed to close the door behind him,

his long face expressionless. This wasn't the first row he'd witnessed between Justin and his father, and by far not the most unusual scene he'd been privy to in this house. With the politeness of a deferential servant he slipped away, leaving Justin and Susanna alone.

'What a memorable first meeting,' Susanna observed drily, her humour failing to raise Justin's downcast mood.

'I can't promise it'll be the last.' At least not until his father's taste for gin finally killed his body. It'd already destroyed his personality.

'You needn't apologise. My grandfather was somewhat like him. He and my uncle used to get into terrible rows when my uncle tried to help him. Some people can't be protected from themselves, or laugh over misfortunes such as a broken bottle of wine. They don't face trials with your happy attitude.'

'I'm not always optimistic.' Justin plucked the fumbled coin from the floor, turning it over in his fingers. This wasn't the image he'd intended to leave her with, of father and son fighting like a couple of cocks in a pit. He wanted the man he'd been on the front steps, the determined, confident one bent on success to be the memory she carried home tonight, but the buoyancy he'd experienced when the duke's carriage had rolled to a stop in front of the Rathbones' house was gone.

She laid a hand on his shoulder. 'Are you all right?'

He slipped her hand off his shoulder and raised it to his lips, pressing a kiss to the slender fingers. If they weren't standing in the Rathbones' entrance hall, with Jane no doubt listening at the top of the stairs, he'd wrap his arms around her and forget himself in the delight of her kisses. Instead he did as he always did and shoved down the frustration and torment of his father to flash Susanna a smile as dazzling as a row of lamps along a Drury Lane stage.

'With you beside me, nothing can be wrong.' He wasn't going to wail in her embrace or admit how deeply his father's insults really struck.

The slight disbelieving arch of her eyebrow matched the disapproving curve of her lips. He wasn't fooling her with all his smiles and wit because she knew exactly what this hurt was like.

'Some day you'll tell me what's troubling you instead of hiding it away.'

'Some day, but not tonight.' He took her arm and led her out to the waiting carriage, stopping before the impressive vehicle to embrace her.

She glanced at the driver, who fixated on the reins before Justin turned her face to meet his. He didn't care what the man thought or what he might say to his employer. The only thing concerning him was their last few moments together. He laid a tender kiss on her lips, the promise of something more than merely physical whispering in the soft caress. In three days, he'd savour every curve and supple mound of her. Tonight, he needed her understanding and compassion as much as she'd needed his in the garden.

The bells of St Bride's began to toll the late hour and Susanna broke away from his kiss, her reluctance to leave as strong in her expression as it was in his chest.

'Goodnight,' she whispered, backing out of his embrace to step into the carriage, her eyes never leaving his.

He closed the door, watching her through the open window, reluctantly moving away when the driver flicked the horses into motion. He wished he could keep her here, but he refrained from calling her back. When she'd stood beside him with his father, the man's insults hadn't cut so deep. She recognised the pain he endured and instead of wanting to dismiss it with a laugh, he'd wanted to take her back to the garden and unburden himself of years of torment. It wasn't like him to complain, but realising how much she wanted to soothe his suffering had almost made him reveal it, and the nagging doubt creeping along in the back of his mind.

For all his efforts to impress her with his determination to succeed, the constant reminder of how easily he'd failed before still shadowed him. There was nothing to ensure he'd be any more successful in this venture than he'd been in his last one. He might avoid the sea and all its perils, but he'd seized enough men's collateral to be familiar with the hundreds of other risks merchants faced.

He turned and made for the Rathbones' house, unwilling to entertain further doubts about his business or how much he missed having Susanna beside him already. There were better things to think about, such as Monday and the life he and Susanna would enjoy. She believed in his ambitions like a wife should and would help him achieve his goals. In return, he'd make her see the wonderful woman she was. Together they'd forget the pain their families had caused them. That was a more pleasant subject to ruminate on than his father's insults, or his own past failures.

Chapter Six

Susanna, dressed only in her stays and chemise, stood on the small stool in the room in the back of Mrs Fairley's shop. She laid her hands on her stomach, fighting against the dizziness creeping over her. The stool wasn't very high, but she felt as if she were teetering on the eaves of a house, with any quick turn sure to send her tumbling to the floor. It'd been like this all morning, and she stepped down to sit in the small chair beside the oval mirror, trying to settle her head and stomach.

The queasy feeling had come on after breakfast when Susanna had begun packing in anticipation of Monday. It wasn't nerves over the uncertainty of her future which had made her stomach swim, but Lady Rockland watching her and the maid as though expecting Susanna to slip some silver teaspoons into the trunk with her things. The duchess hanging over her like a bird of prey had exacerbated the tension still nagging at her after a long night spent tossing and turning in bed.

The memory of Justin's lips on hers last night had teased her until she'd jerked awake with the sheets sticking to her sweaty skin. With the dreams of his hands on her fading, the memory of his argument with his father had slid in to dominate her thoughts. Justin might have smiled jovially at her afterwards, but the pain etched in his eyes as his father had left was one she knew all too well. She'd wanted to soothe his hurt as much as she'd wanted to ease the elder Mr Connor's.

It'd been the same way with her grandfather and mother, when her grandfather had thrown her mother's mistakes in her face, flinging at her the same contempt Mr Connor had hurled at Justin. Back then Susanna had tried so hard to make peace between them, until one day, frustrated by her continued interference, her grandfather had aimed his insults at her. She should have known better than to approach old Mr Connor, but there was a pain deep inside of him, too, like the kind she'd witnessed in her grandfather after her grandmother had passed. It had seemed as if there was too much loss in one room for all of them to endure and she'd wanted to banish it with a touch of kindness.

'Here's the wedding dress for you to try on, Miss Lambert,' Mrs Fairley said brightly as she carried in the creamy silk gown, the paleness of it highlighted by the woman's light yellow dress, the hue of which nearly matched the tone of her blonde hair. Blue satin ribbon the colour of the modiste's eyes adorned the small, puff sleeves and circled her trim waist, emphasising an enviable bosom contained by the crossed material of the bodice. 'I altered it according to the measurements I took last week.'

Susanna rose, rocking a bit as she stood. Mrs Fairley reached out a steadying hand. 'Are you well, miss?'

'Yes. I haven't eaten much today and I was up all night. I'm nervous about the wedding.' She fought the swimming room to focus on the modiste. 'You must know how it is.'

'I do.' She nodded with enthusiasm. 'I could barely eat or sleep for days before my wedding to John. Now let's try on the dress and see how it looks.'

She lowered the dress so Susanna could step into the centre of the silk, then the modiste raised it, pausing so Susanna could slip her arms through the smooth sleeves. The silk kissed the bare skin of her shoulders, reminding her of Justin's tongue against hers last night. He hadn't been greedy or lecherous in his caresses, or pressed her for more than she was initially willing to give. Instead he'd been patient, holding back even as he'd claimed her mouth with caresses to make her knees weak.

Susanna turned to face the mirror, the image of herself hazing a little as her eyes filled with tears.

'What's wrong, miss?' Mrs Fairley laid her hands on Susanna's upper arms and gave her a heartening squeeze.

Susanna wiped her eyes with the backs of her hands. It wasn't like her to be so emotional, but never in her life had she imagined herself in a wedding dress, ready to marry a respectable man who cared for her and her mother's dream for her about to be realised.

'I wish my mother could have seen this.' When she'd been alive, she'd wanted Susanna to have a loving husband, children and a home of her own, all of the things she'd been denied. Her mother had been rigorous in training Susanna to live a merchant's life, convinced those skills would attract a good man, but also aware it would help Susanna make her way in the world if need be. Despite her hopes for Susanna, she'd feared no one, not even the simple men along the high street in Oxfordshire, would offer for an illegitimate woman. Now Susanna was to marry, and well, and all the hours her mother had spent training her to run a business would be employed at last.

'I'm sure your mother would be proud of you,' Mrs Fairley offered.

'Yes, she would have been.' If only she could be here. It would stifle some of the coldness of preparing for Monday with only the modiste to care about her and assist. Perhaps she should have invited Mrs Rathbone to join her today. Their acquaintance might be slight, but it was deeper than anything she'd enjoyed with her so-called family. Neither Lady Rockland nor Edwina had shown any interest in her coming nuptials. She hadn't expected them to. They were too eager to see her gone and overly consumed with their own affairs to trouble with her. This was Edwina's second Season and already there were rumblings amongst the family, and wider society, over her failure to marry last year. Her half-sister was probably jealous of Susanna making her way down the aisle before her.

'I'll do up the buttons so we can have a proper look

at you.' Mrs Fairley began to fasten the long line of buttons along the back. As she reached those at the top, she was forced to pull the two sides of the dress tighter to fasten them.

'It's too tight,' Susanna complained, her breasts sore from the pressure of the bodice.

'My measurements must have been wrong.' Mrs Fairley frowned apologetically at Susanna in the mirror from behind her. 'It isn't like me to mismeasure.'

'My blue dress needs altering, too, it's also snug,' Susanna added, surprised the young lady's work was suddenly so shoddy. It'd always been so neat before. 'And I think I need my stays let out as well.'

Mrs Fairley's eyes met Susanna's in the mirror and then she came around to stand in front of her, looking up into her face with a motherly concern. 'Are you sure everything is well with you, Miss Lambert?'

'I'm quite well, other than a slight bit of dizziness and no appetite. Why?'

The kindly woman studied Susanna, a curious realisation dawning across her round face, as though she was aware of something Susanna was not. The modiste opened her mouth to say something, then seemed to think better of it.

'It isn't my place to pry into your affairs.' Mrs Fairley dropped her hands as she stepped behind Susanna to undo the dress.

'You don't pry, I tell you.' The modiste knew more about Susanna than anyone else, except Justin. Strange he should garner her confidence faster than Mrs Fairley, whose kind patience had relieved some of Susanna's aching loneliness over the last few years. 'You've helped me before. If there's something you think might help me now, please tell me.'

Mrs Fairley shifted on her feet, her cotton dress crinkling with the subtle movement as she silently debated Susanna's request. Then, at last, she spoke. 'Miss Lambert, were you intimate with Lord Howsham, in the married sense?'

Mrs Fairley had been the only other person besides Lord Howsham who'd known about the affair and Susanna's plans to run away with him. Even with the Rocklands paying her bill, the modiste had never betrayed Susanna. Despite the shared knowledge, and Mrs Fairley's discretion, Susanna was reluctant to admit her mistake. She wanted to leave it in the past, as Justin had urged her to do, but she couldn't lie to the one woman who'd been the closest thing to a confidante she'd ever known. 'I was, just once. We were walking in the woods at Rockland Place the day before the Rocklands and I left for London. He kissed me and then insisted on more. I didn't refuse him. I thought it meant he cared for me, but it didn't.'

She rubbed the back of her neck, remembering how the bark of the tree he'd pressed her against had scratched her skin as he'd pawed at her and how much she still regretted her foolishness. She should have known better, she should have pushed him away, but she hadn't.

'When were your last courses, miss?' Mrs Fairley asked, beginning to plant in Susanna's mind the most horrifying of thoughts.

'The week of Lady Day, I think.' So much had happened since then, coming to London, then Vauxhall Gardens, and she'd lost track of time. 'It wasn't long ago.'

Mrs Fairley's eyes widened. 'Miss Lambert, Lady Day was over six weeks ago.'

'It couldn't have been so long.' Yet the modiste's worried expression told her it was.

Susanna racked her mind, trying to determine if her courses had arrived since, but they hadn't. Her hands flew to her mouth as she realised exactly what the modiste suspected. The memory of Lady Rockland watching the maid struggling to do up her dress last night, and then warning her not to delay the wedding, came rushing back to her. Mrs Fairley wasn't the only one who suspected the horrible truth now beginning to fill Susanna. Lady Rockland did, too.

'It can't be. It can't.' The little breakfast Susanna had eaten threatened to come up and stain the skirt of the dress. She held it back, shrugging out of the silk as fast as she could, afraid of ruining it just as she had all hope of a future with Justin.

Mrs Fairley said nothing as she laid the dress to one side and watched as Susanna began to pace back and forth across the small room.

'It can't be. Justin thinks I'm so much more than a bastard, but I'm not and he'll know it. He'll hate me because of it.' The intimacy she'd experienced with him last night, every promise hovering in his kisses, all desire to prove everyone wrong, to enjoy a family and friends who loved and cherished her came crash-

ing down around her. She slouched to the floor against
the chair and pressed the heels of her hands to her
eyes, determined not to cry, and to face this calamity
as she had every other one in her life, but her chest
constricted with her sobs.

Mrs Fairley wrapped her arms around Susanna and
rubbed her back, her kindness making it impossible
for Susanna to stop the tears from coming. A hopelessness she hadn't experienced since the morning of her
mother's funeral crashed over her. If she told Justin, he'd
break off the engagement and nothing but penury and
the dark, ugly streets of London waited for her and the
baby. She could interrupt Lord Howsham's wedding,
insist he do right by her, but she knew he wouldn't.
He'd cast her aside as he had before and Lord Rockland would allow it. He wasn't likely to fight for her,
not against another peer.

'What am I going to do?' She moved away from
Mrs Fairley and rubbed her cheeks with her hands.
Tears and self-pity wouldn't help. They never had before. 'No man wants another man's child foisted on
him. I know, because no man would accept my mother
because of me, not even my family.'

'Perhaps you could go away to the country,' Mrs
Fairley suggested, attempting to bolster Susanna's
hope. 'Once the child is born and settled with a good
family, you could return to London and marry Mr
Connor.'

'I can't. Lord and Lady Rockland would never allow
such a delay, and if I tell them why I need to leave,
they'll throw me out without a shilling.'

Susanna sat back on her heels and stared at the small cutting of ribbon lying on the floor beneath the chair. Her stomach ached more at the thought of giving up a child than telling Lord Rockland the truth. The stories of families who'd fostered infants with farm couples who'd shown their charges little concern, leaving them to near starve or die of illness even when they were paid well, made her cringe. It was the reason her mother hadn't relinquished Susanna despite her grandfather's insistence. She couldn't subject her own child to such a horrid fate, or the lonely existence she'd endured. Her mother had made sacrifices to give Susanna the safety of a family home, even if it'd lacked true acceptance and love. Susanna would have to do the same, though she had no idea how. Her grandfather and uncle wouldn't take in another bastard, and Lord Rockland wouldn't stand staunchly behind her this time as he had the day he'd brought her to Rockland Park and presented her to his wife.

She sagged against the chair, two tears of despair rolling silently down her cheeks. 'I'm going to lose everything.'

'I've heard of a woman, miss,' Mrs Fairley began hesitantly as she handed Susanna a small scrap of fabric to wipe her cheeks with. 'She offers a tonic of pennyroyal-mint oil.'

'I can't.' Susanna cringed. One of the maids at Rockland Place had tried to end her troubles in a similar way and it'd killed her.

'Then you must trust in Mr Connor.' Mrs Fairley

took Susanna's hands in hers. 'I'm sure he'll understand and help you, one way or another.'

'Why? There's no reason for him to care about me.'
He'd tried to raise her up last night and in the curricle
in Hyde Park. Telling him of the child would lower her
in his eyes and turn him, the one person who'd ever
thought highly of her, against her. 'There's no more
reason for him to marry me.'

'What about your dowry?' Mrs Fairley suggested.
'You two wouldn't be the first to marry, one for money,
the other for protection. The better sort do it all the
time.'

Susanna snatched at the hope. Even coming to him
as tainted goods, she did possess some value, if not for
herself and her skills behind a shop counter, then for
the fifteen hundred pounds which would be his. It was
a depressing, if not practical and uncertain, prospect
to hang her future on, and worry gnawed away at the
chance it offered. 'What if the money isn't enough?'

It hadn't been the first time her father had proposed
the idea to him.

'He's a good man. I'm sure he'll find a way to help
you and the child.'

'I hope you're right.' His charity was the only way
she and the baby might avoid being cast out on to the
streets.

Justin's chaise rolled to a stop in front of Gunter's
in Berkeley Square. The sweet scent of the treats inside wafted out of the front door and further turned
Susanna's already knotted stomach. It was early in

the afternoon and unusually warm for the middle of May. The more fashionable members of society who usually filled the tables inside, or sat outside in their open-topped carriages to enjoy their ices, were missing, leaving the shop to merchants' wives and officers courting young ladies.

Justin had arrived at the Rocklands' at noon to finalise the details of the wedding contract and the disbursement of Susanna's dowry. It'd been a brief meeting in the duke's office, with her father agreeing to the time and place of the wedding and engaging him in a short conversation about Susanna's pin money, doing at least that much for Susanna despite the duchess's disapproving glare. The woman had roused herself before noon to stand behind her husband and their solicitor, never daring to second-guess the men and not once smiling, even at the prospect of being rid of Susanna the next day.

During the entire discussion, and the review of the dowry contract, Susanna had attempted to sit still and not twist in her chair or fumble with her bracelet. More than once the desire to reveal her horrid secret had flitted to the tip of her tongue, ready to be freed, but she couldn't do it. It would make everything Lady Rockland believed about her true and Susanna wanted to deny her the satisfaction, if only for a little while longer, though it was a hollow victory. The harsh way Lady Rockland had regarded her when the issue of providing for future children in the event of Justin's death had been raised told her she did suspect the truth. Susanna had waited while the solicitor had read the wording aloud, wondering if the duchess would say anything, but she'd held her tongue. Like Susanna, she'd allowed events to continue, no doubt more relieved than before to be rid of her bastard charge.

Having failed to reveal her condition in the Rockland study, Susanna had suggested the outing in Justin's borrowed curricle, eager to be alone with him where they might talk. She'd intended to broach the subject while they drove, the open top giving them the illusion of being in public while in the privacy of the conveyance, but her courage had failed her again. Justin had been so enthusiastic in his discussion of the wine-shop inventory he'd acquired, and so solicitous of her advice on how best to sell the different quality vintages, she hadn't wanted to ruin his mood.

'I'm glad you suggested coming here.' Justin flicked a coin at a young boy on the pavement and asked him to watch his horse. As he came around to help her down, the bright sun played off the dark felt of his hat, shading his eyes, but not concealing his pleasure in her presence. His hand in hers was confident and sure, but it did nothing to bolster her own spirits and she bitterly regretted again her time with Lord Howsham. This would be the last time Justin would regard her with such joy.

'Given the warm day I couldn't think of anywhere else to go.' And what Susanna needed to tell him was best said in public. Though she'd come to know something of Justin's character over the last few days, there was no guessing how he might react when she delivered the news she was carrying Lord Howsham's child.

She didn't think he'd become violent, or even shout, but whatever his reaction, with so many others around him he would be forced to show restraint and maybe even listen to her reasons why he should go through with the marriage. She didn't want to force another man's baby on him, but she didn't want to lose him either, or condemn her child to the insufferable illegitimacy she'd endured her entire life.

'Are you all right?' Justin studied her with a concern she hoped wasn't as astute as Mrs Fairley's. She didn't want him guessing her secret before she could reveal it.

'Yes, only I haven't slept well.' It wasn't a lie. After leaving the modiste's yesterday, she'd barely been able to sit still, much less lie down.

'Try and rest tonight for tomorrow night may be a long one...' he breathed against her ear, twining the regret tighter around her stomach. There would be no wedding night and soon he'd discover it, too.

He escorted Susanna inside. A few couples sat at the tables scattered throughout the room, but most were empty. The plump older matron in a bright, white mob cap and an equally clean apron moved from behind the counter to serve two tall glasses of ices to two women sitting together on the far side of the room. The small table in front of the bow front window was empty and Justin guided Susanna there, holding out the chair as she sat down.

He took his place across from her. 'What do you recommend?'

'The orange ice. It's what I had when I was here before.' Then, she'd relished the treat. Today, her stomach was so tight with worry, she could scarcely imagine herself consuming something as rich as an ice. It'd been all she could do this morning to keep down two pieces of toast and her tea. She wasn't sure if this illness was the result of the baby growing inside her or sitting across from Justin, preparing to reveal what she wished she could hide. But she couldn't hide it. He'd been open and honest with her and shown her respect. He deserved her respect and honesty in return.

As she stared across the table at him, struggling to match his smile, the realisation the admiration he held for her was about to be flung into the street like an old broadsheet tore at her.

'This isn't my usual indulgence.' Justin laughed. A young boy pressed his nose to the window to admire the coloured sweets displayed in glass jars before his irritated governess pulled him away.

'Is there a public house you prefer?' Her grandfather had frequented one in Oxfordshire. When she'd been little, she'd wondered at this strange male bastion. Then she'd peeked in the window of the dark timber-and-wattle building to view the plain wooden tables inside and it'd lost all hold on her young imagination.

'No, I spend too much time in those places when I'm collecting information for Philip. To wander into one and pay for a tankard would feel too much like work.'

'Then where do you spend your free time?' Susanna asked, though she wasn't sure why. There was no point continuing to get to know him when she was about to bring their growing intimacy to a terrible halt.

'Philip and I regularly patronise a pugilist club. We've been training there since we were boys.'

'It certainly explains your agility the other night at Vauxhall Gardens.' And the sturdiness of his build. He had the bulk of the men who used to carry in the wine casks to her grandfather's shop, but none of their coarseness.

'That wasn't even my most interesting skirmish.' He held up his fists in mock sparring, his knuckles tight, the strength carrying up to his forearms, which bulged beneath his fitted coat. 'And your brother wasn't much of an opponent.'

The serving woman came to collect their orders, then hurried away.

'Surely you don't spend every night at the pugilist club?' she asked.

He rested his elbows on the table and leaned forward, a hunger for more than ices apparent in his rakish smile. 'If you're worried I won't be home to do my husbandly duties, you're quite mistaken.'

The recollection of his mouth against hers and his tongue caressing the line of her lips made her shift in her seat. She wished she could tug him out of his chair, hurry outside and pull up the hood of the curricle. She wanted to lose herself in the caress of his hands across her back and bask in his compliments and praise, but she couldn't, not when she was about to pull down everything between them like a row of houses in the path of a fire.

She resisted leaning in and answering his invitation to flirt and tease. Instead she changed the subject, fear diverting her from her real purpose yet again. 'Given the state I found you in at Vauxhall Gardens, I gather you don't spend all your time at the pugilist club. Who was the woman I saw leaving your carriage?'

He tapped the top of the table a couple of times, not embarrassed, but not exactly thrilled by her question. 'A friend of mine.'

'A friend?' His clothes had been too dishevelled for her to believe they'd been discussing business. Jealousy pricked at her, the sensation as surprising as it was troubling. Very soon he'd no longer be hers to be jealous of. His past mistakes could easily be walked away from while hers lingered to condemn her.

'Mrs Gammon is a woman I've known for some time, most recently in the carnal sense. The night you saw us, I'd suggested we make our partnership permanent. Apparently, I was only good enough for bed sport. She'd decided to marry another.' He slid back upright in his chair, his earlier excitement fading with this admission. Here was another person who'd failed to believe in him and she felt the sting as keenly as she had every time someone in her life had failed to believe in her.

'You loved her?'

'No. But we got on well together, or so I thought. She didn't have the same faith in my ability to succeed as you do. But enough sour discussion.' At once the seriousness which had marked him was gone and he was again the good-natured Justin. 'How's your dress coming along? Will Mrs Fairley have it ready in time for tomorrow?'

For the wedding which will never happen? 'Yes,' she barely managed to say, not trusting her tongue. The news she was carrying another man's child was not something which could be blurted out across a table at Gunter's, yet in the end it would have to be done.

'Then why the long face? Did Mrs Fairley make the wrong dress?'

'No, of course not. She's an excellent modiste.' Susanna's stomach turned over and she swallowed hard. What she was about to say would heap another insult on him. She wanted to spare him the pain of it, but to lock this sin in her heart for the rest of her life, knowing every time he looked at the child it wasn't his, was more than she could bear. 'Justin, before we meet at the church, there's something I must tell you.'

'About what?' He regarded her with a slightly more serious look.

The room swan around her and she laid her hands on top of the table to steady herself. She opened her mouth to speak just as the matron in the mob cap set two tall glasses frosted by the cold ices inside in front of them.

'Here you are, then.' She laid out two pewter spoons and linen napkins, then bustled off to attend to another couple who'd entered the shop.

Susanna met the eyes of the young woman in the red velvet pelisse striding to a table along the far wall, her narrow-jawed fiancé in tow behind her. She was Baron Holster's daughter and she eyed Susanna as though she were a loose woman who'd crept in the shop to dirty the bright, clean establishment. Any other day, Susanna would have stared the woman down until her delicate sensitivities made her flinch. Today, it was Susanna who looked away first. The woman's opinion of her was correct. Susanna was no better than a cyprian.

'If you're concerned about any lingering feelings I might have for Mrs Gammon, you shouldn't be,' Justin assured her, mistaking the source of her unease. 'Her true opinion of me killed all my feelings for her, as I'm sure Lord Howsham's behaviour did for you.'

'Yes, it did.' If only her time with him hadn't resulted in a new life. She rested one hand on her stomach, remembering how her already weak love for the earl had wilted when he'd failed to arrive at Vauxhall Gardens. If he were as honourable a man as Justin, then she might appeal to him and tell him about the baby, but he'd callously walked away from her before. He'd have no compunction about doing it again and would probably publicly disgrace her this time. Once the Rocklands disowned her, there'd be no reason for him not to reveal the story, for it wouldn't risk offending the duke. No one would be worried about offending her because she didn't matter. The only people she'd ever mattered to were resting in the churchyard in Oxfordshire, or sitting here across from her, unaware she was about to crush his regard for her with the truth.

'Speaking of Lord Howsham…' she began hesitantly, swirling the melting ice in her glass.

'I told you the other day we won't discuss the past,'

he insisted, as aware as she of Miss Holster and her fiancé watching them with too much curiosity. Justin shifted his chair, the metal scraping over the wood as he placed his wide back between the couple and Susanna.

'But it's only fair you know—'

'You and Lord Howsham were intimate,' he interrupted in a low voice before she could say the words. 'I'd guessed as much and I don't care. Your time with him is as finished as mine is with Mrs Gammon. There's no reason to discuss it further.'

He jabbed his spoon in the ice, scooped out a healthy portion and stuck it in his mouth with a finality to tell her she wouldn't be able to broach the subject today, and if not today, then never. Tomorrow would see them before the altar.

'Then I won't say anything,' she mumbled, as much to him as herself.

She slipped a spoonful of ice in her mouth. The orange was sharp and she swallowed it down as she did the words of her revelation. Both chilled her, but she forced the feeling aside. She wasn't going to make a public spectacle of either of them by insisting on telling him something he obviously didn't wish to hear. It wasn't a secret she wanted lingering in the corners of her mind, but he'd made her decision for her, just as she'd made her decision to marry him the night at Vauxhall Gardens and again in the Rocklands' sitting room. Her conscience nagged at her, but if he insisted she remain silent about her past then he accepted her as she was and she'd carry the secret the same way she'd carried all the other heartaches and disappointments of her life.

In time, when her child was happy and loved, she might forgive herself, assuming Mrs Fairley's suspicions were correct. She might not be with child, or she might lose it after the wedding. After tomorrow it wouldn't matter. Whether she gave birth to Lord Howsham's child or a puppy, in the eyes of the law it would belong to Justin. No one would ever call the poor little mite a bastard or look down at it the way the baron's daughter looked down on Susanna now. Her child would have the love and care of both parents and a home where he or she would be cherished. It was everything she'd wanted as a child and everything she'd be sure to give to hers. Heaven willing, he'd never discover the truth.

Justin finished the last of his ice, barely tasting the too-cold concoction. Her mention of Lord Howsham, and interest in Helena had turned the sweet sour. He didn't want to hear about her past any more than he wanted to ponder his. He had a future to look forward to and it, not old ghosts, would guide him today.

'I've purchased a shop for the business,' he announced, his spoon rattling in his glass as he pushed it aside.

'Why not lease instead? It'd be cheaper.' She seemed as relieved as him by the change in topic. It settled the storm in her green eyes which had gathered there during the discussion of her past.

'Buying it is a hedge against failure. If the wine

trade doesn't work, at least I'll have the building to rent, or I can sell it and recoup some of the capital.' Unlike a ship it couldn't end up at the bottom of the ocean.

She wrinkled her nose at the last bite of her ice, then dropped the spoon in the glass. 'Once, when my grandfather was doing well, the owner asked if he wanted to purchase the building with his shop. Grandmother begged him to do it, but he didn't want to spend the money. When she tried to insist, he told her not to meddle in a man's work. He should have let her meddle— she was better at business than he ever was.'

Justin reached across the table and took her hand, then slipped his thumb inside the small hole just below the glove's button to caress her smooth flesh. It pebbled under the soft stroke, the tightness of her skin matched by the one in his loins. 'You have my permission to meddle with my business as often as you like.'

Beneath the pad of his thumb the faint thump of her pulse quickened. Her heightened awareness of his skin against hers, even in this small way, increased the need surging through him. He slipped his thumb a little further inside the glove and swept it over the arch of her wrist. Her fingertips beneath his arm pressed into his coat with the same shock which parted her lips in a subtle inhale of breath. He shifted to the edge of his seat, wanting to push the table aside and pull her across the gap to him, but they weren't alone or in some bawdy house. As conscious of his touch as she was, she was more aware of those around them. Her eyes shifted to the other patrons before coming back to him. Someone must be watching them, for the innocent reaction of her instincts faded and she pulled back her hand.

Justin let her go. He wouldn't embarrass her in public, not when tomorrow night they'd be alone and they could both savour her unfettered response to his touch.

'Shall we be off?' he asked, as though a private room were waiting for them and not the imposing iron fences of Grosvenor Square.

'Please,' she choked out, before clearing her throat, gathering up her reticule and rising.

The ride home was no more soothing than their time in Gunter's. Despite the traffic commanding his attention, Justin's focus remained fixed on every shift of Susanna's legs, each slide of her skirts across her knees and thighs. Her voice as she described her mother pierced him as sharply as the faint scent of the orange ice lingering beneath her jasmine perfume. He'd never been so aware of a woman before. Many had amused and intrigued him, but not one had ever exerted such control over his senses without even trying.

At last the noisy streets gave way to the quiet confines of Grosvenor Square. If he could have kept driving right on through today into tomorrow night he would have done it, but he couldn't. Patience was necessary and he pulled the curricle to a halt in front of the Rockland house. They'd have their entire lives together after tomorrow.

Susanna studied the house, blinking against the intensity of the sunlight reflecting off the white stone.

Netley pulled open the door and the cavernous entrance hall yawned, ready to engulf her. She wanted to stay out here in the daylight with Justin as the shadows fell from his hat to deepen the rise of his cheekbones. As agitated as she'd been before Gunter's with her secret boiling inside her, the faint caress of his thumb over her skin had increased the tension until she thought she might jump from the carriage and sprint home. On and on she'd chattered at him, trying to dispel her increased agitation. He hadn't demanded she sit quietly the way Lord Howsham used to do, but listened, deftly manoeuvring the curricle through the crush.

'Thank you, Justin.' She made for the house, needing to be alone and settle herself. How she'd get through tomorrow as the smiling bride everyone expected her to be she didn't know. In the meantime, she'd concern herself with the business of seeing the last of her things packed and sent off to Justin's house, wrapping up the unhappy life she'd endured with the Rocklands.

'Wait.' He caught her hand before she could go, his large fingers curling around hers and steadying her against the rocking which was making the street swim.

'Yes?' She wanted to cling to him and his solid faith in himself and her, even if she didn't deserve it. She'd find a way to deserve it, to assist him in all his endeavours in the hope so much good could absolve her of the one wrong she was about to commit. All her behaviour from this day onwards would make her worthy to take his name and enjoy the protection of him as her husband. The sin wasn't just for her own selfish reasons, but for the future of the child. This was her chance to give it everything she'd never had.

He inched closer until his chest was nearly against hers and she could see the faint ash and dust from the street in the threads of the wool coat. As she peered up into his heavy-lidded eyes, temptation almost overcame her better sense.

'I can't linger on the doorstep with a suitor, even if we're meeting at the church tomorrow.' It would only be a matter of time before Lady Rockland scuttled out from wherever she was inside, most likely making a maid miserable, and accuse Susanna once again of being common, or say heaven knew what to Justin.

'Damn them all. I don't care what they think.' He bent down and claimed her mouth.

There was no evergreen bush to shield them from the view of the governesses parading up and down the opposite walk with their charges, or the nosy maid in the window across the street who'd weave what she saw into a fabulous tale to delight her employer and embarrass the Rocklands. Susanna didn't care. Tomorrow she'd leave them and this world behind. Today she delighted in the firmness of his lips against hers. The heat from the sweep of his thumb beneath her glove ignited again until she was sure the trees of the square would catch fire and burn her and everything around them to the ground. She wouldn't be sorry to see it go, only Justin when he drove away. Tomorrow they'd be together and then nothing, not her past, or his, could separate them.

When at last Justin released her, she staggered back

a touch, barely aware of Netley coughing his disapproval from his place by the door.

'Until tomorrow.' He raised his hat to her, the sun catching in the light strands of his hair before he settled it back down over his head.

'Until then.' She gripped the iron railing along the front walk to steady herself, admiring the tightening of his breeches over the roundness of his buttocks as he raised one leg to step up into the curricle before placing himself on the seat and setting the horse into motion. Susanna lingered on the pavement, hardly noticing the rough iron against her palm as she watched his curricle turn the corner to be obscured by the trees dominating the square.

With heavy feet she trudged inside, ignoring Netley's disapproving scowl as he swung closed the door behind her. He marched off to see to his duties, and no doubt to tell Lady Rockland of Susanna's blatant indiscretion on their front doorstep. Let him chide and snitch, she didn't care. Tomorrow, she'd be done with them all.

Justin arrived home to find an ordered confusion of men and trunks as they carried Susanna's things into the house.

'Upstairs, first door to the right, mind you don't nick the plasterwork,' the housekeeper, Mrs Robinson, instructed, with all the attendance of a general overseeing manoeuvres.

She'd come to him with this house in Johnson's Court, off Fleet Street, when the previous owner had sold it to Justin in a rush to raise money to keep himself out of prison. It'd been Justin's sanctuary for the last six years, the place he'd retire to after a day of either dodging unhappy perfumers, or after yet another argument with his father. The furniture was left over from the previous owner, some of it fine, other pieces in need of freshening, but that wasn't something he concerned himself with. Susanna could do the place up as she liked when she settled here. To him, it didn't matter what his home looked like as long as it was comfortable.

Leaving everything in the capable hands of Mrs Robinson, he retreated to his study. Its walls were decorated with paintings of spaniels and horses left by the former occupant along with the thick leather furniture. One low bookcase sat under the window with a tray of glasses and decanters on top. The rest of the shelves were empty. The books had been sold last year to fund his venture. He should have burned them for all the money it'd gained him.

He poured himself a measure of the American whisky one of his less reputable suppliers had procured for him. He'd have to see what other gems the man could smuggle in for him for the shop. Justin held the drink under his nose, inhaling the stiff burned-oak scent before tossing it back. The smoky shot briefly eased the tension which had marked him before he'd kissed Susanna goodbye and ever since. Their awkward exchange at Gunter's had been forgotten in her savoury response to his lips against hers, the promise of which he looked forward to fulfilling tomorrow night.

'Quite the flurry of activity here.' A familiar voice slid through the room from the entrance, the notes of it souring his drink.

'Good evening, Mrs Gammon,' Mrs Robinson stiffly greeted her.

Justin carried his glass with him as he came to the door to lean against the jamb, a fisted hand on one hip as he eyed the widow. 'What are you doing here?'

A man carrying a stack of round hat boxes and who knew what other frippery tried to shift around the widow before she stopped him. She lifted the lid on a box and peeked inside, frowning with more envy than disapproval. 'Rather feminine attire for a man of your carriage.'

She eyed him with the same suggestive craving which had invited him into her bed over a year ago. Now, not even years of celibacy could drive him back into her arms again.

'Does your husband approve of you being here?' he asked, taking a slow sip of his drink and wishing he'd brought the entire bottle with him.

'We haven't married yet. He insists on reading the banns.' She dropped the lid and allowed the man to continue on his way.

'Probably too cheap to pay for the common licence.'

Her lips pursed and he knew he'd struck at the truth of the matter. So, her furrier wasn't the pampering prince she'd thought him to be, but a businessman like every other penny-pincher in this part of London. 'What are you doing here?'

'I seem to have misplaced a couple of items since the last time I was here. An expensive ivory fan and a tortoiseshell hair comb.'

Justin had no idea if the items were here, or if this was simply her excuse to come back and dally before the banns were read. Either way, he was about to disappoint her. 'I haven't seen them. Mrs Robinson, have you found a hair comb and a fan left behind by Mrs Gammon?'

'No, sir, I haven't seen such things.' The housekeeper held her hands tight in front of her, arms bent at the elbow like some Egyptian statue he'd seen at the British Museum. She'd never cared for the widow, or her late-night visits. On more than one occasion she'd referred to Helena as a wanton hussy. Justin had been more amused than irked by the housekeeper's mutterings, until Helena had proven them to be true. 'I can't imagine how a lady's items could have ended up in the house of a single gentleman.'

Helena frowned at the subtle dig and Justin restrained a laugh. The widow had never once hesitated to enter his house late at night in her cloak, or to venture downstairs after sunrise for all of the servants to see. It seemed, with her pending nuptials, all sense of decency had suddenly returned, though not enough to stop her from visiting him.

'Perhaps I'm mistaken and they were left at my sister's.' Helena pulled her bright red spencer closed over her ample and too-well-displayed-for-so-early-in-the-day breasts, trying to reclaim her dignity. Justin wouldn't allow it.

'If they're here, we'll be sure to find them.' He exchanged a dubious look with Mrs Robinson before fixing his eyes on Helena. 'I wouldn't want my bride to be troubled by the sight of another woman's things when she arrives here tomorrow night.'

Helena's petulant mouth fell open in shock. 'You're getting married?'

This was fast becoming a very satisfying day, though tomorrow would be even more so. 'In the morning.'

'My, you move quickly.'

'I've learned from the best.' He finished his drink, ignoring her acid stare.

'And who's the lucky woman?'

'Miss Susanna Lambert.' He said no more as he set the empty glass down on a bust stand next to the study door. Helena read the scandal sheets and would recognise the name. He wasn't disappointed.

'The Duke of Rockland's bastard daughter?' She let out a low whistle, betraying her fishmonger roots. 'I'm impressed, Justin. You're marrying into the nobility.'

'Yes, can't you just see me in the House of Lords?' he replied sarcastically, enjoying her jealous astonishment as much as he had his contraband whisky. It proved he wasn't the loafer she'd taken him for in the carriage outside Vauxhall Gardens. Now all he needed to do was make a success of his wine business and prove to her and his father how much they'd underestimated him.

'How did you of all people manage to capture such

a prize?' She said it as if no one but she would deign to have him.

'The duke believes in me more than some people do.' He strolled past her to the door and pulled it open before Walter, his valet and butler, could hurry to do it. After his failure last year, he couldn't spare the extra expense for a footman. In time, when his wine business began bringing in money, he'd hire more staff, perhaps even a lady's maid for Susanna. She'd need someone to help her undress at night, though in the meantime he'd be more than happy to assist her. 'If you'll excuse me, I have a great deal to do before tomorrow.'

Shoring up some of the dignity with which she'd entered the house, Helena approached him, pausing to lay one well-manicured hand on Justin's chest.

'If you find your little daughter of a nobleman lacking, my previous offer of the other night still stands,' she purred, her voice like screeching metal compared to Susanna's tender tones.

Justin removed her hand from his chest and allowed it to drop back down by her side. 'That's too kind of you, Mrs Gammon, but I assure you your services will not be necessary.'

Helena whirled around in fury and made for the gig waiting at the end of the pathway. She climbed inside, smacking away the driver's hand as he tried to help her before she settled beside him and they set off.

Justin wandered back to the study, leaving Mrs Robinson and the others to their duties. Despite dispatching the widow, there was more to accomplish before he could claim victory over her and his father's low expectations. He poured himself another drink, not touching the amber liquid this time as he sank into his favourite leather armchair by the fire. Susanna's strained manner at Gunter's made him wary and the unsettling feeling there was something he couldn't anticipate waiting to rise up and crush him nagged. He wanted so much to be successful, but last time, despite all his careful plans, Mother Nature had knocked him down. He hadn't seen the strike coming.

He wondered if a nature more akin to lust was making him blind to a weakness in Susanna. He was normally adept at reading people. It was a skill he'd learned with Philip under the tutelage of the elder Mr Rathbone. If he'd better employed it with Helena, he might not have made a fool of himself outside Vauxhall Gardens. Was he ignoring his better sense with Susanna?

He lifted the glass to the window, observing the labourers, shop assistants and apprentices passing back and forth in front of it through the hazy liquid. Perhaps his father was right about not reaching too far above his station. Maybe he wasn't meant to be anything more than the employee of another. He lowered the glass and knocked back the rest of the liquor before setting it aside.

His father wasn't right. Justin might not have guessed Helena's venality, but all men made mistakes at one time or another. It didn't mean he was any less worthy to strive for something more. Even the nearly infallible Philip had experienced doubts, especially after his first wife had died giving birth to his son Thomas and he'd nearly lost his business. The measure of a man was how he dealt with upsets and setbacks. Justin would face each and every challenge, never allowing his reservations or anyone else's to undermine him, and he would do it all with Susanna by his side. Everyone had their weaknesses and failings; at some point hers would reveal themselves, as would his. There was no reason to brood on them now and sour the honeymoon. Getting to know her and all her little quirks would be as pleasurable as exploring her body and letting her discover his. It was a much more appealing prospect to consider.

Chapter Seven

Susanna sat alone in the quiet of the carriage outside St Bride's, waiting for the footman to return from inside and tell her it was time for the ceremony. She smoothed her hands over the waist of the silk wedding dress draping her body. The bodice had been altered by Mrs Fairley in time for this morning. While she waited, her father's words as he'd escorted her to the carriage rang in her ears like the church bells in the tall spire overhead.

'I might consent to the marriage, but I can't insult Lady Rockland or my legal children by giving you away. I'm sure there's a friend of Mr Connor's who can stand in my place.'

Susanna hadn't argued or begged him to change his mind. As much as this final insult hurt, not having the Rocklands sitting like a bunch of sour-faced gargoyles in the pews during the service was a relief. In the end they hadn't even bothered to rise and help her dress, leaving her to the lady's maid and her own skills to prepare herself. Despite the cut, it'd saved them all from enduring an awkward goodbye.

Taking in the greystone church entrance with its graceful metal arch over the top, she drew in a deep breath, ready once again to face a challenge alone. Hopefully, with Justin soon to be her husband, this would be the last one. They might not enjoy the grand love she'd read about in novels, but she respected him, though not enough, it seemed, to tell him the truth.

She tugged at the lace along the neckline of her dress, wishing the footman would hurry. The carriage was growing hot in the morning sun and she was eager to leave this last trapping of her old life behind. If only her secret was so easily discarded. It was wrong to enter the church carrying this large a lie, but it would be even worse to bring a baby into the world and see it scorned due to no fault of its own. It would do no good to be tossed with it into the gutter where the baby would either die or endure a life of misery at the whims of the unkind streets. She'd endure anything to ensure an innocent child wasn't subjected to a life of suffering.

At this moment, Susanna felt very alone.

'Miss Lambert, you look beautiful,' a feminine voice exclaimed from the opposite side of the carriage. Mrs Rathbone stood in the open window, beaming at her. Mr Rathbone stepped behind her, his opinion of her dress better concealed, but his expression echoing something of his wife's excitement. 'Mr Connor said important business kept your father from attending the service. Philip has graciously volunteered to walk you down the aisle, if that's all right with you?'

'It is, thank you.' Susanna breathed a sigh of relief as she slid across the squabs to where the driver had pulled open the door.

'It's the least I could do for my friend and his soon-to-be wife.' Mr Rathbone offered her his elbow and she took it.

Around her, Mrs Rathbone adjusted the dress, smoothing out the wrinkles and arranging the short veil cascading down the back of Susanna's head. They were the small services a mother, or at the very least a friend, should do, yet they were left to a kind stranger. Smiling in gratitude at Mrs Rathbone, Susanna knew, in time, these people would mean more to her than anyone related to her by blood, except her mother and grandmother, ever could.

'I'll go inside and tell them you're ready.' Mrs Rathbone hurried off to the church with the good news, leaving her husband to escort Susanna.

Mr Rathbone carried out his duty with all the solemnity of an older brother, setting Susanna at ease despite the formal way in which he stood beside her. Unlike her father might have done, he didn't fulfil this position because it was expected of him, but because he wanted to, and for Susanna this distinction made a great deal of difference.

The moment she stepped through the double doors and into the high space coloured by the large, stained-glass windows, the loneliness she'd known in the carriage disappeared. Mrs Rathbone had taken her place in the front pew beside Miss Rathbone and Mrs Townsend and other people Susanna assumed were Justin's friends. They all turned to watch her as she walked on Mr Rathbone's arm up the aisle to where Justin waited with Reverend Clare.

A black coat covered the width of Justin's chest, the lapels trimmed in dark velvet. The blue light of a stained-glass window overhead graced his shoulders and caught the faint blue in the darkness of his coat. His face was set off by the contrast between the jacket and the crisp white shirt and cravat, both of which fitted tightly beneath his chin. The severity of his dress was softened by the cut of his wide smile. It echoed in the brightness of his eyes as they took in the length of her before rising to catch her gaze. Under the spell of his charm, it was all she could do not to let go of Mr Rathbone and rush up the aisle. Instead, she moved steadily forward on her gracious escort's arm, trying to maintain the calm reserve expected of a bride. The time to fling off all restraints would come tonight, when she would at last see what lay beneath Justin's staid black and enjoy something of the teasing touch he'd left her with yesterday.

She reined in her wicked thoughts. Now was no time to think of the marital bed, not with Mr Rathbone handing her over to Justin and Reverend Clare observing them from beneath his severe brow.

It was difficult with Justin's hand in hers to keep her thoughts anchored in the solemn surroundings. While Reverend Clare read the ceremony, every inch of her was aware of Justin standing beside her as solid as any of the pillars holding up the church. It was only when the reverend said to the gathered guests, 'If there is anyone here who has cause to believe that these two should not be joined in holy matrimony then let him speak now or for ever hold his peace', that the present flooded over her like wine from a broken cask.

Reverend Clare paused and waited. Susanna's pulse pounded in her ears. She peered over her shoulder at the empty pews, half-expecting Lady Rockland to appear at the church door and announce to all Susanna's condition, snatching away everything, but there was no one there. Any ideas of revenge the woman possessed had probably been overwhelmed by her inability to rise before noon. Late balls made for such a trying life.

At last, Reverend Clare resumed the ceremony and Susanna shifted a touch closer to Justin, her arm brushing against his as she drew from his happiness and strength to bolster hers. Soon they would be bound together and the intimacy she'd craved with him since their time alone on the Rathbones' portico would be theirs.

All regrets from the past, and worries about the future, vanished the moment the reverend instructed them to face one another. With a steady hand, Justin followed the reverend's words and slid the gold band studded with small diamonds around her finger and repeated the vows. She didn't doubt his willingness to stand beside her through better or worse, just as she would stand beside him.

When at last the vows were said, the rings exchanged and the blessing given, Reverend Clare pronounced them man and wife, linking their fates before instructing them to kiss.

She tilted up her head, eager to enjoy the weight of his mouth upon hers, and she was not disappointed. Settling his hands on her upper arms, he pressed his lips to hers. This was not the passionate kiss from the portico or the stolen one from yesterday, but something deeper, meant to convey to her and everyone gathered the intensity of the promises they'd made.

Afterwards, it was a merry gathering in the Rathbones' garden where the sun highlighted the green of the bushes and the blue sky hanging over a fine day. A hearty selection of food was laid out on a table on the portico for the guests to enjoy as they mingled. Young Thomas toddled between the ladies, cooed over by them as his nurse followed after him, and the Rathbones' young infant slept upstairs. More than one ribald joke about the wedding night made the rounds, especially after yet another bottle of wine was opened by a footman. Miss Jane stood in the midst of it all, listening with interest despite Mrs Townsend's halfhearted attempts to shield her young charge.

'Do you like the ring?' Justin asked when he caught Susanna admiring the way the diamonds sparkled in the sunlight.

'It's gorgeous. Where did you get it?'

'It was my mother's.'

Susanna closed her hand, almost ashamed to be wearing it after the secret she'd kept. Then she stretched out her fingers and looked at it again, determined to make herself worthy of the intimate gift.

'If you'd like, we could sneak out the back gate.' Justin tempted her, his hot breath laced with wine teasing her cheek. 'They wouldn't miss us.'

'Of course they would.' After all the effort the Rathbones had gone to on their behalf, she didn't want to be rude by sneaking away, no matter how much she wanted to be alone with Justin. 'I sense Mr Charton hasn't depleted the last of Mr Rathbone's fine port or his store of bawdy jokes.'

As if hearing his name, the lanky man with the red nose approached them.

'Surprised us all with this wedding, Justin. I didn't expect you to settle down. Just like your father. I was stunned the day he escorted your mother up the aisle.' Mr Charton raised his empty wine glass to Justin before wandering off in pursuit of a footman carrying a tray laden with more drinks.

'Your father isn't here,' Susanna said, at last noticing the older man's absence.

Justin shrugged, his lips drawing up into more of a grimace than the smile he'd worn since she'd come up the aisle. 'The plentiful drink might have lured him here, but he'd have to be pleasant, something he's no longer capable of.'

Susanna wasn't so sure and she intended to find out. She wasn't going to allow the wound festering between father and son to continue.

'I hope you aren't offended by Mr Charton, or anyone else's jokes,' Justin asked, his humour returning.

'No, I love it. A society wedding can't compare to this, unless you enjoy sitting around like a statue with everyone bored and watching the clock tick down the minutes until they can leave.'

He brushed the back of her neck with his fingers, sending a chill racing across her exposed skin. 'I'm counting down the time until we can leave.'

She offered him a seductive look, tempting him as much as he tempted her. 'You aren't the only one.'

'Justin, stop fawning so much over your wife or all us husbands will be expected to show our wives the same favour,' Mr Charton called out across the garden.

Mrs Charton laid a steadying hand on him as he lurched a little to one side. 'Careful, my dear, or you'll have all the wives angry at you.'

'Yes, a fate worse than death, isn't it, Rathbone?'

'Indeed, I'd never dream of making Mrs Rathbone angry.' Philip brushed his wife's lips with a kiss, lingering a little too long for the gesture to be called merely playful.

Once witnessing such intimacy would have made Susanna envious. Today she linked her arm in Justin's, knowing she along with the other wives here would soon be enjoying the pleasure of the marriage bed.

At last the shadows of the rosebushes stretched across the gravel path and the chill of the coming night began to fill the air. The Rathbones' coach was summoned and, with the guests lining either side of the front steps to wish Justin and Susanna well, the newly married couple took their leave.

* * *

Justin's house wasn't far from Bride Lane, but in the crush of carriages on the street it was some time until it rolled up to Johnson's Court and the simple two-storey dwelling wedged between similar unassuming houses on either side. It wasn't as fancy as the Rathbones' or as large, but simple in a way she admired. After years living in the draughty halls of Rockland Place, she was eager for the cosiness of an unfussy home.

Justin escorted Susanna up the steps and into the entrance hall where his servants stood ready to meet their new mistress. He introduced her to the cook, his valet who was also the butler, and the housekeeper, Mrs Robinson. They all received her warmly, even Mrs Robinson, who didn't seem troubled by a strange woman arriving to displace her authority.

'If you'll follow me, I'll show you to your room,' Mrs Robinson entreated.

Susanna went with her up the narrow staircase. From the height she took in more of the house. No panelling graced the walls and the furniture she could see through the open sitting-room door was from another era, though sturdy and of good quality with the exception of one or two pieces which were stashed in discreet corners. The slight formality of the decor didn't seem to have Justin's mark upon it and yet at the same time it did. It was uncomplicated and comfortable, yet sturdy.

At the top of the stairs, Mrs Robinson led her into a bedroom connected by a door to Justin's room.

'I've seen to the arranging and unpacking of your

things. If there's anything you'd like changed, please let me know,' Mrs Robinson offered.

Susanna turned over the brush and comb on the fine but unadorned dressing table beside the wardrobe. On the wall above it hung the gilded frame with the miniature of her mother. This was such a different welcome from the one she'd received at the Rocklands' house. Back then, nearly everything she'd brought with her to Rockland Place, especially her clothes, had been discarded and replaced. Lady Rockland had been too afraid of the lice which hadn't existed to allow Susanna to keep more than the miniature. Even this had been reframed so it would match the decor of her room. It was a wonder Lady Rockland hadn't pried it out of the frame before allowing it to leave the house yesterday. She'd probably considered the loss of the frame a small price to pay to hustle Susanna out of her life.

Susanna moved around the small but comfortable room. Not a speck of gilding or silk marred the clean lines of the suite or made it so pristine one couldn't touch anything for fear of ruining it. A large bed stood against the far wall and was draped with a fine yellow coverlet which matched the subtle weave in the cover of the chair beside the fireplace. Curtains in a similar cheery hue hung from the single window which overlooked the bustling street in front of the house. A wardrobe stood on the opposite wall, carved in a similar dark-and-burled wood as the bed. Susanna opened the wardrobe and fingered her dresses, which had been arranged by colour. She marvelled not just at Mrs Robinson's efficiency, but at how at ease she felt here, as if this room were made for her. Even in the house in Oxfordshire she'd never felt completely at home, or in any of the Rocklands' estates. In this humble dwelling, with her things spread out by a stranger, it was as if she belonged.

'Is everything as it should be?' Justin asked, opening the door adjoining his room to hers. With him the masculine scent of shaving soap, leather polish and spirits drifted in to overwhelm the more delicate notes of jasmine adorning her space. His coat was gone and he stood in his waistcoat, his powerful arms made larger by the billowing fabric of his shirt. The waistcoat was solid against the flatness of his stomach, the slight taper of it widening his already impressive chest.

'It is.' Susanna fingered the banyan draped over the back of the chair by the fire to warm it, noting from beneath her lashes how he eyed her with an eagerness which made her toes curl. She wanted to see beneath his waistcoat, to lift the linen of the shirt from his torso and trace the hard lines of muscle which must lie beneath.

'Shall I help you undress, Mrs Connor?' Mrs Robinson offered, old enough not to blush with the knowledge of what was about to happen.

Susanna stared at the housekeeper, a little stunned. It wasn't so much her question which shocked Susanna, but the new name, home and the station in life she'd gained, a station which suited her better than any she'd previously held.

'No, I believe we can manage,' Susanna answered, the new surety in her life giving her a true confidence to replace the one she'd feigned so many times in the past.

Without another word, Mrs Robinson left, closing the door behind her.

Once the lock clicked shut, the desire in Justin's eyes ignited Susanna's insides like a hot poker added to wine to boil it. In two steps he brought the high-polished toes of his boots up to touch the satin of her slippers. The nearness of him sucked the air from the room and she looked down at the thick carpet, the confidence she'd enjoyed a few moments before deserting her.

He slid one large finger beneath her chin and raised her face to his. 'Don't tell me a woman of your experience is nervous.'

It was a joke, meant to be light and to break the tension making her stomach draw in, but it fell flat.

'I may not be a virgin, but I'm not as experienced as you believe.' She moved to the washstand near the window and fingered the curving arch of the porcelain handle. 'Lord Howsham and I were intimate only once, in the woods at Rockland Place. He was so eager and I was so stupid to not reject him. In the end it wasn't—' She bit her lip, unsure how to explain.

'—wasn't for your benefit, but for his,' Justin finished, coming to stand beside her, the linen of his shirt brushing against the bare top of her arm.

She crossed her arms in front of her, trying to fight back the chill creeping over her. She looked up at Justin, touched he didn't blame her or call her a whore. She shuddered to imagine what words he'd hurl at her if he discovered the result of her ill-fated encounter with Lord Howsham and how she'd duped him. She didn't deserve this happiness.

Justin slid his fingers beneath Susanna's, caressing the tender skin of her arm before he tugged her hand away and raised it to his chest. With a reassuring squeeze, he stilled her trembles, but not the unease curling her shoulders and making her draw away from him. He'd been foolish to tease her about Lord Howsham. He wouldn't make such a stupid mistake again.

Justin brushed the side of her face with the tips of his fingers. With her lips pressed together and her eyes wide, she appeared as fresh as the young milkmaid who'd taken his innocence many years ago while surrendering her own. He was no innocent now, but Susanna was, despite her encounter with the earl. He silently cursed the man for having fallen on her like some overeager schoolboy instead of cherishing her enough to take his time and ensure her pleasure as well as his own.

Justin cradled her face in his hands and lowered his lips to hers. The moist softness of her mouth heightened the desire already coursing through him, but he held it back. There would be no hurrying, no cajoling of her favours, but a willingness in both of them to unite their bodies. He gently probed her lips with his tongue and with a sigh she opened to him, her body unfolding beneath his as she uncurled her arms from her waist to wrap them around him. He explored the taste of her as he ran his hands along the row of ivory buttons along the back of her dress. Starting at the bottom, he began to undo them one by one. When the silk gaped open, she gasped, but didn't startle or cling to the modesty the fabric offered. Instead she drew away from him, allowing him to take the short sleeves of the dress and lower it down over the length of her. He admired the subtle point of her toes in the stockings as she stepped out of her slippers to raise first one foot and then the other from the circle of the dress. He laid the silk to one side, then slid a wide hand along the back of her calves, stopping just behind her knee, not ready to go higher.

A sweep of pink spread across the tops of her breasts as he stood to admire the curve of the ivory cotton of her stays. It followed the roundness of her hips up along her waist to where the pliant garment cupped each full breast. Not wanting to leave her exposed and embarrassed, he shrugged out of his waistcoat and tossed it aside, then tugged off his boots. He undid the knot of his cravat and pulled the material out from around his neck. She watched in silence as he undressed and he flashed her a wicked smile when a small gasp of amazement greeted the removal of his shirt. The heat in her gaze as she took in his defined chest made every hour he'd spent in the ring at the pugilist club worth the effort.

'Now we're even.' He caught her by the waist and pulled her into the curve of his body. As their lips met, her hands lay flat against his muscles, singeing his exposed skin.

With deft fingers, he began to undo the laces of her stays, each slip of the strings through the eyelets taunting him to move faster, but he held back. He'd never rushed with a woman, but he'd never moved quite this slow either. The widows he'd enjoyed had known their way around a man enough to keep pace with him, but not Susanna. She'd indulged, but it was clear she hadn't been allowed to enjoy a man's body and he wanted her to revel in his as much as he relished hers.

At last the stays opened and he let go, allowing them to drop to the floor. She broke from his kiss, moving back a touch in her hesitancy. The crisp white chemise surrounding her body glowed cream with her skin. Through the fine fabric he could just make out the pink buds of her nipples, pert against the cotton. He knew what his own body was doing to his breeches as she glanced down to his hips, a saucy smile pulling up one corner of her full lips. She caught the sides of the chemise and raised it over her head, revealing inch by glorious inch her supple body and her trust in him.

'We're no longer even,' she purred, standing before him in nothing but the sheer silk stockings with the blue ribbons tied in dainty bows at the centre of her thighs. The candlelight danced over her skin and her full breasts were pert above her stomach which led down to the dark sable at the junction of her thighs.

'Allow me to rectify the situation.' Undoing the buttons on his fall, he slid off his breeches, stepped out of them, then straightened to catch her eyes widening at the sight of him. She bit her bottom lip not in fear, but with a hesitation laced with anticipation, which further tightened his member.

Her soft stomach against his hardness made him

groan as he tangled his hands in her hair, dislodging the pins and sending a cascade of curls spilling down over her shoulders. The feathery strands brushed his chest and he pushed one silken curl aside to cup her breast. With his thumb, he grazed the pointed tip, aware of the shiver it sent coursing through her. She raised her hands to his shoulders, gripping them tight as he continued to tease the hard point, her breathing growing heavy with his. He broke from her mouth and dipped to taste the skin of her neck, inhaling the flowery scent of her. As his tongue traced the line of her skin, she laid one cheek against his hair, the subtle move both innocent and trusting. He wanted to be worthy of it as he sank lower to take the tip of one full breast in his mouth. Her grip on him strengthened as he made small circles around it, suckling as she arched her back so he could taste more.

His hands rested on her hips to steady her against him, but he hesitated to move lower and worship the more intimate part of her, afraid the force of her reaction might undo his control. There'd be plenty of time to show her more. Tonight he wanted her to experience the most basic of pleasure, the one denied to her in the past.

Sliding one hand beneath her arms so the side of her full breasts grazed his skin, he moved his other arm beneath her thighs and raised her up. She wasn't heavy, but fitted perfectly against him, her lips light and teasing against his neck as he carried her to his room. A few candles flickered in the holder beside the bed, but the fire in the grate roared, increasing the heat generated by their bodies. He laid her down on the cool sheets, then stretched out beside her.

'You're beautiful...' he breathed as he traced the curve of her waist and trailed his fingertips down over her hips before sliding between her thighs and into her pleasure.

'Justin, I—' She shifted against his hand, searching for something denied to her as his thumb teased her.

'I know,' he murmured against her arched neck, his ability to hold back with her body tightening around his failing. He wanted her as much as she wanted him and she was ready.

She moaned in frustration as he slipped his fingers from her, but she opened her legs to him and he settled between her thighs. With languid, questioning eyes she watched him, moving beneath him until his manhood pressed against her need. He paused, noting her silent entreaty for more in the flush of her skin and the faint parting of her lips. The other women he'd been with had been demanding in their desire to be satisfied, but she waited, eager for him to lead her, and he wouldn't fail her. Here was someone who understood him and what it was to endure the attacks of family and the doubts of many. She supported him, believing in him when those he'd once thought his friends refused to, trusting him even in this most intimate of moments.

He slid his arms beneath her back, his fingertips digging into her skin as the softness of her curves pressed into his angular body and he slipped fully into her, bringing her closer to him than anyone had ever been before.

* * *

Susanna dug her nails into his shoulder blades as he moved slow and steady inside her, solid against her like a wall. She lost herself in the strength of him as he caressed her hip and trailed his finger over her stomach until he reached between them to touch her. She cried out at the sensation of his fingers working her pleasure as his member stroked in time to his movements.

This was no greedy fumbling or a hurried slaking of his need, but a lingering taste of affection and a deepening of the connection which had been growing between them these past few days. In this as in everything, he was careful and kind to her in a way almost everyone else had never been. Lord Howsham had used her body and ignored her, while the rest had torn at her heart, leaving her to bleed. Justin would never be so unkind.

She entwined her legs with his, drawing him deeper into her body. It wasn't just physical desire driving her on, but a more intense need rising up from the place she'd kept hidden from everyone. For the first time since her mother had died, there was someone to protect her and truly care for her and it touched her more than all the play of his fingers across her back. She was his wife. He would keep her safe and give her more than his body and name and worldly goods.

He took one nipple in his mouth and sucked the tender tip, making her writhe beneath him. The pleasure was too intense, too strong, and she craved the release cresting deep inside her. Each press of his lips on her exposed skin and the fierce play of his fingers against her continued to drive her higher and higher until at last she cried out, clinging to him. With a few more thrusts, Justin groaned, his pulsing flesh matching the rippling of hers and heightening her release until at last he lowered himself over her, his chest meeting hers with each struggling breath.

After a long moment, the crackle of the fire and the sounds of wagons on the street outside began to fill the room. She released her grip on his back and the cool air danced over her sweat-dampened chest as he shifted away to one side, then drew her close. Her whole body was alive and yet satiated and she let out a long sigh.

His chest rumbled against her ear with a chuckle. 'I assume you enjoyed our evening together.'

She raked her hand lazily through the light hair on his chest. 'Very much.'

'Good, because there'll be many more. I want you to crave them as much as I do.'

She rolled over and settled her chin on his chest, her hair falling down the sides of her face to spread over him. 'You've certainly succeeded in your intention.'

He brushed a lock of her hair off her face, tucking it behind one ear. 'Good.'

She laid one thigh over his and shifted closer to him, her mouth almost touching his. 'Is it too soon to ask for more?'

He raised one interested eyebrow at her and his fingers entwined in her hair. 'Not at all.'

Chapter Eight

The chaise rolled down the crowded length of Fleet Street, passing the hundreds of people flitting from shop to shop as they went about their day.

'Where are we going?' Susanna asked, stifling a small yawn behind one gloved hand. She and Justin had enjoyed little sleep over the past few nights, yet for all their long evenings she felt as refreshed as if she'd taken the waters of Bath.

Faint circles hung beneath Justin's eyes this morning as well, but it didn't diminish his natural humour or the teasing smile he flashed from across Mr Rathbone's borrowed carriage each time he admired her. 'You'll see, it's a surprise.'

'Like the one you showed me last night?' She kicked off her slipper and ran one stocking-clad foot up the length of his thigh.

'Not quite.' He shifted to the squab next to her and took her hand. He turned it over to expose the skin between her glove and sleeve and flicked his tongue against the sensitive spot. His breath against the moisture raised a chill along her arm which reached deep inside her until she almost insisted he turn the carriage around and go back home. 'There'll be time for more later.'

He lowered her hand, both of them conscious of the carriage slowing to make a turn.

Susanna leaned past her husband to peer out of the window, taking in the red uniforms of old soldiers as they walked with their families, and the rosy cheeks of the young hawkers selling pies, apples and flowers. On one corner, they passed a man peddling newspapers announcing a salacious account of the Prince Regent's latest scandal.

Edwina would be eating up the story, tittering about it with her vapid friends, but the doings of the aristocracy were no longer Susanna's affair. She pressed one hand to her stomach, trying to settle it, wishing she didn't carry such a potent reminder of her time with them. It would ruin all the happiness building between her and Justin if he ever found out.

'You're trying to guess where we're going, aren't you?' He tugged her away from the window and down on to the seat beside him to wrap his arm around her waist.

'I am.' She shifted so his hand landed on her hip instead of her stomach, covering her worry with another lie, adding to the one already hovering over her. 'I wish you'd tell me. I don't like surprises.'

'You'll enjoy this one. I promise.'

She hoped so. Most surprises in her life had led

to nothing but misery, though she couldn't imagine any of Justin's treading such a dark path. If he made a promise, she believed it. He was too good a man to deceive her. Sadly, she couldn't say the same of herself.

'I need to tell you something, Susanna...' Justin began hesitantly, raising a flutter in her belly which had nothing to do with the baby. 'Until the wine business is fully established, I have to remain in Philip's employ. I don't want us to fall into debt. I've seen too many times the horrors it can wreak on men and their families to risk it.'

'Why make it sound so grave? Working for Mr Rathbone seems more a pleasure for you than a burden.'

'It is, but it also means there'll be nights, or mornings, or any time of day, in fact, when I might be called away to help him deal with a matter.'

'Like a doctor?' She remembered the one who had lived next to them in Oxfordshire and how many nights she'd been awakened by someone ringing the bell outside his door.

'Rather, but in the past I've never had to concern anyone else with my comings and goings. I don't want you to be alarmed or startled when it happens, or to worry about me while I'm gone.'

'Given the sudden nature of our courtship and marriage, there's little which can alarm me now.'

'Good. I'll rely on you to manage things when I've been called away. I intend for you to be my full partner in this.'

'You'd give me control?' Even when her grandfather had been ill, he'd refused to allow her mother to run the shop, relying on her uncle, even when he was barely a man, to see to the business. She touched her stomach again, wondering how much longer it would be before she couldn't conceal her condition and would have to pretend the child was his. It sickened her to deceive him when he was so good to her, but for the child's sake, she had no choice.

'Who else can I trust to manage it properly if not my wife? Besides, you didn't really think marrying me would mean a life of leisure, did you?'

'Not after the last few nights.' She flicked her top teeth with her tongue, the memory of their pleasure relieving some of her anxiety.

He pulled her against him and claimed her mouth, his wanting kiss making her forget everything except him and the pressure of his tongue against hers. She slipped her hand inside his coat, following the curve of his side beneath the silk before reaching the waist of his breeches. She began to work her hand inside the buckskin when he caught her wrist and broke away from her lips.

'Not yet, my dear. We're almost at our destination.' His eyes smouldered with his need and she knew, if they weren't so close to wherever he was taking her, they'd have indulged in a little sport in the carriage. The mere thought of such a daring intimacy nearly hollowed out her insides with desire.

She laid her hands on either side of his face and rose up to give him a long, tempting kiss. 'Then let's be quick with our business, so we may move on to more delightful work.'

He pulled her to him so each breath made her already taut breasts brush against his firm chest. 'Not so fast, you don't want me to rush.'

'Indeed, I don't.' She hummed, remaining in the circle of his arms, eager to be beneath him and to forget everything in the pleasure of his touch.

The driver's voice calling to the horses accompanied the slowing of the carriage as it came to a stop. Justin's arm around her eased as the carriage tilted a little to one side when the driver climbed down from his seat.

'We're here.' As soon as the door was open, Justin was out and beckoning Susanna to follow.

She blinked against the bright sun which greeted her as she stepped down on to the pavement. People passed by them in a steady stream, hurrying from one establishment to the next, carrying their purchases.

In front of her was a shop with arched windows, the walls holding them painted a shiny red. The name over the door had been removed, but the oblong ghost of it was outlined in faded paint. Brown paper covered the bottom half of the windows, denying all but the tallest passers-by a peek inside, assuming they could peer through the grime covering the square panes.

Justin tucked her hand into the curve of his elbow and pushed through the people to lead her to the front door. Removing a brass key from his pocket, he slipped it into the lock, oblivious to the scraping squeak it made before it released the bolt and allowed them through.

Justin moved into the centre of the rectangular room

as Susanna closed the door, blocking out the noise from outside.

'Well, what do you think?' He held out his arms and spun in a slow circle, his boot heels thudding against the wooden floorboards and sending up small puffs of dust which tickled her nose. 'The building is sturdy, the previous occupants didn't take out their anger on the woodwork, or the windows, and it's well situated in a good neighbourhood with a great many prosperous businesses surrounding it.'

'Very nice.' There was nothing in the room but an abandoned table and chair, a dark fireplace in one corner and a counter in front of the far wall, but Susanna could picture the space filled with bottles and barrels of the finest French and Spanish wines. The panelled walls only needed a little wood oil and dusting to make them shine again and with some washing the windows would sparkle. 'Is there a cellar?'

'There is and it's being stocked with the first delivery of our inventory as we speak.' He banged one heel against the floor and a familiar hollow sound echoed through the room. 'I'll leave it to you to find appropriate decorations for the windows and to arrange this room as you think best. I imagine you've given some thought to a matter like this before.'

'I have.' The same excitement she'd known the morning of the wedding raced through her. 'When I used to sit in Grandfather's shop while he was out with a delivery, I imagined how I could change things to make it more appealing to our customers. I had so many ideas, though I never said anything. There was no point. Grandfather wasn't likely to listen, or to change no matter how much it might profit him in the end. He was incredibly stubborn.'

'Luckily for you, I'm not. This is your chance to employ all your ideas.'

Susanna didn't respond. She couldn't. After doing little more than sitting in corners reading books for the past seven years, to be given real purpose excited her more than even the shop. As hurtful as her grandfather had been, the work of assisting a wine merchant had always kept her busy, distracting her from the pain and loneliness of her life. It would be wonderful to have industry again, to be a useful partner instead of some unwanted adornment.

The familiar thump of a wine cask being unloaded followed by the melodic roll of it down a wooden ramp filled the room.

'Come, I'll show you the cellar.' He held out his hand and she took it, clinging to him as he led her behind the counter and through the door to the room beyond.

The darker, smaller space wasn't as tidy as the front, and the remains of the past business were evident in the papers scattered about the tables or stuffed in the small cubbies along the wall. At the far end, a trapdoor in the floor stood open. Justin pulled her over to stand above it, as proud of the cellar as Lord Rockland used to be of a new hunting dog.

Susanna bent, hands on her knees, to peer down into the hole. The flicker of candles and the daylight from the outside ramp lit up the faded red bricks lining the walls and rising up to arch over the ceiling. The pungent scent of damp plaster and musty air wafted over her, dredging up memories of the many hours she'd spent in the semi-darkness of her grandfather's cellar, counting barrels or fetching bottles. More than once she'd slipped into the cool darkness to cry in the corner behind a tall cask after some rude comment from a neighbour, or her grandfather. She straightened and moved away from the dark hole, back to the sunlight and Justin's excitement, trying to place some distance between the present and those difficult days.

'You think it's too small? I was worried about that. I'm hoping in time to expand the business, perhaps gain the shop next door,' Justin explained, as though seeking her approval. It was something she wasn't used to.

'I think the cellar and your plans are perfect,' she reassured him.

'Except?' he prodded, having noticed the change in her mood. Far from letting it pass to focus on his own concerns, he wanted to draw it out.

'The smell of it reminds me of my grandfather.'

'Not a pleasant memory?'

'No. The students he sold wine to never cared about my background, only how cheaply they could obtain their spirits. It was the neighbours who were nasty and my grandfather and uncle never stopped them. They were too concerned with maintaining their clients to worry about protecting my insignificant feelings. More than likely they agreed with whatever it was they said.'

'Then they and he were wrong.' He brushed a stray

curl away from her cheek. 'If anyone throws your past in your face, or says anything degrading to you, I'll see to it they regret it.'

Remembering the way he'd pummelled her half-brother, she didn't doubt he would. As tender as he was with her at night, she'd witnessed the way his hands could turn lethal when it came to defending himself. His protection now extended to her, and if her past was any indication of her future he'd be forced to keep his word. 'I don't think it's a matter of if, but when.'

Justin took her by the shoulders. 'Don't invite trouble. It has a way of finding you—there's no need to seek it out.'

'Are you never bothered by things like your father?'

'Every day, but I try not to regret, or wish things were different. It doesn't do anyone any good.'

'I wish I possessed your optimism.' And his ability to stride away from past troubles and mistakes. Hers grew quietly inside her.

'In time, you will. Now, what do you think? Is the cellar sufficient?' he urged, trying to draw her out of her melancholy mood. She let him, eager to be as happy as he was.

'It's excellent.'

'Good.' He glanced past her out of the window to the yard at the back where the men were unloading the barrels. 'Come and see what I've purchased.'

In the small courtyard behind the building, men laughed and talked as they rolled the casks into the cellar. Susanna approached one of the waiting barrels and read the name on the lid, amazed by the words emblazoned on the label.

'How did you come by such a fine vintage so soon?' Her grandfather had known many men in the wine trade and he'd never once been able to secure a cask such as this.

Justin leaned his elbow on the top of the barrel and dropped his voice, taking on the sly countenance of a rogue. 'In the course of working for Philip, I've culti-vated a number of contacts in, shall we say, more dubi-ous corners of London. Usually, I rely on them to tell me who owes money to whom, what brothels potential clients are in debt to and what other moneylenders they might be avoiding. Since starting this venture, I've used my connections to put it about I'll pay for infor-mation about wine coming in on ships. An old source told me about this one and the debts the man owed. I was able to purchase this cask at a fraction of its value and ease the man's more pressing financial burdens.'

He smiled, quite proud of himself. Susanna was impressed.

'How very astute of you, though I wonder if any of these contacts of yours will ever show up on our doorstep?'

'If they do, Walter will handle them. He's quite adept at getting their information and giving them their expected payment.'

'No doubt from years of practice.'

Justin nodded, but said no more.

'Then I won't worry,' Susanna assured him.

'Good.' He picked at the metal band around the top

of the barrel, his roguish smile changing to one serious enough to challenge Mr Rathbone's. 'I want you to know your safety is important to me and I'll always protect you.'

'I know.' Guilt chewed at her, but she smiled, trying to bring back the excitement which had greeted their arrival.

'Sir, we'll be needin' you to check on what we brought,' one of the burly men interrupted from near the ramp as he raised his cap to wipe the sweat from his wide forehead.

'Of course.' Justin made his way down the wooden stairs into the cellar, beckoning Susanna to follow.

She hesitated, wrinkling her nose at the dark, but with Justin beside her there was no reason to fear the memories it conjured up. He was right. The past was over and gone, at least most of it. With any luck, the rest of it would stay buried. She pressed her hand to her stomach as she followed the ramp down to where the delivery men were arranging the last of the barrels.

While Justin compared the number and names on the casks to a list he withdrew from his coat, Susanna explored the narrow space. There were sconces in the walls where candles could be placed, but none were there now. They'd probably been pilfered by street urchins once the business had been abandoned. Even in the quiet of Oxfordshire, Susanna had seen more than one shop broken into after the building had been foreclosed on, others picking over the leavings in search of something to steal or pawn.

Moving through the line of barrels, she tapped the

smooth tops of each one, as so many things she'd forgotten over the last seven years returned to her—the pop of the casks being tapped, the gurgle of the wine pouring into the bottles, the tedious work of corking and labelling each one. Lady Rockland had tried to drive the common experiences out of her, yet the new ones she'd offered in return had fitted Susanna like a cast-off pair of shoes, more abrasive than welcoming. Here, not at Rockland Place, was where she belonged and she was glad to be returning. For all the bad memories of her uncle and grandfather, she remembered the many hours she'd spent working beside her mother, the two of them talking as her mother shared with her all she'd learned of the business from her parents.

Some day, Susanna would pass on the same knowledge to her child, and to the children who were sure to come from her union with Justin. All of them would possess the love of a father and mother and never experience the sting of being a bastard. It didn't make the deceit she'd played on Justin right, but she'd done it for the child. For this reason, perhaps one day she could forgive herself.

Justin finished his inventory, struggling to concentrate on the list as he watched Susanna move along the length of the cellar. She didn't sneer at the damp, but seemed lost in thoughts which brought a sweet softness to her face. There was something delightful she saw in the casks, not just the harsh memories of a neglecting grandfather, but other more comforting ones. Justin knew the sensation. Sometimes, when he walked into the pugilist club and inhaled the sweat mixed with sawdust and leather, he'd remember not his surly, drunk father, but the barrel-chested man who'd introduced him to the ring when he was twelve and taught him everything his own father had taught him about fighting.

She turned at the end of a line of casks and started down the second row. The light from outside illuminated her face and Justin caught the faint promise of their children in her wistful smile. Some day, he'd escort his own son to the club, show him how to defend himself like a man, both with his fists and his brains. Then he'd bring him down to the cellar and prove it wasn't just brute force which made a man or earned him respect, but hard work and industry, which so many thought Justin lacked. He'd raise his children to make themselves better men than him and encourage them to seek a station in life even higher than his. He wouldn't tear them down or hold them back and neither would Susanna. Her enthusiasm upstairs, and the alacrity with which she'd accepted her duties as his business partner, heartened him more than obtaining this fine shipment. In this stranger he'd found a true partner for both his life and his heart, one who wouldn't look down on him or doubt him.

'Are you done, sir?' the deliveryman questioned.

Justin snapped his attention back to the list, finished his assessment and dropped a number of coins, including a few extra, into the man's wide hands. 'If you hear of any more shipments, be sure to tell me.'

The man counted the coins, his thick eyebrows rising at the payment before he palmed them, then raised his cap to Justin. 'I'd be glad to, sir.'

The man made for the ramp and climbed up into the daylight, leaving Justin and Susanna alone.

'Why are these separated from the others?' She waved her hand at the far corner of the cellar where six casks were arranged in a small alcove.

'You miss nothing, do you?'

'Observing is nearly all I've been allowed to do these last seven years.'

He moved between the line of barrels to join her. 'The wines near the front are common vintages and should turn a nice profit with sales to merchants looking to enhance their dinner table. These—' he thumped the top of one lid, eliciting a deep sound from the full wood '—are the best of the lot. I'm saving them for your stepmother's masked ball.'

'I wouldn't hold them all back,' Susanna warned.

'You think your father won't honour his end of our arrangement?'

'He will—after all, he kept his promise to my mother, in his own way. It's Lady Rockland you'll have to contend with. She'll whisper about us to the wives of the other peers, I have no doubt about it.' She picked a small splinter off a cask and flung it away. 'Cultivate your own contacts. Don't rely too heavily on Lord Rockland's.'

'Sage advice.' If not a touch disheartening.

'Don't look so grim.' She laid a hand on the side of his face, driving back the sense of failure nipping at him like the damp. 'A man who can secure inventory like this can just as easily shift it to a notable merchant and other prosperous men.'

Justin took her hand and laid a gentle kiss on her palm, thankful for her honesty and her faith in him. Until the shop was on a secure footing, and trade brisk, the risk of failure still loomed. With her by his side he could face it and keep his worries at bay.

'Now come, we should be getting home.' He led her to the ramp, his confidence restored. 'We have a great deal to plan.'

Justin instructed one of his trusted men to remain behind and guard the store, then he and Susanna made their way home in the carriage. During the drive, they exchanged ideas about the shop, talking over one another in their rush to explain their plans.

They were not more than a foot over the threshold of Justin's house when Walter approached them. 'Mr Rathbone requests your assistance at once with the Jacobson matter.'

'Have you laid out my clothes and other necessaries?' Justin asked as he escorted Susanna upstairs, Walter following behind.

'As usual, Mr Connor.'

They entered his room to see his plain coat draped on the bed, beside which rested the thin leather holster and the lacquered case which held his pistol.

'What is this nefarious matter calling you away?' Susanna asked, her humour unable to completely hide her concern.

'A ship's captain with a considerable amount of

debt.' He shrugged out of his good jacket and handed it to Walter before taking up the plain one. 'He gambled the profits from his last cargo away and the one he has now must be seized in order to repay his loan. Keep your fingers crossed there's a shipment of fine wine in the hold.'

'Even if it's bad we can still sell it for a profit.'

'I like the way your mind works.' He dropped a kiss on her lips, lingering a moment to enjoy the sweet taste of her and wishing he could dally, but business called. Breaking from her, and heartened by the answering disappointment in her eyes, he took up the leather holster and slid his arms through it, settling it at his side. He flipped open the lid of the case, revealing the shiny pistol resting on the blue velvet inside.

Susanna's eyes grew wide at the sight of the weapon. 'Will it be dangerous?'

He hadn't been completely honest with her in the carriage about all aspects of his business with Philip. 'Desperate men who owe money are unpredictable. Best to be prepared.'

He checked the flash pan to make sure it was clear of debris. If things with the captain grew tense, he couldn't risk a misfire. Hopefully, the captain wouldn't put up a fight. The thought of risking his life again, especially with Susanna standing tensely beside him, so concerned about where he was going, didn't sit well with him. Soon he'd give up this portion of his life, but not today.

Confident the weapon was clean, he slid the pistol into the holster, then slipped on his jacket.

'Please be careful,' she urged.

He looked at her. 'I'm always careful.'

'Why do I doubt that?'

He came around the bed to stand over her, resting his hands on her slender shoulders.

'Don't worry, the pistol is only a precaution and I'm as skilled with it as I am with my fists.' He dropped a long, comforting kiss on her lips, his desire to remain strong in the pressure of his skin against hers. However, like her he knew he had to go and all too soon the kiss was over. 'I'll be back as fast as I can.'

In a whirl of his redingote, he went out the door and was gone.

Susanna sank a little against the bedpost, holding on as much to steady herself against her worries as to brace her knees against the intensity of his kiss. His ability to affect her so deeply made her as giddy as when she'd sampled the champagne at Lady Rockland's soirées. However, she wasn't drunk now and this was no sitting room.

If business hadn't called him away, she might have provoked him to linger and lost herself in the smell of the leather beneath his shirt and the heat from their time outside. Instead, she'd let him go, understanding his need to remain employed and his loyalty to Philip Rathbone.

His loyalty was one of the traits she admired about Justin the most and one she was determined to match. There was no better time to begin than now. She couldn't sit here all day fretting over him, not when there was so much work to be done.

Susanna made her way downstairs in search of Mrs Robinson. She found her in the kitchen and discussed with her the need to hire a charwoman to clean the shop.

Within the hour, the efficient housekeeper had summoned the daughter of a scullery maid who worked next door and the stout woman with strong arms was engaged. Susanna sent her off with a note to the man guarding the shop to allow her in so she could set to work at once.

This one item seen to, Susanna settled at the desk in Justin's study near the back of the house and began drawing up a list of necessary items for the window. The list was nearly complete when Walter interrupted her with a cough.

'The elder Mr Connor is here, ma'am,' the formidable butler announced with more warning than welcome. 'He's in the study. Should I give him the usual amount Mr Connor does and send him on his way?'

'No, I'll see him.' With Justin gone and not expected back very soon, she might become better acquainted with the elder Mr Connor and discover ways to soothe some of the difficulties between father and son. It seemed a monumental task, but if she could make things even a little better between them, it would be worth the effort.

'Very well, madam. I'll remain close by, in case I'm needed.'

Having seen Mr Connor's temper, she well understood what he meant. 'Thank you.'

Susanna set down her pen and with some hesitation made her way down the short hall to the cosy room at the front of the house. Before she reached the narrow entrance hall she paused and turned to the butler. 'Ask Mrs Robinson to set out a small tea in the dining room.'

'Yes, madam.' Walter hurried off on his errand, leaving Susanna to face Mr Connor alone.

She nodded a greeting to Mr Green, who waited near the front door, his eyes on his boots as though trying not to be seen. With a charge like Mr Connor, she wasn't surprised by his desire to fade into the woodwork. Her nerves weren't exactly calm as she stepped into the bright sitting room to face her father-in-law.

'Good afternoon, Mr Connor,' Susanna called out, refusing to allow his answering scowl to diminish her smile.

'What's good about it?' Mr Connor grumbled. 'With my son out, I suppose I have to come begging to a woman for my money, as though I were a boy in breeches and not a full grown man who earned every one of those shillings.'

'You needn't beg at all.' Susanna clasped her hands in front of her. 'All you need do is ask and I'll gladly supply you with your usual sum.'

Mr Connor scrunched up his face as though trying to come up with an answer to her invitation as biting as the anger eating at his insides. Susanna spoke first.

'First, you'll join me for tea. I'd like for us to get to know one another.'

He eyed her with more suspicion than disdain and she braced herself for a sharp retort, determined not to fling one back. For all her years of living with her grandfather, no matter how hard she'd worked, no matter how sweet and kind and loving she'd been to him, she'd never once cracked the hard shell he'd surrounded himself with. The same might be true of Mr Connor, but the little girl in Susanna who'd tried so hard to gain her grandfather's affection wasn't ready to give up on this old man, especially not when he was hurting Justin, too.

Despite the hardness deepening the lines of his face, the only thing Mr Connor hurled at her was a question. 'Why?'

'Because we're sure to deal with one another quite regularly and it's better to do so as friends than enemies,' Susanna offered, trying to lower the man's hackles. Like her grandfather, Mr Connor was perpetually surly and she could guess the reason why. Her grandmother's death had ended what little cheer her grandfather had possessed. Judging from what Justin had told her of his father, the same grief had settled over Mr Connor after his wife's passing, weighing on him until there was nothing but gin and hate to dull the pain.

'I'll stay if you can offer me something stronger than tea.'

Like his son, he wasn't one to beat around the bush. 'Come and join me in the dining room. We'll see what we can find to slake your thirst.'

Susanna led the gentleman to the dining room, then stepped into the hall to speak with Mrs Robinson. 'Please see to Mr Green. He looks as if he needs a thimble of gin.'

'Or a tankard,' Mrs Robinson replied. 'Leave him to me, madam, I'll see him calmed, though not so much he can't perform his duties.'

'Thank you. And one more thing.' She moved close to the housekeeper, dropping her voice so as not to be overheard by the elder Mr Connor or his minder. 'Bring me a small bottle of spirits, nothing too strong and only a quarter full.'

Mrs Robinson's normally staid expression bloomed with surprise. 'Ma'am?'

'Trust me, please.'

With a 'whatever you wish' nod, Mrs Robinson made for the kitchen, collecting young Mr Green as she went.

Susanna joined Mr Connor at the table where he was already seated and helping himself to a generous slice of lemon cake. Ignoring his lack of manners, Susanna took her place and poured herself tea, not bothering to offer him any.

'This food is much better than the slop Mrs Green feeds me,' Mr Connor complained, tucking in to the cake.

Mrs Robinson's entrance kept Mr Connor's mumbling from expanding into too loud a complaint.

Susanna took the dark green bottle from Mrs Robinson and passed it to her churlish guest. 'Here we are, something a little stiffer than tea.'

He sniffed the open top with a snarl. 'Is this the best you could do?'

'Our merchandise is in the store, not here, Mr Connor.'

'Don't think you can fool me. I've seen my son carousing enough to know he likes his spirits as well as any man.' He poured himself as much port as the dainty tea cup in front of him would hold. 'Don't suppose a man could get a real glass?'

'Your drink is better concealed in the china.' Susanna raised her cup to her lips, sliding him a conspiratorial glance.

Mr Connor seemed to regard her with a new appreciation and he winked one wrinkled eye at her, then held up his teacup in salute. 'You're a crafty one, I'll give you that.'

'I've learned a thing or two from your son, as I'm sure he did from you.'

'Taught him everything he knows.' Mr Connor sat back and puffed out his thick chest with pride. 'None was as good at gettin' information out of people as me. I could ferret out any man's secret and his debts, and discover where they'd stashed their valuables. I was the one who kept the elder Mr Rathbone safe when his clients didn't want to pay.'

'Justin speaks very highly of your time with him at the pugilist club.' It was a bit of an exaggeration, but it served the purpose of stunning Mr Connor.

'He was the best fighter at the club. Gentleman John Jackson himself once saw him spar and said he could be a professional boxer if he wanted.' Mr Connor's face broke out into a fond smile at the pleasant memory before his expression wilted. 'But he thought himself too good for it, like he thinks himself too good for me. I'm surprised he speaks well of me at all.'

'He wants you to be proud of him.'

'He don't care a fig for what I think.' He drained the teacup, but didn't ask for more.

'I assure you, Mr Connor, you're very wrong.' She laid a steadying hand on the almost threadbare arm of his coat.

He stared at her hand as if this was the first time in a long while he'd been offered any tenderness.

The clock in the hallway began to chime and the quiet moment between them was broken. Mr Connor pulled away his arm and rubbed the whiskers at the end of his chin. 'Best be going before Justin comes back from wherever he's at. He smells liquor on my breath, and we're both in for it. I wouldn't want a pretty thing like you getting in trouble.'

'I assure you, I can hold my own against anyone, including your son.'

'Good. He needs someone to thump some good sense into him every now and again.' He winked at her and she winked back, happy to be colluding with him. In the gesture she felt a measure of trust and the first small step towards easing the prickliness of his relationship with Justin.

'Please come back any time you wish. I'm sure I can find a little something to make your visit a bit sweeter,' Susanna offered as she escorted him to the door.

'I shall.' He trilled his fingertips together in front

of his chest in delight, his look reminding her very much of Justin, especially around the eyes which were the same rich brown as his son's. With a shave and a better-fitting coat, the resemblance between father and son would show even more. 'Now, where's that lousy minder of mine?'

His raised voice carried through the house. A moment later Mr Green came hurrying in from the kitchen, looking slightly more at ease either from one of Mrs Robinson's tonics or just a few moments away from his blustery charge. 'I'm here, Mr Connor.'

'Then let's be off.'

'To the pub sir?' Mr Green asked.

'No, I'm tired and want to go home.' Mr Connor tapped his hat over his head, oblivious to the stunned stiffness of Walter as he passed him and made for outside.

Susanna watched the two men walk off down the street, aware of Mrs Robinson beside her.

'Well done, ma'am,' Mrs Robinson commended.

'Make sure you keep a half-empty bottle of port handy,' Susanna instructed the housekeeper, whose eyes danced with mirth at the idea. 'I think we may be seeing Mr Connor here quite often for tea.'

Chapter Nine

A myriad things connected to the business kept Susanna busy, both after Mr Connor left and for the many days after. There were curtains to be selected for the front windows, accounting books to purchase, calling cards to order and the design of wine labels to approve. Justin was occupied with his own tasks, taking on an apprentice, two shop assistants and visiting and securing customers. It proved an exciting and challenging week, and with each passing day Susanna felt more at ease in both her new role as a wife and her place in the Connor household. Here, no one made her feel like an unwanted interloper, even when she changed the menu or suggested a different arrangement of the sitting-room furniture. The security of it provided a calm she hadn't known since before her grandmother had died.

Despite her happiness, in the back of her mind she couldn't help but feel something was waiting to end it all. In the past, whenever she'd felt safe and secure, death or a rumour had reared its ugly head to steal her peace. The old worry it would happen again continued to pester her during quiet moments when she studied inventory or reviewed the bills. She tried to shake the feeling, but she couldn't. Whatever foreboding she imagined waiting for her, she suspected it would come from Grosvenor Square. Since the wedding, they'd heard nothing from the Rocklands, but Susanna wasn't convinced Lady Rockland was finally done with her. The woman had little else to do except to see to Edwina and be nasty to her inferiors. Every time a letter arrived at the house for Justin, Susanna feared it might be a missive from her stepmother with some insidious reference to Susanna's secret, one which would plant the fatal seed of doubt in his mind and ruin their happiness.

Only at night when she was alone with Justin in the low light of his room, his body covering hers, was everything forgotten in the bliss of his kisses and the playful caress of his fingers.

One evening, a week after their visit to the shop, Susanna entered Justin's room where he sat before the fire reading a letter. The sight of it and the stern contemplation dulling his usual humour made her halt. Whatever was being conveyed held his full attention and not for a good reason.

The old crow has finally written. Her hand tightened on the small board she carried. She wanted to drop it and flee, but she held fast. Whatever the letter said, she would face it.

He didn't glance up as she cautiously approached, trying to catch sight of the signature on the letter through the thin paper, but his hand blocked it. The seriousness in his eyes as he read increased the dread sliding through her as she came to stand in front of him. She braced herself and held out the board with the three samples of a bottle label which had been delivered by the printer.

'Which one do you think we should use for the red wine?' she asked, clearing her throat at the unnerving squeak in her words.

He looked up at the labels, then pointed to the one in the centre, barely seeing it or her. 'This one.'

'I agree.' She set the labels on the table next to his chair, still on edge but glad to not see the anger she'd expected. It still didn't calm her fears. 'Who's the letter from?'

'Your father.' Justin folded the missive and set it beside the labels, visibly troubled by the contents.

She dropped into the chair across from his. 'What does he say?'

'He's asked me to see him tomorrow afternoon to discuss the wine purchase for the lovely Lady Rockland's ball.'

She sagged against the back of the chair with relief. However, she wasn't out of danger yet, she never would be. She wished she hadn't made the deal with her father for his support. A clean break would've been best. Instead they were obligated to deal with the Rocklands for a short while longer. Her father wasn't likely to say anything about the child, assuming he knew, but the remaining ties between them risked Justin encountering Lady Rockland and her vicious tongue. She wouldn't put it past Lady Rockland to let her suspicions about Susanna's pregnancy slip, if for no other reason than to be spiteful.

'Do you want to come with me or shall I go alone?' he asked.

'You should go alone.' Lady Rockland was much less likely to approach him if Susanna wasn't there.

With a sharp knock, Mrs Robinson entered, carrying a parcel wrapped in string. 'This just arrived for you, ma'am, from Mrs Fairley.'

She laid the parcel down on the bench at the foot of the bed, then left.

Susanna went to the package and began to untie the knot securing the string.

'I hope you aren't spending lavishly on clothes,' Justin teased from his place by the fire, the return of his good humour helping her to recover hers.

'It isn't a dress—' Susanna tugged at the knot but it wouldn't budge '—but our costumes for the masque.'

Justin came to stand beside her, gently pushed her hands away, then broke the string. 'You're aware I don't dance?'

'At all?' She winced. She sounded as shallow as Edwina.

He leaned against the footboard. 'Dancing isn't a skill a man of my class is required to possess.'

Susanna pulled the string off the package, balled it in her hand and tossed it to one side. 'It's a lot like boxing, with a great deal of hopping back and forth with your partner.'

'Liar.'

'You needn't worry about standing up with me. As much as I enjoy a good reel, I've found it's much more interesting to remain in the crowd and observe.' She lifted the lid off the box. 'I learned more about society hidden behind a black-silk mask than I ever did sitting quietly in a corner while the women gossiped.'

'And what costume am I to wear?' He shifted behind her and wrapped his arms around her waist to peer over her shoulder. His cheek rested against hers as she folded back the tissue paper to reveal the garments beneath.

'I decided to make it simple.' She lifted a flowing dark green cloak with a hood and matching silk mask out of the parcel. 'Cloaks and masks.'

Justin reached out and slid the mask from her fingers. The silk gliding over her skin raised a line of goose bumps along the length of her arm. 'If the wine business fails, we can take up careers as highway robbers.'

'It'd certainly be an interesting way to fund a venture and quite thrilling.'

'Until we're hanged.'

'I didn't say there weren't risks.' She grinned at him over her shoulder. 'And you'd make a dashing rogue.'

'I like the sound of that.' He flicked the mask on to the bed and turned her around, pressing her to him so she could feel the stirring of his manhood against her stomach.

'That's not all you like.' She twined her arms around his neck, drawing him down to her, eager to be close to him and enjoy the comfort and peace of him. It would banish the worry still hovering inside her.

There was no careful removing of clothes or the slow unlacing of stays tonight. Their garments were discarded in a hurried frenzy of tugging and pulling with one or two snapped buttons plinking to the floor before Susanna and Justin tumbled naked and needy on to the bed.

Against her skin Susanna felt the discarded mask. Pulling it out from under her, she drew it across the span of his back.

'What are you doing, my little minx?' he growled in her ear, his fingers pausing in their tracing of her thighs.

She didn't answer as she draped the silk over the top of his shoulder and then down his chest, pushing it over the solid ripples of his stomach and the sides of his waist. He sat back on his knees and she rose to hers, never allowing the silk to leave his skin as she worked it lower. She slid the softness up and down the length of him, drawing from him a low, deep moan.

'Do you like it?' she asked in seductive innocence, tilting her head down like a coquette.

'What do you think?' he murmured, his fingers tight on his thighs as he closed his eyes, delighting in each stroke of her hand. He grew stronger beneath her palm until at last he pulled her hand and the mask away. 'Careful, we don't want to end things too soon.'

He gently pushed her down into the coverlet and

arched over her to take one taut nipple between his teeth before pressing a kiss against the space between her breasts. He moved lower, tracing circles on her stomach with his tongue before he placed a kiss at the top of the hair between her thighs.

'Don't tease me,' Susanna gasped, wanting to be one with him at once.

'I must.' He smiled like the devil before his head dipped down and his mouth pressed against her most intimate parts.

She gripped the coverlet as he tasted her until she thought she could take no more. Arching her hips against him, he slid his hands beneath her buttocks, his fingers gripping her tight as he continued to pleasure her. She sighed, not ashamed to surrender to him in this most delicate way. It would have embarrassed her a few days ago to be so vulnerable with him, yet she welcomed it tonight, lost in the desire he raised within her, trusting her whole being to him. She knew he would never betray it or her. She cried out as he slid one finger inside her, caressing her with a gentle pressure. Never in her life had she imagined so much passion and intimacy could exist with a man.

She whimpered, eager for release and at the same time holding back, wanting all of him. When at last she thought she might shatter, he withdrew from her and sat up. She rose to her knees and feeling quite bold, pushed him back down against the coverlet. She straddled his thighs until the tip of his hardness pressed against her. He took her hips with his wide hands and eased her down over him, filling her body as he had her heart since the day they'd wed.

He clutched her by the waist and rolled so she was under him. She grabbed his buttocks, pulling him deeper into her as he lay down on his elbows, his chest hard against her breasts, his mouth firm on hers as he thrust into her. Bound together as one, they raced towards their pleasure, each pushing the other higher until at last their release crashed over them like waves against the rocks of the shore.

'I love you…' Justin breathed, his face buried in the silky curls which had slipped from their pins to spill across the pillow.

'I love you, too.' She held on to him, refusing to let him slide away from her, still so afraid this bliss between them wouldn't last. All her life she'd wanted this closeness, this beautiful experience of being cherished and loved. To think it might end with only a few nasty words broke her heart nearly as much as his love had mended it. Tears filled her eyes and one slid down her cheek to wet his.

'What's wrong?' he asked, touching his forehead to hers.

'I'm so happy with you. I don't want anything to ruin it.'

'What could?'

She closed her eyes and inhaled his musky scent. She loved him and she didn't want to lose him. Despite the joy of the last few days, she was still deceiving him in the worst way a woman could. How something wouldn't come from it to ruin everything, she didn't know, but she couldn't reveal her fears.

'Have faith, Susanna, in me and us,' he murmured in her ear.

She pressed her lips to his, struggling to share in his belief all would be well. Perhaps it would and their love would never end. It was a beautiful dream and she would cling to it, and his heart, for as long a she could.

The bell over the wine shop door chimed as Justin entered. From the room behind the counter, Susanna appeared, a welcoming smile spreading across her pretty face like the light falling in through the windows. It heightened the blush of her cheeks and the sparkle in her eyes. He'd been called away at daybreak by Philip, denying him the pleasure of waking with her and perhaps enjoying something more of the delight which had kept them both from sleep for the better portion of the night.

'Do you like what I did with the front window?' she asked, coming around to offer him a kiss which was both welcoming and inviting. If she continued with such sweet greetings, he might have to set up a private room in the back with a bed, or find a way to make the squabs of the chaise much more comfortable.

'I adore it. You're beautiful *and* clever. How did I get so lucky?'

'I jumped in your carriage instead of some bucktoothed old man's.'

'How fortunate for both of us.' He nuzzled her neck, ready to pull her into the room at the back, send away the assistant and the apprentice, slip the lock and while away the hours when the bell over the front door clanged.

Justin straightened, his hand freezing on Susanna's back at the sight of Helena striding through the door. Susanna looked from Justin to Helena, scrunching up her brow in question.

'Good morning, Mrs Gammon. To what do we owe the pleasure of this visit?' Not even Justin's skills at jest could keep the edge from his voice.

'I'm Mrs Preston now,' Helena corrected. 'Mr Preston and I were married a few days ago.'

'Congratulations,' Susanna offered in a sweet voice, but Justin caught the slight hesitation.

'The Chartons told me of the shop and your wedding. I wanted to meet the new Mrs Connor and see your establishment.' Helena fixed her scrutiny on Susanna as though she were an elegantly crafted bottle of fine port with a hefty price affixed to it. If Helena appreciated the vintage, it was difficult to tell through the jealousy which stiffened her stance beneath the red silk pelisse she wore.

'And now you have.' Justin rapped the top of a cask with his knuckles, making it clear it was time for her to take her leave, but it was obvious her curiosity was not completely satisfied. It could kill her for all he cared.

'Mrs Connor,' the bespectacled assistant said, coming out from the back room. 'There's a discrepancy in the ledger I'd like you to see.'

'Yes, I'll have a look.' She glanced back and forth between Helena and Justin as if debating whether or not to leave them alone together. Justin nodded at her. He was more than capable of facing his old lover and seeing her off. 'If you'll excuse me.'

Susanna followed the shop assistant through the far door and into the storeroom behind.

'She's very pretty,' Helena grudgingly admitted, clearly disappointed at finding Susanna beautiful and not horse-faced or buck-toothed.

'I'm not you, Helena. I don't sell myself to the highest bidder to achieve my goals.'

'I didn't marry Mr Preston only for his money. We care a great deal for one another.' She wasn't convincing and she knew it. She lifted a bottle of wine out of the straw-filled crate beside her and read the label, nodding approvingly. 'I'll have to send my man here to purchase a few bottles. Mr Preston does love his Madeira.'

She practically dropped the bottle back in the crate and Justin knew it wasn't all marital bliss at the Preston residence. A part of him felt sorry for her. They'd been friends once, but she'd made her decision and now she would live with it.

'I must say I'm surprised. I didn't think you'd make a go of it.'

He crossed his arms over his chest to keep from tossing the woman out on to the street. 'I'm glad I exceeded your expectations.'

'I never thought you one to take responsibility seriously, especially not all the endless details like inventory and bills.' She flicked a glance around him to the door leading into the back room. 'Or have you left those things to your wife while you enjoy the more pleasurable aspects like sampling the merchandise?'

'He hasn't left all the work to me.' Susanna's voice echoed from behind the counter as she came to stand beside Justin, linking her arm in his and facing the widow. 'It's to Justin's credit we purchased this shop. Without his hard work in securing the merchandise, and our clients, we would've been forced to abandon the venture long before we'd begun.'

'I'm sorry, Mrs Connor. I didn't mean to insult you or your husband,' Helena stuttered, her round face as red as her pelisse with her embarrassment.

'Yes, Mrs Preston, I believe you did.'

Justin held his head a little higher at his wife's response, heartened by her courage. If she could stand up to a woman like Helena, she could face anyone who cast aspersions at her about her background.

'Yes, well, I apologise again, Mrs Connor. Congratulations on your success.' With her head lowered, Helena hurried out the door, all the confidence she'd walked in with gone.

'Quite a charming woman,' Susanna observed, sliding her hand down his arm to lace her fingers in his. 'Whatever did you see in her?'

'Not nearly as much as I've seen in you.' He claimed her mouth, drawing out her tongue with long, smooth caresses. She pressed her body to his, fitting against him perfectly.

'Come.' He pulled her towards the door.

'Where are we going?'

'Home. Mr Spinner, the shop is yours for the afternoon,' he called over his shoulder.

'Yes, sir.' The assistant's voice trailed out of the door behind them.

Justin bundled her inside the chaise. 'Home, Mr Tibbs, as fast as you can.'

Justin climbed inside beside her, smiling to find she'd already drawn the shades. Without a word they were in one another's arms, exploring each other as best they could through the wool and cotton covering them. He slipped his hands under her skirt and traced the line of her calf up behind the curve of her knee, slipping one finger in between her skin and the ribbon holding up the stocking.

It wasn't physical need which drove him forward now, but her belief in him. Never had a woman made him feel so capable of achieving every goal he'd set out to achieve, or stood beside him as Susanna had just now. All the others had considered him only for sport or an evening of pleasure and laughter. They'd never seen him for more, or believed in his dreams.

Sliding his hand up her thigh, he found her centre, his restraint threatening to buckle as he discovered her readiness for him. This would be no rushed fumbling in a carriage, but merely the prelude to an hour or two in which he would pleasure her entire being. She clasped his lapels, breathing hard against his cheek as his fingers worked her tender flesh, stoking a need which had sparked long before they'd entered the carriage.

'Please stop,' she begged, her wanting clear in her

strained voice, but he continued with the relentless pace of his strokes, eager for her to reach her release more than once today.

The noise of the streets muffled her cries as she fell against him. He cradled her, playing with the soft skin of her thighs, his member throbbing with impatience beneath the buckskin of his breeches. He could open the fall and be inside her at once, give in to the urgency near strangling him, but he held back as the chaise came to a rocking halt in front of his house.

Together, they hustled to straighten her skirts and she was just composed when the driver opened the door. Jumping out, Justin pulled her along behind him. They rushed past Walter, who held open the door, and up the small staircase, reaching Justin's room and slamming the door closed behind them.

Together they toppled on to his bed. With deft fingers she slid his buttons through their holes and tugged his breeches down over his hips. The cold air of the room hit him and he closed his eyes, opening them in surprise when Susanna's gentle lips brushed the tip of his hardness. He moaned as her mouth slid over him. With her tongue she teased him and he grew tighter with each satiny caress until at last she sat up and he groaned his frustration, opening his eyes to pin her with a look of pent-up need he could feel deep inside of her.

Pulling her skirts up around her waist, she straddled him, sliding down to take him inside her. He let out a low, guttural sound as she ground her hips against his. He raked her thighs with his fingers and her stocking-clad feet curled beneath her on the bed as she moved with a steady pace over him. As her body began to tighten around him, he clasped her thighs, his strokes coming faster and faster until his cries joined hers and she collapsed on his chest, the ripples of her pleasure caressing his.

She laid down over him and rested her cheek against his chest, closer to him than anyone had ever been. For all his jokes and humour, for all his teasing and pretending not to care, there'd existed inside him a loneliness she now filled. He didn't want to lose it any more than he wanted to let go of her now.

They laid together in silence for some time, Justin tracing lazy circles on Susanna's still-exposed thigh. She fingered the line of his uncovered hip, her gentle touch increasing the contentment their lovemaking had brought him. Helena's insults had struck a nerve he thought his father's condemnation had long made him blunt to, but Susanna's sure belief in him had eased the sting.

'I couldn't have managed the start of my business so well without you,' he admitted, breaking the quiet punctuated by birds and a maid calling to someone across the street.

'You could have. You have a way with people. I've seen how you handle the men who deliver the wine and the ones at the docks who you buy it from. You're a natural charmer.'

'But Helena is right, I don't have a head for the details.' It nearly choked him to say it. 'It's why I've left them to you.'

She lifted her face to his, resting her chin on her hand on his chest. 'And I have no gift with the importers. It's why we do so well together.'

He pulled her closer. 'I lied to you when I said nothing ever troubles me.'

'I know.' She slid down beside him and rested her head on his shoulder.

'Ever since my mother died, it's killed me to see my father drinking himself to death. He used to be like me, capable of charming anyone. It's what my mother said she loved so much about him. I barely remember what that man was like.'

'Perhaps if you talk to him,' she urged.

'I've tried, many times. I'm always polite when we're together, but it never makes a difference.' He wound one of her loose curls around his finger, hating to admit his failure with his father. It was as devastating as the loss of his ship and much more lasting because he couldn't overcome it. 'No matter what I do, it doesn't make a difference to him.'

'Don't be so sure, Justin.'

'It's hard not to be. What hurts the most is what he says about me. Sometimes, I think he's right.' He stared at the ceiling and the small crack in the plaster snaking over the bed, unable to face her, despising how weak and sad the admission made him.

She propped herself up on one elbow to sit above him, caressing his face with her hand. The light coming through the cracks in the curtains glittered in her eyes and caught the wispy strands of hair cascading down the side of her face. 'Don't let others define you, or set your value. It's something I've allowed people to do to me for years and it's never made me happy or changed their opinion of me.'

He stroked her cheek with the back of his fingers. 'You're as wise as you are beautiful.'

He drew her down and her hair fell over him as he tasted her lips, the sweetness of them driving back, but not silencing, the foul insults he'd endured for years and the failures which followed on their heels. He was a better man than all those people believed, one worthy of his wife's love. In time, with her help, he'd silence everyone who thought otherwise.

The clock on the mantel chimed one o'clock. With a sigh, Justin disentangled himself from Susanna. He wanted to linger here, but numerous details now demanded his attention.

'Where are you going?' she asked.

He stood, tugged his breeches up over his hips and did up the fall. 'Your father is expecting me and I have a great deal of charming to do.'

The glow from their lovemaking faded from her face and she chewed her lower lip in worry. 'Be careful with the Rocklands. I don't trust them.'

'What can they do except renege on their word?'

'More than you realise,' she murmured as if she knew something he didn't.

'Such as?'

Apprehension drew down the corners of her lips before she regained her smile. 'Nothing. I'm sure you'll dazzle my father with all the charm you use with your other contacts.'

'Indeed, I will.' He pressed a kiss to her forehead, ignoring the strange sense there was more to her worry than she was revealing. 'I'll be back soon.'

Susanna watched him slip out the door, leaving her alone in the semi-darkness of the room. She drew her knees up to her chest and wrapped her arms around them, wishing she'd gone with him. It wouldn't stop Lady Rockland from lashing out at them if she chose to, but at least it would prevent her from worrying about what might happen while Justin and her father were together.

Swinging her legs over the side of the bed, she rose and made for her room to change her dress, determined not to fret. Nothing would happen. All would be well, just as Justin had promised last night. Selecting a new dress from the wardrobe, she shrugged out of her old one. The faint smell of Justin clinging to the muslin might be a comfort, but she could hardly go through the rest of the day so dishevelled.

An hour later, dressed in a simple white gown with green sprigs and with her hair confined once again to its coiffure, she sat at the writing table reviewing the week's menu. The satisfaction of her lovemaking with Justin had long since eased and had been replaced by the anxiety which continued to prick at her like a pin left in a dress. She didn't want Justin anywhere near the Rockland house, or her stepmother and the secret she held. It would be a long few hours before he returned and she learned if her secret was safe, or everything was coming to pieces.

She was so distracted with worry she didn't hear the elder Mr Connor until he sauntered into the sitting room unannounced.

'A good day to you, Mrs Connor.' He swept off his hat and handed the dented Wellington to Walter.

'And you, too, Mr Connor.' They went to the dining room where Mrs Robinson laid out the tea and set before him the half-full bottle of port. Mr Connor's hands still shook as he poured out a measure of the drink, but he didn't appear as rumpled or careworn today as he had during his first few visits. His coming to the house had become a habit over the past week. He seemed to know with unfailing canniness when his son wouldn't be home.

'Thank you for treating me as you do. I haven't felt this well in a long time.' He patted her hand in the fatherly way which had developed between them during their teas. 'I sometimes think, if my wife had lived and with her the little girl, she might have grown up to be like you.'

Susanna struggled to maintain her smile. He wouldn't wish for a daughter like her if he learned what kind of woman she really was. She settled her hands over her stomach, noting the slight thickness where the child was growing inside her. For all her kindness to Mr Connor and his son, she was still a charlatan, a fallen woman who hadn't had the sense to remember herself in the face of a man's false promises.

'I'd like to tell Justin of our teas and have him join us one of these days,' Susanna offered.

'Don't go ruining a man's meal with such unpleasant business,' Mr Connor chided her, taking a long drink before setting the teacup back in its saucer.

'If you both spoke civilly to one another, you might be surprised how different things could be between you.'

Mr Connor scratched his head, mussing his already wild grey hair. 'Gets to be so many years, a man doesn't know where to start.'

'The simplest, most direct approach is best.'

'But not always the easiest.' With a wink reminiscent of his son's, he held up his cup to her, then took a hearty sip. 'But I suppose nothing worth doing is ever easy.'

'Then you'll see him?' Susanna asked.

'Let's see what time brings.'

It wasn't a promise, but she felt sure he would soon face his son just as she was now certain how much port to place in the bottle, or which tarts were his favourites. There was no denying the change in Mr Connor and even Mrs Robinson had remarked on it. Whether it would last or result in any peace between father and son, she still couldn't say, but she'd continue to try and mend the rift between them. She owed this much to Justin in thanks for all he'd done for her, known and unknown.

Chapter Ten

'Here you are, Mr Connor, a complete list of the wines I require for Lady Rockland's masque.' The duke handed a sheet of paper across the wide oak desk to Justin. The entire room was grand, imposing, meant to make a man like Justin cower before the wealth and influence of Lord Rockland, but it did nothing to intimidate him. Today the duke might own the world, tomorrow his debts might consume him and force him to sell off the full-length Van Dyke hanging on the wall behind him.

Justin took the paper and examined it, careful to conceal his true reaction at the sheer number of bottles and vintages required. It would take all his connections throughout London, and quite possibly in the countryside, to acquire everything on the list. It'd be even more of a challenge given he had only a few days to achieve it, but he wasn't about to fail. Despite Susanna's worries about Lord Rockland's support, Justin was confident a man impressed was a man he'd continue to do business with. 'I'll have this to you in time, Your Grace.'

'Are you sure?' Lord Rockland regarded him with more shock than admiration at the alacrity with which Justin answered. 'It's quite an extensive selection.'

The sense the list was something of a test nagged at Justin, but he wasn't about to give Lord Rockland a gentlemanly way out of their bargain. 'I assure you, I'll have everything delivered in time.'

'Of course you will,' he answered with some disappointment. 'You do understand, after the masque, the two of you cannot expect further invitations or help from me in regards to your business. A man of my station can hardly be expected to meddle in the affairs of merchants. I've done my best to be responsible, as I have with all my other obligations, giving Susanna a most generous dowry which an enterprising couple could make more use of than my limited influence.'

It was then Justin understood why the duke had taken Susanna in, but shown her no real love or affection. She was a duty, not his daughter. He was honourable enough to assume those duties laid at his feet, but once they were discharged, he would wash his hands of them, as he would Susanna and Justin after this order was fulfilled.

'You've been very generous with Susanna and you needn't worry about us. I made my way in the world before I married your daughter. I will again.'

Lord Rockland silently regarded him with, if Justin dared to think it, respect, the kind his father hadn't even grudgingly shown him. 'I have no doubt you will.'

Lord Rockland rose and nodded to Justin, bringing their meeting to an end. 'Good day to you, Mr Connor.'

Tucking the list in his coat pocket, Justin followed the waiting footman out of the high-ceilinged study, down the wide avenue of the hallway and to the expansive space of the entrance hall with the tall double doors set in the far end. For all his bravado in Lord Rockland's presence, the clear understanding there would be no more patronage was a blow. Susanna had tried to warn him, but he'd held out hope she might somehow be wrong. He should have listened to her. This must have been what she'd attempted to caution him about before he'd left. She knew the Rocklands better than he did, but still Justin wanted the great man's business. Lord Rockland's support would've smoothed the way to quicker success and the ability to rub it in the faces of his detractors sooner. Without the high-born patronage, Justin would once again be left to make his own way.

'Here to beg from my husband so soon?' A voice from somewhere above Justin made him stop. He turned to watch Lady Rockland descend the stairs, eyeing him as though he were a bug scurrying across her dinner plate. 'Has your business failed already?'

'I'm here at Lord Rockland's request.' Justin struggled to maintain his smile, seeing first-hand the wickedness Susanna must have suffered under the woman. 'My shop is doing well, thank you. Susanna is proving quite an asset.'

'It's fitting since she was born to such a low station in life.' Lady Rockland came to face Justin in an imperious rustle of black silk, her tight curls unmoving against her head. 'And she's brought you such a great deal beside her support, hasn't she? Money, connection to my husband, a child.'

Justin cocked his head at the woman. 'I have no doubt there will be children in the future.'

'There'll be a child sooner than you think, Mr Connor, one with a bloodline more distinguished than yours, but condemned to life as the common offspring of a wine merchant.'

The house rocked around Justin. He stood still, summoning up everything he'd ever learned from his father, Philip or at the pugilist club to centre himself and keep a hard restraint on the anger, disbelief and confusion rising inside him. Susanna hadn't deceived him. It was this wicked woman trying to cause trouble.

'Saying such a thing can be of no benefit to a woman of your rank and manners.'

'It is if it means you won't pollute my house with your or your wife's presence ever again.' Her tight face sharpened the jut of her square chin. 'My husband might welcome you here, but I won't have you set foot in this house again. He may want to wallow in his sins, but not me. I suggest you don't assist him in the endeavour by not attending the ball.'

Justin didn't answer, but executed the same bow which had shocked her the first time they'd met. Then he turned on his heel and made for the door.

'Through the back door, Mr Connor, where the rest of the tradesmen call.'

Justin didn't break his stride as he marched towards the front door. The butler moved to step in front of it and block his exit, but Justin pinned him with a scowl to nearly fell him dead. The man drew back, leaving Justin to pull open the tall wooden doors and step outside. He left it to the hired man to close them behind him and, with his head held high, climbed into the chaise.

The streets of Grosvenor Square passed on either side of him in a blur as he stared at the empty seat across from his. It wasn't Lady Rockland's slight which had followed him out of the house like the stench of beer from a brewery, but her accusation.

Susanna is carrying Lord Howsham's child.

Justin banged his fist on the side of the chaise. He wouldn't let this consume him, not until he reached home and heard from Susanna it wasn't true. It couldn't be. He wouldn't put it past the old carthorse to lie in an attempt to cause trouble between the two of them, or ensure Justin was so disgusted by the duchess he stayed away from her husband, the house and the masque. Yet the instinct he'd relied on to keep himself and Philip safe prickled along the back of his neck. He'd trusted his senses too many times to his benefit to shake the feeling off as a mistake now.

Justin trilled his fingers on the squabs. Susanna's attempt to speak to him in Gunter's the day before the wedding added to his torment. Something had pressed on her enough to dull the usual sharpness of her eyes and make her appear as worried as a pickpocket before the magistrate. Justin's stomach dropped. She'd been intimate with Lord Howsham and when she'd tried to elaborate, he'd refused to listen, believing with too much glibness nothing from his past or hers could trouble them. By cutting her off, he'd made it easier for her to deceive him, or abandon whatever guilt her conscience drove her to relieve.

Self-disgust whirled in him to muddle with his anger. He should've listened, he shouldn't have been such a starry-eyed fool, too focused on the shop and the future to see what was in front of him. Assuming what Lady Rockland had said was true. He didn't know, but he'd soon find out.

The streets outside grew more familiar as the chaise rumbled down Fleet Street. Justin tugged at his cravat, irritated by the cloying heat inside the carriage. He pulled down the window, but the thick air outside, rank with horses and the river's stench, was no better. He fell back against the squabs, hands tight on his thighs, trying to regain his calm, but one thought kept stealing it from him. What would his father and Helena say if the rumours reached them? They'd laugh and call him a cuckold, and every damning thing they'd thought of him would be proved right by the one woman he'd come to rely on and love more than any other.

He tapped his heel against the floor, pulling back his condemnation. Before he'd left, Susanna had worried Lady Rockland might strike at him and she had. This had to be a lie, it needed to be. With his street coming into view, he'd soon have his answer and surely all his worries would be for nothing.

The chaise hadn't even stopped before he tossed open the door and jumped down.

'Good evening, Mr Connor,' Walter greeted him as Justin strode into the house.

'Where's Mrs Connor?'

'In her room,' Walter stuttered, surprised at Justin's curt query. It wasn't like him to dismiss the man, but he wasn't interested in the butler, only his wife and her reassurance all was well.

He took the stairs two at a time as he continued to chew on Lady Rockland's pronouncement. The woman was probably driven by jealousy at seeing her husband's illegitimate daughter married while her daughter languished for another Season. Justin wouldn't believe her story until he heard it from Susanna herself.

He flung open the door to her room. She looked up from whatever she was working on with Mrs Robinson at the writing table. She smiled at him, bringing Justin to a halt. He could say nothing and trust in this woman who regarded him with an eagerness and faith few had granted him before.

She set down her pen, her pleasure at his return changing to worry. 'What's wrong? Did my father renege on our agreement?'

He glanced to Mrs Robinson who, without a word, excused herself, drawing the door shut behind her.

'No, he's purchasing the wines, but he made it clear there'll be no further help after the masque.'

She drummed her fingers on the desk. 'We never

negotiated for any and we should have. That was my fault.'

'It wouldn't have made a difference. He and Lady Rockland are quite eager to see the back of us, as you expected.'

She didn't gloat over having been correct, but seemed to mourn with him Lord Rockland's lack of support. Again he considered biting his tongue, but the uncertainty tearing at him wouldn't allow it.

'There's more, isn't there?' she asked, twisting the pen between her fingers.

'I encountered Lady Rockland as I was leaving.' He pressed his fists to his hips, unable to hold back the question which had tormented him since leaving Grosvenor Square. 'She said you're carrying Lord Howsham's child.'

The colour drained out of her cheeks as she dropped the pen to clatter against the table top.

'Tell me it's a lie,' he demanded, wanting to hear the words from her mouth, to soothe the anger roiling inside him. 'Tell me.'

Her shoulders slumped in a defeat he felt in his soul, and everything between the two of them shattered as the truth rippled through her eyes.

'Did you know before the wedding?' he demanded, wishing for a leather dummy from his pugilist club so he could pound out the rage rising inside him. She'd deceived him, all the while pretending faith.

'I tried to tell you at Gunter's, but you wouldn't let me.'

'So this is my fault?'

She jumped to her feet, reaching for him before pulling her hand back. 'No, of course not.'

'I think it is, for letting you and your entire damned family take me for a dupe.'

'They aren't my family and it wasn't about how I could fool you. It was never about that.' She raised her voice to match his, balling her hand at her sides. 'I was afraid I'd lose you or you'd reject me and the child. You don't know what it's like to be a bastard, to have people scorn you for something that isn't your fault. To bear a bastard would've meant being condemned twice and subjecting the child to an even worse childhood than I knew. Lord Rockland would have thrown me out if I hadn't gone through with the marriage and then where would I have been? Where would the child have been? I couldn't condemn a baby to a future in the gutter because of my mistake.'

'I wouldn't have turned my back on you.' Justin stared into the fire, following the rise and fall of each flame as it consumed the coal. 'I know what happens to women who end up in the streets. I see it each time I visit Moll Topp's to investigate a potential client's debts. I see the gaunt, disease-ridden women devoid of hope or happiness, with their daughters washing the filthy sheets until they're old enough to earn their keep on their backs while their brothers are stuffed up chimneys until they contract soot wart. I know Lord Howsham forced himself on you, taking advantage of your loneliness and lack of experience to satisfy his own lust. If you'd believed in me enough to tell me the truth, I wouldn't have consigned you or the child to such a fate. Instead you took me for a fool and it burns more than your deceit.'

She laid one hand on his arm. 'I'm sorry, Justin. I'm sorry I hurt you, I'm sorry I deceived you and didn't give you the chance to decide.'

He shrugged off her touch. 'Apologies aren't enough.'

'I don't know what else to say, or do.' Susanna stared into the fire, the pain etching her face touching him. He hardened himself against it. He didn't want to pity her or understand her suffering, not with the storm of emotions surging inside him and the new worry eating at him.

'You're not to do anything which might endanger your life, or the child's, do you hear me?' He wouldn't have them solve their problems that way or lose Susanna to the darkness of death where nothing, no conversation or the passing of time, could ever bring her back. The idea tore at his insides with claws as sharp as her dishonesty.

Susanna nodded. His insistence she not risk her life or the baby's spoke to his integrity and increased the shame draping her like a shroud.

'What will happen between us?' she asked, as though he was as much a stranger to her now as he'd been the morning they'd entered into this agreement.

'I don't know.' Without another word he turned and left, the door lingering open behind him. Then she heard the back door slam and him call out in the mews for the chaise.

In the dim light of the bedroom, she dropped down on her knees to the rug, buried her face in her hands and wept.

Justin jabbed his fists at Philip, first one, then another, each time missing his friend. Justin didn't back up, or try a new position, but swung blindly, his failure to strike anything fuelling the rage hollowing out his innards.

'You're sloppy tonight. What's wrong?' Philip dodged another hit and Justin growled with his frustration. He shouldn't be taking out his fury on his friend, but on the punching bag in the corner. With so many other men crowding the club, he wasn't about to beat the thing into a pulp of leather and feathers in front of everyone.

'I'm experiencing some marital difficulties,' Justin admitted through gritted teeth as he shuffled forward to try and land another hit on his friend who easily dodged him.

'I remember you telling me once to go home and deal with my woman troubles instead of pounding them out.' Philip leaned away from Justin's swing. 'Why aren't you taking your own advice?'

Justin ceased his mindless jabbing, but didn't lower his fists, unable to unclench his hands. 'I can't go home.'

'Why not?'

Justin dropped his arms to his sides, his muscles screaming from his exertion, but not as loudly as his heart. He stared at his best friend, the man who'd seen him cry the day he'd lost his mother, who knew every trouble and grief his father had caused him. He didn't want to reveal this deepest of all his shames, but he had to tell someone. 'Susanna is pregnant with Lord Howsham's child.'

What Justin's fists had failed to accomplish this pronouncement managed, knocking his oldest friend silent.

'Are you sure?' Philip asked after a long pause, lowering his fists. The fight was over.

'Yes.' Justin briefly explained his encounter with Lady Rockland and coming home to have Susanna confirm it. He'd spent years fighting his father, now it would be his wife. This wasn't how he wanted to live. The choice had been torn from him by Susanna and the Rocklands.

'What'll you do?' Philip handed his friend one of the towels draped over the ropes of the sparring ring.

Justin rubbed the stinging sweat from his eyes, then flipped the towel over his bare shoulder. 'What can I do? We're wed. In the eyes of the law the child is mine no matter what villain sired it.'

At once he understood why his father drank. What he wouldn't give to crawl into a gin bottle tonight and forget everything—his mother's death, his father's insults, his business failures and his wife's betrayal.

'Then treat it as yours and never let anyone aside from us think any differently.'

'And the Rocklands? The duchess won't be content to let this secret go.'

'If she sees her vileness hasn't troubled you or driven a wedge between you and your wife, then she will.'

'It has driven a wedge between us.' He tugged the towel from his shoulder and threw it to a passing boy. 'Any other bastard and no one would care, but she's the Duke of Rockland's daughter foisting her child off on another man. It'll give everyone from Mayfair to Seven Dials something to talk about.'

'The better sort don't care what we get up to.'

'They do when it involves the illegitimate daughter of a duke.'

'Then walk away from them and never have anything more to do with them. Then nothing they or anyone else of their class says will ever matter,' Philip suggested.

'I can't, not yet. It would mean missing the ball, forfeiting the chance to cultivate clients and getting stuck with a lot of inventory instead of selling it to the duke.' It wasn't so much the wine motivating him now, but the craving to stick a finger in Lady Rockland's eye by attending. He'd have to do so with Susanna at his side, the two of them grinning like idiots and pretending she hadn't hurt them. It'd be worth it to spite the old dragon. 'I refuse to let him out of his agreement, or to allow his wife to sneer and look down on us.'

'And Susanna?'

'I don't know.' Justin opened and closed his fingers, the knuckles smarting beneath the bruises forming there. He didn't want to care about how facing the Rocklands might affect her. She hadn't shown him the same consideration when she'd marched up the aisle to meet him, giving him no say in a future so carefully planned out with the Rocklands. They'd all thought him stupid enough to accept a woman carrying another man's bastard and like a dolt he'd fallen in neatly with their plans. 'I love her, as you love Laura.'

It made her betrayal hurt so much more, dragging him down further than the day he'd learned the ship had sunk. Failure dogged him again, predetermined by forces he couldn't control or account for, just like before.

'Which gives you more reason to overcome this. I've seen the two of you together. You get on well and are good for one another. You can be happy if you find a way to move past this and you must.' Philip dropped a steadying hand on Justin's shoulder. 'You know what might happen when she's brought to bed.'

'I do.' Justin shrugged off his friend's hand, not wanting to face the truth the way he had the morning his father had told him about his mother's passing along with the infant they'd anticipated for so many months. His mother's loss had ruined his father. What might Susanna's do to Justin? Nothing. Her lie had already destroyed everything.

Justin pinched the bridge of his nose with his fingers. Spite for the Rocklands burned a hole in his chest, not just because of what they'd torn from him, but what it meant for the future.

'What'll I do if the child is a boy?' Another man's son would be heir to everything he might build. He could amend his will to cut the child out, give his rightful heirs their due, but it would mean admitting to the world their secret and tainting the child the way Susanna had been tainted. Given what Susanna had suffered, and having been scorned by his own father, he couldn't visit such misery on an innocent boy. He would have to bring himself to love this child, as much as he disliked it and its mother right now.

'You'll have time to figure it out. Nothing needs to be decided tonight,' Philip reminded him, but it didn't help.

He needed time and distance, a chance to reclaim the centre which had been knocked out of him by Lady Rockland's nastiness and Susanna's grudging honesty. With the masque only a few days away, it was a luxury he didn't possess. He couldn't walk away from the Rocklands' wine order any more than he could from his marriage. He'd see to it the duchess didn't win, but to do it he'd have to choke down his pride, especially where Susanna was concerned. It was a vintage he wasn't ready to swallow.

Susanna sat listlessly by the fire in the sitting room, her eyes sore from another night spent crying alone in her bed. She hadn't seen Justin in two days. He'd come home well after dark and risen before dawn. She didn't know where he went. She was afraid to ask and powerless to stop him. All she could do was continue with her routine, going to the shop every day and seeing to the endless tasks. Every time the bell over the shop door rang or the back room door to the alley opened, she held her breath, waiting to hear Justin's voice, but it was never him.

Coming home to the empty house again today, the stiff upper lip she'd tried to maintain in the presence of the shop assistant and the servants began to flag and her spirits ebbed nearly as low as they had in the days after her mother had died. She sat in the window seat, trying to read, but tears kept clouding her eyes. She dropped her head in her hands. It was too much and she hated herself for what she'd done, but she despised Lady Rockland more. There'd been no reason but sheer spite for her to tell Justin of the child and ruin everything.

The front door knocker banged and she raised her head, unable to see who was waiting outside from where she sat. Rubbing the tears from her eyes, she hoped it was just another messenger with a note for Justin. She picked up her book, attempting to appear composed to whoever might happen to see her, but the pages blurred through her unshed tears.

'Mr Connor,' Walter announced.

Old Mr Connor stepped around the man and beamed at her, a new fullness about his crinkled eyes and beneath his square chin. His clothes appeared neater today, though they were still near threadbare around the elbows and collar. He wore his old Wellington, which he swept off his now combed hair and handed it to Walter. In the entrance hall, Mr Green even smiled as he left Mr Connor in Susanna's care to seek out Mrs Robinson.

'You look very well today, Mr Connor,' she remarked, his transformation lifting her for a moment from her own sorrows.

'Good food will do that to a man.' He patted his fuller stomach before taking her in with a critical eye. 'You aren't looking very well. Justin isn't running you ragged with the shop, is he?'

'No, he—' The brave face she'd worn the entire day began to crack. She wouldn't cry in front of him, she refused to, but the tears fell in steady streams down her cheeks to drop on to the front of her dress.

'What's this, then?' Mr Connor sat down next to her in the window seat and wrapped his arms around her.

She buried her face in his soft dun-coloured coat. It smelled of tobacco and the coal-filled London air. The scent was as comforting as his large hand rubbing her back, soothing her as she'd wished her grandfather would have done so many times as a child.

'Tell me what's wrong, lass. There's no reason you should be crying.'

His sympathy made the tears come harder for herself, Justin and everything she'd never had in her life and wouldn't have in the future. For a few short days she'd discovered what it was to be loved and through her own weakness she'd ruined it all. She wished she'd never enjoyed such happiness with Justin so that losing it now wouldn't be so bitter.

'Come now, tell me what's wrong,' he urged.

The story came tumbling out, all of it, as she cried against him. He'd find out about it soon enough and the patient way he listened made it so she couldn't hold back the words. While she spoke, he never once stopped in his comforting or pushed her away. Instead he continued to hold her, calming the sobs until only the dried tears on her cheeks and the sense of being wrung out like a rag remained.

She rubbed her wet face with a small handkerchief from her pocket. 'You hate me now, don't you?'

He shook his head. 'I don't hate you and what's done is done. I'm not saying it's right, 'cause it ain't, but I understand why you did it.'

'Do you?' It didn't seem possible.

'I'm a man of the world. I know how it works. Why, Justin was almost born on the wrong side of the blanket. Molly and I were so in love and young and foolish. We couldn't wait for the church's blessing, so we did what nature drives a man and woman to do. I hadn't thought of marrying yet, but when she told me, I did right by her. Never regretted it because I loved her and she loved me.'

'But that wasn't how it was with me and Justin.'

'It's how it is now.' He patted her hand with his calloused one. 'You have a good heart and you did what you did because you care for a child which ain't even here yet. You treat me kind because you are kind and you care for my son.'

'I love him. And now he hates me.'

'No, he doesn't, but you've given him a shock and it'll take time to gain back what you two had before.'

She twisted the handkerchief between her fingers. 'Do you think he'll give me another chance?'

'All the times I've come in here cursing at him like the devil and still he hands me money, keeps me fed and housed, talks to me with a respect I should show him.'

'But you're his father.' She didn't have the same claim on Justin's affection.

'There's plenty out there who don't give a fig for the hardships of their folks, or their children.' He rubbed his chin, a pensive look coming over him. 'I've been hurtin' so bad these many years, ever since I lost my dear Molly. I took it out on him and he didn't deserve it. Still, he treats me as a son should treat his father. He'll do the same for you.'

It wasn't Justin's regard she wanted, but his love. 'There's no reason for him to be kind to me.'

'Yes, there is. You're his wife whether it's been for three weeks or twenty years. He'll do right by you, but you'll have to work for it, keep the anger from festering like you've done with me. Don't let him pull away as I have, but hold him close and cherish him. He loves you. Bring it out and I promise you, all will be well.'

She hugged him, hoping he was right.

It was well after dark by the time Justin returned home from another day of scouring London for Lord Rockland's libations. His father's gig sat out front and whatever brief ease he'd found in his work today vanished as his shoulders and neck tightened. He was in no mood for his father's acid tonight. He thought of turning around, climbing back in the chaise and going to the Rathbones', but he wasn't a man to run from his problems. He'd face them, as he always did, but with a little less humour tonight.

Justin strode into the sitting room, dug some coins

from his pocket and held them out to his father. 'Here, take the shillings and be gone.'

His father waved the money away. 'I don't want money.'

Justin pocketed the coins, eyeing his father suspiciously. Something about him seemed different tonight. 'What do you want?'

'To talk to you.'

Ice crept through his veins. The last time his father had sought him out to talk had been to tell him his infant sister hadn't survived and neither had his mother.

'Is Susanna all right?' Panic nearly sent him hurling from the room and up the stairs to check on her.

'She's well, but she ain't all right.' He sounded weary and for once his hands didn't shake, nor did the agitation which usually marked his visits send him grumbling and pacing across the room. He was the calm, steady man Justin remembered from his youth and for a moment Justin saw the shadow of his childhood, before his mother had died, when the three of them had been happy and his father had been his hero. 'I spoke with her this afternoon.'

The fact his father and wife enjoyed a confidence startled him as much as his father refusing the coins. 'I didn't think you two were on such intimate terms.'

'I've been coming here for tea for a while now, always when you're gone. We decided not to tell you. Wanted it to be our secret.'

'Yes, she's good at keeping secrets.' He wondered what else she was upstairs hiding. If he hadn't seen the bank account for the dowry, he'd wonder if the fifteen hundred pounds were real or another one of her lies. 'She's told you, then?'

'Aye, she has.'

Justin crossed his arms. 'Go ahead, belittle me for trying to rise above my station, tell me I deserve to be made to look like an idiot by the better sort.'

'I won't, because you don't deserve it. She's been telling me about your shop and the clients you've got.' Pride coloured his father's words. 'I went there once and she showed me the cellar and the front room. She's done it up very pretty, tells me you're to supply Lord Rockland with wine for his masque.'

Justin lowered his hands. He couldn't believe after so many years of insulting him for wanting to better himself, his father was praising him now. 'I thought you said I wasn't good enough for such things?'

'I was wrong to say it,' his father admitted, knocking Justin more off centre than any of Philip's or his trainer's punches. The man he'd once admired was standing in front of him again. 'I was jealous of you, afraid if you made something of yourself, you'd look down on me. I was wrong to treat you the way I did, to blame you when it was me who was at fault. The young lady made me see it. It's why I can't condemn her for what she's done. She was kind to me when I was making my mistakes. I can't help but be kind to her and you.'

Justin stared at his father in disbelief. He'd waited years to hear this kind of apology, hoped his patience would bring it about, but it hadn't. Susanna, the woman who'd deceived him, had caused this. He should be glad for it, but it was tainted by everything else he was mired in.

'What you're dealing with ain't easy,' his father offered. 'But don't let this trouble come between the two of you. You're a good and caring man, keep being one where she and the child are concerned. She's already worn thin worrying about how you'll treat her. Such a thing is dangerous to a woman in her condition.'

The worry which had gripped him at Philip's similar warning seized him again. She might die in childbirth, whether it was with his baby or another man's. He couldn't shake free of the possibility, or how much losing her would reopen the hole in his life he hadn't realised existed until he'd met her. It didn't move him to forgiveness, but increased the cut of her deception. All the time he'd been falling for her and coming to rely on her support, she'd been lying to him.

'Put aside your anger like I should've done all those years ago after your mother died. Instead, I wallowed in my grief and you suffered because of it. Don't turn into me.' His father tapped his hat over his grey hair and made for the door. Mr Green rose from his place in the hall to follow him out into the night.

Justin didn't stop him, he couldn't. He hadn't expected this any more than what Lady Rockland had told him about the child. The change Susanna had wrought in his father was nothing short of a miracle and an answer to at least one of his long-held wishes. Whether she'd done it to ease her guilty conscience or for a nobler reason he wasn't sure and he wasn't ready to find out.

He wandered to his study and dropped down into the leather chair, catching Walter's curious glance from the doorway before the valet hurried away. They knew. Servants always knew gossip first and now his father did, too. Yet the one man he'd expected to laugh the loudest at his misfortune had pitied him and advised him with as much insight as Philip.

He took up the whisky and poured himself a healthy measure, then drained the glass. It didn't matter how much the smoky liquor fogged his brain tonight, it was already muddled beyond reason. He grabbed the decanter and filled the glass again. If she'd told him the truth before the wedding, he could have recommended her to Philip's charity. They would have looked after her and the child as they did all the other unfortunate women whose husbands and fathers had fallen into debt and left them in dire straits. It would've meant leaving her and all the hope he'd felt in her presence behind, abandoning the one person who'd believed in him and his dream.

He stared into the tawny liquid, his thirst gone.

She'd made him happier than he'd been in years, working alongside him in the shop. He'd accused her of not caring for him and lying simply to save her own hide and that of the child's, but she'd befriended his father before Justin had discovered her secret, working to bring about a change not to redeem herself, but to help him. It made the veracity of his accusation difficult to maintain. If nothing else, he owed her for this kindness.

He finished the drink, then set the glass on the table

with a clunk. He might have been taken for a dupe, but he'd be damned if he'd prove himself any less of a gentleman than the duke. She was his wife and he'd honour the commitment he'd made to her and do right by her and the child the law would view as his. Whether it meant loving them both, especially her, he couldn't say, but he was stuck with her and would make the best of it, as he'd made the best of his losses after the ship had sunk. He wouldn't give up and he wouldn't let this ruin him. He was too good a man and if others couldn't see it, it didn't matter. He knew and so did those who cared for him the most, even his lying wife.

The sound of whispering pulled Susanna from a restless sleep. Light flooded the room and made her blink as she opened her eyes. Justin stood at the foot of her bed. At once she sat up, but the trials of the past few days, the lack of sleep and a proper meal made her stomach rebel and the room spin. She closed her eyes and took a deep breath, glad when she opened them to see everything as it should be, except for Justin.

His face was drawn as tight as it'd been the night she'd first met his father. The time he'd spent away from her hadn't changed anything between them or brought him any closer to forgiving her. It was evident in his hard expression and the stiffness of his hands by his side.

She tugged the coverlet up a little closer to her chest when she noticed the distinguished older gentleman standing behind Justin and carrying a black leather bag. He was tall with grey hair along his temples and vivid blue eyes which took her in with a strange sort of curiosity.

'Susanna, this is Dr Hale, Philip's father-in-law from his first wife.' Gone was the laughing, smiling Justin she'd come to love. She barely recognised this taciturn man.

'Good morning,' the doctor said brightly. 'Justin tells me you might be with child.'

She let go of the coverlet, stunned someone would announce it in such a merry tone. She'd greeted the news of her pregnancy with nothing but dread.

'Yes, I believe so,' she stuttered, amazed Justin would reveal this to a near stranger, even if he was a physician.

'You two have wasted no time,' Dr Hale teased as he pulled the chair from the dressing table next to the bed and sat down beside her. He took her wrist and slid a watch out of his waistcoat pocket to check her pulse. 'When were your last courses?'

Susanna exchanged an uneasy glance with Justin, looking to him for what to say, unsure if she should tell the truth, or try to concoct some lie. If the doctor examined her, he'd know at once she was further along than simply the three weeks since her wedding. 'The week of Lady Day.'

Dr Hale's fingers stiffened on her wrist before he released her. He slipped the watch back in his pocket, all business as though he hadn't calculated the date and realised exactly what it meant. 'I see.'

Shame weighed on her as much as a lack of rest. This wouldn't be the first awkward encounter Justin would have to endure because of her mistake. There'd soon be many more when her condition could no longer be hidden, though if he'd wanted to avoid this one, he shouldn't have brought the doctor here. It didn't lessen her humiliation at the embarrassment he was forced to endure thanks to her. She was sorry and would have told him so if Dr Hale hadn't been there. Although no apology could undo the damage her lie had wrought or make him look at her as he had the morning before he'd gone to the Rocklands'.

Dr Hale asked her a few questions and she answered honestly, all the while conscious of Justin's presence. There was no pretence during the exam to their being a happy couple, not for her sake or Dr Hale's. If the physician noticed the tension between husband and wife, he never revealed it, maintaining his courteous chatter until, at last satisfied she was well, he snapped his black bag closed.

'Now get some rest. I'll return in a few days to see how you're doing.'

'I'll see you out,' Justin offered.

'Justin,' Susanna called, unwilling to let him go. Something had drawn him to her this morning, a care or concern which, for the first time in days, offered some hope of lifting the darkness which surrounded them. If she could draw it out, like the long-buried goodness in his father, perhaps they could begin to repair the rift between them.

Justin hesitated, but didn't answer. It was Dr Hale who made the decision for him.

'I'll wait downstairs.' Dr Hale strode into the hallway, his steps fading off down the staircase.

'Why did you summon him?' Susanna asked, confused.

'Mrs Robinson tells me you've been tired and you haven't eaten much.' He might not have seen her these past few days, but he'd taken an interest in her wellbeing. It should've comforted her, but it didn't. It was probably Mrs Robinson who'd informed him of Susanna's lack of rest and food, rather than he who'd asked about her.

'But now he knows.'

'You're my wife. It's my duty to see to your wellbeing.'

'Your duty,' she whispered, understanding why he'd endured humiliation to summon the physician. Like her father, he'd honour his obligation, but there'd be nothing more, no love or the affection they'd shared during the past three weeks. The loneliness of the years when she'd lived with her grandfather and uncle, tolerated instead of cherished, was suddenly fresh again. Bitter tears stung her eyes, but she fought them back, wishing he'd been this way from the beginning. The joy they'd found in one another was gone, leaving nothing but the cold, empty shell of what might have been to taunt her.

'I must see the doctor out.' He left before she could stop him. She wasn't sure he would come back unless some other obligation drove him to it.

She laid her hand on her stomach, trying to summon up the resolve which had carried her through the long years in Oxfordshire and then with the Rocklands. She could endure the heartache and disparagement of a cold spouse. It was the child which worried her. Justin would look on it as her grandfather had looked on her, with grudging acknowledgement, not love, never love. Lady Rockland had stolen the chance from her and the baby. At least the child wouldn't endure the suffering of being illegitimate. Having lost the love of her husband, it was Susanna's only consolation.

'Congratulations, Justin.' Dr Hale held out his hand as Justin came down the stairs.

Justin gritted his teeth as he shook the man's hand. Whatever Dr Hale suspected about the parentage of the baby, he'd decided to ignore it, as he suspected most people would. It was what they'd say behind his and Susanna's backs he wondered about. Dr Hale wasn't one to gossip, but many others would. Justin had never cared before, having created more rumours than he could recall, but this burned along the back of his throat and there was nothing to do but silently tolerate it.

'Is she well?' Justin asked.

'Many women suffer from fatigue in the first months of pregnancy. A few days of rest and some good food will see her set to rights very quickly.'

To Justin's ire, the doctor's proclamation sent a wave of relief through him. He shouldn't care whether she felt well or not. She'd never considered his feelings once in the matter. 'When do you think she'll be brought to bed?'

'Early winter, I'd say, though babies have their own schedule and will arrive when they're good and ready.'

'Do you think she'll be delivered safely?' Justin asked, though there was no physician who could predict such a thing. It was up to nature which women survived and which didn't and whether the infants joined them or not, just as it'd been up to nature to sink his ship and his last business.

'She's young and healthy. I'm sure she'll come through her confinement. I shouldn't worry.' Dr Hale clapped him on the arm. 'Summon me if there are any problems, though I don't think there will be.'

'Thank you, Dr Hale.'

Justin watched Walter close the door behind the doctor. He would go through the motions of being a dutiful husband as he'd gone through the motions of being a dutiful son for years, all the while fighting back the bitter bile of the situation which at his lowest times would creep up to almost consume him.

The whisper of a lady's step on the stairs made him turn. He expected to see Mrs Robinson, but it was Susanna. She stopped, the hem of her wrapper fluttering around her legs. Over one shoulder her hair fell in a long braid, its darkness echoing in the circles beneath her eyes. In their time together, he'd never thought of her as frail, but seeing her leaning heavily on the banister, Philip's warning about what might happen if she were brought to bed seared through his mind. Despite Dr Hale's assurances, Justin worried about her.

'What are you doing up?' Justin demanded.

'I have too much to do to sit in bed all day.'

'It can wait until tomorrow. You need rest.' He marched up the stairs, took her by the elbow and gently turned her around. She didn't fight him, but allowed him to lead her back up to her room.

Her exhaustion was evident in her slow pace and the heaviness of her arm beneath his palm. Dr Hale had said it was to be expected but it raised the worry which had tormented him all night until he'd been forced to summon the physician early this morning in order to put his mind at ease.

They stopped outside her room, Justin making it clear he wouldn't follow her inside.

'Will I see you tonight?' The sadness marking her questions reminded him of the times she'd talked of her childhood. For a moment, he wanted to banish it, but he couldn't. Nothing right now could make him take her in his arms or forget how she'd deceived him.

'No, collecting the wines for your father's party will keep me occupied for some time.'

'And will we attend the ball?'

With her so tired and pale, he couldn't imagine forcing her through the rigours of the ball, or the strain of facing her dragon stepmother. Nor could he stand before Lady Rockland and act like some Drury Lane leading man, grinning like an idiot and pretending all was well. Lord Rockland had made it clear there'd be no more support for Justin's business so there was no point pressing the flesh with the better sort, or putting either of them through the strain of a long evening which might garner them nothing. 'No. We need to distance ourselves from the Rocklands for good.'

Her shoulders relaxed with a relief he couldn't share. This one difficulty might be surmounted, but there were many others facing them, along with disappointments. Despite her warning about cultivating the patronage of the *haut ton*, he'd held on to the hope of securing more clients at the masque. The plan was now as good as dead.

'I must go.' Without another word or a kiss goodbye, he made for downstairs. Things might be all confusion, but the simplicity and focus of his work remained. He had a job to do, wines to procure. Even if he despised his client, he'd be damned if he'd fail. He'd never let Philip down in all their years of business. Now he was in charge and he would fail no one, least of all himself. Everything else could wait.

Susanna dragged herself back to bed, thankful for the soft sheets and pillows. She was tired, wrung out by crying, worry and the demands of the infant growing inside her. Nothing with her and Justin was settled, but a small relief made resting easier. They weren't going to the masque. He would fulfil her father's order and then their time, her time, with the Rocklands would finally end. Lady Rockland had done her worst and now Susanna never had to face the evil woman again. Even if she continued with her whispers, the distance between Fleet Street and Grosvenor Square was vast enough to keep Lady Rockland's vinegar from tainting her life more than it already had. Insulated by his friends and his business, she and Justin would find some way past this. They might never enjoy again the closeness of last week, but they'd find a way to live with one another and make the best of the union. Sleep began to creep over her as she snuggled down beneath the coverlet. No matter what happened between her and Justin, the Rocklands would never be there to trouble them again.

Chapter Eleven

Over the next three days, Justin had paid a call on
every contact he possessed and made a few new ones
in the processes of assembling the required vintages.
He had even managed to secure a case of the Spanish
port which had nearly eluded him and left the order
unfulfilled. The morning of the masque, he personally
saw to the wine's delivery, unwilling to trust even Mr
Tenor with its safe handling.

As he finished going through the list with the tart
Netley, Lord Rockland joined them in the wine cellar.
He inspected the casks and crates of bottles stacked up
in the dank, dark room with a critical eye, as though
looking for any reason to reject the wines, or deny Justin his money. After what Lady Rockland had done,
Justin wouldn't put it past the man to leave Justin on
the hook for the stock and the bills which went with it.

Lord Rockland picked up one of the bottles of Spanish port from the shelf where the butler had set them.
His eyebrows rose with admiration before he set it

down, offering no congratulations for the effort it'd taken to secure it. It was as if he was owed the thing simply because he'd asked for it and had been given by providence the means to pay for it. His surety in himself and his place in the world nearly made Justin sick. The man's wife had thrown Justin's life entirely off kilter and yet nothing mattered more to this man than whether or not his guests could drink themselves into a stupor. Neither he nor his wife had done a day's work in their entire lives, or knew what it was to scrape by on little more than ambition, yet they thought nothing of ruining those people who worked hard. Despite hating to admit it, Susanna was right. These weren't the kind of people to build a business or a future upon and he couldn't be free of this sort soon enough.

'Well done, Mr Connor. I'm impressed.' Lord Rockland at last faced him and Justin made sure to maintain his deference. He didn't want the man to suspect the loathing he carried for him and his wife. 'I'm very impressed.'

Whether it was because Justin had procured the wine or defied his low expectations he wasn't sure, although he could well imagine. 'Thank you, Your Grace.'

'See to it Mr Connor receives his payment, then set things up as we discussed yesterday,' he ordered Netley, who didn't work to hide how he felt about having to pay Justin as he dropped a leather bag of coins into his palm.

With the matter concluded, Justin tucked the pouch in his coat pocket and picked up the crooked lid of a crate to straighten it, ready to see this strange part of his life laid to rest.

'Lady Rockland tells me you and Susanna won't be able to attend tonight,' Lord Rockland observed. 'She says Susanna isn't well.'

Justin's fingers tightened on the rough wooden edge of the crate lid as he set it down over the bottles. His determination to walk away now and leave the Rocklands to their lives while he and Susanna went about theirs came rushing back. He could agree with the duchess, graciously bow out of tonight and heed her warning to not sully her precious party with their presence. Until this moment, it was exactly what he'd intended to, but he couldn't. He didn't want her or Lord Rockland to think they'd triumphed over them. Lord Rockland had agreed to their invitation to the ball as part of the marriage contract. If Justin declined to attend now it would relieve the duke of this last duty and Lady Rockland would win. Justin wasn't about to allow her to think she'd defeated them, or to let Lord Rockland out of even one of his obligations, no matter how small. Nor was Justin about to surrender his own ambitions and miss the opportunity to acquire a few new clients. With his marriage in tatters, Justin's work was the one thing remaining to lift him up. He would succeed, despite what anyone, even Susanna, thought.

'I'm afraid Lady Rockland is mistaken.' Justin brushed the wood and dust from his hands. 'Susanna is quite well and we will be there tonight.'

'Good, I'm glad to hear it.' Lord Rockland hummed.

If he was surprised by the answer, his laconic demeanour didn't change to show it.

Justin realised it didn't matter to him one way or another. It was Lady Rockland who'd seethe like a cornered cat when he and Susanna appeared tonight. He wanted her to fume; she deserved it.

Lord Rockland reached up to a nearby shelf and ran one finger over the embossed label, the one Susanna had designed with the printer. Then he turned to face Justin with a strange kind of scrutiny. 'I think a man of your ingenuity will do well tonight with my guests in establishing your name.'

Justin stilled. At least there was one person who saw something of worth and promise in him. He hadn't expected it to be Lord Rockland. 'I hope so.'

'Until tonight, then.' Lord Rockland made his way back up to the kitchen, his business done and other needs awaiting his attention.

Justin didn't linger in the cellar, but gathered up his men and made for home. It would be a press to prepare for the masque. Susanna wouldn't be pleased, but it didn't matter. It was time for her to resume her duties as a wife and stand beside him.

Susanna sat curled in the chair by the fire, trying to read, but not one of the sentences she'd skimmed in the past half hour had remained with her. In the three days since Dr Hale's visit, she'd seen less of Justin than she had in the days after her secret had been revealed. She knew he was securing her father's order for the masque, and understood once the delivery was made she and Justin would be free of the Rocklands at last.

It seemed such a strange idea and at the same time it was the only one which gave her any joy. For years she'd wished them to be a part of her past as much as her grandfather and uncle. Soon, they would be. Despite the fact Lady Rockland had risen up one last time to destroy all chances of a happy future for Susanna, she was glad to never have to face her again. She would remain here, quietly living her life with Justin in whatever shape it decided to take, while the duchess and her father lived theirs.

The door to the room swung open and Justin stepped inside. She set aside the book, her heart fluttering not so much with hope at his arrival, but in anxiety over the stern set of his jaw. Had her father rejected his order or refused to pay? She knew the cost of the wines Justin had procured. She'd taken a glance at the list during one of the many nights she'd been awake, pacing in her worry. There was more than one bottle only a man like Lord Rockland could afford, the cost of which would ruin Justin if Lord Rockland didn't pay.

'Did all go well?' she dared to ask, almost afraid to hear the answer. She wouldn't put it past Lady Rockland to try and ruin Susanna's livelihood as well as her marriage in the hopes she and Justin would sink from all society for good.

'It did. Your father was very pleased. So much so, he believes I can cultivate some of his friends as clients.'

Her stomach dropped. They weren't supposed to have anything more to do with society. 'What brought about his change of heart?'

'I impressed him. There's no reason why I can't impress his friends.' He marched to the wardrobe and flung open the doors, then plucked from inside the green domino and gown. 'We're going tonight and we have to make a good show of it.'

'We can't.' She jumped to her feet, rocking a little with dizziness before the room settled around her. 'Lady Rockland won't allow us to walk in there without finding a way to punish us. You saw what she did when you were alone in the house. Imagine how she'll strike if we dare to show ourselves at her ball.'

'Lady Rockland can go hang. Her guests are the only people I care about.'

'You used to think nothing of them before. Now, because you want their patronage, you're willing to risk being insulted or humiliated by Lady Rockland to curry their favour.'

He whirled to face her, the domino hanging limp in the hand by his side. 'I want to succeed and if that's how I can make it happen, then so be it.'

'There are other ways to do it without them.'

'Not tonight, there isn't. With everyone there enjoying their drinks, I can slip among them and spread the word about my business.'

'You won't win these people over, especially not if Lady Rockland is set against it. These aren't merchants who appreciate the effort it takes to procure things they believe their due. They won't admire you like the duke, but look down on you for meddling in trade.'

His fingers played with the sagging cape while he considered what she'd said. He knew she was right, but it was plain something more than ambition was driving him tonight. He'd told her in Hyde Park not to care about these people; now he was willing to set aside his pride to wander among them and it frightened her. This wasn't the Justin she'd come to love, the man she wanted so much to be with again.

'I understand your desire to prove wrong all those who've doubted you,' she sympathised, desperate for him to give up this course. 'But I don't want to see you ridiculed for my mistakes.'

He reached into the wardrobe and plucked out the mask, the one she'd so carefully laundered after their intimacy together, a closeness they might never take pleasure in again. 'You didn't mind so much the idea of ridiculing me when we wed.'

She swallowed hard against his insult. 'If you're determined to attend, then you'll have to do it alone. I won't face them or their insults and snide remarks again.'

Especially not on the arm of a man who could barely stand to look on her.

He marched up to her, coming toe to toe with her, but with nothing of the adoration or care he'd shown her the first time they'd stood so close. 'Whatever discomfort you experience tonight, it isn't even a measure of what I've been forced to endure, what I'll continue to endure because of your lie. We will arrive there together and appear like the happiest of couples.'

'How will we, when we aren't?'

He started and in his silence she caught the regret before his anger buried it. 'You lied to me to get me to the altar and for all the days afterwards. Surely you can lie as convincingly for one more night.'

'I lied about the child, but I never lied about how I felt about you. I love you, very much.' She reached up to touch his face, but he flinched away.

'Then it shouldn't be too difficult for you to act like it tonight.' He flung the domino across the foot of the bed as he made for his room. 'Be ready within the hour.'

Chapter Twelve

Susanna entered Lady Rockland's masque on Justin's arm. There was no footman at the door to announce the names of each arriving guest. Instead, they strolled in with their costumes, some with their hair powdered in the fashion of a few decades before, others with togas draped around the men's shirts and golden asps wound around the ladies' arms. Each one paraded through the main floor of the house in the guise of a different historical figure, laughing and drinking the wine, unaware of how hard a man had worked to procure the libations they enjoyed. They didn't care. This was all for their amusement and tomorrow it would be forgotten as they moved on to the next, trying to fill their vapid lives with meaning.

Elaborate masks covered many of the guests' faces, and Susanna wished she'd opted for something more substantial than the thin silk covering her eyes. Despite the cape allowing her to blend into the shadows along the edges of the room, it wouldn't be long before someone recognised her. Then it would all begin again, the whispering behind fans, the reminders she wasn't one of them, but someone to be pitied and ridiculed. This time the rumours would be more cutting, for surely Lady Rockland had let Susanna's secret slip and it was now making the rounds through the sitting rooms and dressing rooms of society.

At one time it would've been a comfort to have Justin walking beside her. Tonight his hardness added to her isolation. He'd all but ignored her when she'd come downstairs to join him, offering a stiff arm as he'd led her to the chaise. They'd sat beside one another in the darkness as it'd rattled towards Grosvenor Square, more tension icing the air between them than the night when she'd first jumped into his vehicle at Vauxhall Gardens. The silence had left her to wallow in her fears about what might happen both tonight and in the many more days to come. She hoped like most worries the reality would pale in comparison to what she imagined, though at present it didn't seem likely.

'At least try to smile,' Justin demanded from beside her.

'Why? It doesn't matter to these people whether we're happy or crying in some corner.'

'It matters to me.'

She forced herself to smile as wide as he did, hating this act. She'd pretended so many times in places like these to be honoured when some lord evaluated her to determine whether a connection to the Duke of Rockland and a thousand pounds was worth marrying a bastard. She'd appeared gracious as she'd danced

with men who'd thought her as loose as a cyprian because of her illegitimacy. She'd stood behind Lady
Rockland and Edwina, pretending not to notice how
they ignored her. She never imagined she'd be here
pretending to be happy with her husband while her
entire world was falling apart.

Her smile sagged and she didn't bother to bolster
it. She was tired of play-acting for these people and
longed for tonight to be over and to finally leave this
rotten, ugly world behind.

'Please, Justin, let's leave,' she begged, tightening
her hand on his arm. 'There's nothing we can gain
here.'

His smile stiffened, turning as hard as his muscles
beneath her palm. 'Of course there is. There's Lord
Pallston. Introduce me to him.'

He pulled her through the crowd to where Lord
Pallston stood stuffed into a doublet as red as his nose
and near bursting at the seams under the strain of his
bulk. The earl finished his drink, depositing the empty
glass on a passing footman's tray and taking another.
He tossed it back, then grabbed the tall footman's arm
to stop him so he could take one more before sending
him on his way.

'Lord Pallston—' Susanna began, enduring the
nasty curl of his fat lip in displeasure as she introduced him to Justin.

'The champagne is a fine vintage, isn't it?' Justin
plucked a flute off a passing tray and handed it to the
man. He regarded Justin suspiciously as he finished

his other glass and exchanged it with Justin for the full one.

'Definitely better than many I've enjoyed at such gatherings,' Lord Pallston mumbled through a tongue thickened by his enjoyment of the duke's hospitality.

His confidence buoyed by Lord Pallston's appreciation of the champagne, Justin produced one of the engraved calling cards Susanna had printed for him and held it out. 'I'm the man who procured it and I can acquire more for a gentleman who appreciates the finer vintages.'

Lord Pallston took the card with two sausage-like fingers and eyed it as if it were a biblical tract condemning strong drink. Then he flicked it away. 'I don't trouble with merchants. My steward deals with them. Talk to him.'

He waddled off in the direction of another footman with a full, glittering tray of drinks.

Justin snatched the discarded card from the floor and stuffed it back into his coat pocket, then dropped the empty glass on a passing footman's tray.

'Go ahead, gloat over my failure, tell me you were right and how I'll succeed in the pubs of Fleet Street, but not in the ballrooms of Grosvenor Square,' he said, the knock to his pride so palpable it made Susanna's chest hurt.

She wouldn't gloat. She couldn't, because his failure didn't feel like a victory. She wanted him to succeed as much as he did. 'You're determined to continue?'

'I'm not leaving here without one good contact.'

She studied him. It was difficult to read his expression behind his mask, both the silk one and the one he'd worn in her presence over the last few days. She wanted so much to be with the laughing man she'd come to love during their marriage, the one who didn't care about what all these people thought of him or her or their situation. But that Justin wasn't with her tonight and she'd have to do her best with this sullen one.

'Then speak to Lord Felton. He's a baron and not as rich as Lord Pallston, but his mother was a merchant's daughter. He might be more inclined to patronise us. Come, I'll introduce you.'

Without waiting for him to agree, she wound her way through the crowd to where a man draped in a cape and hidden by a mask similar in simplicity to Justin's leaned against a column. He watched a set of masked ladies and gentlemen move through the tortuously slow steps of the minuet, the long notes of the violin accompanying them grating on Susanna's nerves.

'Lord Felton, it's a pleasure to see you tonight.' Susanna held her hand out to the man who recognised her at once, responding to her greeting with enough charm to almost raise her fallen spirits.

'Miss Lambert, I thought you'd left us for a better place,' the distinguished older gentleman drawled, his enthusiasm for the night's festivities lacklustre.

'I have.' She told him of her marriage and her new name, speaking of it with as much pride as if she possessed as grand a title as anyone here, hoping Justin might notice. Then she introduced Justin to the baron and explained about their business. Lord Felton listened with an interest not usually seen in great men unless they were discussing hunting. By the time the man was summoned away by his wife, Justin had given him his calling card and extracted from him a promise for an order for a dinner party the man was hosting next week.

'That was unexpected,' Justin remarked with a touch of his old humour, their accomplishment appearing to have tempered his foul mood.

'You mean his not flinging your card away?'

'No, you helping me, even after I dragged you to this sixth level of hell.'

It wasn't an accusation tossed in her face, but almost a surrender of some of the vitriol he'd carried against her since learning her secret. It was as if for a moment he'd been able to see the love she still held for him. She wished she could work another miracle for him, demonstrate again the depth of her dedication to their union and remove some of the anger still clinging to him, but there wasn't another man here with Lord Felton's background or a soft spot for merchants.

'You asked me in Hyde Park to help you and I said I would. I might not have told you of my condition, but it doesn't mean every other promise I made to you was false.'

He didn't respond, but looked past her to focus on the room, his brown eyes behind the mask thoughtful, as if he was considering not just the guests, but also what she'd said. It gave her some hope, not for tonight, but for their future.

'My father says the two of you have been taking

tea together,' he said at last, fixing his eyes on her instead of the room.

She pressed her lips tight together, regretting her decision to keep even this seemingly innocent secret from him, especially in light of her more nefarious one. 'I'm sorry I didn't tell you, but I thought if I waited a little while longer, I might make some progress with him. I'd hoped by showing him some kindness, he might return the favour with you.'

'He did,' Justin admitted, the stiffness which had marked him since they'd left for the ball easing around his lips and in the set of his shoulders. 'We spoke the other night. It was the first civil conversation we've had in years. Thank you.'

'It was the least I could do after all you've done for me.'

A couple passed behind him, forcing Justin to step so close his chest nearly brushed against Susanna's. Standing over her, his breath sweeping across her cheeks, he regarded her not with the stern distrust of the last few days, but as if realising for the first time since learning of the baby she hadn't acted to trick him and didn't think him a gullible fool. She'd done her best tonight, despite the strain between them, to demonstrate how much she still cared for him. In his acknowledgement of her efforts both tonight and with his father, there lingered something of what they'd once had together. Their love wasn't dead, only hidden beneath his resentment and distrust.

'I think we should go.' He held out his arm to her. With relief, she wrapped her hand beneath it, allowing her fingers to rest in the crook of his elbow. Nothing was settled between them, or forgiven, but in the tenderness with which he laid his hand over hers, she felt in time it would be.

They were not two steps towards the door before a sight across the room riveted her to the spot.

'What's wrong?' he asked.

'Lady Rockland.' She nodded to where the duchess held court near the windows leading out to the garden. Edwina stood beside her, her roundness stuffed into a black Tudor dress with a high ruffle behind her which did nothing to flatter the increasing size of her waist. Susanna's half-brother stood beside his sister, looking as bored and sallow as he always did at these events, less interested in displaying himself to a future wife than sneaking off to his club to drink away his evenings along with his health and a good bit of Lord Rockland's money.

It wasn't so much her family together which chilled her, but Lady Rockland speaking with Lord Howsham. She recognised him by the red hair peeking out from beneath his domino.

'Let's leave before she spies us,' Susanna insisted, eager to avoid both Lady Rockland and Lord Howsham, but Justin refused to move.

'Let her see us.' He drew himself up taller beside her, the tenderness which had marked him a moment before gone as he stared at the woman in defiance. 'I want her to see she hasn't won.'

At last, sensing their scrutiny, Lady Rockland slid

aside the mask she held on a stick, her eyes narrowing in disgust as she spied them.

Susanna shivered, for the first time truly afraid of Lady Rockland. Having realised the depths to which the duchess was willing to sink to strike at Susanna and Justin, she could only imagine what damage she intended to inflict now. Her intentions revealed themselves when she turned to Lord Howsham and levelled her mask at Susanna, drawing his attention to where she stood.

A wicked smile broke beneath his elaborate white-plaster half mask, the same conquering jeer he'd pinned her with after he'd taken her innocence. She could practically hear him laughing at having been relieved of any consequence for what he'd done.

'Please, they've seen us now, let's go.' She tugged Justin towards the door, but he wouldn't move.

'Who's the man in the white mask?' Justin asked as Lord Howsham started towards them.

A slight sweat broke out on her neck beneath the cloak. She didn't want to be here or face the earl and endure the nasty things he might say. 'Lord Howsham.'

Justin's jaw ground beneath his mask and a new fire burned in his dark eyes.

'Let's go.' Susanna begged. 'Please.'

'No, we'll face him.'

'We can't.' If Justin had been willing to come here tonight simply to spite Lady Rockland, she could well imagine what he'd do to Lord Howsham. The man deserved it and more, but not here, not when his title gave him privileges Justin could never hope to possess, or use to protect himself.

Lord Howsham cut a deep swathe through the guests until he was in front of them, as arrogant as ever as he swept Susanna's body with a disgusting, lascivious look. 'Susanna, what a pleasure it is to see you here tonight.'

'Her name is Mrs Connor,' Justin corrected, the same force she'd seen in him at Vauxhall Gardens curling through him now.

Susanna slid her hand down his arm to intertwine her fingers with his. Even after everything that had happened, and all the doubts and heartache still lingering between them, he was standing beside her, defending her, making her and everyone see she was worthy of respect. Neither Lord Howsham nor anyone else here had the right to look down on her and she'd allow it no more. She wasn't the bastard daughter of a duke any longer, but the wife of an honourable man she loved.

'I'd forgotten you married her,' Lord Howsham snorted. 'Quite convenient for me since it relieved me of not one, but apparently two very minor problems.'

Justin's hand tightened in hers and she noticed many masks turning to face them. She let go of Justin and came to stand toe to toe with the earl, defiant against his haughty triumph.

'It isn't you who was relieved of a burden, but me. To think I nearly saddled myself with a man so deep in debt he must chase after every heiress from here to York or lose his estate,' Susanna shot back, noting with pride how Lord Howsham's eyes widened in surprise beneath his mask before they darted to those around them who moved in closer to gather more gossip.

'Such words from a bastard married to a mere merchant,' Lord Howsham sneered, colouring beneath his mask at this first public confirmation of his debts and all the rumours surrounding them.

'I'd rather be the wife of a merchant than countess to a man like you whose estate is mortgaged to the rafters, yet who still doesn't have the fortitude to work hard to save it. While you sweat and worry about your bills, afraid to lift a finger to do anything more than turn over a few cards and waste even more blunt, I'll be far from here and happy. I'll never, ever give you another thought.'

Stepping back, but not flinching from the hate in Lord Howsham's eyes, she took Justin's hand, bolstered by the pride in his gaze. It was the same pride he'd shown her the day they'd ridden through Hyde Park, when she'd faced Lady Rockland's wilting sneer on the stairs, refusing to back down. She never would again. These people and their opinions of her were nothing and when the door to the Rocklands' house closed behind her tonight, they'd never matter to her again.

Without a word, she and Justin turned to make for the door, the show of solidarity he'd craved on display for Lord Howsham, Lady Rockland and all society to see. It wasn't a lie or an act, but as genuine as the diamonds around Lady Rockland's thin neck.

'How does it feel to have married my whore?' Lord Howsham called out to their backs.

A gasp of shock rippled through those around them.

Justin spun on his heel and rammed his fist into the earl's face. Lord Howsham's mask cracked in two, falling away as he staggered back to hit a pillar. Blood slid down his nose and stained the front of his shirt as he blinked, trying to recover from his shock. The commotion brought the music to a halt and the dancers stopped, craning their necks to see what was going on.

'I demand satisfaction for your insult to my wife,' Justin cried, drawing the attention of the entire ballroom.

From her place near the window, Lady Rockland turned a deep shade of red with a fury Susanna had only witnessed once before—the day Lord Rockland had brought Susanna to Rockland Place. Back then, Susanna had cowered before the imperious woman; tonight she stood strong beside her husband, her defiance further darkening the crimson blotching her stepmother's cheeks.

'You're no gentleman to be challenging me.' Lord Howsham blanched more at the challenge than the blood on his fingertips.

'Too big a coward to face me?' Justin prodded, tearing off his own mask so everyone could see his face.

Lord Howsham looked around at all the masked people watching him, as if hoping one person with a cooler head might step forward and settle the matter. No one, not even Lord Rockland, who must have been among the disguised merrymakers, moved. Justin was backing him into a corner. Lord Howsham would have no choice but to accept. Without the anonymity of his mask, everyone would witness Lord Howsham shying from a challenge, one from a man beneath him in rank no less. He'd never be able to show his face in society again if he didn't agree to the duel.

'I accept your challenge,' Lord Howsham declared for everyone to hear, but there was no mistaking the flutter in his voice. For once he'd have to deal with the consequences of his actions. If the man he was facing wasn't Justin, Susanna would cheer for the duel. Instead she stared back and forth between the two men in horror. This wasn't how she wanted this to end. 'We'll meet at dawn with pistols.'

'My favourite weapon.' Justin smiled darkly at Lord Howsham, who cringed back, hiding his fear behind the handkerchief he pressed to his still-bleeding nose. 'Bring your physician. You'll need him.'

Justin grabbed Susanna's hand and pulled her towards the entrance. People parted to let them pass, gawking in disbelief. Behind them the crowd closed and the whispers rose to drown out the now playing violins. They were the talk of society, a spectacle to amuse and disgust all the lords and ladies and for the first time in her life Susanna didn't care. All she could think about was Justin and the danger waiting for him tomorrow morning.

Susanna nearly tripped in her effort to keep up with Justin's hard stride as they marched down the pavement outside the Rocklands'. He pulled her along the line of carriages until they found his chaise, the small vehicle obscured by the massive town coaches filling the street. She climbed inside, struggling to breathe against her stays and the panic making her heart race.

Justin thudded into the seat beside her and banged on the roof to set the vehicle in motion.

'Maybe he'll send his second to apologise, then you won't have to meet. He's a coward. He might do it.' Susanna rushed on. This wasn't how she wanted things to end, for Justin to put his life in danger for her honour or his. 'He can refuse you and he might since you aren't—'

'A gentleman?' Justin finished in a tone as hard as a grinding stone.

She didn't care if his ego was bruised. She wanted him alive, not dead with his pride intact, especially not in defence of her. 'He won't lose face if he does, at least not among his class.'

'I struck him, he can't refuse me now.' Justin crossed his arms as if welcoming the coming fight, so sure he wouldn't die, but she knew better. A duel was an unpredictable way to settle a matter of honour.

'At one time you didn't care what these people thought of you and urged me to do the same. Now you're willing to risk your life to prove yourself to them?'

'I won't be mocked, not by Lord Howsham or by anyone.'

'What good is your dignity if you lose?' Susanna pressed, refusing to allow the darkness filling him to make him risk his life. In the ballroom when he'd thanked her for her friendship with his father, it'd seemed the beginning of a fragile peace between them, one Lord Howsham's insults had killed. If she could call it back, build it and him up again, maybe he might not meet the earl in the morning.

'Dr Hale will be there,' Justin scoffed, focused on the quiet London streets passing by outside the chaise. The late hour had drained the lanes of traffic and any impediment to a quick journey home.

'He can't put your head back together if Lord Howsham shoots it off.'

He jerked upright, his hands tight on the edge of the squabs. 'Still you have no faith in me. You think I'm nothing but a reckless idiot. He insulted you. Don't you care?'

'No, not any more. I only care about you and keeping you alive.'

'Don't fret too much. If I die you'll get everything for yourself and the child,' he mocked.

'I don't want it if it means losing you.' She was determined to remain steadfast in the face of his derision. This wasn't the Justin she'd come to love, the one who met adversity with an easy smile and a quick wit, but one driven by a pain she understood. She wouldn't allow it to consume him as it'd once consumed his father or her so many times. 'Everyone I've ever loved and who ever loved me has ended up in the churchyard—my grandmother, my mother. I won't see my husband buried there, too.'

He stared at her, the mockery knocked out of him by her honesty. His eyes softened, but not his tight grip on the leather. She waited, hoping her words were enough to help him see beyond this crisis to the future they'd planned and the love they could rebuild.

The chaise slowed, leaning to make a turn before rocking to a halt in front of their house.

'It might not have come to this if you'd thought me a better man and not hidden your child from me,' he said at last, throwing open the door and stepping out of the carriage.

She climbed down into the sharp cold of the night, facing him on the pavement.

'I did it because I was afraid and I didn't know you as I do now.' She took his hand and raised it to her lips to press a tender kiss against the skin. He didn't jerk away from her or accuse her of playing him for a fool, but allowed her to hold him and it gave her hope. 'I love you and I'm certain you still love me. Forget the duel and society and everyone. They don't matter, only we do.'

His fingers curled around hers and she held her breath, praying the man inside him, the one whose optimism had captured her heart, would win against the one so determined to fight.

Then his fingers eased and he withdrew his hand. 'I have things to see to before tomorrow morning.'

He climbed back into the chaise and without a second look set off.

With a heavy heart she watched him go, his demons driving him on. She prayed clearer heads, or Lord Howsham's cowardice, might prevent their meeting at dawn.

* * *

'Is that all, then, Mr Connor?' Mr Woodson, Philip's solicitor, asked, looking up from the will he'd been summoned to draw up according to Justin's instructions. As sure as Justin was of his aim, he still needed his affairs to be in order before sunrise.

'No.' Justin ceased his pacing of Philip's office to stare out at the moonlit garden and the dark corner of the portico where he and Susanna had first kissed. The roses had faded since then, leaving only a few buds clinging to the thorn-ridden stems. Susanna's pale and worried face from across the chaise haunted him, as did her pleas for him to end this, but he couldn't. He wasn't about to allow Lord Howsham's insults to stand or to prove himself the gullible idiot they believed him to be. 'In the event I die, all is to be left to Susanna, including the care of my father.'

'Might not Mr Rathbone be a better guardian?' Mr Woodson asked. Having fought to make Justin his father's guardian, he knew something of Mr Connor's reputation.

'Susanna will do. She and my father have become friends.'

The man nodded in surprise. 'I suppose every man has it in him to change.'

'I suppose he does.' His father's apology and the contrition and regret which had lengthened the lines of his face came back to him. If Justin hadn't been wallowing in his own pain and heartache, he could have hugged his father and put to rest for good the turmoil between them. His father had changed for the better under Susanna's influence. How different things might be now if Justin had allowed her influence to work on him.

Shifting, he caught his reflection in the window pane, the serious man who met him in the glass barely recognisable. She was right, he wasn't the same person who'd driven with her through Hyde Park as if nothing in the world could diminish his spirits. He was a hypocrite, telling her not to care what others thought while he left their insults and derision to fester until he was willing to risk his life to prove they were wrong about him.

'Is that all, then?' Mr Woodson pressed him again, covering a large yawn with the back of his hand, not the only person in the room feeling the late hour.

Justin opened and closed his fingers by his side. The memory of Susanna's warm hand, and the faint brush of her lips against his flesh, crept through him more than the fury which had driven him away from her. On the pavement, she'd almost made him believe she truly cared for him. He'd wanted to believe it, but he'd ignored his intuition one too many times before and it'd cost him. Whether his instinct was still worth employing as a guide he wasn't sure. Everything was clouded by his hate of Lord Howsham and everyone who'd ever looked down on him. 'Yes.'

'Mr Rathbone, I'll need your signature as a witness.' Philip stepped forward from where he'd been observing from behind the desk, took up the pen and put his name to the will. Then the solicitor held out the pen to Justin who, without much thought, scrawled his name above Philip's. The solicitor rose and tucked the paper into his satchel.

'Good luck to you, Mr Connor.' He left, taking Justin's will with him.

With any luck, neither Justin nor Susanna would need the cursed document.

'Is everything ready?' Justin asked, sagging down into his usual chair by the window. Beside him a decanter of port shimmered with the candlelight, but he ignored the tempting liquor. This was no time to indulge.

'It is. We're to meet at dawn on Primrose Hill. As we have no duelling pistols, Lord Howsham will provide them.'

'Make sure to check them before I fire.' He didn't trust Lord Howsham to fight fair, even when it was in his best interest to do so. If the earl tampered with the weapons, it'd be society's judgement, not Justin's he'd have to face when this was over. He knew how cruel the toffs could be, especially when it came to matters of honour.

He laced his fingers over his stomach. Seeing Lord Howsham disgraced wouldn't amuse Justin if he was shot dead by the man.

Philip took his chair behind the desk, rested his forearms on the blotter and fixed on Justin. 'Are you sure you wish to do this?'

'No, but if I walk away, they'll call me a coward. No one wants to do business with a coward. Besides, my honour is about the only thing I have left.' He clung to his distrust of Susanna, despite her tempting words of love which had played on him in the chaise. There'd been nothing in them, or in the faint tears shimmering in the corners of her eyes, to tell him her love for him was false, yet still he refused to believe it. 'You'll be sure to look after Susanna if anything happens to me.'

'I will.'

'And the child?'

'The child as well,' Philip agreed and the relief which eased Justin's tension surprised him. He'd spent so many days despising the baby and what it meant to her and him and their future. He couldn't despise it any longer. It was as much a part of its mother as her beautiful voice, or the smile which had eluded him for the last several days, the smile he missed.

'Have you made your peace with her?' Philip asked.

'No.' He couldn't. Even if the hardness he'd born against her had begun to soften beneath her love and concern for his life, his suspicion of her motives continued to play on him. 'Why do you think she kept her pregnancy from me?'

'She was afraid of losing you.'

Justin banged his fist against the arm of the chair. 'Because she thought so low of me.'

'Because everyone has always thought so low of her. I imagine she couldn't conceive of a man she barely knew standing by her when those bound to her by blood never have.'

'No, I don't suppose she could.' Yet she'd believed in herself tonight, standing firm against Lord Howsham, proclaiming her faith in herself and Justin to everyone.

He picked at the thick stitching of the chair's covering, unable to ignore the pride he'd felt when she'd stood up to Lord Howsham, defying the man who'd treated her like an old coat to be worn and then discarded. In doing so, she'd demonstrated to him and everyone her deep belief in herself and Justin. It wasn't the first time her faith in him had prevailed during the masque. She could have stayed silent after Justin's failure with Lord Pallston, refused to offer any assistance and let him blunder his way through who knew how many more meetings. Instead, she'd demonstrated to him the manners it took to win the influence of a baron, as well as the necessary information to target the right man.

He wished she'd gloated. It would make shunning her easier. She'd stood beside him against Lord Howsham and Lady Rockland exactly as he'd asked her to do. He couldn't even promise to come home to her without a hole in his stomach.

Philip rose, coming around the desk. 'You'd better get some rest.'

'I'd like to stay here.' It almost seemed an easier thing to face an earl at dawn than to go home and face his wife. He possessed enough concerns about tomorrow without adding Susanna's to them, and he couldn't face her pleading green eyes and expect to stand firm. She'd nearly swayed him on the pavement with her tender kiss, her chestnut curls glistening in the carriage light until he'd wanted to twine his hands in the locks and draw her lips to his. As much as he tried to ignore his instincts, tonight they told him she loved him. It was as disquieting as the coming duel.

Chapter Thirteen

A soft mist settled over the green grass covering Primrose Hill and wound through the few trees near the bottom of the rise. In the distance, London spread out, its chimneys spewing thin tendrils of black smoke into the air, which the wind carried away to obscure the orange of the rising sun. It wasn't high enough in the sky to cast off the early-morning gloom and Justin stood in his greatcoat, gloved hands in his pockets to protect against the chill air. Behind him, horses tossed their heads and jingled the equipage of the many carriages lining the road. Inside the vehicles sat those brave or curious enough to rise early after a long night at Lady Rockland's to watch the duel.

'I've drawn quite a crowd,' Justin remarked to Dr Hale who stood beside him, looking over his shoulder at the people standing along the edge of the field waiting for the spectacle to begin. What little sleep Justin had snatched in the Rathbone house hadn't eased the anxiety tightening his muscles, or the second thoughts which continued to fight with his determination to see this through.

'Not too late to reconsider,' the doctor advised. 'Better to go home to your wife in a chaise than a coffin.'

Justin let out a long breath and it curled like smoke in front of him before fading away. If he came home unscathed, Susanna would be waiting for him and with her every ambition for his business and a long life ahead of them both. Whether it was one of happiness or marked by the bitterness which made Lady Rockland such a prune he wasn't sure. In the end it would be up to him. She'd made her love and belief in him clear, and during the few dark hours of last night, as he'd lain in the Rathbones' guest bed contemplating the past few weeks, he'd come to realise, like his father had, it was time to choke down all the hate and hurt and cross the wide chasm separating him from Susanna. No matter what secrets she'd brought to their marriage, she was his wife for better or for worse and he'd prefer better, assuming he survived the morning.

'Lord Howsham made the first insult. It's up to him to apologise.' Justin rolled his head against the stiffness in his neck, eager to get on with this business.

Across the field, Philip stood talking with Lord Sutton, Lord Howsham's second. Justin wasn't surprised to find one coward standing beside another, Susanna's half-brother throwing in his lot with the man who'd stood against his own sister's husband. A small part of him wished the arrogant earl would relent and apologise. Judging by the sneers he tossed at Justin from out of his two blackened eyes, it wasn't likely.

While they waited for the seconds to finish their conversation, Justin didn't pace. He wasn't about to fret in front of all these people, or his opponent. As much as he might dream of a life with Susanna after this morning, once the duel was over, there could be other problems to face. He didn't doubt he could kill Lord Howsham. Every time he thought of what he'd done to Susanna, Justin wanted to put a ball through the earl, but duelling was illegal. He might drop the man for his crimes, then find himself on the long end of a short rope for murder. He'd been audacious enough to challenge a peer to a fight, he didn't want to risk execution. It meant winging the earl and hoping he didn't die of gangrene. He should have sent Mr Tenor to book passage for him on a ship out of England, just in case. Fleeing was safer than avoiding the constable, assuming Lord Howsham didn't get off a lucky shot. They might both be dead before noon.

Justin glanced at the carriages along the ridge, wondering which unadorned one carried Lady Rockland. No doubt she was here to watch her son stand with Lord Howsham against Justin with great pleasure. In a short while, Justin would see to it Lady Rockland choked on her relish.

Susanna wasn't amongst the crowd. He hadn't seen her since leaving her on the doorstep last night. There'd been no note, no good wishes or sudden appearances before sunrise to talk him out of the duel. She'd pleaded her case with him last night and he'd ignored it, so there was no reason for her to be here and nothing she could say which would stop him. It was too late.

The conversation between the seconds ended and Philip strode back across the moist earth to Justin and Dr Hale.

'Well?' Dr Hale asked, more anxious than Justin when Philip returned.

'He won't apologise.'

'Good.' Justin tugged his gloves off, then stuffed them into the pocket of his coat. 'Time to satisfy my honour.'

He marched across the grass, the soggy earth giving way beneath his boots as he approached his adversary. Dr Hale and Philip followed behind him in the silence which swept through the waiting crowd at the sight of the two men coming together.

'I didn't think you gentleman enough to appear this morning, Mr Connor,' Lord Sutton taunted.

'How's the stomach?' Justin smiled coldly at his despicable brother-in-law.

'You'll get yours this morning.' Lord Sutton glowered.

'Let's begin,' Lord Howsham demanded, but not with his friend's bravado. His hand shook as he waved his manservant over, his eyes darting to Justin's, then everywhere around the park as he shifted from foot to foot.

Justin stood straight as an oak, his eyes boring into the earl's as the manservant approached with the burled wooden case carrying the pistols. If sheer bravado could force an apology out of Lord Howsham, he'd stare him down until sunset, but the earl, with his honour at stake, refused to yield. Good, Justin wanted a fight.

The manservant opened the case, revealing two shiny pistols resting on blue velvet. Justin picked up the closest and examined it, looking for any evidence of tampering. He wouldn't put it past the man to rig the duel, but with so many of his peers watching, it seemed he'd decided to rely on his talent instead of more nefarious methods to win this challenge. If so, it wasn't a fair fight.

He handed the pistol to Philip who looked it over and, silently agreeing with Justin's assessment, handed it back to him.

'The pistols are acceptable, then?' Lord Howsham questioned.

'Quite.' Justin dropped the weapon to his side, adjusting his fingers on the handle and getting a feel for the weight of it. He'd handled many weapons, none as fine as this, but in the end they were all the same whether they were polished to a gleam or tarnished with grime.

The manservant closed the case, then handed it to another. 'Twenty paces, gentlemen. The first to draw blood wins. You have both met here and proven your bravery. Mr Connor, do you feel your honour is satisfied?'

'No, not unless Lord Howsham publicly apologises to me and my wife.'

The man paled before seeming to revive what little

courage he'd mustered for the morning. 'You'll have to shoot me first.'

'If you insist, though I want it noted, he demanded it.' Justin turned his back on the earl, waiting for him to do the same.

The grass shifted behind him and he heard more than felt Lord Howsham's back meeting his.

'You'll regret this, Connor,' Lord Howsham hissed.

'If I do, it won't be because of your bad aim.'

'Twenty paces, gentlemen,' the manservant announced. 'One—'

With each call of the number, Justin and Lord Howsham moved away from one another.

Justin cleared his mind, caressing the trigger with his finger, figuring out the distance between him and the earl and where best to aim. The calculations would come together in an instant the minute the manservant reached twenty and Justin turned to fire. He didn't know much about the earl, but he'd heard more rumours of his debt than his duelling abilities; yet even a poor shot could get lucky once in a while.

In the distance, where the field met the road, a gig came racing up the hill. Justin was about to look away, to centre himself again on the weapon and what he was about to do when he noticed his father at the reins. Susanna sat beside him, gripping his arm as his father pulled the gig to a stop. She jumped down and with Mr Connor close behind her, hurried across the grass, the hem of her white dress growing dark from the dew wetting it. She stopped as close as she dared, but she was so near Justin could see her green eyes made more vivid by the red of many shed tears.

'Ten, eleven—'

Justin's pace didn't slacken, but his grip on the pistol tightened. Around her people whispered and pointed, but she saw none of it, focused on him with a worry which could melt a man's heart.

I love you. Don't do this, she mouthed as he continued to step away from his opponent.

His determination threatened to desert him and he struggled to maintain his grip on it and the weapon. It was too late, he couldn't back out now and hope to save face. Once the two men turned, fate would decide if one, both or neither of them walked away. If Justin died, what would it be for? These weren't his people. He'd never given a fig for their opinion or approval before, yet he'd allowed his pride, his need to prove himself to her and everyone, to drag him to this field. There was no reason for him to do it. He already possessed her faith in him and he always had. She'd believed in him enough to help him, not just with the business, but with his father. She'd cared for him. Yes, she'd deceived him, but it'd been to protect her child and because she'd been afraid to lose him and the life he'd offered her.

The pain in her green eyes in the chaise when she'd told him about losing everyone she'd ever loved echoed between them now. She clung tight to Justin's father's arm, his skin as pale as hers with worry. They both loved him and he was hurting them by risking his life.

His death would crush his father like his mother's had and it would destroy Susanna, too.

Her eyes held his and it wasn't pride in what he was doing which wrapped around his heart, but shame. Nearly everyone who should have loved her had failed her and Justin was throwing his name on the heap, shoving her aside and risking their life together for his own selfish means. The toffs might respect this display of honour, but this wasn't who Justin was or the kind of man he wanted to be.

'Eighteen, nineteen—'

'Stop. I withdraw my challenge,' Justin announced, sending a gasp racing through the crowd. He saw Susanna sag against his father in relief before he turned to Lord Howsham and lowered his pistol.

'Are you too much of a coward to face me?' Lord Howsham taunted, puffing out his chest in victory.

Justin flung the gun away and marched up to the earl. The man shifted one foot behind him and raised his pistol as though he expected Justin to fall upon him. Justin had no such designs. He brought his chest right up to the snub, the cold metal hard against his shirt.

'Go ahead, shoot me. Show everyone here what a brave man and how superior you are by killing me,' Justin growled.

'No!' Susanna cried, her voice carrying over the mist of the morning settling on the grass.

The silent crowd watched, mesmerised.

'You should listen to your wife,' Lord Howsham

suggested, but Justin sensed the tremble in his hand through the barrel of the pistol.

He continued to stare down Lord Howsham until the arrogant sneer he'd worn since last night began to fail. The earl's attention darted from Justin to the spectators then back again. Beneath Lord Howsham's red hair, a small bead of sweat slid down to his round jaw. He wouldn't kill him, Justin knew it as well as he knew the bookseller would never come back. Everything Lord Howsham had done, from his relationship with Susanna to his smearing of Justin's character, had been executed either in secrecy or from behind the anonymity of a mask. Now he was in front of everyone who mattered to him, his deed made public for all to see. If he killed Justin, he'd be killing an unarmed man. If society didn't shun him for it, the law would certainly hang him.

Somewhere behind him a horse whinnied and the sound was joined by the faint call of a bird far off in the high grass.

At last, Lord Howsham lowered his gun. 'I'm sorry for the offence against you and your wife.'

'Say it again and this time so everyone can hear,' Justin insisted.

Lord Howsham took a deep breath, screwing his lips tight in defiance before he at last spoke up, silencing the birds in the trees. 'I'm sorry for the offence against you and your wife.'

'Apology accepted.' Justin turned his back on Lord Howsham and strode across the field towards Susanna.

She let go of his father and raced to him, the same joy he felt in his chest making her glow.

She threw her arms around him and buried her face against his neck as he hugged her tight, her love more precious than even his honour.

'You're safe, you're safe,' she sobbed, her tears as tender as her body against his.

'You doubted me?' Justin laughed as he curled his arms around her, inhaling her jasmine scent as though he'd come back from the dead.

'I've never doubted you, I couldn't.' She shifted back within the circle of his arms, her tear-stained face wrinkling in displeasure at his carefree smile. She clutched at his lapels and pulled herself up on the balls of her feet to better face him. 'Don't you ever scare me like that again. He might have killed you.'

'I knew he wouldn't.'

'How could you have known, you arrogant fool?' she hiccupped.

'The same way I know I love you.'

She let go of his jacket as two tears spilled down her cheeks kissed with red by the morning chill. Justin slid his hand behind her neck and bending down, took her warm lips with his, not caring for anyone or anything except the flutter of her pulse beneath his fingers and her hot breath mingling with his.

Epilogue

Four years later

'Did the delivery to Lord Pallston go well?' Susanna asked Justin as he stepped through the door of her bedroom.

Pausing on the threshold, he took her in, as awed by her beauty today as he'd been the night she'd first climbed in his chaise. She sat in the chair by the window, nursing their infant son. Behind her the sheer curtains softened the light which fell over her chestnut hair and danced in her green eyes. Beside her on a small stool sat Emily, reciting her letters from her horn book, her hair as dark as her mother's and bound up in a large red bow.

'Exceedingly well, as always.' He dropped his hat and gold-tipped walking stick on the table by the window, then made for his wife. 'I told you a thirst like his could make us rich.'

'His and all his friends,' Susanna added with a lopsided grin. 'I'm quite impressed with your ability to make the lords pay their bills. You're the envy of every merchant in London.'

'I suppose my reputation for collecting money for Philip precedes me.' After the duel, most of London had read of the incident in the paper and even the toffs had gained a new respect for Justin, leading to a flood of orders which had poured in from every corner of London, including the better parts.

He placed his hands on the arms of the chair and leaned in to lay a swift kiss on Susanna's lips. Between them, their infant son gurgled and fussed before settling back to his suckling. Justin pushed himself up, ruffling Emily's big bow.

'Daddy, don't!' She swiped away his hand and he reached in again, truly mussing her hair this time, much to the girl's amused irritation. 'Daddy!'

He tapped her on the nose, then straightened. 'I think it looks better that way.'

'Daddy, are you going to take me for a drive in the new chaise like you promised?'

'I will. I'll even show you the new shop with its cavernous cellar.' He picked her up and whirled her around, making her squeal with laughter. 'Perhaps we can convince your mother and brother to come, too.'

'Grandpa,' the girl screamed in Justin's ear.

Justin came to a stop at the sight of his father in the doorway. A wide smile drew back the wrinkles at the sides of his father's mouth and made his faded brown eyes twinkle. His coat was well tailored, if not a little large to accommodate the fullness of his body.

'Spin a young lady around like that and you'll bring

up her nuncheon,' he warned. His grey hair was as wild as ever as he entered the room, with his arms held out to Emily. 'Besides, that's what her Grandpa is for.'

'Good afternoon, Father. We weren't expecting you until supper,' Justin greeted him as he set his daughter down and she ran to hug her grandfather.

'I had to bring you this.' He withdrew a slender newspaper from his coat pocket and held it out to Susanna. 'Have you seen it?'

Susanna took the paper with her free hand and read the headline, then gasped. 'Lord Rockland is divorcing Lady Rockland.'

Emily let go of her grandfather's leg and rushed to her mother's side. She peered at the paper with her green eyes, her mother's eyes, studying the words she couldn't yet read before she wrinkled her freckled nose. 'Who's Lady Rockland?'

'No one of any importance.' Susanna rubbed the small girl's back. They hadn't had anything more to do with the Rocklands after the morning of the duel, each family leaving the other in peace.

'But I want to know,' the child insisted as only a three-year-old can, as unaware of her mother's heritage as her own.

'You're too little to hear about grown-up things,' Justin chided, hoping she never learned the truth. He loved her as if she was his own and he never wanted her to learn the truth.

'Come on, young lady, we'll leave your parents to talk and see if Mrs Robinson has any of those mince pies we love.' Justin's father took Emily by the hand and led her out of the room in search of a treat.

Justin turned to his wife, who continued to read the paper, her lips twisting into a small frown. Reaching the end of the piece, she laid the paper on her lap and shook her head. 'Lady Rockland cheated on her husband with the Earl of Colchester and Lord Rockland has brought a suit of divorce against her in Parliament.'

'He certainly has the means and influence to do it.' He took the paper from her and skimmed the story. 'Makes for quite salacious reading. I suppose what is good for the goose is forbidden of the gander.'

He handed the paper back to her, but she didn't finish the story.

'It serves the nasty woman right to taste the poison she spewed on so many for so long.' Susanna did up her bodice and laid the squirming boy on the pillow across her lap. 'She can have her troubles. I don't care.'

She tossed the paper in the glowing fire beside her. In a rise of flames it ignited, the story turning black beneath the curling paper.

Justin knelt beside her chair, perching his elbows on the arm and laying a kiss on the top of his son's head. 'How's he doing?'

'He's hungry, as always, like our daughter was.'

He rose up, taking Susanna's face in his hands. 'And how are you?'

'In love with you, as ever.'

'As I am with you.'

As their lips met, the fire crackled in the grate, consuming the gossip and all the memories attached to it, the sound of it eclipsed by the contented snore of their infant son in his mother's arms.

* * * * *

LET'S TALK
Romance

For exclusive extracts, competitions
and special offers, find us online:

f facebook.com/millsandboon

⊚ @millsandboonuk

🐦 @millsandboon

Or get in touch on 0844 844 1351*

For all the latest titles coming soon, visit
millsandboon.co.uk/nextmonth